THE BANKER'S
DAUGHTER

THE BANKER'S DAUGHTER

Nesta Wyn Ellis

BLAKE

Published by Blake Publishing Ltd,
98–100 Great North Road, London N2 0NL, England

First published in Great Britain in 1989
by Sidgwick & Jackson Limited

ISBN 1 85782 090 8

British Library Cataloguing-in-Publication Data: A catalogue
record for this book is available from the British Library.

Typeset by BMD Graphics, Hemel Hempstead

Printed by Cox and Wyman, Reading, Berkshire

1 3 5 7 9 10 8 6 4 2

Acknowledgements

To my husband, Edward Moss who, for many years before this story was born, encouraged and educated me in the techniques of story telling and character creation.

To my friend, Cynthia Geller for her enthusiasm, encouragement and advice, before, during and after the writing of the story.

To Dr Patricia Sohl and Dr Richard Pearson for their advice on medical detail and to Nicky Gardiner for his guidance on police and court procedure.

To my agent, Micheline Steinberg whose encouragement enabled me to begin writing the story.

To my friend and lawyer Ann Mosseri for her thoughtful and useful advice.

To my friends and therapists who listened, encouraged, diverted, inspired and nourished me during the hard months of late night and weekend writing.

For Tony

*For all those who love with passion and truth,
and for my muse*

Prologue

The big gold Mercedes bit into the miles: the speedometer flickering around 120. The distance from the coast seemed shrunk. He liked to drive like this, in the small hours of the night, the roads empty but for a few long distance lorries, the world dark except for the white spears of his headlights.

His mouth curved, though his eyes stayed hard: it was a victor's smile. The risks of high speed, the car's power gave him a sense of conquest. He thought of her then, too. She never left his mind. The image of her eyes looking into his during her climax haunted him. Now, other images of her flooded his head; her laughter, her tears, of how she was the first time when he pulled up the skirt of her evening dress, threw her down and took her like a rapist.

He felt himself harden but the pleasure was tinged with pain. Desire brought anguish. He must not go on with it. It would end in a death, his own or the other's. He pushed her to the back of his mind and the hardness abated.

Now he thought of the job, virtually done. The goods were safely on their way. He had not needed to be at the rendevous, but he enjoyed the danger. It was the part of the game he liked best. And it was a game, a sport. It was also a drug he could never give up.

1

He checked the mirror. Of course, no one had followed him. It was just a habit: he'd trained himself to keep watch always. He didn't want to be caught speeding either. Especially not tonight. He grinned, then with a curt laugh, stepped on the accelerator. The needle leaped to 140 and the car seemed to fly down the motorway as it curved out high above the flat Kentish fields. He felt again the surge of excitement, the sense of power and his mind crowed with triumph. He was beating them again, the bastards. He thought again of his private motto, 'I'm one of the doers, not the done to', and a husky laugh rose like a cough from his throat.

Miles behind him, headlights sliced across the land's soft blackness and scratched at the moonless, starry sky. Ahead, London's orange glow signalled the motorway would soon end. He glanced at the car clock. 3.05. South London's winding streets would slow him, but he would be home in half an hour.

He doubted he would sleep, though. His adrenalin was running very high, as it always did after one of these nights. He needed a woman. Then, his mind went to her again. She was not just any woman. She was both what she was to him and what he needed now. He wanted to complete his triumph. She would lie there under him and moan with the ecstasy he gave her. That rich, upper class woman would cry out that she loved him and rise to him, rippling in waves of soft warmth around his cock, sucking him down into a dark whirlpool. She would love him, even knowing what he came from. But he could never tell her that.

He was driving through South London's wastes. She was there. He could almost feel her soft moist sex under his hand. He never had to arouse her. She was always wet for him. And she said she had never seen him other than erect.

He could hear her soft voice as if it spoke to him now. 'You always want me. It never stops: your wanting never leaves my head or my cunt. And I don't want it to. I can feel you in there as if you were part of my body. When you're there or not there, when I work, talk, eat, sleep, whoever I'm with, I'm hungry for you. I don't want to lose you, ever. You're part of me, the part I never knew I'd lost until you came to me. You are me, another me and I am you. No matter how far away you go or for how long, to the other end of the universe or of time, we are each other.'

His throat seemed to swell. He swallowed. His cock was very hard again. His eyes seemed to water. He blinked and pushed the rising feelings down. He had to be strong. It had been five or six weeks now since he had touched her. He had seen her. He had watched her leaving her office. He had not been able to stop keeping watch on her. But he was staying away.

He had never known he could crave a woman as much. He had never intended to become involved. But, involved or not, it was better he stay apart from her. There was too much he could not share with a woman like her. He sighed. The pain softened him. For a moment he felt weak, vulnerable, tired. He longed for her. Her love for him was like a watchfire in his life's loneliness. And her body. His thoughts evoked her smell, the feel of her tight cunt. He wanted her. Now. Desire battled with his mind's voice.

He accelerated across Westminster Bridge, turning left with a scream of rubber into a deserted Parliament Square. The House was in darkness: the politicians had gone home to bed. His mouth made a sardonic downturn. Then impulse made him pick up the car phone and dial her number. He was crazy. Her husband might answer. But, he shrugged, he would say it was a wrong number. A sense of daring aroused him again. He had never gone into her house before. And while her husband slept? He grinned.

She answered. There was astonishment and relief in her voice. She said, 'Where have you been?'

He felt again that sense of power over her. He said, 'It's where I'm going that counts. I'm coming to see you now.'

He heard her long gasp. She said, aghast, 'He's here. Asleep.' A moment's silence, then, in a whisper, 'But I

3

don't care. Come anyway. Don't press the bell. I'll be watching. How long?'

'I'm just around the corner. Three minutes.'

She had not told him about the police guard. He drove into her street and saw the uniformed constable standing outside the door, the other one strolling opposite. He grinned again. That added some spice to the game.

He parked down the street and strolled up to the door. The officer stepped forward to stop him, but she was there.

She said, 'It's all right, officer. This is a friend. I'm expecting him.' And he went in.

As soon as he touched her he knew he would have to kill the man who wanted to keep him from her. Or be killed.

1

'You can't be leaving?'

Catherine felt Gerald's arm slide over the taut silver lamé moulding her hips. His hand came to rest on one buttock and patted gently.

She turned her smile on him: 'I have to put away the April issue tomorrow, darling, and it's late.' She lifted her wrist where the dainty diamond watch barely showed the time, then continued the arm movement, pushing the long skein of heavy silver blonde hair back over her bare shoulder. There was an unconscious sensuousness in the lifted arm moving the breasts under the soft silver folds of the dress while the neck arched, raising the chin so that the green eyes looked down her cheeks at him.

Gerald noticed it – as no one could avoid noticing Catherine's sensuousness: but he was unmoved. He pouted at her and then turned the pout into an offered kiss. She was not tall, but her silver heels brought her lips almost level with his. He took hold of her by the shoulders and pulled her towards him, landing the kiss lightly on her lips. 'I can't let London's most beautiful magazine editor leave my fiftieth birthday party before dawn. Everyone will think the party was a flop. Dempster will be catty. You can't do it to me, my love.'

Gerald's face under his thinning tufty brown hair wore a mock pleading expression. His American voice, softened by almost three decades of living in England, rose and fell in campish undulations. He played the fop and advertised an appetite for young men, but no one was fooled by the manner he had designed to hide one of the publishing industry's sharpest brains.

Catherine laughed. She and Gerald had been friends for years. She leaned over now to kiss his cheek. 'I'll make it up to you, Gerald, I promise,' she said softly. Her perfume leaked into his senses. He was aware of an animal warmth that so contrasted with the cool, ice maiden looks. If he was ever to bed a woman, he thought, it would be Catherine. He felt a sudden curiosity about her sexuality. What was she like, loving a man? What would it be like to love her?

She stood back, smiling at him, reaching for both his hands, suddenly innocent as a schoolgirl.

Gerald bounced up and down on his toes, hamming excitement. 'You mean you'll get me the rights to your father's life story,' he squeaked. 'Or better still, your first novel, the one American Vogue says you're going to write. It must be autobiographical, about your love affair with the Afrikaner.' He wriggled his rounded body inside the Saville Row dinner jacket and breathlessly gabbled on: 'My dear, every passionate detail recalled, against a background of intrigue and subversion, laced with puritanism and perversion. How that would sell and sell. I want you to do it, we must talk. And there's someone I want you to meet. Now. Have some more champagne.' He was vamping wildly. His well noted resemblance to a famous American character actor was more marked than ever.

5

Catherine felt a twinge of pain at the even joking reminder of Jan. But Gerald was unstoppable now. He took hold of her hand and pulled her into the long, still crowded drawing room, heading for the bar.

She protested feebly. She was tired and wanted to leave. She had too many preoccupations to listen properly to what people were saying and the party, filled though it was with London's literary elite, had bored her. She wanted to be alone in her car, driving through the night. Yet, her feet followed Gerald's determined steps through the elegant, peach toned room.

The groups of guests swayed and parted to let them through, smiling, quipping, flattered to be invited, eager to be on the best terms with this publishing genius. Gerald Marks had spent the first twenty-three years of his life in California and taken his first degree, in psychology, at Berkeley. He had decided to settle in London after doing a doctorate at Cambridge, on a Jungian view of literature. The intention to go into publishing had been forming in his mind for years and had eventually crystalized when, acting on his intuition, (for which he had since become famous) he had obtained the rights to an unusual novel written by a friend. He gambled everything he had and more to publish and promote it and it had become a bestseller and formed the foundation for his very successful business.

He had met Catherine once or twice before she came to him with her book on Rhodesia's last days before independence, War in Heaven. A committed black rights supporter who wanted to express the white man's point of view was unusual. Catherine was offering a controversial book that melded the cry for political justice with compassion and understanding for the offending side.

Gerald had a reputation for liberal publishing: black poets, books on human rights and left wing novels were his indulgence among an otherwise commercial output of tight thrillers and hyped romances. He liked controversy, and the occasional risky book that might turn out to be an attention grabber, like this one. Some, on the intellectual left, had damned him for publishing it. He put Catherine's face on the cover, promoted it and let their criticisms bounce off.

Since, he had been angling for Catherine to write her father's life story. Sir Arnold Clyne had been a teenage war refugee from Nazi Austria. While a footman in the house of a White Russian Count in post war London, he had eloped to Kenya with his employer's under age daughter, the Countess Marina Catherina. He was now a leading City of London banker and political patron, friend of the Prime Minister, of royalty. It was one of the best untold stories and Gerald wanted it, but Sir Arnold was uncharacteristically unwilling for a man who was known to court publicity for his business deals and his political contributions. It was rumoured he was waiting for a peerage before baring all.

They reached the bar by the huge bay window. The curtains were drawn back to show the snowy garden, a floodlit negative of angled branches and lumpy shrubs edged in white. Leaning on the bar, a suavely posed black man in a dark blue velvet dinner jacket was listening to one of Marks Publishing's publicity girls.

Gerald waved at a barman. He took the black man by his velvet sleeve. 'Have you met Catherine Clyne, Ndawe? What, no?' He pulled Catherine forward and she smiled uncertainly at the handsome African.

She wondered, fleetingly, if the man was Gerald's lover. Then realized he could not be. Gerald kept business and pleasure strictly apart and this was clearly business. He was saying, 'Catherine my darling, this is Sam Ndawe, one of our latest political imports from South Africa. We're publishing his first novel in June. It's going to be a bit too close to the truth for comfort in South Africa, eh Sam?'

Ndawe nodded cautiously. His face seemed to Catherine to be deliberately expressionless, that of one used to hiding his feelings under a mask. She gave him a straight assessing look from her blue green eyes. He blinked and shifted his weight against the bar, propping his elbow on it.

Behind him, the barman poured champagne

7

into chilled flutes. Gerald was a stickler for detail, a perfectionist. Even at 3.00 a.m., long past the middle of a successful party, the glasses were still being put on the ice and the champagne was still an exact cool. It was one of the qualities that had made Gerald a publishing success. Catherine approved. Gerald's perfectionism matched her own. Everything she did, from her magazine and her TV programme and her writing, to her personal appearance, was hallmarked with that same elegant perfectionism.

Gerald was still introducing her, addressing Ndawe in the manner of an impresario bringing on a star, 'This slip of a beautiful woman was thrown out of South Africa, eight years ago, for trying, single handedly, to overthrow Apartheid. Deported, unceremoniously. In her nightie. But she's a heroine there now.' He tightened his arm proudly around Catherine's shoulders and beamed as if she were his own achievement. He added, confidently, 'You've probably read War in Heaven.'

Ndawe nodded, cautiously. An expression of interest overcame the sudden censorship in his eyes. He opened his mouth, but Gerald was still talking. Catherine stood patiently. Her face showed polite interest, concealing a powerful desire to run screaming out into the snow. South Africa was a subject she avoided. Since her last departure from Jan Smutts airport, seen off by the security police she had tried to forget that piece of her past. The only time she would recall it, she had told herself, would be when she wrote the novel based on her love affair with Jan.

After three years as a correspondent for the Associated Press in Southern Africa, she had immersed herself in a completely new life. She had taken a job with The Sunday Times in London, and made some initial moves to stand for Parliament. Later, changing her mind about politics, she had persuaded her father to bankroll her own magazine, and that was a satisfying success.

Writing War in Heaven, the book about White Rhodesia's final days, had been part distraction part catharsis after her grief of parting from Jan without even saying goodbye. Pages turned swiftly in her mind, flashing images of Jan, bronze, blond, hard bodied. Her stomach churned. Jan Fourrie, her dearest love in all her life. She had not seen him since or spoken to him after that self-torturing call she had made from London after her arrival. She had left him without a kiss and he would never follow. Never. She closed the book.

They were all staring at her. Ndawe was looking impressed, friendlier now. Tessa, the publicity girl was giving her a slightly perplexed look. Catherine had not been listening to what Gerald had been saying about her.

Gerald said, 'Come on, Catherina, let's have some of that Tsarina sparkle. Why so tongue tied after I've been singing your praises?' To Ndawe, he said, 'Cat's mother was a White Russian aristocrat, you know. Her staff at Vanities call her the Tsarina when she's being impossibly exacting, which is most of the time.'

He handed Catherine a glass of champagne. She sipped gratefully. There was a pause.

Tessa broke the silence. She said, 'I was in New York for Christmas and I saw a profile of you in American Vogue.'

Catherine smiled with strain. 'Oh, yes?'

The writer of the piece had put her finger on a sore spot. The pages with their glossy pictures sprang up in Catherine's memory. One paragraph in particular had pinned her with its painful accuracy:

'For a woman who has everything, a rich banker for a father, a likely future Prime Minister for a husband, wealth, beauty, a successful magazine published in London and New York, her own TV programme, she seems remarkably wistful. She pines. Something remains beyond her reach. Money cannot buy love or happiness: Catherine Clyne is a walking advertisment for that.'

They were all waiting for her to say something. Turning to Gerald, she acted pulling herself together, smiling collected charm, 'Darling, I'm so tired. Please forgive me.' To Ndawe, she said, faking enthusiasm, 'I'd like to interview you. We could do it for "Person to Person", my regular piece in Vanities. Maybe for my TV show when the book comes out.' She smiled at him. She had not heard him speak yet. He might not make good TV.

To her surprise Ndawe bowed slightly. He said, shyly, deep voiced, 'I'd be honoured to do that, Catherine.'

'Good.' She smiled a wide happy smile. 'I'll get your number from Gerald. Now if you'll all forgive me, I really do have to go.' She put down her barely touched wine.

Gerald followed her into the hall, helping her slide the heavy quilted velvet cloak over the clinging silver dress. Music flowed out into the hall from the dining room which had been turned into a disco. Serious now, and with an anxious look, he said, 'Did something upset you, Cat?'

She shook her head, answering breezily, 'Nothing, Gerald dear.' She could see he did not believe her.

But his expression relaxed a fraction and he said, caressingly, 'Well, you're still the most beautiful woman in London. You outshine them all, like a rose in winter.'

'Don't you mean a frozen rose?' She had turned from him and her loose hood hid her profile; her tone was jaunty, but she did not conceal the bitterness in her voice.

Gerald leaned over and kissed her cheek. He said gently, bantering, 'Someone should thaw you out.'

'If that happened I should probably die, end up like melted ice cream in a sickly puddle.' She said it lightly, stepping out into the crisp snow. Her smile hid nothing from him as she added, 'This way, at least I'll last as long as refrigeration.'

'We'll have lunch soon,' he promised. He wanted to talk to her alone, and not only about her father's biography. He was her friend, although she was also a very valuable publishing prospect. On both counts, he was interested in her wellbeing.

He watched with a concerned frown as she walked to her car. Again the sensuousness of her movements struck him. He thought, I wonder if she's aware of it. Looking at Catherine was like watching a leopard pace a marble cell. Caged passion with nowhere to go. He wondered if her husband had noticed. He thought, probably not. James wouldn't notice a Marilyn Monroe double on his lap at breakfast. He's too busy with his dispatch boxes. Come to think, Catherina is as sexy as Monroe. I should try to find her a lover.

*   *   *   *

The Aston Martin slid sideways and spun in a complete circle. She went with it, knowing not to brake. Haverstock Hill was slick with freshly fallen snow and the windscreen blinded by flakes that came spiralling out of the night. She straightened out and lifted her foot off the accelerator, letting the car slow naturally. Just after Belsize Park station, she turned off the slithery hill, driving cautiously down a side street into the Primrose Hill Road, following her nose. From the hill she saw London spread in sparkling folds to the horizon. Stars prickled, thorns of light between petalled snow clouds. The flakes had faded into the wind.

It was a long time since she had been to Hampstead at night and even longer since she had been to Gerald Marks' enormous house. It had been a lively party. They served the caviar and lobster supper at midnight. Dessert came on at one. Usually she loved to stay late, dancing, but tonight, she felt tired and depressed. Life had lately begun to taste like sawdust. She carried sadness within her like a dead child. The Vogue writer had seen it.

She snaked around the foot of Primrose Hill and turned right past the Zoo. The hill loomed white to her right and Lord Snowdon's Aviary on her left was outlined in two or three inches of crisp icing. She put out a hand and slid a tape into the deck. Soft jazz late at night soothed her. Oscar Peterson. Hmm. She leaned back in her seat, putting her hand up to cover a yawn. The road opened up, free and empty, slushy and less slick. She put on more speed.

On impulse, she decided to take the Outer Circle into Baker Street and turned into the park at Hanover Gate, slowing to a bare fifteen miles per hour on the freshly covered road. Crazy maybe, but she wanted to see the snow-touched trees with every bare twig outlined in white. She thought about taking a stroll in Regent's Park. That might be the maddest thing to do yet. If it wasn't crazy enough to stay up until nearly four when she had a full day at the office tomorrow.

She thought, so, why not walk in Queen Mary's Rose Garden? There might still be roses blooming there. It had been a mild winter and they might not yet have cut the bushes down. The thought of roses laden with fresh snow leaking their perfume into the midwinter night drew her. She would have to climb the gate in her evening dress to get in. She grinned then at the challenge.

She wanted to see them, smell them, those roses burning and blazing with summer passion in death's barren season. The image lifted her mood, brought a wavelet of hope that seemed to surf over her secret melancholy's dark lake. No one suspected her of having this Stygian undercurrent running below her bright, stylish life. She kept it well hidden under sophistication, masked it with sharp wit that only now and then cut too sharp, like broken glass and made people wonder, as she knew Gerald had wondered tonight.

But then she dismissed the notion. Out loud she told herself, 'Go home to bed, Catherine Clyne, you crazy woman, you have a magazine to edit tomorrow.' She glanced left at the white expanse beyond the hedge. The lake, deep and dark as death, not yet frozen, and around it, all that untrodden whiteness scattered with sleeping birds. It looked very tempting, pure. If only . . . she began a sentence in her head, then abandoned it.

She moved her long silvery blonde hair back over her shoulders and put her chin up slightly. She had to avoid those thoughts. She turned up Oscar Peterson. She turned on the fog light. It shot ahead, lasering the whitened road.

She felt a sense of desperation, so familiar, surging into her chest, blocking her breathing. She clenched her teeth and thought, I can't go on feeling this grief. I'll have to do something about it. She trod gently on the accelerator as a wild impulse possessed her to live dangerously and fly the powerful car down the slithery white river of light. Into nothingness. Into a blinding white instant death.

The engine choked and faltered in its smooth beat, once, then again. The car failed to surge forward. She looked at the gauge. She still had enough in the tank

12

surely, though it was a bit low. The revs missed another beat and suddenly died altogether. She guided the silver car into the kerb and turned off the lights. So much for a spectacular suicide, she grinned grimly into the driving mirror.

Now what? She was halfway between the mosque and Baker Street. She tried the starter. No luck there. With a sigh, she released the bonnet and climbed out into the snow. She pulled the hood of the velvet cloak over her head and bent over the engine, flashing a torch at its intricate and still shining beauty. The car was less than a year old and never gave a hint of trouble. It was a long time since she had had to do anything like this with any car, let alone this beauty.

She decided the gauge must be wrong and went around to the boot where she kept a gallon of petrol. She unlocked the cap and poured it into the tank. But when she tried the engine, it still failed to start. Was there dirt in the pipes? she wondered. Whatever it was, she would not spend any more time worrying about it.

There was no traffic on the Outer Circle, probably precious little on the main street at this hour. She would have to walk down to Baker Street and find a cab, if there was such a thing to be found at nearly 4 a.m. on a bitch of a January night. She picked up her evening bag from the passenger seat, buttoned her coat firmly up to her neck, as much to hide the diamond and sapphire necklace as for warmth, and locked the car.

Then, from the corner of her eye, she saw something move against the whiteness about fifty yards away. She jumped. Someone was walking towards her. She saw a bulky outline and a large brimmed hat. A man walking with a large dog. She thought, What kind of a man comes out here on a night like this? She stood, hesitating, fear prickling at her nerves. Then she unlocked the car again. She was getting in, planning to lock herself in until he passed, when he stopped beside her.

He said, 'Are you having trouble? Can I help?' It was not a cultured voice, but it sounded safe, courteous.

She looked up and saw very little apart from the black

13

fedora and the part of his face between it and the collar of his heavy fur coat. She said, 'It just stopped and it's not out of petrol.' Her own voice sounded suddenly too upper class. She smiled up at him. 'I've decided to dump it and hike.'

He didn't smile. He said, 'Does the starter work? I'm no mechanic, but maybe I can do something.'

She pulled the bonnet lever and said with a grin, 'Help yourself. I'll pay for the dry cleaning.'

She thought he smiled then but he was already moving to the front of the car. She brought him the torch and they both peered into the engine. He reached out a black gloved hand and undid the carburettor.

Holding the flashlight, he said, 'It doesn't look dirty.'

She said, 'It must be something radical. Please don't bother now. I'll get a cab.'

He shrugged. 'It won't be easy. I'm going down towards Baker Street. You can walk with me, if you like.' He spoke with a studied carefulness, elaborately courteous. His accent was London, his voice husky.

'Thanks.' She closed the bonnet and locked the car again, leaving the parking light on and they set off.

Her silver shoes were soaked already and she slithered on the crisp snow, the fantail of her silver dress trailing behind her. He turned and offered her his arm, hamming a little, saying, 'If you're not wearing your snow boots, you'd better hold on to me.'

She took his right arm. He was tall, built strongly and there was something in his presence that made her feel unsure of him. There was a kind of menace in his reticence. Yet she felt secure on his arm. They walked on silently, the dog plodding ahead on its short chain. She wondered what to say to him.

He broke the silence. 'Have you been to a party?'

'Yes. I'm not always out so late.' She laughed slightly, ill at ease with their social difference. He said nothing, so after a few more paces, she said, 'Are you usually out at this hour?' Her voice seemed too coy. She bit her lip.

'Quite often. I walk my dog.'

They lapsed into silence again. They had reached the

head of Baker Street now, and Catherine turned to look up Park Road but there was no traffic. The Abbey National clock said it was ten past four. They walked towards the traffic lights at Marylebone Road. Baker Street station was long closed up for the night.

He said, 'How far do you have to go?'

'Westminster.'

He nodded. 'You can't walk it in those shoes. If we don't see a cab in a minute I'll fetch my car and drop you.' He added, 'I live quite near here.'

She said, 'Oh goodness, I couldn't bear you to have to do that. We can telephone for a cab from somewhere surely.' She looked around, helplessly.

He said, 'It's all right. It's no trouble really. I'm not going to bed just yet.'

They walked half way down Baker Street without seeing a cab. Catherine's shoes were beyond recall, her feet soaked. He said, 'I'd better drive you.'

She looked around. There seemed no alternative. She said, 'You're very kind.'

He led her left and they walked some way down the side street, turning eventually into a mews. At last he stopped in front of a garage and reached in his pocket for keys. He unlocked the garage and went inside. She saw a pale gold Rolls-Royce. He went to a door at the far end and opened it for the dog. She heard an alarm buzzer sound, then he came out again. He brought the car out into the street and got out, coming towards her.

He held the door open for her and took her elbow ready to help her in. He was very careful with her, as if she were made of glass.

She said, again, 'I'm so grateful for your help.'

He closed her door.

As he climbed into the driver's seat she said with a little gasp, 'I'm so sorry, I haven't introduced myself, have I? How very rude of me. I'm Catherine Clyne.'

He nodded, then reversed out of the mews and drove back towards Baker Street. He said, 'Where exactly would you like me to take you?'

'Queen Anne's Gate, please.' She felt intimidated by

his silence, like a small child with an adult.

Still, his silence was restful, reassuring, carried a strength and a trust. It was not a barrier. She sat back looking at the snow masked streets. There were no other cars, few lights now. It was like an abandoned city and she and her silent companion were the only people alive in it. They drove through Mayfair and on down Constitution Hill and the Mall, like pioneers over the virgin snow. It was like the beginning of the future in a world with no past.

They arrived at Queen Anne's Gate. She saw the light on in the drawing room. She and James always left that one on when one of them was still out. He must have been in bed some time now. The House was only just back after the Christmas recess and would have risen early.

He stopped the Rolls where she directed him and kept the engine running, got out quickly and opened her door, putting out his hand to help her out.

Standing in the snow, she said, 'Won't you tell me your name and let me have your telephone number? I'd like to thank you properly.'

He shook his head, 'There's no need.' He seemed embarrassed, suddenly shy. He was not looking at her.

'Please.' She turned her charm on him. He looked at her and, at last, she saw his eyes in the street light. They were black holes, unfathomably expressive. She could not read them. He moved his head and the hat brim cast its shadow again. Then he stepped forward and closed the car door.

She thought, Why doesn't he want to tell me his name? She said, 'I know where you live, you might as well tell me your name. What is it?'

Turning away slightly and lowering his head, he almost mumbled, 'Christopher. Christopher Angel.'

She smiled broadly and lifted her head and the white satin lined hood slid back revealing her shining hair. 'Thank you, Christopher. You have been rather an angel.' She laughed lightly.

He laughed, a low, husky, short laugh.

She said, appealing, 'Where can I reach you?'

He put his hand in his pocket as if looking for something. Then shook his head: 'I don't have a card, I'm afraid.'

She said, 'Tell me. I have total recall of telephone numbers.'

He shrugged. She thought, he doesn't believe me. Was he disappointed? Or was he evading her, still? She waited.

He spoke slowly. '486-5930.'

'Oh God, every digit different.' She repeated the number. 'I'll remember it though.' She smiled at him.

'You mustn't stand out here any longer.' He stepped forward and put his hand under her elbow, leading her carefully towards her front door. She felt immensely protected. He did not leave her until she had turned her key in the lock. Then he smiled slightly, nodded and turned away, walking quickly to his car. He raised his hand in a brief wave as he drove off.

She did not close the door until he had left the street. Then she walked into the drawing room and wrote his number and his address on the telephone pad. She thought she might send him some wine or some flowers as a thank you gift. She had not really needed his telephone number for that. Still, one never knew: it might be useful.

2

It was almost eleven when Catherine arrived at her office in Covent Garden. She looked fresh and elegant, but felt tired and edgy. She had awakened feeling exhilarated by her midnight adventures, but had found James in a tense, dour mood that had wiped away her lightness. She had started to tell him what had happened over breakfast, but he was immersed in papers and had clearly not been listening.

She went straight to her desk at one end of the huge sky lit room overlooking the rooftops and the piazza. The whole of the south section of wall and roof had been glassed, which gave the room's occupants a sense of being in the sky. This morning, they could also see snow shimmering on the rooftops in bright sunlight that flooded the white-walled room with a crackling blue light.

Catherine loved this. She had especially sought out the huge rooftop studio and commissioned the architects to turn it into a glasshouse. She loved light, the brighter the better. The roof space was hung with huge old film lights that turned the place as bright as any TV studio on cloudy days. Ionisers swung among suspended plants from the same rails as the studio lights, and at the far end a fountain played. The walls were decorated with huge blow-ups of bodies and faces, some of the magazine's best work.

The whole space bristled with the kind of energy Catherine remembered from her childhood days on Mount Kenya at seven thousand feet on the equator. That was what she intended. She knew people worked harder and thought livelier in a bright light and Vanities was a magazine that needed the brightest talents at peak performance. Catherine took care to hire them and create the conditions in which they could flourish.

This morning, the office was humming with even more activity than usual. The April issue was going to press today. Writers and editors crouched in rapt concentration over their computer terminals. The intensely light room seemed to flicker with images from a fast running film projector as brightly and fashionably clothed assistants and secretaries raced from editorial desk to editorial desk with proofs and pictures, artwork and problems.

'Your father called, Cat.' Catherine's personal secretary, Janie, leaned over the elegant glass-topped, brass-legged trestle that Catherine used for her desk.

'Is it about lunch?' Catherine pushed up a sleeve of her brilliant scarlet cashmere dress and picked up one of five phones on the desk top. This was the gold personal phone shaped like an egg. It had been a present from Sir Arnold Clyne for the magazine's fifth birthday, a year ago.

Janie nodded. 'He said the Savoy at one. Ring to confirm you'll be there. Or he said I can go instead.' She laughed. She was a tall, slim brunette with long legs and waist length hair. It had been a contest in the office during the past year to see whose hair would be longest. Catherine had cried off with her hair below her shoulder blades. It was already too heavy for comfort. Janie's finer locks were still growing.

Now, Catherine smiled. 'I'm afraid I am going, Janie,' she said, firmly. She knew Janie Barnes had a tremendous crush on her father, despite his age, and she had no intention of encouraging it. Good secretaries were too hard to find. One did not want them turning up as one's stepmother. She punched in her father's personal number. 'Find me some tea please, love.' She smiled affectionately at Janie who turned away disappointed that she would not be able to dangle on the edge of Catherine's conversation with her father.

'I'm coming, Daddy.' Catherine spoke briskly as her father picked up his personal line with a barking 'Yes?'

'What kept you? I rang at nine-thirty.' Sir Arnold Clyne usually got to his Chairman's suite on the third floor of Clyne Johnson's prestigious office near the Bank of England by 8 a.m. each day and could never understand the publishing world's late hours.

'We work late too, Daddy,' she always told him.

'So do I', was the invariably gruff reply.

This time, she said, 'I had a very late night. The Aston broke down when I was coming home from Gerald's shindig. I was stuck in the snow without a ski.'

'Where?' He sounded anxious.

'Right in Regent's Park at nearly 4 a.m.' She had the shadow of an American accent still. She had developed it during her college years at Columbia School of Journalism and allowed it to grow in during three years in New York as a reporter for the New York Post.

'Good Lord. How did you get back at that time? How did you get a taxi in this weather?'

She laughed. 'A sort of spirit of the night came along with a big black dog and whisked me off to Baker Street.

He ended up driving me home. The car's still up by Hanover Gate.'

'What do you mean, spirit of the night? A man? I don't know what kind of a man you could meet out there at that hour of the morning. You're lucky he didn't mug you or worse. You're crazy getting into a car with a stranger.' Sir Arnold sounded horrified. He spoke rapidly in staccato sentences. His Germanic humour was not engaged by Catherine's frivolous description of events. His Viennese accent, which he had been unable to lose despite fifty years in Kenya and England, seemed especially pronounced this morning. He added, as if giving an order, 'You'd better get the car moved.'

'Of course, Daddy darling. My very next call. I'll see you at lunch.'

Smiling, she replaced the receiver. She would get Janie to have the Aston Martin towed to a garage. Now there was a mound of proofs to read before lunch.

She poured pale Oolong tea from the Minton pot on the small silver tray Janie had brought her and dropped a sliver of lemon into the delicate flower patterned cup. She never drank coffee. The tea's gentle stimulation would bring her to peak function in a few minutes. She called it her poor girl's cocaine. Though she never touched drugs, and poor she had never been.

*   *   *

The Thames was grey and stiff with cold. Catherine watched the ebb tide toy with a six foot piece of timber at the edge of Waterloo Bridge and waited for her father to finish his monologue. It was a shame to waste lunch at the Savoy on such a topic, but still, the view was always worth coming for. And the food and service compensated for the conversation. She sipped at her one glass of champagne, an exception at lunch time, but much needed today, then meditatively raised it towards the light and gazed through it at the brilliant sky. At last, she turned her large sea blue eyes back to her father.

Sir Arnold Clyne was easily the most handsome man in the room. His thick, slightly long hair was pale silver,

20

having only a hint of its former blond. But he looked vigorous and in perfect health. His face, tanned from last week's skiing holiday, lit up very pale blue eyes which had the brilliance and changeability of opals.

The impression of this fine head combined with his slim body in the formal dark grey pinstriped suit was of calm authority. He seemed above and beyond the traumas of day to day living, a rich, successful man savouring life's delights without in any way going to seed. He looked no more than fifty-six or seven. No one would guess he was a good ten years older.

They were an ornamental couple. It was not immediately obvious that Catherine was his daughter. With her pale blonde hair and faintly tanned skin she could have been a young wife or mistress. But most of the other diners in the River Room knew who they were.

Arnold Clyne, the immensely successful, recently knighted merchant banker, was often featured in the business pages of the better newspapers and the business magazines. He occasionally appeared on TV as someone whose financial advice was always accurate and who was known to advise the Prime Minister. Sir Arnold had some very senior political connections and, thanks to his daughter's marriage to the Prime Minister's most talented minister, they included the highest. He was admired by some, though disparaged by others, as a man who had started out in life as a footman in a Russian emigre's house in London after fleeing from Nazi Austria before World War II. Catherine's face was known too, from TV, gossip columns and her own magazine's pages.

They were both envied and admired. But at present neither was concerned with the interested glances that came their way. They were occupied with a discordant private matter. Sir Arnold was winding down, satisfied that he had expressed his argument satisfactorily. 'So, you see, my dear girl, divorce should be quite out of the question for you at present.'

She smiled at him, coolly. Her expression masked her irritation, but the eyes stayed moody and her words carried a sting. Her voice was oddly colourless as she spoke. 'You know I always want to please you, Daddy, but don't you think staying in a dead-end marriage to satisfy your political aspirations is pushing things a bit too far?'

Sir Arnold stopped breathing a moment, looking at her, surprised. There was a moment's silence. He had not heard her speak in that cold tone before. When he replied, his voice was gravelly with anger.

He said, slowly, 'First of all, it's not a dead-end marriage. James is obviously going to be Prime Minister when Major goes. Just give it time and things will improve between you, I'm sure. All marriages go through this kind of phase. He's working too hard, that's all.'

Catherine coloured. She spoke rapidly and breathlessly. 'Daddy, you know this phase has been going on since about three months after the honeymoon. We've been married five years and he gives me almost nothing of himself. We don't spend time relaxing together, don't laugh or talk trivia. We only discuss affairs of State or domestic problems. James doesn't pay me any attention as a woman. He makes me feel like a necessary and unattractive piece of furniture and I've lost interest in him as a man. But I'm too young to go into sexual hibernation. I need a loving relationship and I must be free to find one honestly.'

She put down her glass and leaned her elbows on the table. 'Have you any idea what it's like for me? Anything I felt for James has just gone dead. If I didn't have a wonderful life through the magazine I'd just die sitting at home every night while he hangs around the Commons or burns the midnight oil at the Ministry. And when I do see him he's about as much good as a stone floor for conversation, let alone anything more romantic.'

Sir Arnold glared at her and snapped. 'Well you won't help his career at this present point if you start a divorce. He's running into a lot of opposition now with the Development Scheme. His enemies inside the Party are watching for an opportunity to devalue him. Moreover, with a possible leadership election next year, he doesn't need the emotional pressure of a divorce. You should at least wait until he's been made Secretary of State in the next reshuffle. Then maybe you can see how things look.'

Catherine swished her hair back over her shoulders and threw up her chin so that Clyne could see the small cleft in it pointing straight at him. Her eyes slanted above the wide high cheek bones. They glittered like a rough sea under a harsh sun. She was so like her mother.

Her voice went up an octave. Heads at nearby tables turned towards them. The sound, if not the sense of her words alerted them to her anger. 'Why should I think of James, Daddy? He evidently doesn't think of me. Here I am, thirty-five. I want a child. It's a fat chance he's ever going to be the father. What am I supposed to do, find a stud somewhere and pass the kid off as James Waring Junior?' She sagged back in her chair and glared at him.

Sir Arnold looked anxiously at his daughter. They had always been close. Ever since the loss of her mother less than an hour after Catherine was born, he had been both mother and father to her. Though Brenda, of course, dear devoted Brenda, had really done the routine work of raising her.

She had been rebellious, though, always fighting him, and she still did, over everything. She evidently had inherited those same rebellious genes that had caused the seventeen-year-old Countess Marina Catherina to run away with the twenty-four-year-old refugee footman at her father's house.

Catherine had been a rebellious young girl. She had refused to listen to reason over her choice of university, had insisted on going to Columbia and becoming a journalist. Sir Arnold had planned that his daughter would go to Oxford where she could have mingled with the cream of the Establishment's children, enjoyed parties and balls and love affairs with society's future leaders, perhaps found herself a well-connected opportunity in publishing, or gone into politics like Margaret Thatcher.

Instead, she had made things worse by taking a job with the New York Post. He had just about lost patience with her completely when she joined Associated Press and became a foreign correspondent, a war correspondent no

23

less. Risking her life, her health, for what? Excitement? Adventure? Was that self destructive streak also one she had inherited. From whom? Marina Catherina? Or himself?

Catherine was a romantic, that was clear. She had been involved in an impossible relationship with a South African dissident. Now, heaven knows what she had in mind. She had no lover, he was sure. She was too honest to cheat on her marriage, however unsatisfactory, too serious to break her vows without trauma. Divorce would be Catherine's most honourable option, but even that would not be an easy way out. She and James, who was divorced, had had their Registry Office marriage blessed in church. And Catherine, although she never went to church, still believed in the sanctity of marriage and the darkness of sin.

That much, he knew, she had got from Brenda Roberts, the deeply religious woman who had been her nanny and governess. It was the same strict Calvinist morality coupled with Marina Catherina's spirit, he knew, that had got her into that South African business. His White Russian Countess had been a revolutionary in an ivory tower. She had said, so often, that she wished she could have been a member of the red blooded proletariat of her father's time in Russia, able to fight their cause without arousing class suspicion.

Arnold's ambitions were the reverse of his dead wife's. He had dedicated his life to his rise from Vienna's slums into the chandelier-lit salons of power and prestige. Now he had achieved almost everything he had set out to, except a peerage, and he had the PM's promise that that was coming. His only other remaining ambition was to see his daughter as a Prime Minister's wife.

James was in line for Number Ten one day. It was rumoured he was soon to be promoted. The Prime Minister was putting all the right opportunities in his way. Now, Sir Arnold's rebellious daughter wanted to divorce the man. And for what? An ideal of romantic love that no real man could fit or fulfil? With no one in mind? It was ridiculous.

24

Sir Arnold was a good judge of women. He had known many. He behaved, though, as if he had never been deeply in love. True, he had loved Catherine's mother. He had even eloped with her, but what other option had a penniless young man infatuated with a rich aristocratic girl? Anyway, that had turned out well. His fortune had been founded on her family's remittances, paid to keep her and her ex-footman husband out of England. In fact, it was among his best kept secrets that he had loved deeply once since. He had never remarried for there were too many secrets in his heart with which to burden any marriage. Looking at Catherine now, he understood her need for love. For a moment, his glance was softened by sympathy.

Clearly, she was very unhappy in her marriage to James Waring. He felt concerned, not only because he had engineered their meeting and encouraged the marriage, but because his only daughter's unhappiness was now threatening to disrupt the man's career.

'Rina, Rina,' he said soothingly. He used the pet name, short for Catherina, which she had been christened after her mother. 'Don't be so pugnacious. Think about things for a while. Take a lover if you must. Have a discreet affair. Satisfy your needs, but don't start to break up your marriage now. You know James divorced once to marry you. Two divorces in six years begins to look like carelessness and you know how the Prime Minister feels about the sanctity of marriage.

'Well I know how you feel about it, that's for sure,' she spat in good imitation of her Russian mother. 'If you thought marriage was a good thing you might have taken another wife for yourself in thirty-five years.' She pushed her chair away and picked up her handbag, softening her voice to add, 'I've got to get back to the office, darling. Do forgive me.'

She stood up and bent over her father to give him a kiss, then turned and walked out of the restaurant. She did not see the ripple of sadness that deadened his pale eyes, crumbled the confident expression. She might have misinterpreted it if she had: there was plenty she did not know about her father. She loved him dearly, but his addiction to her marriage to James Waring was getting too hard to live with. He is an unreconstructed social climber, she thought, just dedicated to getting his daughter into Number Ten, as a wife, if not Prime Minister. As she took her coat and moved into the cold street, her brisk walk was stiffened by anger.

She knew Sir Arnold had liked the idea of her having a political career. When she showed interest in standing for Parliament after her deportation from South Africa he had pledged his financial and other support. She could have got herself a seat fairly quickly if she had been prepared to fit the mould required by constituency parties for women Parliamentary candidates. But Catherine had not been prepared to dress conservatively, behave diplomatically and spend hours at committee meetings. She had not liked the way the MP's job looked from the inside, glorified social work she decided, and she had backed off.

Catherine had serious ideas but could not stomach dullness. Starting Vanities had been much more appropriate: the magazine world satisfied her need for excitement, variety, experiment, being on the leading edge of people, ideas, places in the news. It had taken a little while and some very smart accountants to convince Sir Arnold to give her the necessary half million to begin. But she had made a success of it and he was pleased, at least with that.

She walked quickly through the piazza without pausing to look in the shop windows as she often liked to do. She was breathing quickly, trying to unwind her tension. The air was scrubbed clean with coldness, a little raw as the night's snow softened into a sorbet under the pale midday sun. But by the time she had reached her office she felt very little better. Everyone was still hard at work and as the litter of half eaten sandwiches showed, they were taking a working lunch. She sat at her desk and stared at the sky. Little puff-ball clouds moved effortlessly over the blue, travelling on some high, sky wind that had not reached the world below. She thought, Life should be that way, light and floating. The weight of her unhappiness pressed in on her, dull and dark, seeming to shut out the brilliant light. She quickly lifted herself out of gloom. She looked over the heads of her hard working team and felt gratitude for them, for her magazine and its success, for her wealth and for her father's love and goodness to her. But she could not dismiss the knowledge that she, too often, felt empty, lonely.

She took out her handbag mirror and retouched her lips bright scarlet, examining her face with a critical eye. Her beauty should have brought her love and joy, something special. It brought her would-be lovers in hordes. It brought her men who wanted to buy her diamonds and who sent her flowers and invited her to dinners in Paris and weekends in Venice; gifts and invitations she never accepted. It had brought her marriage to a Minister of State who was clearly going to be Secretary of State quite soon and probably Prime Minister not long after. It had helped to bring her success as a magazine editor and some fame as a cable TV talk show host. In short it had brought her everything almost anyone could want, but it had not brought her love or a child, though she had only recently begun wanting that, or a deep sense of peace or happiness. And these, she felt were worth looking for, perhaps more worth having than all the rest, though there was no reason that one should exclude the others.

She thought of her father's words. 'Take a lover, have an affair.' Break her marriage vows? She had married with such hope and idealism. Now to junk it all and have an affair, admit defeat, admit her marriage was like almost every other one she knew? Could she do what other women did, amuse herself without being involved, keep her marriage going as a superficial social arrangement? The idea disgusted her. It was so dishonest, so futile. She knew she should try to take a lover, now, try to do as her father proposed, for the sake of James' career. That made it more honourable. Perhaps she could have an affair that was at least honest and true in the feelings it engendered, more than just entertainment, distraction. Perhaps she could find love and still do her duty by James, by his career? But who with? She thought

27

of the men she knew, married and unmarried and knew there was no one she wanted. Perhaps she would meet someone? She had no desire, had had none for years. She was truly a frozen rose.

The thought of roses drew her mind to last night. The man's face as he dropped her outside her house seemed to hover before her eyes. She remembered she had not yet sent him the wine she had intended as a thank you gift. She had a sudden impulse, then, not consciously thought out. It was like a dream action, but decisive, all the same. She put the mirror back in her handbag and picked up the golden phone. It took her a moment to recall the number but then she had it. She dialled 486-5930.

A soft, husky voice answered and she asked for him by name. She felt acutely aware of his intake of breath and the interest in his voice as he replied.

She said, 'I want to thank you for last night. I can't think how I would have staggered all the way down Baker Street in those idiot shoes without you to help me.' There was only a hint of laughter in her voice.

She was rewarded with a soft laugh at the other end of the line. He said, 'I'll provide the service any time it's needed.'

She said quickly, brightly, 'Well it's needed again, tonight.'

He was silent and she felt his hesitation. He didn't know how to react to this. She went on, 'Would you have dinner with me, then I can thank you properly?' She was both relieved and disappointed when he said he could not. Then, after a brief silence, he asked for her number.

He said, 'Perhaps you'll let me invite you one evening.'

She said, 'That would be nice, goodbye for now, then,' and rang off. That's that, she thought. He's not really suitable, anyway. She stared down at her red fingernails. Suitable? Suitable for what? What was she thinking about?

An hour later, he called back. He said, 'If it's not too late, I'd like to change my mind about this evening.'

As she would be working late, she arranged to meet him at a little restaurant in Covent Garden at nine o'clock.

3

The phone on the fur rug rang twice and he reached for it, flicking the TV down with the remote in his other hand. He leaned back against the green sofa cushions, one leg crossed over the other at the ankle, and spoke crisply into the receiver. He was pretty sure who it would be. 'Yes.'

The male voice had a strong cockney accent. The words poured out fast and strung together. 'I've goddit for yer, Guv. She's the b . . .'

He snapped, 'No names.'

The exaggerated cockney voice continued. 'Your bird, Guv'nor. She is who you think she is. She's 'is little blue eyed darlin' all right. He'll do anythin for 'er I'm told. But she doesn' ask f'much. Independent, y'know.' The caller sniggered. 'I could be independent wiv wot she's got, I can tell yer.'

He spoke slowly, quietly, and his low voice carried an authority that was within a hair of being a threat. 'Thanks. Keep it to yourself. Understand.' The last word was also a command.

'Right, Guv.' The caller rang off. He understood. You didn't mess with the Guv'nor.

He dropped the phone into its cradle and sat back, a slight smile on his face, his eyes thoughtful, staring but not looking at the images on the silent TV screen. He did not move to put up the volume. He had other pictures in his mind and another voice in his head. The call had only confirmed information he had received earlier, information he had to have before he gave his answer. His instinct to get background had been right, as usual. But then, getting information on whoever he dealt with was an ingrained habit.

He was cautious by nature, even more cautious by experience, so cautious that he should not be going where

29

he was going now. But then, it was the excitement of danger, added to the other, that he felt in his groin. He had already given his answer, straight after the first call had come through with news of the surprising, but guessed at, connection. Instead of acting as a brake it had goaded him, had given him an even better reason to take this one.

Now he had double confirmation. He had better be very careful. He knew the man could be dangerous and he would have to use more than his usual care with what he was planning to do. Care never to be found out, by anyone. Or at least by anyone who might live to tell tales.

He frowned. It was still not too late to change his mind. He went over it again, looking for his reasons for what he was doing, his reasons for not following his usual instinct, to keep away from this kind of connection.

He stood up. He was still going. He couldn't let this one pass. Something stronger than reason was driving him. Well, at least he knew what he was getting into. And there would be compensations. He laughed softly. He flicked off the TV and went into the bedroom, shedding his clothes quickly as he went. He just had time to take a shower before dinner.

4

He watched her come in. She stood in the doorway, looking around her, waiting to be led in. The cold air still seemed to cling to her pinkened cheeks. Her breath was coming quickly from her rush up the street. She did not see him sitting far back along the wall and as he watched her, unobserved, the sense of insult he had felt at being kept waiting melted into a growing confidence. Watching her made her his prey. He began to know her, then, to feel a power over her. It would only be a matter of when and how it would begin.

At last, a waiter reached her and he saw her smiling as she gave up her heavy white coat, saw the graceful gestures, the undulation of neck and shoulders as she spoke, took in the shapely legs, the figure under the short red dress. She swept her long silvery hair back over her shoulders and seemed to hesitate again, then threw up her head as the waiter led her to him.

He stood over her and was aware again of that fragility, but also of a strength that he had not noticed the previous night. She held out her hand in a rather grand social style, smiling brilliantly. He thought, She gives this smile to everyone. It's a barrier. I want what lies behind it. He took hold of her hand in both his, and for a fraction looked straight into her eyes, saw her falter as she met what lay there. It was enough. He released her and pulled out her chair. It had been her invitation, but she was now, clearly, his guest.

* * *

He dropped her outside the house in Queen Anne's Gate and she thanked him with that same polite formality of the previous night. She wondered whether to invite him in, for coffee, since he did not drink, then offered, hesitantly. He refused.

He walked her to her door and said, 'You'll have dinner with me again, won't you.' It was not a question.

She smiled and gave him her hand. 'I'd love to. Next week?'

He nodded. 'I'll ring you.' He turned and went briskly to his car.

This time she did not wait while he drove away, but let herself into the darkened hallway and closed the door quickly, leaning her back against it like someone who has had an escape.

*

31

5

Why was she going to dinner with him after deciding she would not? After all, what had she in common with him? Her fingers ran gently over the piano keys, absently picking at the Chopin waltz. She had told no one about him, had not mentioned him after the first explanations of how she had got home from Gerald's party.

She thought of their last meeting. He had a certain charm and presence. She liked him. She felt attracted to him. His big body gave her an exaggerated sense of her own fragility. There was a subtle emanation of power from him that was both comforting and threatening, and which excited her.

He was uneducated, of course. He had left school as soon as possible and run around doing any job he could find. He was a rebel, a maverick like herself, but not her kind. Not her class, she had known that from their first accidental meeting. As it turned out, he was not out of any class at all, not accepted by anyone as one of their own: he had told her he was the son of a Jewish woman who had got herself into trouble with a black man who had then vanished.

'I'm the result,' he laughed softly, watching carefully for her reaction.

She said, wonderingly, 'I hadn't noticed.' And it was true. She had not seen what he now made her see. His skin was pale and this distracted from her observation of his features. She now looked and read his blood in the slope of his rounded cheeks, the heavy unlined lids of brown eyes that were the shape and, at certain times in certain lights, seemed the colour of black olives. His hair was bushy, and abundant with the tight curls of Africa. She had not looked at his body either. Now she did. Had he meant her to do that? She had run her eyes rapidly over his heavy shoulders in the tailored pinstriped suit, down to the powerful thighs on the chair next to hers. She felt a shiver of sensuality as she recalled his eyes meeting hers after that assessing glance. They were knowing, searching eyes that told her his intentions. He seemed to project his sexuality at her then. She thought, Is it because I told him I was brought up in Africa? Does he want to see how I react to a black man? Did he think she was waiting for a black lover, or that she was afraid, like so many white women in Africa, of rape?

She told him then about her partisanship in South Africa, about her deportation. He seemed to relax somewhat. His blackness that he had seemed to thrust at her like a challenge receded. He was an Englishman again. With an English and Christian name, Christopher.

She said it seemed a strange name for a Jewish boy, and he laughed. He had been named after his absent father. His surname was from the German, Anglicized when his mother's family left there three generations before.

She came to the end of the waltz. Her fingers now moved randomly, running arpeggios and chords together into a subtle jazz theme. He was late. Half an hour late. Perhaps he was not coming. Did she feel relief or apprehension? Both. Perhaps his lateness was to punish her for keeping him waiting last time. She felt he had resented that. Had it made her seem rude or patronizing?

Abruptly, she stopped playing, stood up and walked across the light blue carpet. She surveyed the room. Its classical dimensions pleased her: the high, ornate ceiling, carefully restored with gilt, the chandelier and Venetian mirrors, the elegant, deep blue and gold silk sofas and chairs, the good watercolours and oils, the shelves of books. Perhaps he was held up by business. He had told her he was involved with restaurants and bars. She supposed that kind of business made demands at all kinds of hours. But he had a phone in his car. He could have called. Then she remembered, he did not have her home number, only that of the office.

She felt a stab of guilt. She had begun a deception, of James. But how honest was she being with Angel? At their previous dinner, she had told him briefly about her marriage. He could deduce her feelings from her words and must realize that she could be available. But was she? Was she misleading him? She must be mad to have him pick her up at the house. How would she explain it if James came home from the House just as Christopher Angel came to take his wife to dinner? Angel did not seem the kind of man she could claim to be having a business chat with about Vanities. Would she be able to pass him off as a financial adviser or a major advertiser? Could she say she was thinking of interviewing him, say he was a musician, an author? She thought, I don't want lies. I don't think I even want this man as my lover. What am I doing? The doorbell rang. She took her coat from the sofa and went into the hall.

Angel stood on the doorstep, unsmiling. He said brusquely, 'I'm sorry I'm late. I had some business problems.'

She nodded and walked into the street. Her movements were meant to tell him she was unimpressed by his ungracious manner. Surely he should conceal his mood when he knew her so slightly? Could it be something she had done? The evening went awkwardly after that. He drove fast, saying nothing, along streets that seemed curtained with cold. If she made comments or asked questions, he answered reluctantly. He drove into Belgravia and then across Hyde Park without telling her where they were going, stopping eventually outside a small Greek restaurant in Bayswater. Once inside he seemed more relaxed. They talked more easily over the highly-flavoured dishes. Bazouki music played on a tape and the restaurant was small, warm, dark and noisy. Cigarette smoke seemed to enfold them like fog. But she was uneasy. The strain between them did not dissolve and Catherine pleaded tiredness early. She felt him take offence, again. He drove her back across the park without speaking.

She thought, I won't do it again. He won't ask me. We don't get on. The encounter had reached an impasse. They would have so little to talk about, once the biographical stuff was laid out: it was just as well.

It was a relief to know she would not have to feel guilty any more. But it was strange that there should be so much feeling between them. So much energy in the silence that was alive with unsaid things. He pulled up outside her house and got out quickly to open her door. His movements were abrupt, angry, his face stern.

She put her hand out to offer her farewell. She said, in her best charming manner, 'Thank you. That was so nice.'

He ignored her hand and said, still unsmiling, 'Aren't you going to invite me in for coffee?'

She said, 'I think I'm probably rather over tired this evening. If you don't mind, I'd rather like to just go to bed. Please forgive me.'

He caught her to him then, roughly, furiously and pressed his lips onto hers. She felt his hands inside her coat running over her back, her buttocks, her breasts, under her skirt.

She pulled herself away from him. 'Stop, stop, please.'

He said, 'You must spend your life fighting men off? You're too good at it.' There was no humour. Bitterness jerked the words out of his mouth, harsh and coarse.

She said, coolly, 'I don't usually have to fight. Most men take a civil no for an answer.' She turned and walked towards her door.

He followed her and grabbed her hand as she put the key in the lock. His grip was strong. She trembled. She thought, I think he'd rape me if I let him in. She gave him a long look and then the tension broke. He kissed her again, more softly. She did not resist.

She felt herself soften and alarm began in her mind. She had to stop. She had to think. She had to decide what she was going to do. To decide if she really were going to take a lover. She pulled her lips away from his and for a moment they looked into each other's faces.

He said, 'Do you want to change your mind about the coffee?'

She shook her head. She whispered, 'Not now. Perhaps another time.' Her eyes looked into his and a small smile seemed to reflect back and forth across the space between them.

He said, 'I'll ring you.' There was a look of triumph on his face. Then he was gone.

She went into the drawing room, dropping her coat onto the floor. She was disturbed, aroused. She had to think about what she would do next. Her body was screaming with desire for him. But how was she to reconcile her sudden need for him with her marriage, with her life, her views? Mental arguments seemed futile against this overwhelming physical urge. How could she have not seen this coming? How had she thought she could simply choose to have or not to have a lover, or this man as her lover, as though she was buying a dress or a new car? How had she lied to herself for so long?

Now, she was up against a tough truth. She wanted him very badly. She sat at the piano, staring at the keys, her whole body open like a screaming mouth. Wanting. Wanting. She had not felt desire for months, or was it years. She could not ever remember feeling anything this intense. She could not be alone with herself and her need. She had to calm herself, to take her thoughts somewhere else. She began, slowly, to play a Beethoven sonata. She played for an hour thinking of nothing but the music. Slowly the screaming ache of longing to be touched and entered became a memory. But it was not a memory she was likely to bury. When she stood up to go to bed she knew she would be Christopher Angel's lover next time they met.

6

'Darling, I'm so sorry.' Catherine stood up and went towards her hostess. She slid an arm around the woman's waist and kissed her cheek. She smiled apologetically. 'You know, I mentioned I'd have to go early.'

The woman smiled back, regretful at losing one of her guests so early. It would break the cosy conspiracy of a successful party. That reward that came as the guests, having enjoyed her carefully chosen dishes and wines, now loosened their belts, stretched their legs and prepared for the more intimate giving away of gossip and trading of professional intelligence. The dinner party of ten was now all together in the cream and black drawing room. Catherine had waited for the ritual of the women leaving the men to their port and cigars, waited through the women's talk of clothes, parties, houses, lovers, husbands; waited until the women had come out of the bedroom and filed, chattering into the drawing room where the men had joined them. She had waited an agonizing ten minutes longer while talk of the latest book, the latest publishing coup, the newest sale of film rights, the most recent debacles in a certain television company had been tossed lightly back and forth among the replete, brandy supping company. Waited while cigar smoke rose over the elegant chairs and sofas, until conversation ebbed and flowed about her.

Catherine was on edge, hiding it behind her party front. No one seemed to notice, she thought, that she was silent, sipping Perrier, watching the men, mostly in dinner jackets, the women in an assortment of evening clothes, feeling bored. These were not people Catherine knew well, though she had met several before, knew of them, liked them well enough. Her hostess was a social friend, not an intimate, a woman who sought her as a dinner party ornament and social scalp: banker's daughter, Minister's wife, media success.

Perhaps she should not have come, knowing where she was going later. But it had been a professional duty to attend. In her position, one had to go everywhere, meet everyone, be seen and see. One had to pick up the gossip and contribute those subtle pieces of information about one's own business that would be retold at cocktail and dinner parties, at lunches and drinks; that would convey the impression she wanted. She would have preferred a more private life, more true friends and fewer smart acquaintances. Mostly she was bored by the predictable conversation, the received, fashionable ideas, the rehashed enthusiasms of youth offered as the sophistries of middle age, the often malicious, though wittily-told gossip.

She often felt alien, alienated from these drawing room superficialities and from people who had always lived in middle or upper class security in a democracy with safe streets. She silently held up her memories of Africa's bush wars and their casualties, her knowledge of cruel and real political struggles and injustices, for comparison against these dinner party opinions. She mildly despised and yet envied the innocence and indulgence of being educated and prosperous and safe from the experience of real suffering. Yet she hid this successfully enough behind an ironic wit and was popular, sought after, admired.

Tonight, it was worse. Her preoccupations were over-whelming her ability to think at all, let alone join in the dinner table conversation or the gossip. The guests that night were from publishing and TV, a terse newspaper editor and his morose Slav wife; a serious documentary film maker and his babbly girl; a woman newscaster, a newly successful woman publisher of literary novels; a recently Oscared filmwriter and his actor boyfriend; the newly appointed Controller of a TV channel whose wife was working abroad.

It was a carefully matched list of arrived but still upwardly mobile people in their thirties and forties, who would not feel overshadowed or in competition with any of the other guests, but who would harmonize well, would talk freely in each other's company. Many knew each other from other dinner parties in other, similar houses in Kensington, Holland Park, Chiswick and Hampstead. They were not the top league, the kind Catherine met at James' State functions, at Chequers, or even her father's power dinners at Charles Street: but in ten years, some of them would probably be as high as anyone could go in their professions.

The women were not particularly well dressed. Catherine, for whom clothes were an expression of her perfectionism as well as a defensive disguise, had chosen to wear an understated St Laurent black velvet, with a few equally understated diamonds.

At dinner she had sat between the TV controller and the newspaper editor. No one seemed to notice that she sent almost every course away, barely touched. In the candlelight reflecting from the deep polished table, scattering from crystal, silver and porcelain, Catherine's bare gold shoulders and her face framed by the curving fall of silver blonde hair glowed, irridescent against the strapless velvet sheath. No one noticed that her cheeks were paler, the lines around her mouth more taut, her eyes more intense than usual.

No one, that is, except the dark, watchful wife of the newspaper editor, who sat opposite, and who believed she had the gift of clairvoyance. She, alone, perceived Catherine's suppressed agitation and evident distraction, read the simultaneous brightness and darkness of the sea coloured eyes with their dilated pupils. She recognized the signs of fear and unsatisfied intense desire. She had watched Catherine pacing the bedroom, while the other women chatted, brushing her silky hair in front of the long mirror, stopping to stare at herself, with her bare shoulders, her black stockinged legs, lengthened by very high heeled black suede shoes, and visible to the thigh through the slit at the back of the short narrow skirt.

She had watched as Catherine stood, oblivious of the chattering women, still and silent before the mirror, an expression on her face that was part fear and part self discovery, as if she was seeing herself for the first time. The eyes had the look of someone who had seen an unbearable truth, but the editor's wife was sure that that truth was still in the future. She was watching Catherine now, in the drawing room, apparently growing mysterious and far away, as if slipping into another dimension of time, through the mist of cigar smoke rising above the conversation's river. But it was not only the smoke that created this impression. Catherine was receding from them like Euridice at the gates of hell, as if some dark Orpheus was summoning her into another life.

As Catherine left, the editor's wife shivered with a thrill of arousal and forboding that was not her own.

* * *

Catherine reversed the Aston out of its parking space and drove out of the quiet side road into Kensington High Street. It was not quite 10.40. She would be at the meeting place before 11.00 without effort. She drove fast all the same, jumping the lights, swerving left at Alexander Gate and then illegally right into Hyde Park. The needle reached 90 along The Carriage Road. She swung into Park Lane, crossed into Mayfair going past the Dorchester, waited, tapping impatiently at the wheel for the long light at South Audley Street. She was ten minutes early outside the block of flats on Hill Street. She found a space in Waverton Street and parked, turning off her lights, keeping her engine running and the heat on against the cold February night.

She reached out a hand to turn the mirror towards her face. The eyes that stared back at her seemed wild. Her body shook. She had spent days in a state of pulsating awareness of her sexuality. All evening the wetness and the throbbing in her groin had dominated her. Usually, Catherine was detached and observing, cool, clear, untouched. She lived in her head, and her quick, flickering emotions were always subjected to mental analysis, always transformed from murky sensations to clear thoughts, like grubs into moths. A feeling was only an incoherent thought, she believed. And thoughts could be perfectly understood, assessed and contained, once translated into words. But her feelings for the past few days refused to be turned into cool logic. They remained where they began, in tumult, in her sex. Her desire for that man seemed to have burned through some invisible barrier between her feelings and her mind. Her thoughts were now feelings recognized as truth.

But there was also fear. She was afraid of him, but she had no idea why. It seemed, there was some threat. It was as if he could kill her. And perhaps he might. He could be anything. She knew so little about him, only what he had told her, his name, his address, his work or what he told her of it, his origins. And no one knew she was meeting him. No one knew she even knew him. No one knew where she was now, where she would be, when she went to him in a few minutes.

She looked at her watch. It was still only five to eleven. She opened her handbag and pulled out her lipstick, to retouch the lips she had licked and chewed all the way here from Kensington. Her black silk and lace knickers were crushed into the small bag along with her comb and her keys. She had removed them when the women had gone upstairs at the dinner party. Since, she had been sitting on her throbbing sex, feeling the wetness that was surely seeping into the silk lining of the dress, so much so she was afraid there would be a mark on the velvet when she stood up.

Now she slid her hand under her skirt and touched the soft warm wetness that was swollen with readiness, ran her fingers tentatively over the silky hair, into the soft petalled heart whose perfumed dew was now a sticky nectar. She moved her fingers, shivered and gasped. The longing for him, for his hands, his mouth, his cock inside her, swallowed her whole. She was nothing now except desire. She was a pre-universe waiting for creation, waiting, dark and silent, inchoate and breathing as in sleep, waiting for the single pulse of light, the seed, the awakening.

Her sense of capitulation was complete. After the three weeks of fending him off, she thought she would not care if he killed her now, after they were lovers. All she wanted was to give herself up to him, to melt under him and be nothing except feeling. Mindless. Only womb and woman's wanting of the man's latent power made real in her body. Man to her woman. Body to body. Made one. She could remember nothing like this before. She had felt desire for men, experienced passion, fallen in love. But she had never felt compelled, beyond reason, like this. She felt helpless, fated, destined for whatever lay inside the block of flats, whether it was death or new life.

She took her hand away and tissued off the moisture.

41

Her fingers smelled of the sharp erotic sea and honey-suckle scent she knew was hers when she was aroused. She had been smelling like this for days, made more aware by the number of men who followed her, accosted her, approached her in restaurants and on the street, that she must be exuding some animal signal.

She glanced at her watch. It was time. She took another look in the mirror. Her face was alert, fearful. The eyes were almost black in the street's amber light. Her cheek bones stood out. Her lips looked full and moist. She tossed back her hair, got out of the car, locked it and walked, quivering, up Hill Street and into the block. She took the lift as she had been told and pressed the sixth floor button. Her balance was unsteady and her knees trembled. As the lift rose she was acutely aware of the bareness above her stocking tops, the nakedness caressed by her skirt's soft lining, the wetness between her thighs, like the wetness made by a man's semen as it leaks slowly out during the hours after love. But she had not yet been loved. She had not been loved for ten months, since James last touched her. And that had not felt much like love.

The flat was a distance down the hallway from the lift. She pressed a bell on the right side of the handsome teak door. It opened almost immediately. He stood there, a dim light casting his shadow onto her, like a presentiment. He wore a light grey pinstriped suit which fitted perfectly over his muscled body and a pink shirt open at the neck. His eyes were completely black in the shadow.

She moved towards him as if he, not she, willed it. He wrapped his arms fully around her, kicking the door closed, putting his full soft lips down on hers in a kiss that she was never to forget.

It was a kiss that merged her with some greater whole; a kiss of such intensity and softness, such heat and bliss that it was as though two elements of complete chemical compatibility had come together and fused. And in that fusion, that incredible flash of light and heat, it seemed nothing would ever be the same.

Catherine felt herself helpless, her legs giving way under her. Her cape fell to the floor. She was melting, merging, dissolving, her form and structure vanishing as he kissed her. Everything in her body seemed to be soft: even her bones had melted. His body too, was strangely soft in its power and size and muscled development, but his cock was hard against her belly. She could feel its size, its aggressive bulk. She felt his determination to have her swelling in intensity, to violence, felt his enormous strength, his physical power over her. She was afraid, but resigned to whatever he would do with her. Whatever he would do, she wanted. She was completely and willingly in his power.

And now his hands hunted for her skirt hem. She felt him lifting, pulling, felt his fingers stroke her thighs, his pause of breath as he explored above the stockings, the lace suspenders. He pulled the skirt again, impatiently, roughly and his hand roved higher. He held her tightly with his other arm, tight against him, against the full chest, the hard cock, the heavy muscular thighs, running his hand up to her buttocks. She felt his body swell and subside with his sigh of surprise at the discovery that she was naked under the dress.

He turned her now, pinned with her back against him, pushing his cock hard against her buttocks. He pulled one of her hands around to feel the cock straining under the trousers. Then he took her two wrists in one hand, holding them roughly behind her back. His free hand now pulled the skirt up high over her hips. His fingers ran quickly between her thighs, found the soft, wet place.

She cried out with relief and want. She was breathing with little gasping breaths like sobs. She went limp, collapsed against him, leaned her head back and he put his mouth on her throat, ravenously kissing and sucking, running his tongue into her neck sides.

He said, huskily, 'I'm going to rape you. You know that, don't you? I've waited for you too long. You're going to let me fuck you because you haven't got any choice now. You can't say "no" any more. I've got you.'

She groaned with pleasure again, as his fingers surged around her swollen desperate place. Then he took his hand away and put both hands on her shoulders, gripping

43

them. He pushed her along the hallway. She let him steer her, ready now, as never before, longing, and frightened, like a virgin, to have him do what he wanted, whatever that would be.

The bedroom was unlit but light fell through the doorway from the hall onto the large curtained bed that stood a few feet from the door. He pushed her towards it, then turned her to face him. He held her again, kissing her, while with one hand he undid his trousers. He pulled her hand to him and laid it on the big cock that was swollen and hot, curved, its skin stretched tight without a fold, the head bulbous, with moisture already forming at its tip. He wrenched at her skirt which had slipped down as they walked. She heard a seam tear as he pulled it violently upwards. He pushed her backwards onto the bed, pulled her legs apart and thrust himself into her with a growl, ramming the big cock deep into her soft warmth, and she cried out with surprise and momentary pain. At once, he was avid, panting, pumping hard, driven, it seemed, beyond self control.

With one strong hand, he caught both hers and held them over her head. He said, roughly, 'I'm raping you. Do you know that? I've wanted to do this since I saw you that night. I should have raped you there in the park in the snow. I shouldn't have waited. I should have fucked you in my car outside your house.'

She cried out once as he thrust into her. For all her wetness she was tense with fear and he hurt her. Then his cock filled her but its thrust was a devouring caress, a command that craved her response. He was panting now, desperate, fast. She felt herself totally controlled by his intensity as if indeed it was rape. And the fear was still there. Fear and excitement and longing to be annihilated by his power. But she wanted everything he was doing to her. She cried in ecstasy at what he did to her. No, it was not what he did to her. It was the passion with which he did it. It was his desire, the violence of his lust for her, and her response, her need for him, for him alone above all men, now, that made this the greatest ecstasy she had ever known. It seemed to go on for ever. She wished it would. She thought, is there any other heaven?

He paused, and, still deep inside her, pulled off his jacket, then resumed his thrusting. He lay on her and his weight was what she wanted, pinning her, overpowering her. He stopped thrusting and kissed her long and hard, and then ordered her, breathlessly, 'Keep your eyes open. Look at me, look into my eyes.'

Everything he said was a command. 'Move your leg. Turn over.' She did as he asked, and he entered her again from behind, pushing a pillow under her belly, lifting her and teasing her soft place in his so gentle fingers until she gave long shuddering gasps of pleasure.

She felt his testicles bouncing against her vulva as he rammed her. She reached her hand up and caressed them and heard his answering sigh. She squeezed the pumping cock with the muscles of her vagina and heard his pleasure in the short hissing groans coming with each rasping breath. She was afraid he would come then, before her, but he was rapt, entranced, lost in sensuality.

She was wound up beyond words into some mystic passion. He turned her again onto her back and held her buttocks up close to his pelvis and pressed deeper, harder, wilder; pressed and pushed into some deep spot that opened before him allowing him into her temple. Something happened then. Some totality of experience that made them lose awareness of their separation. As he probed, slowly now, into that secret source as if longing to be fully inside her like a child in that womb whose entrance he now unlocked, it was suddenly as if some seal was broken, as if she had been a virgin. But this was not physical. This was some occult seat of life he penetrated, some source of power that seemed divine. Something exploded in their minds.

Then their senses were heightened as if drugged, their bodies, crazed, demanding beyond fatigue, drove them beyond perception of pain, beyond any normal desire. They passed into a trance that was a higher kind of union. And she began then to feel her body merging and flowing to him, unable any longer to hold back the softening and

45

quivering and loosening of that beginning that builds slowly and can be controlled to give the greatest pleasure, that long slow climb towards the climax.

He held her shoulders fiercely. 'Tell me what you're feeling. What are you doing, Catherine? What are you doing with my cock?'

She said nothing, letting herself go into some deep abyss, just crying out in inarticulate release. Her orgasm was a growing crescendo of rising force, like oil rumbling and gurgling out of the earth's depths seconds before the strike, before it spurts into the world.

The rising wave culminated in some convulsion that shook them both and her cry seemed out of an archaic womb, an ancient deep-throated moan that came from the depths of her body and that was as long and undulating as the wave motion of her flesh that held and swallowed his cock as though it would never ever let him leave her. All the while she gazed into his eyes and he watched for her surrender.

He went on then, deeper, ever deeper into her as if trying to reach again that source of power in which her orgasm began. She cried again as he penetrated her inner space and thrust again and again until his sweat poured off his face and onto hers. He sought with his lips and then his teeth on her throat and cried out himself, a wild, animal cry. She thought he might kill her then, the violence in him was barely checked. It was as if he would bite her throat, like a dog, and shake her until she was dead. But he rose on his hands now, and moved rhythmically to his climax, his eyes on her, his expression frantic, desperate as if with some need to reach his lost paradise. He put his hand on her then and played her like a sweet guitar, while he thrust. Then his hand fell away and his movements grew faster and more violent and she contracted her muscles and held him tight inside her, guiding his cock down a narrowed channel to the place where it belonged. And as he loosed his semen into her she let go and came again, with him now, sucking his seed deep into her womb, her cry joining his own.

His eyes never left hers. But when his ejaculation

came, she saw them glaze and turn upwards like a dead man's and he seemed no longer there. He slumped on her and seemed to die. Only his long deep slumberous breaths showed he was alive.

* * *

She lay with his good sweet weight on her, and his body was strangely but deliciously soft in relaxation for a man so muscular. She ran her hands over his back, and where the trousers had slipped down, the full, tight runner's buttocks where she had held him close as he held her, so they were one writhing creature. She heard a clock somewhere in the flat strike the three quarter hour but could not move her left wrist from under him to see the time. She had no idea how long they had been together, lost in each other.

He slept on, his rhythmic breathing deepening to occasional snores and she lay under him, entranced by his body's magic, this stranger with whom she had shared something beyond ordinary lovemaking, beyond life, knowing him more in sleep even than in sex. It was as if his soul became alive while he lay trapped in sleep's net, and came to her, glowing with light.

There was less to fear now. His lust seemed to be for some goal beyond sex, for her response and need for him, an urgent need to consume and be consumed in union. But, their coming together had tapped a powerful core of something dark and violent within him. An obsessive lust whose source lay deep in some dark deprived anger which was the secret of his powerful sexuality. Something as close to hate as to love. Something that reverberated within her and called out her own response, from her own dark depths of secret buried violence. She too had to consume and be consumed in the fire of love. Now, she knew that.

Whatever she had to fear, then, it was not death. Unless, and the thought flickered like a light going out, unless this passion itself would lead to some danger for them both. For a moment there was the shadow of a precognition, then it vanished.

47

If there was to be death, it could be a death of a self that stood between the past which had ended here, and the miracle of new life. A self that might refuse the path now opening before them both. A self that would run screaming from the purifying flames that this love offered. It seemed to Catherine that there was no retreat from this fire, except into the past. And that was cold and empty. She shuddered as if she knew that joy was not the only experience likely to come from this initiation. The fear had not gone away.

The clock struck one and she knew then that she should go. Their lovemaking had lasted almost two hours. She had to get home. She could not be missing from her bed without a pre-arranged plan. She moved under him, stroked the full silky head with its soft, tight curls, tried to reach her mouth to his, and finding she could not, stretched her tongue out and licked his cheek until she awakened him.

He roused and began kissing her. He had fallen asleep with his cock still inside her, and now she felt him hardening again. He began to move and in seconds was fully erect again, and probing for her response. She sighed with delight, raising her knees and letting them fall wide apart, and he moved faster, deeper, pulling one of her legs up over his shoulder, making her gasp.

He said, 'I want to fuck you for ever.'

He was impassioned again, moving deep and hard and fast, panting and muttering what he would do to her, using his fingers now to arouse her, his eyes on hers. He brought her to climax quickly and then let his semen go. Then he held her, kissing her face over and over again.

At last, they dressed and left. She found she could hardly stand and had to let him hold her as she walked. He saw her to her car and told her she would see him very soon. She sat in the driver's seat and he bent his head in and kissed her gently and took her hand and placed it on his cock. It was hard again. Then he left her.

*

48

7

She sat at the breakfast table, playing with the lychees. They were cold from the fridge. Ridiculous of Anna to put fruit in the fridge: she kept telling her not to do it. Anna came for a couple of hours every morning, to clean up for the day, and shop for and prepare dinner if it was needed. There was room for her to live in but she preferred not to, and Catherine was happier not having a servant live in the house, to avoid the accidental intrusions on her moments of solitude, of small domestic issues, and of a presence when she needed the whole house empty of all but her own thoughts.

Unlike her father who kept a staff of butler, housekeeper, valet and chauffeur living in the mews and the upstairs flat of his Charles Street house, she was content with informal help and brought in extra people only when needed for entertaining. Sir Arnold, however, entertained a great deal. In fact, she and James were due at Charles Street tonight for one of his more intimate dinners.

She took one of the rough, cold fruits and cracked the brittle shell between her teeth. The juice spurted onto her tongue, sweet and lively. She thought of him and the way he had spurted his semen into her while his eyes fixed hers, and then sunk down like a dying man. With long red lacquered fingernails, she delicately picked the crusty shell away from the slippery white flesh and dropped the naked fruit into her mouth. Its succulent flesh fell away from the hard kernel and she sucked the slippery brown seed recalling his hardness within her.

It was seven hours since she had left him on Waverton Street, but her body tingled and flowed, as though its boundaries had dispersed, opened and glowing, newly alive, alight. Her senses were near some delirious edge. Music seemed to radiate from every cell, stirring and evoking strange energies that coursed up and down her body like tides of light, a surging of life where before she had been numb.

Looking at herself in the mirror she had seen that she was quickened. Her skin glowed and her eyes seemed luminous, her lips appeared fuller. It was as though she had been sleeping, for years; Sleeping Beauty who pricked her finger on a spindle. She smiled gently at the analogy, he must be the Prince who fought through the thicket of her antagonisms, her prejudices, her clinging resistances to life, and had come to kiss her alive.

After that kiss, it seemed as though her soul had split like a sprouting seed. She was awakened as though she had been a virgin... But surely not? She tried to remember Jan's lovemaking, his vigorous quick passion and the way she had risen to his demanding drive with her own. Surely she was awakened, then? But, not in this way. Not as though she had passed through a rebirth. As for James, she looked at the lychee in her fingers. Its toad's skin mingled subtle greens and pinks. She thought of frogs turning into princes and smiled sadly. James was a prince who had turned into a frog. Their sex had been rewarding while he had still found her a forbidden excitement, while she had been his mistress and he married to Jane. After their marriage he had placed her beside their elegant furniture. She had become an accessory to his career, and one of which he did not much approve, since she had her own life and not much time for his. She bit the crisp shell hard, and it fell open easily. This fruit was riper. Its cold sweet flesh seemed to explode against her palette. She fished the sleek brown seed from under her tongue and dropped it onto her plate.

James came, absent mindedly, into the sunlit kitchen. The stark white light bouncing off the cupboards and tiles washed unkindly over his grey complexion. He wore a short dark blue velour robe that showed his former rugby player's knees. His rather lank straight brown hair was uncombed. He had not yet shaved and a darkish stubble exaggerated his thickening jaw and chin.

He looked around and then reached for the coffee pot that was already primed with fine ground filter grains of his favourite Uganda blend. Catherine had prepared the pot for him and then made herself China tea in the Wedgwood pot. She poured herself another cup and added a sliver of lemon and looked up at James.

They seldom met in the morning. Catherine usually took a tray up to her room and read the papers, often going off to her office around eight-thirty, while James, after a late night in the Commons would sleep until about nine. Today, Catherine was running late and had decided to eat her usual breakfast of fruit and yoghurt in the kitchen. James was up early. He looked ill humoured.

She took The Daily Telegraph from the pile of unread papers on the chair beside her and scanned the front page. The lead story held her attention briefly. She had no feeling for the news today. Her mind was full of a fluttering excitement that infused her with a sense of her own life, vivid and real. She could not give her attention to the world outside when the world within seemed haunted by the sound of a great aria being sung, while her whole being vibrated to this inner turbulence. She heard this music now as her eyes flicked across her newspaper. Its inaudible power burned its way through her body's secret channels, arousing and elevating her senses from the dreaming wound in her groin to some high inspiration that soared into a paradise of light above her head.

James opened the fridge and leant inside to reach eggs and bacon. He bustled about, making irritable clattering sounds that set Catherine on edge. He broke two eggs into a pan and put the bacon under the grill. He poured coffee from his filter pot and the kitchen swam with its scent. Catherine loved the smell and taste of coffee but had not been able to drink it for years. It made her jumpy, irascible, and manically energetic for all too short a time before plunging her into irritable fatigue. She thought it did the same for James but he had not seemed to notice.

James sat at the other side of the round white table and leaned across to pick up The Times from the chair between them. She heard him snort and then push the chair away with a rude scrape as he remembered his breakfast.

51

She opened The Telegraph at the foreign page, picking up an item on South Africa. She heard James mutter as he sat down again, heard the sound of his plate being placed on the table and then the rattle of The Times in his hands.

His voice scarred the rhythmic quiet. He said, 'Have you seen this?'

She looked at him over her paper. His round face was vivid with colour, his light brown eyes agitated, but she could not tell whether he was pleased or angry.

He snapped at her, 'Have you seen this story, Catherine?' There was indignation in his voice. Was she in some way to blame? He turned The Times' front page towards her, and jabbed with his finger at a headline halfway down the page.

She leaned across and read: 'Lambeth Protesters Demand Inquiry into Minister's Vested Interests.'

James passed the paper across the table. She read:

Michael O'Leary, leader of the Lambeth Preservation Group, last night accused the Minister of State for Environment, James Waring, MP, of standing to gain personally from the South London Redevelopment Scheme.

Speaking at a meeting of the Lambeth group opposed to the Scheme at the Town Hall, Brixton, last night, O'Leary claimed that James Waring has private interests which he has not disclosed in connection with the SLRS.

He said, 'James Waring stands to make a personal fortune from the passing of the Bill he is preparing to push through Parliament later this year. Companies connected with his wife's family own large tracts of property in the Redevelopment Scheme area.'

This property, O'Leary claims, is bound to increase in value considerably if the Bill is passed, thus enriching the Minister of State's family and benefiting himself.

Any redevelopment in the Lambeth area under the circumstances, O'Leary claimed, would be a further indication that the Government was putting the interests of big developers before those of the house-holders. People would not be able to afford to live in their present neighbourhood if the Minister's plans were permitted to become law, but the Minister himself would walk away a rich man.

She looked at James: 'What are you going to do about that?'

'I'd better ask Arnold what he's playing at before I do anything, don't you think?' James' tone was cold.

Catherine shrugged. She said, 'Is there anything to stop his companies investing in South London just because you're putting through a Bill? It's public knowledge that the whole area will go through a metamorphosis and it's fair game for developers. Anyone can take a risk and make an investment. If the Bill fails, they'll lose. If it succeeds, they'll gain, so long as they're prepared to develop their property according to the zoning.'

James had picked up the Guardian. He now threw it down on the floor and glared at her. 'Damn it, Catherine, you know as well as anyone that Arnold's up to his neck in raising development finance for the area in partnership with the Ministry. He absolutely should not have any undeclared interest in the scheme.'

'Then you'd better ask him, hadn't you, my dear?' Catherine was cool: she did not want to play tantrums with James. She stood up, gathering her flowing red silk dressing gown around her and lifted her teapot and the flowered cup and saucer onto a small silver tray. As she went upstairs to dress she carried the image of James' belligerent face looking at her over his untouched bacon and eggs. She shed his mood. Nothing that had passed between them had seemed to matter. Her feelings were tuned to another source. James could no longer upset her.

She reached her bedroom and put the tray down. Going into her bathroom and turning on the shower she found her thoughts already far from the problem of her father's South London interests. She stood under the soothing deluge of hot water and was again conscious of the melting excitement that aroused her body and of the sensuous images that obsessed her mind.

8

The Angel has become a bit of a tourist attraction. It has one of those unspoilt views, if you think the river is unspoilt by driftwood and paper cups, old bottles, the diesel oil floating on its opaque greyness.

You can get a good view of Tower Bridge from the verandah. And from the first floor restaurant too. There you can eat a Dover sole and look across at the Docklands. That's what it used to be before they ponced it up with fancy housing developments and converted the old crumbling warehouses into flash apartments for overpaid City types.

The pub too: it's never been the same since the building started. Used to be, the bit between the Jamaica Road and the wharves was sacrosanct. Desolate. The perfect jungle. You could hide anything there. It's not like that now. Worse, the creeping blight is spreading South and West from Greenwich right through to Lambeth...

*   *   *

The man they both knew under a pseudonym had left an hour ago, but they were still there, sipping pints and dropping their cigar ash into the Thames from the creaky old verandah, watching the barges toiling through their bow waves, or the occasional police launch speeding, stern down towards the bridge. It was dark and the river had a kinder look, rolling liquorice wavelets under the far shore's lights, slick as wet tar under Tower Bridge. Clouds hid the moon. Their breath on the cold air was thicker than their cigar smoke. Not surprisingly, on such a cold damp night, they were alone on the verandah.

The short man with the limp blew out his last gasp of rich Havana smoke and dropped the butt over the wooden rail, leaning to watch the glowing end snuffed as it hit the water. He spoke with a deep, resonant voice that had only a touch of accent in it, but the accent was not London: and as he spoke he wrinkled up his eyes and gazed out into the river's night. 'We'll be beginning the work, then?'

The other man said, 'If he's providing the cash, the sooner the better. But it won't be easy.' His voice was higher, thinner and London suburban. He went on, 'I'll organize a meeting, get some of the lads moving. Word'll spread fast enough once we've had one protest meeting. In no time we'll have demonstrations. It shouldn't be a problem.' He paused and looked questioningly at the other man. 'If the goods come through.'

He turned up the collar of his heavy winter raincoat. He was a tall man, with light brown waving hair that was going fairly grey at the temples and around the ears and that curled over his forehead in damp weather. He had been a Parliamentary candidate once or twice and fancied himself an MP, but had never quite been to the tastes of Labour constituency parties. Too middle class for most of them. That was his trouble. He had made it into local politics, however, and had a good job now, too. Business was also thriving. And now, there were some fair pickings coming up. He was ready to cash in on both sides of the option, whichever way it went. This was the big one, he was sure.

The short man nodded. 'We'll do our bit. We'll be ready when you are.'

The taller man swallowed his beer and put his glass down on the splintered planks at his feet. He too flicked his cigar butt into the cold thickened Thames. It floated for a moment before sinking and extinguishing itself. 'I'll be off then.' He patted the other on the shoulder and made his way along the narrow platform.

The man with the limp watched him go and shook his

head thoughtfully. He never had much time for bent politicians. He'd rather a bent copper any time. But none of them were his kind. It all came down to the same thing in the end, with them, how much they were going to make. That's what made the world go round for the greedy bastards. And that's what was ruining his waterfront. He took a last look up towards Tower Bridge then took up the gnarled walking stick that leaned against the rail and limped painfully down the empty verandah.

9

Catherine bolted out of her office just before seven, late and wanting to get home to change before her father's dinner party. She almost fell over him in the dark.

'Hello, Catherine,' he said softly, a hint of challenge in his husky voice.

'Oh, hello,' she gasped and then laughed nervously at her own surprise. Of course she knew what he was doing there. He had an extraordinary knack of finding her without arrangement. Ten days had passed since their first lovemaking and she had been with him again three times. Once he had called her first, but twice before he had sprung out at her and waylaid her on her way home. She had not seen or heard from him for four days since the last time.

He looked pleased with himself, perhaps for catching her again. He said, 'Can I drive you anywhere? You look in a rush.'

'Oh yes, I am rushing, but I do have my car...'

He cut in, 'Leave your car, I'll drive you wherever you're going.'

She dithered in confusion. Sir Arnold hated her to be late and dinner was at eight-thirty, drinks at eight. And a very important crowd. Wanting him, she said, 'Well, I don't want to make use of you. I can very well drive myself. I have to go home and change, you see. And then I must get to a dinner. I won't have time to stop.

He took her arm and steered her off the pavement and out over the cobbles. Where was he taking her. She surrendered to his kidnap as she did to his lovemaking, suddenly not caring where they went or how long it took.

'Did you wonder why I hadn't called you, yet?' he said softly, teasingly.

'No,' she said firmly and laughed.

He chuckled. He stopped near a gold Mercedes and unlocked it. She was faintly surprised, having seen him every other time in the Rolls. He opened the passenger door and helped her inside.

They eased their way out of Covent Garden and down onto the Strand. He did not speak.

She said, 'I've been very busy. Have you?'

He shrugged. 'So so.'

He went straight into St James's Park from Trafalgar Square and drove quickly, accelerating into gaps. Her watch showed barely seven-fifteen when they pulled up outside her door. Big Ben chimed the quarter hour. James would go to Mayfair directly from the House. She turned to him. 'I think I've got time, if you'd like a quick drink . . . I . . .'

He cut in: 'No. I don't want a drink.' He took hold of her wrist.

She took a deep breath. What would he do? Had she meant a drink or... She felt herself quiver and melt. He leaned over and kissed her and she felt his hand slide under her skirt and between her thighs, his fingers probing the space inside her silk French knickers until they found her softness. She gave a little shuddering moan.

He said softly, 'Have you wanted me, Mrs Waring?' The words held mockery.

She jerked her head back and looked hard into his eyes.

He stared back deeply into hers. 'Do you feel guilty?' He was still mocking.

57

'Do you care?' She raised her eyebrows and looked coldly at him.

'I might.' He took her hand and placed it against the hard ridge in his trousers. He went on, 'I might care if you felt too guilty to meet me again.'

'Is that why you didn't telephone?'

He laughed, triumphant. 'So you did wonder.'

'It's what I'm wondering now.'

He smiled and brought his lips down on hers again. He held her hand where he had placed it then let it go and she felt him undoing his zip. His other hand was still between her legs, touching her gently, stealthily, like a thief. He drew her hand onto his erect penis and she stroked it softly.

He said, 'We mustn't make you late.'

She bent her head quickly and put her mouth over his cock. He felt the warmth and softness of her lips, the hard ridges of her palette. She sucked him deeply into her mouth, and then she withdrew, caressing him with her tongue as she let him go. She said, smiling, 'You're right. I really must go.'

He held her wrist again and kissed her hard. He wanted her furiously. In a moment he would have her here, in the car, no matter who would see them. She put her hand on the lever and opened the door. He pushed his finger into her and found her slick with her nectar.

He said, 'Tomorrow. Come to the flat.'

'When?' She thought rapidly over her diary for the evening.

'I'll ring you at your office.'

She nodded and turned to get out. He held her back and then kissed the finger that had touched her and brought it quickly to her lips, pushing it between them. She smelled and tasted the sea sweet pungence of her own desire. Then pulling her skirt down she swung herself quickly out of the car and almost ran into the house.

* * *

Sir Arnold's private dinners at Charles Street were occasions where selected groups of the people who really mattered were brought together so that they could work out practical new ideas that would help the politicians improve the world. As Sir Arnold was in and out of Ten Downing Street everyone knew where the ideas would end up so there was no shortage of acceptances for these dinner parties. In fact the invitations were a treasured accolade, a sign that one was one of the practical doers and thinkers who helped the Government carry out its work.

Tonight there were just eight and Catherine was the only woman. There were five strategically important businessmen. Strategically important for James Waring's political career, that is. Sir Arnold was as keen as his son-in-law on the idea of James becoming Prime Minister. But these things required careful planning and even more careful nurturing. If James had a disadvantage it was that he had a tendency to be too crisp and direct. He suffered fools very badly. Sir Arnold, on the other hand, was adept at concealing impatience or boredom, and a master at appearing to admire those he despised. He would have been a success anywhere from a Byzantine court to Hollywood.

Tonight he had invited the senior businessmen who were playing a key role in James Waring's precious South London Redevelopment Scheme. It was Sir Arnold who had created the consortium which was working closely with the Ministry to finance redevelopment projects. These were to be factories for high tech industries, studios for crafts people, office suites for small and medium-sized businesses, a college for retraining in high tech skills, sports centres for gifted athletes, low cost housing estates for rent and purchase by the local workforce and complexes of shopping centres and market places that would serve the whole.

Sir Arnold's guests this evening included Joe Staines, the entrepreneur Chairman of SASCO, the fast burgeoning computer company; Lord Lewenthorpe, Chairman of the Southern Banking Corporation; Robert Ward from the Ward Mason Property Group; Sir Aidan Denton, Chairman of the Kentish Building Society and

Charles West, head of one of the City's largest stock-brokers. These were leading members of the consortium put together to assist the Minister in his ambitious plans for the redevelopment of a huge swathe of South London. The proposed redevelopment area extended along the waterfront and inland where a large loop of the Thames between Lambeth and Greenwich formed a natural boundary. The area included most of Brixton, Southwark, parts of Camberwell, Deptford and Greenwich. The scheme was controversial but had the qualified support of the Prince of Wales.

The Secretary of State for the Environment was known to be less enthusiastic about the scheme than the Minister of State, though it was also known that the Prime Minister was one hundred per cent behind it. No one in the room had any doubt that at the next reshufffle, the present Secretary of State would find himself moved sideways and James Waring would be installed in his place.

Tonight, the conversation had started over cocktails in the first floor drawing room and had continued in the spacious dining room downstairs. The staff had served a seven-course dinner which began with the best Beluga and passed through turtle soup and scallops mornay before reaching the roast beef. A green salad had been followed by a delicate pavlova and then the ripest stilton. Now the fruit bowl was being passed by Clive, the butler. Port, brandy and liqueurs would be served upstairs with the coffee and petits fours.

Catherine made her move and left the men to follow her. She was wearing a long white crepe sheath with long sleeves and a low plunging back. Her fair hair was coiled and plaited into the nape of her neck and a superb string of pearls hung down the back of the dress, swinging gently as she walked. Not one man failed to watch her admiringly as she walked out through the double doors into the wide hall and up the staircase to the drawing room. James watched her thoughtfully. He always noticed her more when she was in her father's house, acting the hostess. She was remote enough from him then for him to see her clearly as a separate person rather than a rejected part of himself. He could not help noticing the effect she had on the others.

She was breathless when she reached the top of the stairs, but not from lack of fitness, since she exercised at the Grosvenor House Health Club almost every day. But since she had left Angel's car she had been dominated by images of their lovemaking and these now oppressed her with a suffocating sensuality that she could not shake off.

At dinner she had kept herself in control, doing her job of moving the conversation along, linking one man's thoughts with another's. Now, briefly free of her role of hostess for these few minutes she let the full effect of those images work on her. She felt almost too weak to make it up the stairs. She went into the bathroom on that floor and looked at herself in the mirror. She looked on fire, cheeks burning, eyes diamond bright. She wanted him so badly that she doubted she could keep her mind on the conversation.

She had only one recourse. She leaned against the locked door and watching herself in the mirror opposite, lifted her long dress. Her fingers found her clitoris swollen and sticky. She brought herself quickly to climax, gasping and sucking for air in her need and suppressing the cry that broke from her as her body surged into orgasm with the empty agony of his cock's absence. She wanted to weep. Relief flooded her but there was the hollow sense of unappeased hunger. Her need was for him and it did not go away with the brief release of tension. He haunted her mind and she could not forget his touch. She washed her hands and retouched her face. She looked as lovely as ever.

She went into the gold and rose drawing room and by the time they followed her she had resumed a cool collected poise, a perfect lie. Her secret lay within her painfully, like a pearl in an oyster. She was still aroused and burning for her lover. It was as if his thoughts would not let her forget him. Whoever she talked to, he was there, a presence so strong she could almost taste his cock in her mouth and feel it inside her. Now, she looked along the long sofa at her husband, who sat at the other end, talking to Lord Lewenthorpe who sat between them. She wondered how she could ever have been in love with him, let alone felt desire for him. But then the desire she had felt for James was a mere whisper of a breeze compared with this storm of passion building inside her. In comparison, her marriage seemed to have been arranged and she wondered how she could have been so misled. She blamed her father bitterly for this. It had been his match, after all.

The coffee was being brought along with a trolley of brandies, port and liqueurs. The guests had broken up into groups but she now heard her father's voice addressing them all.

'Gentlemen,' Sir Arnold began in the vibrant Germanic voice, 'I do believe I must ask my brilliant son-in-law James Waring to say a few words about the project which is so dear to all of our hearts. James, my boy...'

James cleared his throat but remained sitting on the sofa next to Lord Lewenthorpe. He said, 'I really want to bring up something which has cropped up and which could prove a continuing embarrassment to our group of supporters.' He cleared his throat again and went on, 'I suppose most of you will have seen an item in The Times today which referred to my private interest in property held by companies said to be owned by my father-in-law. I should like to say that I have had a full and frank discussion with Sir Arnold and he has promised me that his companies hold absolutely no property in the area affected by the Redevelopment Scheme, nor are they likely to do so. I have consulted my solicitors and they are issuing a writ against O'Leary and an injunction against his making any more statements of the same kind.'

There was a growl of approval from the men. James took a sip of Courvoisier and smiled a tight little smile. He said, 'I believe we are likely to experience many more attacks of this nature and of other kinds. I have, I must say, been amazed at the vitriolic nature of the opposition we are encountering to this scheme and I personally find it hard to understand quite why so much heat is being engendered about something which is so clearly going to improve the environment and the lives of the local people, not to mention creating jobs and a new heart for a community that is suffering from all the symptoms of decay and alienation, street crime, drug-taking and so forth.

'It is, gentlemen, as you know, my opinion that the Redevelopment Scheme and its many sub-projects will destroy the social substratum on which the criminal culture thrives, once and for all. By sweeping away the decayed infrastructure and replacing it with a new one we will eradicate the breeding ground of the criminal community and replace it with a healthy, vigorous and normal way of life.' He sat back and there was a rumble of approval.

Lord Lewenthorpe applauded loudly. 'Well done, my boy,' he said, gruffly. 'That's the stuff of leadership. We'll have you in Number Ten one day if you keep on with that sort of fire in your belly.'

James blushed and gave a modest smile.

'Hear, hear,' Joe Staines chimed in, with his cockney voice. He was standing by the marble fireplace. He put his liqueur glass down by a silver jug of pale yellow roses and took a cigar from the gold box being proffered by Clive. He allowed the butler to clip the cigar for him and strike a match, then as he drew on the cigar, he turned to James with a worried expression. 'I must say,' he said, 'I think you're chewing off a big one. The opposition looks rough and it's likely to get rougher. Some of the lads down there who're making a living out of crime are going to get nasty if you try and dig up their turf.'

Waring looked at him sharply. He said, 'I get the feeling we might see some pretty heavy stuff in the Commons once we get this Bill out of the draftsmen's hands and into the legislature. The Opposition is plotting its tactics already.'

'I don't think you realize what you're up against.' Staines blew out cigar smoke. 'You're not dealing with ordinary political opposition, you've got your embedded, ingrained villains out there and you're going to break up

63

their little breeding grounds. Once you create jobs and new housing and give the local population in places like Brixton something else to live for, you'll take away the breeding stock of crime as well as the breeding grounds. There's going to be a backlash from the criminal leaders. You watch. You'll disrupt the traditions and the culture of generations. There are huge vested interests pitted against you throughout the redevelopment area. The drug masters in Lambeth are another bunch you're taking on. They don't want you breaking up the party either.'

He had their attention and they were listening seriously. As Staines finished, James was looking around the room and saw the others felt the computer man had hit on something believable. This was the first moment it occurred to him that he had anything other than political opposition to cope with.

There was doubt in his voice when he said, 'I can't see that that will have any bearing on the passage of the Bill through the House.'

Catherine, sitting on the other side of Lord Lewenthorpe on the long sofa, said: 'Joe's got a very good point, James. I can see now that someone like O'Leary could be a conscious or unwitting pawn for a really serious group of criminals who wanted to stop your Scheme.'

James smiled and said, 'Don't let your journalistic imagination carry you away, darling.' His tone was patronizing.

Sir Arnold said, 'Catherine's a political animal, James. Don't forget that. She has the right instincts.' Catherine looked at her father gratefully. She thought he looked more worried than the situation merited and wondered why.

Robert Ward stretched his legs out in front of him. He was a tall, thin man in his fifties with a distinguished head of thick dark hair streaked with grey. He was a Yorkshireman and had a Yorkshireman's matter of fact manner. 'You'll find out soon enough who's behind your opponents when you see their methods,' he said crisply.

'I'm afraid we're beginning to see them already,' Catherine murmured.

Lord Lewenthorpe leaned across and touched her hand in a fatherly gesture. 'Don't worry yourself, my dear. Your husband is quite capable of taking care of himself. Besides, this group is much too committed to give up at the first sign of a smear campaign.'

Catherine smiled gratefully at the distinguished banker.

'Well, now that we've got that little matter over with,' Sir Arnold said briskly, rubbing his hands, 'Let's get down to some serious talk. How much money are we all thinking of contributing to the Redevelopment Scheme's first stages?'

The conversation moved on and Catherine sat listening as the group talked about the finance they and others in the private consortium would provide. She found herself watching James with objectivity, for the first time since they were married. Her feelings of need for love and of rejection that had been at the root of her unhappiness for the past few years were no longer so powerful. She felt a sense of freedom from James. She had forgotten it was possible to feel so separate. She breathed more freely and it was as if a weight had gone from her chest.

Her mind drifted again to Christopher Angel. He was a mysterious man and she must find out more about him before she got any more involved. A frisson of excitement ran through her as she remembered tomorrow's meeting. Once again she felt the melting sensation in her bones, the moisture and burning need between her thighs. A shadow of anxiety crossed her mind and she wondered if it was not already too late to choose how involved she would become with him.

*

10

Sir Arnold Clyne sat at his desk in the large dark panelled room that looked out over the Bank of England. The February afternoon light was dim and monochrome and the Bank appeared dark and oddly threatening. He stared at the powerful Grecian columns that supported the portico and thought of the temple to which Samson had been chained. And of the consequences.

He swung his chair around to face the room and his desk. The room was unlit, but for an antique brass lamp on the huge leather-topped desk. This cast a spotlight over Sir Arnold and encircled the small engraved silver tray with its delicate Limoges tea cup and saucer, the Georgian silver tea pot and hot water jug, and the plate of his favourite Liebkuchen. There were no papers on the desk: the day's paperwork had long since been cleared away by his personal secretary.

Miss Andrea Werner was in her late forties and, like Sir Arnold, of war refugee stock. Her Jewish father had been killed by the SS during World War II and her Jewish mother had fled, pregnant, to England, and after the war, married a former British Army sergeant and settled in London's East End. The marriage had not lasted and Andrea had kept her German name. Her own marriage history was no luckier: she had got pregnant at seventeen and her marriage, to the child's father, had been brief. She had gone to earn a living for herself, her small son and her mother, as a secretary in the City of London.

She was Sir Arnold's right hand and, some said, his left as well. She spoke German and English with equal fluency. She was also as understanding as she was effective and, as she had been with Sir Arnold Clyne for over two decades, since he set up the Clyne Johnson Bank after his return from Kenya, she was as familiar with his ways as a wife.

Sir Arnold was thinking mainly about last night's dinner. It had gone well. James had spoken with inspiration and had helped to convince the group that he was a man with a future, despite any dirt the opposition would try to fling at him. As for O'Leary's allegations, they were alarming and would have to be stopped. Sir Arnold leaned back in his leather chair and ran a hand through his pale hair. He did not think it would be diffficult. But, in the meantime, damage would be done. He frowned and swung his chair around so that he was facing the window again. What was O'Leary really up to? Well, he would find out pretty soon.

He looked at his watch. It was 4.35 p.m. The street lights were on and the slowing traffic formed lighted chains running to the five roads that converged on the Bank. Sir Arnold could not conceal from himself the fact that he was deeply worried. His plans were threatened now, more than ever before. He stood to gain or lose far more in the next few months than at any previous time in his life. It was not only his own future but Catherine's which was at stake.

It had always been his ambition that his daughter should succeed in becoming a member of the British establishment. It was true that he had succeeded himself: financial achievement, social recognition and a knighthood were all evidence of that, but he knew very well that he was not accepted in the heart of the City Establishment.

Sir Arnold Clyne was not the only one who knew that Arnold Kleinwort had come out of Vienna's slums and had come to Britain as a destitute refugee. He was not ashamed of his origins or the way he had achieved his start. After his arrival in Britain in 1939, the authorities had sent him with other refugees from German occupied countries to work on a farm in Scotland. After the war he found himself in London with nothing but his old clothes and a handful of ration coupons, some of which he had traded for cash. He'd had to use his wits to survive. He had been lucky immediately. One night, in the Cafe Royal Bar, while spending the fruits of a bet, he had met

Rhonda, a rich widow in her forties with an entre into London society. His stunning good looks got him into her bed and soon into her life. Sir Arnold thought fondly of Rhonda, of the way she had taken him in to her Mayfair flat and passed him off to her friends as her nephew: how she had then groomed him, taught him the social graces, persuaded him to drop Kleinwort and change his name to Clyne. She had even taught him how to convert his raw sexual energy into bedroom arts. A smile reached his eyes and dispelled some of the anxiety showing there. He owed a great deal to Rhonda. When Rhonda found a duke who wanted to marry her, she had, with much regret, found Arnold a job as a footman with Count Starlinsky. She had continued to see him on an occasional basis: the strong sexual attraction between them had not died with the duke's arrival.

Running away with seventeen-year-old Countess Marina Catherina had been a risky escapade that had, in the end, brought him good fortune. He had adored the girl at a distance for months, but eventually it was she who had let him know she wanted him. One afternoon when she was at home for half-term from her expensive ladies school, she had rung and he had answered. He felt a burning nostalgia as he remembered the way she had looked. Her pale hair, the same hair as Catherine's but curled into the post war page boy style, haloed around her as she sat on a Victorian love seat in the bow window of the house in Kensington.

She had a clear, rather high pitched voice, a very aristocratic way of speaking but with the faintest Russian accent absorbed from her family. She sat upright and held out her hand to him as if it should be kissed. 'Aha, Clyne,' she said, rather imperiously, he remembered. 'Come here.'

He went over to the window and stood in front of her. It was winter and the view behind her seemed a pencilled sketch in which bare trees scratched the sky for warmth. But an early blackbird sang on the small lawn beneath the window. He could almost hear it now, that voice predicting spring.

'Would you like to kiss my hand?' she said, cool as ice,

and he had gazed at her like a love-sick dog, unbelieving.

He had dropped to one knee and taken the small hand and kissed it. When he looked up at her face, she was smiling with an invitation he was sure he was imagining.

She had asked him when he came off duty and he had told her. Not until the family was in bed. She had smiled again, her eyes full of mystery, and said, 'I'll expect you in my room at midnight.'

He had shivered and shaken for the rest of the day in an anguish of anticipation. He thought he knew what she expected of him, but there was the nagging doubt that he was deluding himself, perhaps she only wanted him to carry out some task for her, to take a secret message to some more suitable lover, perhaps.

But no. When he had crept into her room that night at midnight, still in his footman's livery, she had been lying naked on the bed surrounded and covered by dozens of red roses which he remembered seeing delivered in the morning. He had jealously assumed she had someone madly in love with her who was starting to court her lavishly and romantically. But now it looked as though she had planned the whole thing for him.

And she had. She had taken on a bet with her school friends that she would lose her virginity in the half-term break. She knew Arnold wanted her and thought it would be easier to keep her secret with him than with some man of her own class who would talk around their circle and give her a reputation.

But Arnold turned Marina's light hearted wager into a serious affair. He used the arts taught him by Rhonda, and Marina had fallen quite as deeply in love with him as he was with her. He had crept to her bedroom every night for a week and when it was time for her to return to her school on the South Coast, they had made their plan. She would leave as if returning to school and she would ask if Clyne could drive her on the pretext that she wanted to practise her German en route. They would then drive to Scotland and be married at Gretna Green.

Their plan went perfectly. Her father had been outraged. He knew nothing of young Clyne other than his reference from Rhonda, now a Duchess. He was clearly not the right husband for his younger daughter. Attempts to buy Clyne off, dissolve the marriage and keep it secret, were abandoned when Marina told them, untruthfully, that she was pregnant. The only thing to do was to give the couple an allowance and send them overseas. Kenya had been the answer. Marina and Arnold had lived happily there for eight years before Catherine's birth.

Sir Arnold smiled sadly. He had made good with his wife's money. He had justified Marina's love and faith in him. But still, he was not accepted by the real elite. He was an outsider, a foreigner without social background. He had not come out of the right stock to be accepted fully, even in this enlightened age where the doers and achievers were the real aristocracy, whatever their origins. The real Establishment remained untouched, their doors never opened. They were like a secret society which one could not penetrate except by the stealth of birth or the outright theft of power.

It was completely dark outside now but he continued to gaze at the Bank's facade, carved with deep shadows. He had resolved then, he remembered, as clearly as if it were a few minutes ago, that he would enter the heart of the Establishment and that his daughter would marry into it. He swore again, as he stared unseeingly at the Bank of England's bulk, that his background and his past would not impede Catherine.

He muttered to himself, 'If they can't accept me, they will have to accept the Prime Minister's wife.' He was determined that James should become Prime Minister and that Catherine should stay married to him.

He laughed a short bitter laugh, swung his chair back again and leaned on the big desk. It was almost completely dark in the room now but for the disc of gold light on the burgundy leather desk top. He looked at his watch. Four minutes to five. He wondered if his next appointment would be on time. He would have liked a drink but he had to stay clear-headed. He pressed the buzzer beside the phone and it was answered instantly. He said softly, 'Andrea, bring in the iced water, would you.'

He stood up and stretched his arms over his head, pulled his shoulders back and wound his elbows around to try to ease the stiffness in his neck and shoulders. He had to erase the lines of tension, assume a relaxed and confident expression before his visitor arrived. The buzzer on his desk went and he snapped on the intercom. 'Yes.'

'Your visitor is here, Sir Arnold.' Andrea's voice was distorted by the intercom into a nasal snarl.

'Bring him in, Andrea. And the water, if you please.'

He pulled his jacket straight and moved behind the desk. As he sat down, the heavy mahogany door opened and Andrea walked in carrying the silver tray with the silver bucket of mineral water. She walked to the antique cabinet where the drinks were kept and put the tray down. She turned on the lamps, as she went out. She came back leading the visitor. The man came jauntily into the room. Andrea watched him going towards Sir Arnold, taking a proffered chair beside the desk. Sir Arnold did not offer him his hand nor was he smiling, though the man smiled at him.

The visitor's suit was dark and well tailored, though not Saville Row, Andrea thought, watching him. She had never seen him before and had no idea what Sir Arnold was meeting him about. That was unusual. He norma'ly told her who everyone was. After she had served them both, Sir Arnold with iced mineral water, his guest with a gin and tonic, she took the tea tray from the desk and went out. Sir Arnold had not asked her to stay at her desk, but he had not dismissed her either. So she busied herself and waited. It was only half an hour before the man left. He walked swiftly out of the room, gave her a cheeky grin and went out to the lifts. He had no coat or briefcase. She assumed he must have a chauffeur waiting outside.

She waited some minutes but Sir Arnold did not buzz her. She wanted to go home. It was a long day. She decided she would check to see if she were still wanted. Instead of calling him on the intercom, she went to the door and put her head round it. She was astonished to see her employer with his head on his desk and cradled in his arms. She almost ran across the room. She stopped beside him and hesitantly put her hand on his arm.

He jumped and sat up. 'Oh, Andrea,' he said grufffly, 'I think I am very tired tonight. I almost fell asleep.'

'Are you sure you're all right?' she asked anxiously.

'I'm fine, my dear.' He straightened himself and smoothed back the full pale hair. He stood up. 'I'll just make myself a whisky soda and then I'll go home. I had a late night last night.' He patted her shoulder. 'You look tired yourself. I'm sorry if I've kept you late for nothing. You'd better get John to drive you home. I'll get myself a taxi.'

She opened her mouth to protest but he cut her off. 'Please do as I ask, Andrea.' He spoke in German, then moved to the phone and as if to ensure her obedience, called down to the security desk and summoned the chauffeur to drive her back to Essex.

She thought she had never seen him look so tired and worried. She gave him an anxious backward glance as she went through the door. He was already at the liquor cabinet pouring himself a whisky. She hesitated long enough to see that he did not add any soda, but downed the stiff measure straight.

11

The morning after the dinner party he rang her as arranged and at one minute past ten she stood outside the door of the flat wondering how she had the strength to stand there, let alone go inside. She was trembling and breathing in little short gasps. Her whole body was tingling and there was a silky wetness between her thighs that seemed to soak the knickers she had forgotten to remove. She pushed the bell. The door opened almost immediately. The hall was dark. He must have been standing behind the door and as she walked in he came out from behind it, pushing it closed with one hand and seizing her with the other.

He pulled her very close and put his soft lips onto hers, kissing her avidly, yet with tantalizing slowness, while his hands ran over her body. Then he sharply pulled up her skirt and reached behind her where the curve of her buttocks began and ran his fingers under the lace and into her softness. She felt again the same fear and complete surrender to his strength that she always felt with him. But now she surrendered to him without caring what he did, without letting the fear matter. She was his, absolutely to do anything with, his plaything, his victim, his woman, his whore.

She thought her knees would give way and sagged weakly against the arm that held her. He held her up and then led her by the hand into the bedroom and pushed her onto the bed. In seconds he had his cock out and into her, wrenching aside the loose gusset of the French knickers and thrusting it all the way into her soft space. His eyes were fixed on hers in that desperate way of his that showed his need. And with his cock in her, she felt again that sense of relief at her completeness, of being whole at last after the days of hollow need. Days of longing for him so badly that she would almost have given herself to anyone to assuage her cunt's craving. He slithered his cock up and down her wet spaces, probing and plunging into the deep corners where she gave and opened into that other space he sought to plant his seed. She felt again whole and greater than whole, as if mastered by a new will; and helpless, allowing his power over her as if he had bought her and she was his willing and adoring slave.

Perhaps she was more conscious of everything he did, now. Now that she had experienced him several times, she was able to observe every feeling he created in her. And he seemed to be creating not only her feelings, but a new person with new needs and desires, new tormented longings. She shared his fantasies, perhaps, compelled by their secret's growing power, that they were watched as they made love. She knew, now, as he drove her higher and higher into that state before her climax, the meaning of renewal by death. And as she released her orgasm, she seemed to give herself so completely to him that she died, letting her life flow out into the universe, letting some primeval female cry escape her, asking nothing but to surrender, to be annihilated under his cock.

Was it so for him, when he came, when he drove desperately into her, crying to her what he was doing, then sighing and dying as his essence emptied into her? 'What is it like?' he asked her. 'What do you feel?' he said as she writhed and moaned under his strength and brought her consciousness back for long enough to analyse her senses. 'It's like giving yourself up to God,' she gasped and he drove again and again into her, as if mad with need to fill her and command her, to reach her secret heart and wrench it open like a conqueror crashing into the vanquished temple. To reach her God.

'Do you want my soul?' she asked him afterwards.

He laughed and looked down into her revealing eyes. 'I want everything. I want to control you completely. To have absolute power over you.'

She stroked his still clothed back. 'You have . . . a chance,' she whispered. And then her thoughts retracted what she had said. No one should have power over her, she knew. No man should replace God. And she shuddered at the thought of how, under the drug of passion, how close she had come, to making him God.

12

Gerald leaned back on the sofa and lit a cheroot. He beamed at Catherine who sat, elegant in a black cashmere sheath, on a chair, opposite. Catherine was concentrating all her energy on the act of pouring China tea. The low white-clothed table was a mess of crumbs. Gerald had claimed lack of lunch and made himself a pig over the Savoy's full tea. Further evidence lay in a small smear of cream on his upper lip and a sticky patch on his right thigh where blackcurrant jam had dropped on his sharply creased dark blue suit.

He blew out a stream of bluish smoke and fixed Catherine in an X-ray gaze. 'So tell me, Catherina,' he drawled in his light affected voice, 'why are you looking so divinely glowing these days?'

'I can't imagine,' she replied, still pouring tea very precisely into Gerald's cup. 'We need some more hot water,' she added and looked around for a waiter.

'I can wait,' Gerald smirked and drew on his cheroot. He recrossed his short legs and smoothed scone crumbs from the rounded curves of his waistcoat. 'It has to be a lover. At last.' He grinned triumphantly.

She held her hand up and one of the white coated waiters started towards them. 'Suppose it is, you wretch?' She snapped at him in playful anger as the waiter reached her. 'Some more hot water, please,' she said sweetly and then turned back to Gerald.

He smirked again and said confidently, 'You haven't asked me how I know yet.'

'You already said. It's my glow. But, for all you know, I might have made myself some deal that put the roses in my cheeks. Like start a new magazine.' She bit into a strawberry. 'Ugh,' she said, 'it's just like a turnip.' She chose another and popped it into her mouth.

'Have you?' he asked.

She looked questioningly at him, her mouth full of strawberry.

He continued, 'Started a new magazine?'

'I'm going to.'

'My dear. How exciting.' He beamed. 'What is it going to be and do for us all that Vanities isn't and does not?' He uncrossed his legs and leaned forward. The cheroot wafted blue smoke at Catherine and she waved it away. Gerald ignored her gesture. He stared keenly at her as if she were lying. 'Why do you need a new magazine, Tsarina?'

Catherine leaned back in her little chair and stretched out her legs. She tilted her head back and put her hands under her great silken mane of platinum hair and lifted it up onto her crown. She smiled and said coyly, 'I'm empire building.'

'Tsarina, tut tut. Is this going to make you happy?'

'You said it yourself, Gerald darling. I have a glow.'

He leaned back again and his expression was bafffled. He said, 'Why are we having tea, Catherina?'

She looked at him quizzically, her head on one side. 'Because you didn't have lunch, Gerald.'

'Oh, bosh.' He picked up the napkin that he had tossed onto the sofa beside him and flung it at her. He was glowering. 'I know perfectly well you wanted a heart to heart. Why else would you ask your Uncle Gerry to tea at such short notice?'

'I might want to write a book,' she said soothingly.

He gave her a disgusted look.

Catherine let her glance drift towards the window. It was getting dark outside. She felt suddenly tired and rather vacant. She had wanted his company. But had she wanted to confess anything? Or just be amused, distracted from ever-present images and the desires they inspired?

Usually Gerald was very entertaining but today she felt he was wasted on her. His company was not distracting her enough. She wanted to get up and leave. Wanted to drift out into the street and make her way to Hill Street and into his arms. She missed him intolerably. It was a week since she had seen him or heard from him. He did not answer his phone. His silence was killing her.

'Catherina?' Gerald said softly. He was watching her intently. 'My legendary powers of intuition tell me something is preying on your dear little mind. Tell Uncle Gerry . . . Hm?'

Catherine looked at her watch. It was five fifteen. 'Let's have a glass of champagne,' she said, lightly.

Gerald's expression changed. His lips became a straight disapproving line. He stood up. 'I've got to go,' he said in a bored voice. He stubbed the cheroot out viciously in a puddle of jam and picked up his cashmere scarf and his gloves.

She smiled up at him and held out her hand. 'Goodbye, darling.'

She'd called his bluff. 'Damn it, Catherina,' he spat, sitting down suddenly and whipping off his gloves. 'Spill it. Stop playing this game. It's a man, isn't it?'

To his astonishment, Catherine looked at him with a completely shattered expression. Tears spilled out of her eyes and she grabbed for a napkin. 'Oh Gerald,' she said, gulping, 'I was so afraid this would happen if I talked about it. I wanted to tell you but I was afraid it would make me cry.'

'For heaven's sake, Tsarina,' Gerald was aghast that she should cry in the Savoy. He had never believed the ice maiden cried at all.

She dabbed her eyes. She looked mournfully at him. 'I'm so happy but I'm just so unhappy too.' She reached in her bag and drew out an enormous pair of dark glasses and slipped them over her tear-stained eyes. 'Is that better?'

'You look like a gangster's moll.'

'Oh dear.' She ducked her head in a strange mixture of laughter and tears. 'I think,' she choked, 'that may be exactly what I am.'

*   *   *

They sat in Gerald's peach drawing room in Hampstead. Catherine lay on a long peach silk sofa, shoes off, feet up on the cushions, a box of tissues resting on her stomach. She had cried. She had not known why she was crying. She had no idea what dam had burst inside her. She was limp and drained but quiet at last.

Gerald came out of the kitchen carrying a tray of herbal tea and a large vodka. 'You can drink them both. They'll do you good, Tsarina, especially the vodka.'

'Gerald, why do you treat emotion as though it's an illness?'

'I don't. But if I seem to, it may be my adopted British

77

way. Why do you treat emotion as if you've just discovered it?'

She giggled. 'Maybe I have.'

'Yes,' he said, looking at her seriously, 'maybe you have.'

She had told him a great deal of her involvement with Christopher. Gerald had read psychology at Berkeley and done a doctorate in something Jungian at Cambridge. That, with the legendary intuition he often joked about, was said to be his secret weapon in the signing of astute deals. He seemed always to know what his opposite number was thinking and to be a jump or two ahead. Catherine often used him as a sounding board for her new ideas and had come to rely on his startling insights into people and situations.

It was now five weeks since she had met Angel. She had been to the flat in Hill Street eleven times and had begun to suffer from a mixture of guilt and anxiety about Angel, who he was and what she was becoming involved in. He had dropped hints and made vague references to things which she felt connected him with some shadowy world of illegality.

She was in a miasma of uncertainty. He hinted, but he was also secretive. She knew he had night clubs but not which or where they were. Or what went on in them. She had begun to think of the consequences of loving a man, for love him she knew she did, now, who worked in what he described as 'a murky world full of murky people'. She wondered often about these people of the night and their sordid, perhaps criminal pursuits. She had to think of James. She might ruin him if she was found out and if Angel was . . . well, outside the law.

But she could not turn away from Christopher. Tugged back and forth by her need and her conscience, she felt at one moment relief that the involvement might be over, at another, hysteria, that she should have to go back to the emptiness of her life without him. That seemed, on looking back, to have been like a coma compared with the razor nerved excitement and joy of her life, the tremendous vitality and blossoming of her being that had come with the feelings he unlocked in her. How could she turn away from something that seemed an elixir, a magic potion that brought new shoots from dead trees? She needed the passion he generated in her.

She had called his number, the only one she had, but no one answered. Intuitively, she was sure he was as involved as she was, and that he would return to her, but she was the kind of woman who needed to act not to sit and wait. She felt completely powerless to control her feelings or the direction of the relationship and was astonished that she should allow herself to be so drugged by sex as to become addicted to one man.

She said, 'I've never been hooked like this before, Gerry.'

'It was overdue,' he replied, drily.

She smiled. 'Do you think so? Is that why it's hitting me like a ton of TNT? Am I normal now? Is this what other people go through?'

'No. You're one of the few. One of the lucky ones.'

'Lucky!' She was sitting up, leaning on one elbow sipping the tea.

Gerald was drinking the vodka. He said, 'You're very lucky, Cat. You have discovered the secret of the universe. The secret of life. Something more powerful than nuclear energy and ten times as dangerous. What you have discovered is as deadly as plutonium unless you know how to handle it. But, if you can harness it, you'll find it a thousand times more beneficial than the cleanest fusion plant.'

'Whatever do you mean?'

'Sex is the secret path to the divine. Sex can release magic energy. White magic or black magic. Once you open that locked casket where the sexual energy is stored – and you could go a lifetime of enjoyable sexual intercourse without doing so, and I'm not talking about orgasms, I'm talking about some metaphysical explosion that blows the top off your head – once you open that you are on the path of sex magic. Whether you use the energy for black or white purposes is your choice. The dark path of sex leads to debauchery and depravity. The

79

light path leads to love. Everyone is looking for the key to that casket. Promiscuity may be explained just by this search for the right partner who will help one create this nuclear explosion of human energy that will then be manifested in art, literature, music or just a happy creative life full of love for humanity and the world.' He gestured blowing kisses to her with both hands.

She was silent, watching him over her hunched up knees, clutching the teacup in both hands. He went on quietly and slowly as if telling a story to a child. 'Those who find it are in charge of the most tremendous power. I think, from what you say, you have found it. So you have no choice. You can't put it back in the casket. You have to follow this path wherever it leads and somehow manage not to get lost on the way. Getting lost means getting sidetracked into negative emotions, being gobbled up by dragons and snakes of jealousy and possessiveness, anger and hate, or getting sucked into perversion and games and sex for sex's sake.

'You have found the key to paradise, little Catherina. That key will eventually unlock another state of mind, a state of grace, if you like. To unlock that door you have to channel that dangerous energy and pass it back to the divine, from where it originates before passing through your partner's own sexual generator. Together you form some kind of circuit for communicating love, which is the highest form of human energy. Sex into love, plutonium into light. If you don't generate love you fail and you abuse the gift. And you may be destroyed, burned out, by a voltage you are not strong enough to carry.'

He went over to the drinks trolley and poured himself a big shot of vodka, putting the heavy cut glass tumbler down on the glass table beside Catherine's tea. He sat on the pouff at the end of the table near the fireplace and leaned his elbows on his knees. 'Are you still sitting comfortably, little girl?'

She nodded and took another sip of chamomile. Perhaps Gerald had explained the wave of energy that passed up her body after climax. And why loving Christopher was like loving God. Gerald went on, 'What you've described to me, my little ice maiden, is not simply the awakening of a professional virgin of the emotions to the powerful stimulus of exceptional sex. What you have told me lets me think something more profound may be going on. You, Catherina, on your path to the divine, have come to the abyss and looked down. What you have seen down there, I can only guess at. But I would suspect you are looking at the biggest nest of serpents any ice maiden ever kept at the bottom of her garden.'

She gave a faint snort. 'Gerald. Explain yourself.'

'All right. You've told me the man may be a gangster. You don't know this. He may be trying to impress a rich bitch with things beyond her ken.'

She shrugged and took another sip of tea.

Gerald shifted himself to the sofa beside her and stared at her over her knees. He went on, 'But, little ice girl, whether your suspicions do or do not mean a thing, you are still going to be looking at your nest of serpents, dragons, or whatever, because they are all yours and they've been squirming around in your psyche all the time. It's just that this sexual explosion has blown the lid off the snake pit. That's why you are wrestling with your pythonic conscience now. Your beast from the abyss is trying to strangle your love with, on the one hand, guilt about your marriage and, on the other, fear that your dark Angel has gone off and dumped you.'

She put down her cup on the table and leaned her head back looking at the ceiling. She sighed. She looked bored. 'Come on, Gerry,' she said, 'cut the Grimm's Fairy Tales stuff and get back to the Heroic Quest of the Plutonium Path.'

'Now hear me out.' He wagged his finger at her. 'If you want me as a shrink you have to put up with the insults. Everyone, Catherine, has a nest of serpents, but some have bigger ones than others. You just happen to have the biggest one this side of hell. You have those serpents because you have kept the lid on all your wicked urges, on all your sexual passions that your upbringing told you were no good and not nice and definitely sinful. And they have turned into serpents which are ready to come and swallow you up.' He turned his hands and arms into the likeness of a squirming snake with open jaws and waggled them at her.

'I didn't know you were a Freudian, Gerald,' she mocked.

He remained earnest. 'I'm not. I'm a Jungian. And what I'm telling you is you've been piling up one hell of a black monster behind that perfect exterior and it's going to control your life until you face up to it.'

'Why?'

'Because it's subconscious. It's made by the truths about your desires and fantasies that you won't face up to, things which are natural and innocent until you load them with censorship and guilt. You've buried them in your subconscious where they act like a puppeteer pulling strings that make you do things you don't understand. They block your light, your spiritual light and cause you to cast a shadow which can eventually obscure your better self. Acknowledging and forgiving your guilty drives redeems them and lightens the shadow. One's ambition should be to cast no shadow, to be transparent to the light.' He threw his hands out towards the ceiling as if to the sun.

'Stick to the point. What have I got to acknowledge, Gerald?' She was faintly interested now.

He leaned back and smiled. 'Well. This is only the first lesson, honey. So I would say for now just get used to the idea that wild sex is something you want and need and like and, whether or not you have to hide it from your husband, it is also something you had better accept as part of your life and stop feeling guilt over. Enjoy it, for heaven's sake, you lucky bitch. Since your husband wasn't giving you anything and this mysterious Angel is, you don't have to feel guilty. And, when you stop feeling guilty and stop telling yourself you shouldn't have anything to do with the man, he'll probably appear again. Just like magic. The mind is a very powerful machine, Tsarina. The more you know about what's going on in it, the more power you wield over yourself and your life. If you don't face the truth in your heart, your shadow personality of secret desires and fears will control you without you even knowing it. It will make you do things you don't understand. Things you certainly won't like.'

She let her knees drop and stretched her legs across Gerald's lap and lay silently staring up at the ceiling. It was true, she had felt the most tremendous guilt about wanting Christopher so badly. Not guilt about James, but guilt that went back years. Brenda Roberts was the source. Brenda who stood out in her memory as a paragon, a nun-like figure who had never married. Who had been her surrogate mother. Brenda was the one who had formed her sexual standards. Catherine felt a sense of discovery and remorse.

She said, 'I can't get rid of what I'm feeling, the guilt and everything, just by telling myself.'

'Just start telling yourself and go on telling yourself that your feelings for your Angel are all right.'

She wriggled her toes childishly and smiled a rueful little smile. 'Okay, Gerald. I'll try.'

'Good.' He leaned over and patted her knee. 'And now let's go out to dinner. It's a long time since tea.'

She went out to the powder room. She splashed cold water on her face and repaired her make up. She stared at herself in the mirror and in the eyes that looked back at her, heavy with unshed tears, she seemed to see a portent of future griefs. Despite what Gerald had said, helplessness overwhelmed her. She was being controlled by something fated. She shivered and went back into the reassuring room.

13

The Prime Minister, with his characteristic attention to details which should not concern him, was supervising the coffee service. James wished he felt less like a good nap. The roast beef and claret had brought on an unfortunate degree of relaxation. He knew the PM wanted him on his toes. Hence the coffee, offered with a motherly touch by one of the women Royal Navy ratings who were currently staffing Chequers. A brandy would help, too, he thought, but that was not offered.

Catherine had said little through lunch, though she had exchanged a few words with the Secretary of State who had been sitting between her and the PM. James preferred her to keep quiet, though he knew the PM liked to hear her views and regarded her as an objective and astute observer of the fashionable political view among the young and trendy. James was afraid of her unorthodoxy and irony and her flippant wit. Catherine rebelled whenever people seemed too sure of themselves, too complacent. She got on well with Major, who liked and listened to clever women, but there were moments when she would upset others. Although Catherine knew very well the delicate game he was playing for his promotion, he feared she would wreck him and his other backers with some candid quip.

Today, James thought, the Secretary of State for the Environment, John Browning, had the look of a man who knew his time was up. The sooner the better as far as James was concerned, and as far as the SLRS went, too. John was gumming up the works, slowing things down. James thought it might be on purpose. Browning had been against the Scheme from the start. Too ambitious, too big, too cumbersome. No comparison with the Docklands for potential, had been his verdict.

But the PM was keen. South London was his home ground and he was taking a close personal interest in every twist and turn of the development scheme's progress. The Cabinet and the Party were solidly behind him. With the Government committed to stopping crime at source, the march of the Inner Cities Development Programme was unstoppable. The SLRS was the key to some big political prizes. Some even bigger profits, too, by the look of the way the businessmen were stepping in with support. Arnold's crowd were definitely committed and there were more rushing in.

James' thoughts were curtailed. The Prime Minister was quietly checking that everyone had their coffee. He sat down on an upright chair, took a few quick sips from his gold lipped demi-tasse, put the cup and saucer down on a nearby table and said, 'Good. Now let's get down to business.'

Catherine would have liked some lemon tea but that was not the kind of aberation one indulged in at Chequers. She also wanted to go out into the crocus-studded garden. Now, wondering if the conversation would be confidential, she said 'Shall I go, Prime Minister?'

'Oh no, Catherine,' Major said firmly in his soft voice, 'We won't be touching on anything you don't know about already.'

James thought the PM was well aware that husbands told their wives most of the Government's secrets, anyway. He would have told Catherine more but he saw so little of her. Since she worked so hard, she wasn't like a proper wife.

The PM was looking at him questioningly through his rather thick lensed glasses. 'There's a great deal of interest being generated by your baby, James,' he said quietly. His usually soft voice was husky from the remains of a cold. He looked tired and vulnerable, his pale eyes a little watery which Catherine thought made them seem more evasive than usual. He seemed to be waiting for James to speak.

James cleared his throat. 'It's not all desirable, Prime Minister. As you may have seen in the papers, we're attracting some rather negative comment. It has no substance to it, I might add'. 'He glanced at Catherine who sat demurely on a hard chair, slightly outside the group. She wore a simple navy blue suit with a white silk blouse, pearls and a small diamond pin. He thought her skirt too short and frowned. She looked back at him without changing her expression which was one of polite interest.

'I trust there are legal measures being taken?' The PM glanced questioningly back and forth between James and Catherine.

Both nodded. James said, 'An injunction and a writ for slander.'

The PM shook his head. 'I'm sorry you're having this malice, James,' he said. Anger flickered in the blue eyes. He went on, his voice suddenly gravelly, 'The press have no interest in supporting constructive policy. They take every opportunity for muck raking.'

John Browning said, 'I do think this mud slinging is inevitable, John. Property prices are beginning to rise alarmingly across the whole area. The Opposition will soon be accusing us of putting poorer families on the streets and giving developers a blank cheque. It's not much of a stretch of plausibility for them to start accusing Her Majesty's Ministers of trying to line their pockets, especially after the spate of scandals we've had in the past few years. They are already complaining that the business interests are only in it to milk huge profits out of the scheme.'

'But I want businessmen to make decent profits, John.' The Prime Minister looked slightly pained. 'I don't expect them to be giving their time and expertise and their capital as charity. I don't expect them to be motivated by good causes. I expect them to be interested in the business opportunity which will benefit everyone, including the poorer people and the homeless and jobless. We are intending to appeal to their business instincts.'

'It's the way it will be interpreted by our enemies, John,' Browning said, sticking his feet out and lying log-like in his comfortable chair.

'Tell me, James,' The PM turned to him again in a rather irritated dismissal of Browning, 'Do you know anything about a man called John Leach?'

James wrinkled his brow and pursed his lips. It was a habit of his when stuck completely for an answer. Catherine thought it made him look like a remorseful orang-outang. No one spoke.

Catherine said, 'Is that the John Leach who used to be with the Docklands Development Board and had to resign about something? He was a Labour candidate somewhere once, I think, and he's still a councillor in

Lambeth, or is it Southwark?' She looked from the PM to the two men, both of whom were sunk down in their chairs with their ears under their collars.

'Well done Catherine. I shall have to have you in my Cabinet.' The PM's attempts at praise came off a shade patronizing, but Catherine smiled. Later, no doubt, James would tell her off for interrupting.

'Well, anyway,' The Prime Minister went on, 'His name has come up in a report from Special Branch. I thought you should have a look at it, James, since it concerns you particularly.' He went across the room and rummaged in a pile of papers parked on a window seat. He took a brown folder from the pile and handed it to James.

James opened it. Everyone watched him. There was just one sheet of typed paper in the folder. He read it and look up. 'I'm astonished,' he said crisply.

'Do have a look at it, John.' The Prime Minister looked at his soon to be outgoing Secretary of State for the Environment and gave him a worried little smile.

James passed the folder to Browning. He said, 'It's quite conceivable, of course, that the Opposition would have the idea of organizing the different protest groups into a cohesive whole, but I'm surprised they would choose a man like Leach to be their organizer.'

'Really? Why do you think that?' The PM wore a look which said he already knew the answer to that one.

'Because he is discredited and may have all sorts of nefarious connections and he will drag their campaign into disrepute. But then', James chuckled, 'that's fine as far as we are concerned. In fact, all the better.'

The Prime Minister's naturally upturned lips seemed briefly to smile. But his face quickly reverted to his usual more worried expression. He said, 'There is one rather sinister suggestion in that report, which I'm sure you have noticed.'

'Good Heavens.' Browning sat up. He looked at James and spoke animatedly. 'This is too bad. Special Branch are investigating a criminal connection with this man Leach . . .'

'Exactly,' the Prime Minister said. He went on, 'And

he is closely involved in the protest campaign with Michael O'Leary, who, as the report reminds us, is a Russian-trained agitator with a track record of fomenting dissention in the motor industry and others. That is why you must be especially on your guard when it comes to your personal interests and your private lives'. He leaned forward and spoke very softly but with great emphasis, going on, 'These people may be inspired by a collection of motives, some of which range beyond the political. They will do their best to smear you and to discredit your plans. Moreover, there is the possibility of some personal danger. The demonstrations we are seeing, especially the one outside the Department of the Environment last week, are increasingly violent. And now that they are apparently being coordinated centrally by a very unsavoury pair of men, we must take extra care of ourselves.'

The Prime Minister looked at James. 'I think you are the most likely target of any trouble-makers, James. I'm going to have a closer eye kept on your house and an extra security guard with you when you travel in your official car. John has these already. If things get worse we'll have to start a 24 hour police watch. And Catherine may need a guard too. But so far that is not necessary.'

The Prime Minister made it clear then that the discussion was over and that he had work to do. So they left. The daffodils along the driveway were bouncing like a celebration in the breeze. It was like being let out of school. Catherine was dying for tea.

* * *

They came into Queen Anne's Gate from St James's Park. James was driving the Aston. Catherine noticed a gold Rolls Royce driving out at the other end. She felt a rush of sudden excitement, but grew quieter as he told herself it could not be Angel.

They went into the house without talking and James went immediately into his study and closed the door. He had a dispatch box to go through, Catherine knew. It was still light. She decided to have a walk and buy herself a cup of terrible tea at the café in St James's Park. The air at Chequers had been so springlike and the flowers so lovely, she had longed to be walking in the garden after lunch. Now, she needed to unwind after the tense drive back, with James talking all the way about John Leach and John Browning, and Michael O'Leary and the Prime Minister and his many anxieties over the scheme.

She changed her shoes and slipped on a cashmere cardigan instead of her suit jacket. Putting a heavy red wool cape over her shoulders she unlocked the heavily secured door and stepped into the fading afternoon. She started walking up the street towards the Gate, looking down towards her feet as she went, adrift in the sense of loneliness James's obsession with work always gave her. She felt shut out. When they were together he talked about work. She was never able to tell him anything about her own problems or feelings. She heard only of his. They never seemed to joke or talk about silly, inconsequential things, goof around for fun. It was always a discussion to a point, James's point. And then he would walk off and start reading his papers.

She lifted her head and took a deep breath. Well, it was too late now to change all that. Thank God for her friends. And . . . she supposed she should thank God for Angel. But she could not quite bring herself to do that. It still seemed unlikely God would send her such a lover with whom to cheat on her marriage. Her guilt took hold of her again and dimmed her pleasure in being at last free to walk.

She reached the corner and turned right. He drove around the corner from the direction of Birdcage Walk. He was in the gold Rolls. He pulled up a few metres away and she went on walking towards him, unsure if it were he. Then, he got out of the car and came towards her. She had seen him twice since her talk with Gerald, but the last time had been several days ago. As usual he had not called her inbetween their meetings. He evidently was a creature of impulse. Or he liked to surprise her. She liked that too. It added excitement to their meetings. He had an uncanny way of knowing when to find her and she wondered if he had her watched.

He took hold of her hands in his. 'How are you?' he said, appraisingly, looking her up and down.

She said, blithely, 'I've had lunch at Chequers and now I'm going for a walk in the park. Will you come too? I want some tea from that little café over by the lake.' She giggled. 'It's terrible tea but you can watch the birds.'

He frowned. 'I'll give you some tea', he said and pulled her by her hand towards the car. He opened the passenger door and hurriedly ushered her in. 'How was Chequers?' he said rather sourly. She answered him with irony and he said nothing more. They drove past the Palace and around Hyde Park Corner, turning into Mayfair by the Dorchester. He parked in Waverton Street and helped her out of the car.

As they walked up the street she was trembling and when they were in the lift she shook when he put her hand into his trousers and let her feel how big he was. Outside the flat door, he pulled her cape around her and raised her skirt. He pressed her against the locked door and pushed his cock past her loosely cut lace pants rubbing it against her wet place.

He started undressing her there. He unzipped her skirt and pulled down her pants. Then he pulled the cape aside and took off the cardigan and the blouse. He lifted the cape away entirely and put it over his arm while he removed her camisole and brassiere. When she was naked except for her stockings and her pearls, he stood back and admired her. 'You're very beautiful, aren't you?' he said. 'What are you doing with a rough man like me?' The last words held disgust.

She looked at him with glowing eyes and she would have spoken, but they heard the lift start moving. He lifted the cape and put it over her shoulders.

'Turn around', he said and she did so. He put his key into the lock and then she felt his cock between her thighs and his fingers as he sought the place to enter her.

'Bend over,' he said, 'I want them to find us here.'

Perhaps she wanted them to because she did as he asked and let him enter her. He held her very close to him with one hand while with the other, he turned the key in the lock. He moved in her, jabbing, and she gasped. The lift stopped at their floor and they heard the doors opening. He quickly withdrew. He pushed her into the flat and then swept up her clothes and went in after her. He was closing the flat door as the voices came towards them.

She gave a little laugh. 'Chicken.'

He pushed her into the drawing room and turned on the lights. He propelled her towards the sofa and bent her over the arm and entered her again from behind. He said, 'This is rape, Catherine. You'll do what I tell you, now.'

He took her roughly, without thought of her need, driving into her. She reached for his hand and pulled it around her hip, drawing his fingers to the place she wanted him to touch as he thrust with a violence he had not shown before. She felt fear again, then. It was as though she was not herself to him but any woman, faceless and without past or future. He seemed to be expressing something, was it a destructive hate of women, or of something else. He seemed, for once, out of control.

She thought he would come before her. He was thrusting rhythmically, jabbing, not talking now, but breathing hard, leaning over her with one hand on the sofa. She moved his fingers on her clitoris, desperately wanting to respond. He pulled her to him and teased her but without finesse. She realized the lights were on and curtains undrawn. Anyone across the street could see them. Perhaps they both wanted that. Their secret needed to be shared. They both needed the world to know they were each other's.

He brought her to her climax, almost ripping the orgasm out of her with his hand while he thrust deeply and violently into her and let himself flood into her with a sigh. He withdrew quickly and she felt a rejection as he walked out of the lighted room, leaving her lying face down without dignity, naked except for her navy stockings and belt and her double row of pearls.

He had remained fully clothed in jeans and a light sweater, his trousers simply pulled below his hips. He came back into the room with them fastened and turned out the light. He said, 'I've got to leave now. Let's get you dressed and I'll drive you home.'

He had not even kissed her. There had been no affection, no feeling that she was loved. He had treated her like a whore. He brought her her clothes and she dressed quickly, feeling shamed. As they went down in the lift he did not touch her or look at her. She wondered what this mood was. She said, 'I thought I saw you drive into my street earlier. About ten minutes before you saw me.'

'No' he said. 'It couldn't have been me.'

She was sure he was lying. She thought, he can't have me legitimately so he has to pretend it's rape. And he wants people to see us because he hates the fact that I have to keep it a secret. Is that why he treats me so coldly? Perhaps her lunch at Chequers had something to do with it. It placed her beyond him, gave her advantage.

In the car, he said, 'What's this I'm reading about your husband and the South London Redevelopment Scheme?'

She said quietly, 'I don't know what you're reading.'

'Secret is it?' There was a sneer in his voice. He smiled, looking at the road, going on in the same tone, 'Is your husband a crook? Is he a bent politician?' His voice turned mocking, now. He turned towards her and she saw his eyes glittering with some unreadable emotion in the streetlights' black and yellow flicker.

She said, 'That's rubbish. There's no family connection.'

He smiled.

She said, 'Mud sticks, doesn't it?'

He said, grinning, 'It sticks better when it's got something to stick to.' They turned down Birdcage Walk and he went on, 'How close are they getting to publishing the Bill?'

She said, quickly, 'The Green Paper was out a while ago.' Her heart had gone cold.

The car stopped out of sight of the house on the corner at the end of Queen Anne's Gate. 'Will you be all right from here?' he said. He spoke as if she was a stranger he had given a lift to.

She nodded and opened the door. He made no move

to come out and do it for her. She stood in the street, holding the door open, not wanting to leave it this way. Then she leaned in to the car to say goodnight.

He said, 'You'd better take a bath. Your husband will smell my spunk on you.'

She closed the door and walked quickly down the street.

14

The early British Airways flight to Paris was crowded and silent. Croissants and coffee had left their trail of debris on dark suited laps. The crackle of folding newspapers accompanied the swift tread of air hostesses collecting plastic trays. Catherine put her unopened papers on the empty seat beside her and stared at acres of white cloud. Her mind drifted to those light plane flights in Kenya when, as a child, she was allowed to take the controls from the co-pilot's seat and practise her 'straight and level'. In Africa you flew by the seat of your pants, not by instruments. Later, in England, she had gained her licence, flying from Biggin Hill over Kent's swimming pools and gardens, learning to trust that innate sense of balance the pilot needs to fly by; her instruments in dense cloud without sign or sight of land below.

She wished now that she was flying her own plane. Flying demanded such concentration that there was no space for thought. She wanted to displace recollections of last night's pain and misery. Thank God she had this trip planned. She could not have sat in her office today. She needed to be here now, on her way to meet a challenge, enjoying this interlude among the clouds. She lolled back in her seat. In the early, slanting light, the endless white cumulus had the appeal of snow fields to someone who will walk forever and fall asleep in a drift, never to wake up. A sweet suicide of sleep. A natural death from fatigue and freezing. From passion spent like a final drop of blood. Her thoughts had turned to death again. How clear it was that he had brought her new life: and now she had cut him out of it in shock and anger at last night's cold violence, she went back to dying. Dying softly from a lack of love. She needed love. But she did not need a man who treated her that way. No. That would be the end. Dying had more dignity.

Besides, she had her work, which had kept her sane through the recent years of marriage and emotional death. She was going to Paris to talk about a French edition of Vanities with the head of France's most dynamic magazine empire. They had been talking for months. Now, she wanted to settle the final terms and conditions. She wanted control, of course, and they wanted more than they rated for their participation. But she would haggle them out or walk away from the deal.

She was in the mood for walking out on things today. She was walking out on Angel. It had been a short and desperate affair and it was over. She breathed out with a sense of relief and escape and slid regret under her thoughts. She would walk out on anything that did not give her happiness, wouldn't she? She wondered about that. It was taking her a long time to leave James. But then that was her father's influence. He was exerting his own pressure, moral conscience. With Angel there was no moral consideration. The reverse. Leaving him was more moral than staying with him. What she had been doing was wrong, clearly. Otherwise it would bring her happiness.

She took her gold mirror and a lipstick out of her soft black crocodile briefcase and started to retouch her face. She stared assessingly into her reflection, and met the hurt in her eyes. She thought she looked less than good this morning, the result of crying herself to sleep last night. And she was angry. Anger was not a beauty treatment. The light that had animated her these past few weeks since she had begun her liaison, was gone. What had that been; excitement, sex, hormones, hardly or she

94

would look good today. Love? Yes, she loved Christopher and that was the explanation for her changed looks of recent weeks, from ice maiden, to firebird. As Gerald said, 'Love is the source of life.'

What would Gerald say to the end of the affair, she wondered. He'd try to find her another lover, she had no doubt. Gerald had been planning love affairs for her for years. Now he knew she was willing to stray from her marriage, he would try harder to produce a man. Well, fine, let Gerald see who he could come up with. She needed a man who would entertain her and amuse her and be good in bed. An uncomplicated man who had no murky associations to worry her. A man who would make her feel happy, even if she cared for him less than he for her. She had had enough of being made unhappy in love. She wanted adoring.

She was looking forward to seeing Jean-Michel. He had been chasing her for several months during the negotiations for French Vanities. Married, but sophisticated, he would have her as his mistress and bring her back and forth to Paris in his private jet. He had already booked her for dinner tonight. Perhaps she would let him seduce her at last. The plane had started its descent. She fastened her belt and took a last look at the clouds before the plane plunged through them. Then, like the other passengers, she began gathering herself for the day's realities.

*　　*　　*

He was not taking no for an answer. She had had her way in the negotiations and he was going to have his way tonight. He had waited long enough. And she had been flirting outrageously. He insisted she come with him to the little apartment near the Champs-Elysees that he kept for his liaisons. She would not mind? He had had other women visit him there. She would not feel like a whore?

No, Jean-Michel, she would not feel like a whore. She would come to the apartment but she would make no promises. Or he could have a Cognac with her in her suite at the Ritz. Certainly not. That was too much like a whore. They laughed. She told him she knew what a whore felt like and he looked questioningly at her. But she did not elaborate.

They left the demure candlelight of the little Left Bank restaurant and stepped out onto glistening cobblestones. The rain had stopped now and the air was fresh and had that lilting magic Catherine aiways associated with Paris at any time of year. It was spring, yes, and she was on the arm of a very rich, attractive man, who knew how to treat a woman, a man with whom she had also reached a very satisfactory business deal. She was about to be made love to in the very special way of a practised lover who enjoyed the pleasure he gave women as a compliment to his skill.

Jean-Michel Barre had been running his Paris-Modes publishing business for fourteen years after inheriting a small provincial paper from his father. He had started small and built his business carefully. He was forty-seven and confidently successful. He was slightly built and not quite six feet tall, with soft curling dark hair going slightly grey. He had a tenderly expressive face in which his blue eyes set in large sockets were the dominant feature. They were lit with humour and the kind of instant sympathy that always made people, especially women, ready to open up to him.

Jean-Michel's chauffeur dropped them in the Rue de Berri and they went into a small apartment house. With a smiling nod to the concierge, Jean-Michel led Catherine into the elegant brass and mirrored lift. He took her gloved hand and brought it to his lips. She looked back into his eyes. She felt soothed and caressed by Jean-Michel's presence, yet she felt no desire for him.

But he had a seducer's touch. He took her into his arms immediately they closed the apartment door, and she felt herself softening like a stroked kitten. He led her into the bedroom and slowly started taking off her clothes, kissing her body and her face softly and sensuously all the while. When he had undressed her he stood back and admired her and then stripped himself with expert speed to reveal a slim, well-formed body and long slender legs.

Catherine had been wearing a simple black dress that showed her shoulders and a single strand of a diamond choker. He now removed the necklace, too. He said, 'I want you completely *au nature*.' Then he lifted her onto the satin covered bed. He started kissing her toes and worked slowly up her legs licking and kissing her fine gold toned skin.

He gently parted her thighs and made love to her with his tongue and then progressed to her breasts and her neck and her mouth before he slid into her exquisitely prepared centre and brought her slowly with him to a climax that was as liberating as a sudden flight of doves.

All the while Catherine did nothing other than stroke his back and his head. She held his cock once briefly while sliding a condom over it, but otherwise, she had been a completely passive lover, allowing him his freedom of her. When he had finished she felt as if every cell in her body had been loved and caressed. She felt freed and uplifted, floating, but otherwise quite untouched by an experience that might have been just a rather superior massage. She lay absolutely relaxed under his arm as he slept. She stared at the elaborately decorated ceiling, the gilt Empire furnishing and turquoise silk window and bed hangings and felt at peace.

But she knew perfectly well what was missing from this delightful symphony of erotic pleasure: and that was the passionate music of love whose majestic dark and light sound seemed to reach her from another place. She stroked Jean-Michel's dark head and wondered if he had ever heard that music.

*

15

The snow came suddenly, covering crocuses and leaving daffodil heads stranded and dusted with white. Catherine's return from Paris coincided with the first fall. She reached her office in the late morning driving in from Heathrow in the Aston which she had parked there the day before.

The day was a busy one. Meetings with her financial advisers and lawyers to discuss the deal with Paris-Modes took up lunch and most of the afternoon. Then, before she could leave, there were some protracted discussions with the Art Editor about the June cover. She was very tired when she left for home, driving slowly down Whitehall and into Parliament Square with the thought that she should go to her Health Club for a workout now shelved. She would have a bath and an early night instead.

As she drove around the corner into Victoria Street she saw the Abbey's north door was open and lights on inside. She pulled, on impulse, into the parking area before the great wrought iron gates and got out. The snow had stopped but there was a skinning east wind. She pulled the light spring coat around her and ran over the cobbles in her high heels. She entered the Abbey's still chill with a sense of reaching sanctuary. The building seemed to welcome her and she felt a sudden rush of tears to her eyes. She felt like a waif brought in from the streets and offered soup and a fireside.

A rehearsal was taking place at the end of the long nave. Choir boys in cassocks were singing a high chant. Catherine went quietly into St George's Chapel and knelt, putting her elbows on the rail and resting her chin on her gloved hands. As she knelt she dissected her fatigue's elements of grief and anger, and her sorrow came welling into her chest, choking her. As the energy of her silent prayer streamed upwards, she desperately sought words to frame her longing. But found none.

She stopped still, her eyes on the ornate brass above the altar and checked her mind. What did she want? What was the need that drove her in here out of the night to plead with whatever God would hear her? Could she ask her God to sanction this illicit love, let alone to bless its continuation? She questioned her right to call on any God. She questioned her purpose and her right to bring this unworded prayer into this holy place. She bent her head onto her hands and groped with her mind. Pleaded for divine forgiveness. Forgiveness for what? Forgiveness for not loving enough. For not being good enough to withstand the tests of loving.

Was she heard? Catherine felt no pulse of response, no spiritual comfort. The world, the whole universe seemed an icy tomb, sealed and silent, imprisoning her without hope of life. If there was a source of light and warmth anywhere, she was locked outside it. The moment of sanctuary, as she entered the Abbey had been an illusion.

Words reached her mind from some forgotten source and formed an offering. She would let him go and return to whatever conventional obedience the divine willed. But no, those words were wrong. Suppose she should love him? Suppose God willed that? Silence. Emptiness. Fatigue brought her head lower to touch the rail. It was as if she would sleep. If only she could have her decision taken from her.

Then, at last, the tears damning her heart, choking her so that she could barely breathe, flowed like water from a roof guttering that comes after the snow melts. And when she could cry no more, she knew her answer. She let go her hold, let go her responsibility for loving or being loved. Let go her will to direct her life. She raised herself and sat back on the small wooden chair behind her. She felt too tired to move, but at peace and warmer, as if life was returning. She was smiling: it seemed a burden was gone from her shoulders. The rehearsal was over and the Cathedral still. Somewhere she seemed to hear that music, the sweet, high sound. It called her, that siren sound. Her mind followed it and was met by joy. She did not understand.

She gathered her strength and stood, moving stiffly. She must have been there half an hour. The choirboys were leaving, stripped of their red and white robes, returned to the less angelic form of schoolboys. Catherine walked out into the melting snow. The wind seemed to have dropped. Big Ben was striking 8 p.m. She got into the Aston and drove slowly around the corner into Queen Anne's Gate, thinking longingly of food and sleep.

He was parked a little way up the street in the Mercedes. He got out, as she parked, and came towards her. She went on locking her car, deliberate, but clumsy with fear. When he reached her she was shivering. He put his arms around her and pulled her to him. She laid her head on his chest, feeling the softness of his coat under her cheek and let the remaining tears bleed from her eyes.

16

The meeting was breaking up but there were still some major loose ends. Michael O'Leary separated himself from the tight group at the dining table, taking his stick and leaning on it while he pushed the weight of his short, thick legs against his chair to move it backwards.

He limped across the huge room towards the great windows that overlooked the river. Tower Bridge was a net of lighted girders filling the windows. Better than those postcards of Brooklyn Bridge any day, the old Irishman thought. He had spent some of his youth staring up at the Brooklyn Bridge, night or day. His Irish parents had taken him to New York when he was three. They had wanted to get away from the rain and the peat smoke and the endemic poverty beyond their prosperous gates.

After a few years, they returned to Galway Bay, where they had their comfortable estate, and declared it good to get back to the soft life of long sleeps and rain smelling of the sea and myrtle, and rabbit stew and peat fires and nights in the pub with the local lads that were there spending their dole.

But Tower Bridge and the Thames were his great loves. He had come to London as a teenage tiger who could drink any man, even much bigger men, under the table. He had gone to Cambridge, and got a First in politics and economics, but that was a secret as he earned his living on the construction sites of the post war City. That's how he'd got his limp, too, when a great girder had pinned his leg and he'd damn nearly lost the wretched thing. It was held together with a piece of metal much like a steel-cored concrete girder itself. But it had not held him down too badly. He could still manage a fight and the old stick was a help there, too.

He propped the stick against the wall and leaned his good hip against it. He took his matches out of his pocket and placed them on the narrow window sill. Then he reached into his breast pocket for the cigar and his cutter. He'd developed the taste for a good Havana during his time in Cuba. He'd done Fidel a service or two, and life even in post-revolutionary Havana had been good enough. O'Leary's tastes were simple now but in those days, before the leg had been smashed, he'd enjoyed a good meal with wine, a dance with a senorita and a bit of a fling afterwards.

He gazed out at the slick black stream with its shivering sizzle of underwater fires. The cold north-easterly which had brought this morning's snowfall was bucking the outgoing tide. The air was clean as new glass and as sharp as a broken window. The stars over the City had a sardonic glimmer. He made out the Great Bear dangling over the old Stock Exchange and gave a low snort of laughter. It would be the Budget in a couple of weeks. The analysts had been issuing warnings and there were jitters. Some civil unrest might help to stampede the Bears. If the market fell badly, the SLRS would lose potential investors. He would hit the target twice, with one shot and a ricochet.

O'Leary turned and leaned his back against the brilliant view. Half the group was standing now. Smoke from their cigarettes hung around them, isolating the dining alcove from the rest of the great penthouse room. Leach had done well for himself in the Docklands to buy this place. O'Leary grinned a twisted grin. The bastard. He knew how to use the fruits of capitalism. But then he was not a red blooded socialist like himself. Michael O'Leary had served his time in the trenches from Cuba to Belfast. And now he was firing his missiles across the Thames at the City, and Parliament.

He levered himself off the wall and grasped his knobble-headed stick firmly and limped back across the room. No one had minded his abrupt departure from the table. O'Leary was the acknowledged master. They knew he was the great thinker, the arch plotter. They greeted his return to their smoke-filled corner with expectant glances. Had he thought of some new strategy that would put them all back in their chairs, chewing it over for another hour? That would keep them until after closing time. There were some fidgety movements of apprehension as O'Leary approached.

'Well then,' he said, grinning, 'you'd better be telling me what you've settled.' He tugged the empty chair and fell heavily into it, leaning the stick carefully against the table.

Reluctantly, they settled into their chairs again and one or two fumbled for fresh cigarettes. Their heads turned to the man at the head of the table who leaned back with an air of propriety. John Leach was very much at home in his own castle and also the group's apparent leader. O'Leary was the elder statesman to whom they all deferred, the old campaigner of many successful wars, but he was not in the confidence of the man they spoke of with awe and called by the pseudonym.

Leach was the link there. O'Leary had met the man once, that night at the Angel when he had told them to begin their work, and he had asked to meet O'Leary.

But Leach was the one who ran back and forth, they assumed taking orders. O'Leary took his from another source and that was his secret. It was O'Leary's source that had given the order to make the allegations about the Minister's family interests in the SLRS. O'Leary had had his fingers rapped for that by Leach. Leach thought he was in charge. He knew what was wanted of the man with the pseudonym but, as O'Leary knew, he did not know the composition of the larger picture, did not even know there was a larger picture. O'Leary was the real master of the plan and knew the whole thing but it was not in the plan's interest that anyone else should see more than a small section of the big jigsaw to which he held all the missing pieces.

Leach turned the corners of his mouth down. His long, knobbly fingered hands were on the table, fingertip to fingertip, as if they held some object within their cage, something he was about to reveal. O'Leary was confident they would have reached a decision. He had said enough to move them there before he left the table.

Leach said crisply, speaking like a major in charge of a military exercise, 'We're more or less in agreement with your proposal to move the street violence up a couple of gears in the next two weeks. We'll coincide our big demo with the publication of the Bill, which takes place on March 20th.

'The offficial demonstration will march from the Bank of England to make the point that this is a plan to enrich the capitalists. It will then go over Tower Bridge and through Southwark and Waterloo, across Waterloo Bridge, up the Strand and into Trafalgar Square. Since demonstrations are not allowed within a mile of Parliament while it's sitting, we'll send a small deputation by car from Trafalgar Square to Downing Street to deliver the petition.

'The unofficial demo will head across Lambeth Bridge. At the Embankment it will break into two. The smaller group will head up Horseferry Road to the Department of the Environment. The other group will run through the gardens along Millbank and storm St Steven's entrance. They'll break across in front of the security check point into St Steven's Hall. They will run through the Hall and out into New Palace Yard where they'll hold the main demo. Meanwhile small groups from the official demo will have left Trafalgar Square and filtered down towards the House. They'll run into New Palace Yard when the fight gets going in there . . .'

O'Leary cut in. 'Lambeth Bridge is too far from the House. The police'll be ready for you by the time you get to St Steven's. But we could keep that group as a decoy from the real assault force.' He grinned and looked around the table. Seeing he had their rapt attention, he went on, 'Suppose you have a third group, say fifty or sixty good lads who'll wait in the underpass at the north end of Westminster Bridge. Another thirty can be scattered around down Westminster underground station and can emerge at a given signal. These two groups can emerge on the Commons side of the street, run round the corner into the square and rush the gates to New Palace Yard. The Lambeth Bridge group can then join them while they engage the police. While that's going on reinforcements can come over Westminster Bridge to swell the ranks. By that time the police will be so busy with the three demos they won't know what's hit them.'

Several members of the group looked admiringly at O'Leary. Here was the master's touch. Leach turned his mouth down again and nodded sagely. In his thin, London voice, he said, 'We can put it to the vote. Comrades? Does anyone have a comment before we vote on Comrade O'Leary's suggestion?'

A pale, moustached youth with narrow, feverishly bright eyes leaned forward on his bony elbows. In a nasal London accent, he said, 'I'd like to know if the Parliamentary brothers have any idea what we're planning?'

Leach shook his head. 'We're not advising them. The less they know, the more this looks like a spontaneous rising of grass roots people – no party links. We have to keep the red banners out of this demo, comrades. Is that understood?' He looked from one to the other, fixing each one with a cool authoritative gaze.

The only woman of the group, a plump, amiable looking girl of about thirty, with red cheeks, and tousled black hair spilling onto her big pillowy bosom, spoke with a northern accent. 'I take it the black brothers are being invited?' she asked Leach.

Leach nodded. 'They are fully involved in our discussions and I hope to have their representative with us at the next meeting. Are there any further questions?' he added briskly, looking pointedly at his Rolex. 'No? Then let's vote on Comrade O'Leary's proposal.' He glanced around the table. 'For? Against? Abstentions?'

It was unanimous. The group got gratefully to its feet with a scraping of chairs against the hand-painted ceramic tiles that floored the dining area and the kitchen that branched off from it. They had been talking for almost three hours. The pale boy led the rush for the pub. They still had twenty minutes.

The room emptied quickly, leaving the shroud of tobacco smoke hanging over the table like Banquo's ghost. O'Leary gathered himself together and hobbled slowly towards the door. Leach followed, turning out the lights and setting the burglar alarm. He wouldn't want anyone to steal his David Hockney.

17

They lay, gazing into each other's faces and the great mirror hanging among the folds of the heavy blue satin bed curtains reflected their nakedness and stillness. They had made love for almost an hour and he had slept while she watched over him in the faint light from the hallway. To Catherine, it seemed their silence was a revelation of the depths of feeling that joined them. In their stillness and silence there was a communion even deeper and stronger than in the heights of their lovemaking. Communion of another sort.

She had not known a time of repose with him. Had not experienced the gentleness of being together and still. She did not want to throw speech into this silence and, when he awoke, it was he who spoke first. A moment before, she felt a shadow pass into the clarity between them.

He said, 'Catherine . . . you shouldn't be with me. You shouldn't be seeing me . . .' Then, as she tried to speak, 'No. Not because you're married. It's because of me, because of what I am.' He moved, then, away from her, pulling himself up and sitting with his back to the mirror, knees drawn up, looking away from her.

She caught his hand and tugged it and said urgently, her voice low but filled with alarm, 'Why, Angel? Why? What are you talking about? What you are is what you are. Whatever it is I love is what you are.'

His head was lowered and there was a half smile on his lips that did not reach his eyes which were brooding and gazing ahead. He said, quietly, 'I'm no good, Catherine.' Then he turned his head and looked down at her, and said it again, the words spaced and isolated from each other, 'I'm . . . no . . . good.'

There was a pause, and her puzzled eyes searched his oddly gallant, mocking ones. She whispered, 'What does that mean?'

He put out a hand and stroked her head, pulled in a breath and spoke in a suddenly jaunty tone. 'It means you shouldn't be with me, my little innocent one. A nice girl like you shouldn't be mixed up with a man like me.' He swung his legs off the bed, turning his back on her.

She felt a stab of anger and flung herself upright, sitting cross legged facing him. Her voice was clear and sharp, 'Just what are you like, Christopher Angel?'

He got up slowly and stood facing her. 'I'm a crook. I'm mixed up with all kinds of people you shouldn't have anything to do with. Your background and your class, your money, your husband, your life, your reputation . . . you don't want to risk them for a man like me.'

Defiantly, she said, 'Suppose I didn't care? If I said it didn't matter? Suppose I thought knowing you worth any risk?'

'I'd say, think again. Think about it when you're not thinking about that.' He leaned forward and touched her soft pubis. 'You could have an affair with a nice respectable man from a good background. You don't need a man like me. You can get your fun somewhere a lot safer.'

'Do you think my feelings for you are just sex?' She was angry again, her face lit with it, her voice higher than usual, spirited and affronted. 'Don't you think that after seven weeks of being your lover, I might have tired of you if it had been just sex?'

He smiled and turned away from her. He walked towards the adjoining bathroom, stepping over their fallen clothes. At the door he turned on the bathroom light and stood silhouetted in the doorway. She admired his developed body, his muscular legs and high rounded buttocks, his strong shoulders and chest, the rise of his neck and his head. His body showed his black genes in every curve and posture, but his skin shone pale, paler than her own. He looked like a black man sculptured in white marble.

'Try imagining what we would do together if we didn't have sex.' He closed the door.

She lay down again and looked up at the corona with its gathering of draperies. Was he trying to say they should not meet again? Pain surged through her. Pain of losing him. How could she let him go when she was sure he wanted her as much as she wanted him? Was it sex alone? Was it the body's pleasure drugging her sanity? Was it mere addiction? Was it time to think about her background, her responsibilities to James and her father? Where, after all was this passion leading? Where could it go?

He came out of the bathroom and started dressing. She watched him a moment, then got up and walked into the bathroom herself. She ran the shower and let the water roll off her shoulders, soaping herself, cleaning away the smell of him that she loved so much. Clearing her thoughts.

He was fully dressed when she came out of the bathroom, wearing the dark suit he would go to work in. She walked up to him naked and put her arms around his neck, looking into his face, her hair hanging in moist tendrils around her neck and shoulders. He looked back at her, smiling, then took hold of her wrists and pulled her hands away. He held her hands down by her sides and said, 'It's time to go, baby.'

She looked steadfastly at him and said, 'I don't care what you are, Christopher. I don't care. Whatever it is, I love, I want. To accept as a whole.'

'Do you, baby?' he said, smiling at her. There was cynicism but also hope in his voice and in his face.

'Yes. I can't just take bits of you, can I, and say I like this, I like that. I have to love the whole package or nothing.'

'Nothing would be best for you, my baby.' He looked down.

'No.' She looked determinedly at him, forcing him to raise his head, then adding, 'I know what's best for me.'

He released her and she turned to her clothes. He sat on the bed and watched her.

After a bit, she said, 'If you're just making an excuse. If you want to end this, I'll understand.' She watched his face and saw that it was not that. He reached out and pulled her towards him, into the space between his knees. He ran his hands over her buttocks and the spaces between her stockings and her silk pants, sliding his fingers into her softness and delicately touching her clitoris.

She sighed and her knees started to soften, her secret spaces to open and moisten again. She bent her head towards him and kissed his soft, full lips. He moved his fingers more and pressed more deeply into her. She sank to her knees and saw he was undoing his trousers again.

He brought his cock out hard and curved as a sword and gently pushed her onto her back onto the Chinese rug. He pushed into her past the light loose gusset of her pants and as she let him hold her and move her and drive himself into her, she knew he would not leave her, that this was more than any ordinary love.

He had his mouth close to her ear and was whispering hoarsely, telling her why he wanted her, what he wanted to do to her and how he wanted their loving to go on. And as he spoke, she understood more from what he did not say between the short hot sentences of love.

She realized her class was a barrier and that he felt unworthy of her for that and other reasons. And she thought of what he had said earlier and wondered if there were things she would not be able to countenance in his life, the things he had hinted of and tried to make her realize were dark and secret, the murky, shady things.

All these things ran through her mind as he grasped her to him and thrust deeply into her with the energy of a fighter. Then she could think of nothing except what he was doing to her body, of what he was making her body do, of what he was doing to her very soul.

18

Catherine usually had dinner with Sir Arnold at least once a week. Sometimes she and James had lunch there on Sundays, if her father was in town. Tonight, she went straight to Charles Street from the office. She found her father in his burgundy velvet smoking jacket, sitting before a bright fire in his study. To Catherine coming from work on a cold night feeling pinched and hungry, the sight of him in the red wing chair with his feet on a stool, reading and with a large scotch on the small tapestry-topped table beside him, was immensely reassuring.

'You look the perfect parent,' she laughed, coming in and kissing him and then dropping to her knees in front of the fire, holding her hands to the flames. Sir Arnold looked at her over the top of his reading glasses. She thought, amused, that he was studying to be an old man with some of the mannerisms he deployed at home. He raised an eyebrow and went back to his book, evidently wanting to finish a chapter.

'Can I take your coat, Madam?' Clive had come in behind her, having been surprised by her rush through the hall after opening the front door to her. She gave him the bright scarlet hooded cloak that always earned her the call of 'Hello, Little Red Riding Hood' from workmen and news vendors.

Without asking, Clive brought her a tall flute of chilled Veuve Cliquot which had been waiting in a silver bucket, and she thanked him.

Sir Arnold was still buried in his book. It was an anonymous one, enfolded in a monogrammed pigskin cover. Catherine sipped her champagne gratefully and stared into the fire. The texture of the Chinese rug, prickling faintly through her stockings, reminded her of yesterday evening's surprise encore and she smiled into the fire. She had not heard from him today, of course. Most lovers would call the morning after and say how wonderful it had been. She had, for instance, received red roses from Jean-Michel at her office after her return from Paris, yesterday. Angel did not comply with romantic ritual. When he wanted her again, he would call or simply appear before her. Until then she had to be content with his thought. The telepathic currents of his desire never left her. She was always aroused now. Always waiting for his cock.

'We have lobster tonight, I believe.' Sir Arnold had put his book down now and was looking at her. 'You can go on drinking champagne all through dinner.' She often did anyway as she usually ate fish or her preferred vegetarian dishes. Her father liked his Clarets and Burgundys and she had not succeeded in persuading him to eat less meat for his health's sake, mainly because it would mean drinking less red wine.

'What are you reading?' she asked him now, looking up from her place on the rug with a childlike open expression.

Sir Arnold snuggled more deeply into his chair and altered the position of his legs on the stool. With a masked yawn, he said, 'The story of the Brinks-Mat bullion robbery, my dear. Not as big as the more recent Clairmont robbery or as brutal as the Great Train Robbery, but a fascinating tale of skulduggery and financial trafffficking. You should read it.'

'Oh no thanks, Daddy,' she laughed. 'I don't share your fascination with crime.'

'Not any old crime, my dear,' he smiled, 'but the intricate processes of big time crime which involve the laundering of money. Money is my business, you will recall?'

She laughed and sipped her champagne. He went on, 'We bankers have to be very alert to the movement of money through our banks. Some turn a blind eye, but, well, others find it's better to be more observant. That way you don't end up in trouble with the law.'

She was staring into the fire again and for a moment was silent. When she turned to him next it was with a questioning frown. She said, 'Daddy, you've never told me, why did you never marry again after mother died?'

'Oh, my dear. What prompted that question?' He smiled at her and took a sip of scotch. He went on, 'Are you going to start questioning me about my views of your marriage again?'

She shook her head. She had her knees drawn up under her chin and the full red velvet skirt of her suit spread around her. Sir Arnold looked down at her, admiring her beauty, reflecting on Marina's loveliness.

He said, 'It's a long story, Rina, but I'll give you the popular press version, short and few-syllabled. I never wanted for another wife.'

She looked curiously at him, her head on one side. 'Didn't you ever fall in love again?' she said incredulously.

His expression was serious when he answered, 'Yes. I did.'

'Tell me about it.' She hugged her knees closer like a child waiting to be told a story.

He moved his legs from the stool and crossed one over

111

the other. He lifted the cut glass whisky tumbler and drank slowly from it. It was still half full. He must have poured himself a very large one, she thought and the thought bothered her, because her father drank spirits only lightly. His love was wine.

'So much curiosity before dinner,' he said and his voice was very heavily accented then.

He was hamming it up, she thought and wondered why. She felt he was putting on an act now, ready to give her a story. She wanted the truth.

'Come on, Daddy,' she said coaxingly. 'Tell me about your love life.'

He looked evasive. 'I don't have one now.'

She looked closely at him. She said, 'I don't mean now. I mean yesteryear. '

Clive opened the study door. 'Dinner is served, Sir Arnold.'

'Thank you.' Sir Arnold stood up and drained his whisky glass in one. Catherine was surprised. 'Was that your first drink?' she asked.

He nodded. But as she followed him out to the dining room, he lurched slightly. This was not the first time she had noticed lately that he was drinking more than usual, more than he should. When they were seated close together at one end of the long polished table, and their first course of hot asparagus was in front of them, Catherine went back to her subject.

'Ach. The trials of having a journalist for a daughter.' Sir Arnold lifted his napkin to catch a drip of melted butter from his chin. He looked at her in the light of the single three-stemmed candelabrum. He said, 'I have had many women in my life, my dear.' His tongue was firmly in his cheek.

Ignoring his act, she persisted, 'But wasn't there anyone special, anyone you really loved, someone you couldn't stay away from? Was there anyone who opened the doors of paradise when you made love?'

'What a curious phrase. You are being carried away by some strange metaphors, my dear. Is that wise? Shouldn't a journalist be more . . . ah, shall we say, acerbic?'

'Love is not acerbic,' she came back quickly.

He looked sharply at her and swallowed the last of his asparagus. Catherine had barely touched hers. 'Don't let your asparagus get cold,' he reproved her. 'It costs a fortune at this time of year, I believe. And the more so if Susan buys it at that robber's in Shepherd Market.'

Susan Hammond was the housekeeper who had replaced Brenda Roberts five years before when Brenda decided to go and live in the country. Brenda had been more than a mother to Catherine. Something of a father too, during the days in Kenya when she had lived on the farm in Nanyuki while Arnold was setting up his bank in Nairobi and living at the Muthaiga Club.

Catherine smiled at the reference to money. Her father, like most self-made men, was deeply cost conscious and accounted for every penny spent by his staff on his fairly extravagant lifestyle. She ate her asparagus quickly.

When the lobsters arrived, freshly boiled and smelling of the sea, she said, 'I know you've been in love, Daddy,' and smiled shyly at him.

He counter-attacked. 'I want to know why you are asking me this, Catherine.' He reached into the ice bucket and lifted the bottle of Cliquot up by its neck. He topped up their glasses and put it back.

She said: 'I'll tell you if you'll come clean.'

He sighed and picked up a claw, getting ready to crack it. He said, 'If you must know my secrets, Rina, be discreet. I don't want the world to know about my love affairs. And I don't want Gerald Marks scenting a new angle for some wretched book of my life.' He smiled gently and with a sad look went on, 'Yes, you are right. I was once very much in love. When I say once, I mean after your mother and I mean for a very long time. It was an affair that lasted many years.'

'In Kenya?' she cut in.

He looked anxiously at her. 'Yes. In Kenya.'

She regretted cutting him off. He would have said more.

'Why did you never marry her? Was she married to someone else?'

He took his time, cracking the claw and picking out the

113

soft meat with intense absorption. 'No,' he said, at last, his eyes on the starched white linen cloth. His feelings seemed to weigh on him. He lifted his glass and sipped, then leaned back in his chair and looked at her. As she was evidently waiting for him to go on, he continued, reluctantly. 'She was not married. In fact she was infinitely available. But, Catherine, I did not marry her because there were too many great differences between us. I could not marry her. It would not have been right.'

Catherine knew her father was a snob. She said, 'Was it class?' Then an idea struck her. 'Was she black?'

'Oh my God, no.' He laughed and looked at her in amazement. 'You know I'm not interested in other races. I am a European purist.'

'Like Hitler?' She couldn't resist it. But he had, after all, run from Hitler's Austria as a youth of seventeen. It seemed unfair. But she always had to fight him, eventually, whenever they were together. She needled him through some impulse she could not prevent.

'Rina. That was not called for.' He gave her an irritable look. 'Now,' he said with a brisk change of tone, 'I want to hear what you have to say. It's your turn.' He leaned over his plate with renewed energy and started wielding the shell crackers again.

With an air of triumph, she said, all in a rush, 'You know you told me to find a lover? Well, I have.' She looked at him expectantly.

He held the fine lobster fork in mid-air and turned his still open mouth towards her. She could see he was not pleased.

'Who is it?' He put down the fork and spoke sharply.

She said coolly, 'The man who rescued me, the night the Aston broke down in the snow after Gerald's party.'

'But who is this man?' The accent was very strong now. His tone was that of a cross-examiner.

She wanted to shock him. 'He's a night club operator.'

'Catherine. What are you telling me? You are the wife of a Minister of State. James will soon be in the Cabinet. Maybe in a year or two there will be a leadership election. And you are risking his career for an affair with a night club owner?'

Clive put his head around the door to see if they were finished and then withdrew quickly. He couldn't help hearing the last part of what Sir Arnold had said.

Catherine looked at her father sorrowfully. 'He is making me happy, Daddy. You know I needed that.'

'Yes, I know, but surely you meet men with more social position, men who are not in a risky business like night clubs, who can make adequate love to you and keep you happy. You know the vice links with these places are inevitable, the protection rackets, drugs, prostitution. Night clubs are not all like Annabel's, you know. Where is his club? What is it called? What is the man's name?'

'Daddy, Daddy. Stop this inquisition. I'm having an affair so that I can keep my marriage going a bit longer for James' sake. That's what you want, isn't it? Don't behave as though I'm telling you I'm going to marry Christopher.'

He pounced: 'Christopher? What is his second name?'

'Angel,' she said, bemused, shaking her head and smiling with a puzzled expression in her eyes. 'Why should it matter? Do you know him?'

Sir Arnold put his knife and fork together. All appetite for the remainder of his lobster had vanished. He took a long sip of champagne and put the glass down thoughtfully. He had seen the change in Catherine. He had suspected it was a lover. He had seen her face seem to fill out, although she was if anything slimmer than before. He had noticed the brighter eyes and clearer complexion, the happier manner, the altered body language that suggested sexual satisfaction.

Her earlier questions now rang alarm bells in his mind. He said seriously, 'Catherine. How far has this affair gone?'

'What do you mean, Daddy?'

'I mean, are you involved emotionally?' He looked deeply at her.

She toyed with her fork, looking down, not sure now what to tell him. But he read her face and said, more gently, 'You are in love with him, aren't you?'

She looked directly into her father's eyes and he read

115

her answer. He was appalled. He put his hand on hers and spoke very softly, gravely. He said, 'Rina, I advise you to do everything you can to end this relationship.'

She said, alarmed, 'Why? Do you know Christopher?'

He shook his head. 'It's not the man. It's the ambience, the environs, the associations. If anyone found out, this could lead to blackmail. The man might blackmail you himself. You don't know what his motives are. A rich man's daughter. A Government Minister's wife. Perfect pickings. You have fallen into disreputable company and worse, you have left yourself wide open to the worst kind of association a politician or his family can risk.' He held her wrist in a strong grip and leaned towards her. 'I beg of you, Rina. Ease up, cool off and just drift away quietly. Take yourself to New York for a few weeks. Just avoid seeing him. It will die.'

'Is that what you did, Daddy?' The still small voice of acid anger at her father's direction of her love life brought this knife out of her sleeve.

He coloured. He said sharply, 'No. It is not what I did. But I was not involved with riff raff dealing on the criminal fringes of society. I . . .'

'Daddy!' She stopped him with an anguished cry. 'Please don't say any more.' She felt hurt and upset. She was suddenly thrown into complete doubt as to her reading of Christopher's feelings for her. His affection might be a ploy to get her involved, to . . . Oh, she felt sick. 'I think I'd better go home now, Daddy, if you don't mind. I'm sorry if I've spoiled your lovely dinner for me. I do love you, but I'm going to have to think about all this. I can't make any promises tonight.' She stood up.

He rose too, feeling suddenly bent and old. His back seemed to have stiffened and his old wound from a street accident in Vienna, seemed to pull back his left leg as he moved so that his limp returned. He hobbled to the door with Catherine.

Clive was coming towards them from the kitchen. He looked surprised to see them. 'Will you have dessert in the drawing room, Sir?' he asked.

Sir Arnold shook his head. He said, 'Mrs Waring has

to go now, Clive. Just bring her coat and then I'll have a nightcap in the study and make it an early night.'

He allowed Catherine to kiss him. He gave her a gruff goodbye and walked stiffly to his study. The fire was burning brightly, still, filling the room with friendliness. Without putting on a light, he went to the drinks cabinet and poured himself a stiff malt. He moved across to his chair and sat down, leaning forward on his knees with the glass clasped in his two hands, staring into the fire.

* * *

Catherine drove home down Constitution Hill and through St James's Park. She felt very weary and went slowly. She put her Oscar Peterson tape on and let the soft music soothe her. She realized she had not played the tape since the night she met Angel, and it revived her memories of that night. She remembered his house and wondered why he had never taken her there. She suddenly realized, too, that she had no idea where his night club was, or what sort of place it was, not even its name. She knew she had been foolish to take so much on trust. It was time to be more circumspect. She usually went against her father on principle. But this time, she had a sneaking feeling he might be right and the thought filled her with unease. At least she should find out a few basic facts about the man she was now sure she loved. In the morning, she decided, she would start.

19

'Gerald. It's not funny.' Catherine's face and voice expressed her anger at not being taken seriously.

'I think the idea of you sleuthing around in a black wig and dark glasses is hysterical, Catherina.' Gerald rocked on his stool. They were sitting in Harry's Bar in South Audley Street, drinking Gerald's favourite Taitinger. It was barely seven and fortunately quiet, in a lull between the cocktail crowd and the pre-dinner drinkers.

She relented. 'Oh, all right, but I haven't got to that stage yet.' She looked down into her glass, feeling foolish.

He reached out and took hold of her arm, leaning forward and peering up into her averted face. In a hoarse whisper, he said, 'Believe me, darling, I do understand why you need to check up on this character but I don't want you to take it all so seriously. It's not a matter of life and death.'

'It is,' she blurted and turned tear-filled eyes on him.

'No, no,' he soothed. 'It can't be. It's only a love affair.'

'Love is life, Gerry. And no love is death. I know that now. I wanted to die for years, remember?'

'And now?' He had not let go her arm, but now he transferred the grip to her hand. 'Are you any better?'

She smiled. 'I'm a lot better.'

He shook his head and sighed. 'Catherina, you are a Russian drama queen with manic depressive tendencies. You have a dark Slav temperament and a persistent death wish. No matter what happens in your life you will pick up its tragic aspects and wallow in them. You keep wanting to be punished, which is so ridiculous for a woman who has everything.' He took her hand and kissed it, looking pensively at her. He added, cautiously, 'It's not your fault your mother died giving birth to you. You don't have to bear guilt for it.'

Her head came up and she looked as if an idea had just struck her. She said, 'My mother? Do you think I feel guilty about that?' She shrugged and looked around the bar, then took a sip of champagne. She said, acting brave, 'Yes. I'm a lucky lady. I have everything. Except the man I love.'

He sounded baffled, 'You do have whatsisname.'

'I don't have him. He's too damned elusive. And I also have a husband, remember? That tends to get in the way.' She sighed. 'Anyway I must find out the truth about

118

Christopher or I can't go on.' The words piled out faster. 'I've found out a bit these last few days. But, he has told me very little about himself, except all these hints which make me think he's some sort of criminal. I'm a little corner of his life. Just a secret mistress. Maybe that's all he wants. But if I go on even with that, I have to know what I'm mixed up in.' She looked helplessly at him.

'Perhaps he thinks you keep him in a little corner. You have your life, your glamorous power circuit, your social background. How can he muscle in on that?'

'I've asked him to private viewings and things and he doesn't want to come. He doesn't want to be in my life at all. But, he could still talk to me about his own life, couldn't he?'

'It depends what he wants to hide. Are you sure you are prepared to find out more?'

'Gerry, would I have gone to all this trouble to dig things up if I wasn't?'

'Your journalistic curiosity is a natural reflex, Catherina. The thrill of the chase and all that. But the answers you may turn up could hit deep. You have been brought up with a black and white view of good and evil. You could be very shocked by what you learn about Christopher and he may realize that. He doesn't want to lose you so he keeps his life a secret.

'On the other hand, he may just think he's too low class and boring for you and that you would lose interest if you knew all about him. Mystery is his strength. That's what makes him interesting. He may really be awfully banal. Or think he is.' He sipped his wine and said, 'On the other hand, Catherina, you risk a great deal. How will you react if you discover he's married or a bullion robber or a Mafia associate, or worse? What then?'

She was looking at him and he saw her eyes filled with flickering uncertainty like a candle guttering in a draught. He went on, pushing to see how much she was prepared for. He lifted a finger and waggled it at her. He said, 'You realize you are doing more than digging up your lover's secrets, don't you. You are exploring your own deadly secrets, your own unconscious fears. So, be

119

cautioned. The unconscious contains the dark night of the soul. You are trying to blow the lid off. I'm truly worried about how you are going to cope with a jackpot of revelations about your Romeo's dark secret life . . . assuming he has one. It might even be better not to find anything out at all. Ignore the challenge. Just drift. Take things as they are and forget about what he doesn't tell you. Get bored with him and then you won't care any more.' He lifted his hands and opened them like someone freeing a bird.

She smiled, suddenly cool and confident. 'To love is to risk, Gerry. I will cope. I have to or else the relationship stagnates. I have to know more for the thing to grow and I want it to, otherwise what we do together just becomes a repetition of some ritual. That's why, if he won't tell me, I'll find out for myself. And if I can't put up with what I find out, well, that's the end of it. I'll have to walk away from it.'

Gerald said, wickedly, 'Of course, he may not have any dark secrets. Are you sure he's not really an accountant who's trying to impress you with a fiction of an exciting back street life? Rich girls are notoriously willing to go for the bad boys. He might have thought that was the only way to keep you interested.' He giggled. 'Perhaps he has a wife and two children in Surbiton and the other house is an office. The reason he doesn't take you to dinner is he's so boring he can't make conversation, but he happens to be a good lover so he sticks to meeting you in bed.'

'Stop it, Gerry.' Catherine was laughing. She looked around. The bar was filling up and she felt exposed. She said, 'Let's go somewhere where I can tell you what I have found out. And you can hold my hand and make sure I don't disgrace myself.'

*   *   *

They sat in a quiet corner of the Grosvenor House coffee shop, looking out at the night traffic speeding along Park Lane. They had ordered food and were already sipping their drinks.

'Are conditions right for you to reveal the results of your daring investigations now, oh intrepid lady?' Gerald patted Catherine's thigh.

She gave him a sideways glance. 'I didn't do much myself. I got one of the secretaries to get a list of licensed night clubs in Mayfair and their licencees from the city council. Then I got another girl to go to Companies House and get me the names of the director of every one of them.' She stopped and smiled at him.

'And?' he encouraged.

'And. Full stop. No Christopher Angel connected with any of them.'

'Well. Did you give up?'

'No. I stayed late at the office and started ringing all the clubs on my list in alphabetical order and asking for him.' She looked smugly at Gerald. 'I got him. It's called the Sirocco and it's in Bruton Street.'

'Oh. Classy, huh?'

'I'm afraid not very. I asked around and no one who's anyone seems to know it. So,' she smiled, 'I made another call and put on a little Scottish voice and asked about membership. There isn't any. You just pay on the door. And so I asked about their hours and whether there was dancing and so on. They have a topless cabaret and they stay open until 3 a.m.' She grinned.

'And now you want to don the black wig and the dark glasses and go round there?'

'No. This is where I need you, Gerald darling. I have a feeling this is the sort of club where out of town businessmen go. They open about ten, and I thought you might like to ring up a couple of your pals and have a night out on me.'

'You could probably come with us, dressed as a drag artist.'

She pushed him. 'Don't be silly. He'd spot me a mile away whatever I wore. It's our amazing mutual chemistry.'

'Do you know, Catherina, I think you're beginning to enjoy this, and I know why.'

She looked archly at him. 'Oh why, pray?'

'Because you're doing something. You're not the

victim of his secrecy any more. You've taken the decision and the initiative. You can't bear not to be in control, can you, Tsarina? It's all very well wanting this macho customer to lay you on your back or whatever else he does to you, but when it comes to real life, you have to be the boss.'

She gave him a challenging grin in which he saw the measure of the woman who was building a successful magazine empire. The same woman who had enjoyed working secretly against the South African government, who relished in breaking down authority or restrictions. He saw, not so much the Russian countess's moody and passionate heritage, but the banker's vigorous, resourceful and wily character. He said, 'In fact, I think you'd make out quite well running the KGB or whatever they used to call it when they had Tsarinas.'

She tilted her head and smiled mysteriously. In a voice that blended steel and silk, she said, 'If you say so, Rasputin.'

20

'How many can you muster?' O'Leary sat forward in the old overstuffed armchair with the torn print cover. It faced the big TV whose screen now danced with black faces and which issued the sounds of a Reggae band. The scuffs on the coffee table marked where the owner's boots so often rested as he watched his favourite programmes.

It was hard talking against the music but they needed to leave it on in case someone somewhere was listening. That was O'Leary's view. But it was not a new ploy to his contact, either. The black man sat opposite on an old sunken sofa. Behind him, the beige paint was peeling off the wall and the plaster was blistering from damp.

They were in a basement in a Georgian terrace house in Brixton.

'This is not my pad, y'know.' The black man had greeted O'Leary in a sing song drawl.

It did not look that way, either. The man was expensively dressed in tan leather trousers and a matching bomberjacket. A big gold Rolex decorated his wrist and a gold chain with a large gold medallion on it hung around the open neck of his bright green silk shirt. He had several gold rings on his fingers, one in the shape of a skull and one gold earring decorated his left ear lobe. His shoes could have been Gucci.

The flat belonged to a Rastafarian. O'Leary was here on important business with the Rasta's employer, the man opposite, whose name was Rex and whose nickname was The Flick, on account of his skill with the small knife.

'How many you want?' said Rex. His Caribbean accent was quite strong. He was sprawling back in the sofa, one ankle resting on the other knee. He fingered his gold chain, thoughtfully.

'Ideally, a couple of thousand, but anything over three hundred would do for what I have in mind.'

'I can get you a few hundred,' Rex said, calmly. His eyes were half closed. He seemed ready to fall asleep.

O'Leary said, 'I need them rough and ready for a fight and I want them to be divided into groups. Each of the sub groups will need one man in charge of it. There will be three main groups but one of the groups will have a special assignment. I need the best ones for that group.'

Rex reached into his breast pocket and brought out a half smoked joint. He fumbled again and brought out a gold lighter. Then he lit the joint. The sweet smell drifted out from where he was sitting and tickled O'Leary's nose. It wasn't time yet, or the place for him to enjoy his daily Havana.

'It's an expensive business,' Rex said. 'The boys'll want a bit of duty free.' He made circles in the air with his joint, then drew on it and pushed out a long stream of blue smoke. He said, 'I can get plenty from my sources, but I'll need cash up-front.'

123

O'Leary shrugged. 'Either way. We have the cash. We can get the goods.'

Rex said, 'Goods. How much can you get me?'

'Enough,' O'Leary said cautiously.

'I need plenty.' His black eyes suddenly sharpened between the half closed lids and focused intently on O'Leary. They were like suddenly drawn knives.

'Moroccan?' O'Leary said. He was longing for a cigar, now. And a drink. He should have brought a bottle. He didn't know the place was a squat. He'd thought he was going to Rex's place from here. But Rex was too shrewd for that.

'Moroccan is all right. Say, three hundred kilos. And a bit of the other, say, twenty kilos.' He lifted his fingers to his nose and sniffed obtrusively.

O'Leary nodded. 'Sure.' Most of the drugs would be Rex's payment. Some would help inspire the troops.

'How soon can I have it?'

'A couple of weeks.' O'Leary cleared his throat. It was strange how his throat got foggy when he needed his cigar. He said, 'I'll let you know where to take delivery nearer the time.' He stood up and reached for his stick. 'I'll have to have another meeting with you to give you the exact plan of action, before the day. I'll leave a message in the usual place.'

He limped towards the door.

Rex lifted the hand with the joint in it in a vague gesture of farewell. Then he picked up the remote and slammed up the volume on the video.

Michael O'Leary closed the door thankfully against the assault. He could still hear it as he unlocked his car. Funny people, these Jamaicans, he thought. As for Rex, the man was just plain dangerous.

*

124

21

'What's going to happen at midnight, Gerald? Do we turn into a pumpkin or does the fairy godmother appear and invite us into the Sirocco?'

'I'm going to give you the low down on your low life lover and in the meantime we might see something interesting.'

'Like what?' Catherine pulled the Hermes scarf more tightly around her chin and tucked up the collar of her black trenchcoat. She adjusted her dark glasses and waited while Gerald developed an answer. He was taking his time. She looked at him anxiously, but his eyes were fixed on the Sirocco's lighted sign.

It was four days after their supper at the Grosvenor House. She had arranged to meet him after dinner in the Ritz bar from which they had driven in Gerald's car to Bruton Street. Now, they were sitting in the Ferrari a few doors up from the Sirocco. It was two minutes to midnight.

'Gerald?' She was becoming impatient.

'Wait. Do you see that?' He was whispering.

'What?' Catherine whispered in return. She looked up the street. Bruton Street was slick and black from the rain and completely deserted.

'Look at the sign.'

'What are you talking about?'

'Do you see, the sign is flickering?'

'What of it?'

'Hold it. Let's wait and see.'

A few minutes later, a large dark red saloon coasted around the corner from Berkeley Square and came slowly towards them. It stopped immediately outside the Sirocco and a man got out of the near side rear door. He went into the Sirocco. The saloon stayed where it was.

'I'm on the edge of my seat,' Catherine said in a bored

voice. She yawned and covered her mouth with a black gloved hand.

Gerald said, 'Now, I can tell you what happened the other night. You see, I was in the Gents . . .'

She cut in, laughing, 'Oh, darling. Not again.'

'Shush, Tsarina. It's not what you think. I was in one of the cubicles and having rather a struggle, sorry to bore you with the detail but it is significant, and a couple of chaps who had come into the pissoir, singly, started having a cryptic conversation. All I could see were two pairs of shoes. One rather nice suede pair, actually. Not that a gentleman would go out at night in suede shoes, of course.'

'Oh Gerry, do get on with it.' She yawned again.

He did a cockney accent that was a passable imitation of a TV East End villain. 'One said, "the goods'll be 'ere tomorrow. Come in around midnight but look at the club sign first. If it's flickering, don't come in. It's all clear when it stops flickering." I had to hold back so badly at that point that I nearly did myself an injury. But, fortunately, the other man just said "Okay, Guv", and walked out. The other one followed him and I was able to complete my mission satisfactorily.'

She looked at him. 'What do you suppose they were talking about?'

'I dunno, duchess.' Gerald still spoke in the TV voice. 'However,' he continued in his normal accent, 'that was a police car that just stopped over there and the man that went in was a plain clothes officer.'

'How do you know?'

'Look closely, my dear sleuthette. There is a uniformed officer at the wheel.'

She removed her dark glasses and saw that he was right. She said, 'So how long do we sit here and what are we expecting to see?'

'I dunno, do I?' The TV voice was now a high pitched whine.

'Well tell me about the rest of the visit, while we're waiting.'

'You won't like it.'

'Oh come off it.' She was getting tired and the suspense was killing her. Gerald had first called her this morning to let her know he had been to the Sirocco. She had been holding her breath all day and now here they were playing cloak and dagger in Mayfair and she still had not heard his story.

'It's a knocking shop.'

'A what!'

'The hostesses are tarts who sit on your lap without invitation and pour champagne that costs £115 a bottle onto the carpet while they think you're not looking. They dance with you in between topless floorshows and rub themselves up and down your organs, and they ask you if you want to take them home for a small fee.'

'How much?'

'What d'you mean, how much? How much are the tarts?'

'Yes.'

'I don't know because I never got into negotiation. There weren't any male ones. Anyway, the risk of disease must be horrendous whatever sex one prefers.'

'Is it legal?'

'So long as you don't screw them on the premises, yes.'

The plain clothes officer came out of the club and got into the car. It drove past them and across Bond Street and up Conduit Street and signalled it was turning right at Saville Row.

'I'll bet it's from West End Central,' Gerald said.

Catherine felt depressed. She wished she smoked to alleviate the boredom and her misery. Gerald leaned over and removed her glasses. He took hold of her chin and turned her face towards him. 'Cheer up, Catherina. It's just a business.'

She said, 'Whores and God knows what else. That's a business?'

He reached across to the glove compartment and took out a silver hip flask. 'Brandy?' he offered.

She put out her hand and he put the small cup into it and filled it. 'Drink up, Tsarina.'

Her voice small and miserable, she said, 'What shall I do, Gerry?'

He took the cup from her and filled it again, tossing the cognac back quickly. He looked at her and then said, lightly, 'Whatever the heart dictates, pretty lady. Follow your heart.'

'What about my head. Doesn't that get a say?'

'What is your head saying, princess?'

'Run.' She leaned her head back on the headrest and groaned.

'And does your heart agree?' he said gently, his hand on her knee, leaning forward and trying to peer into her face.

She shook her head. Her voice was choked and husky and she said, 'I could walk in there now and put my arms round him and tell him I want him for ever.'

'I don't recommend you do it.'

She smiled and turned towards him. 'Gerald. You're my salvation. How much do I owe you for your night out?'

'Oh Tsarina. It's my treat. I'm only sorry you weren't able to join us.' He leaned over and gave her a kiss on her cheek.

She took his hand and held it. 'I should be in love with you, Gerry. Do you think we'd be happy?'

'In love is not a happy state. It's a form of insanity. And you and I could never be happy, together or separate. We're too idealistic and want the impossible perfect union.' He sighed. 'Apart from not being the right sexes for each other, of course.' He grinned at her and stroked her hand.

Just then a large white car came around the corner. It was the latest model Cadillac. It coasted past the Sirocco and turned up the side street to the right.

Gerald said, 'Wait here,' and leaped out of the car. She saw him running with an agility she had not realized he possessed down the street as far as the Duke of York pub. He also disappeared into Bruton Lane. She looked at the sign and saw that it was no longer flickering.

After a few minutes, a man came around the corner and walked towards her. He crossed the street and went into the Sirocco. He had on a smartly cut suit that looked grey in the street light and a light coloured trench coat draped across his shoulders.

Gerald followed him out of the lane and then ran the rest of the way to the car. He got in and started the engine. 'That's him. The suede shoes. I'm sure of it. I had a hunch when I saw that Mafioso motor. I'm going to drop you at your car and I'm going back in there. I'm sure it's a drug pick up.'

'If it is won't we see him come out again with the swag?'

'Maybe. But I could also see what he's doing inside. He might sit around and have a few drinks before he comes out again.'

'Let's wait.' Catherine snuggled down into her seat.

Gerald shrugged. He turned off the engine but he was restless. They waited about ten minutes then he said, 'My intuition is screaming to me to get back in there, Catherina.'

She put her hand on his arm. 'Don't, Gerry. I don't want you to. You've told me quite enough now for me to see what I've got myself into. And I don't think I want to know any more just at the moment. I've got to digest this. Thanks, though. You've been a dear.'

'Whatever you say, Tsarina.' He patted her knee. He sounded disappointed. He drove her back through Berkeley Square to where she had parked in Arlington Street and dropped a kiss on her cheek. 'Let me know if you need me.'

She nodded and went to her car. She gave him a wave and he drove away. Gerald was going back to the Sirocco. He wanted to know a lot more about the man she was in love with and the business in which he was engaged.

22

She walked into the dark hallway and then on into the lighted drawing room without removing her coat or scarf. James was not yet home. She went to the antique styled telephone on the miniature partners' desk near the

129

window and dialled Angel's house. The phone rang four times and then she heard his soft, questioning, 'Hello?'

'Hello,' she said. Her voice was a husky breath.

He gave a soft laugh. 'Well,' he said, mockingly, 'what are you doing up so late?'

'I don't feel sleepy,' she lied. Her voice was teasing. She felt exhilarated at finding he was at home. Perhaps he had been there all the time she had sat outside the Sirocco with Gerald. She tried to picture his house, wondered what he did when he was alone, how he sat when he answered the phone.

'What are you doing?' The words were a seductive purr.

She answered demurely, 'I'm standing in the drawing room. What are you doing?'

He sighed, 'I'm just ready to leave for work.'

'Must you?'

'Yes. But I could meet you later . . . About two?'

She was very tired and it was not yet one. But she felt herself tingle and tremble. She knew this was what she wanted. She must see him. The things she was learning haunted her. She had to touch him and see him to be reassured that he was still the person she knew.

He said, 'I'll see you in the usual place.'

'Yes.' A shiver ran through her as she put down the phone. She had to kill some time. Still in her trenchcoat, she went upstairs to the room adjoining her bedroom that she used as her study.

She went to the small locked file and drew out her private journal. She crossed the small, cosy room which was her refuge from James, and sat down at the desk. She had spent weeks searching for the right piece of furniture, elegant and feminine, in the antique shops of the King's Road and had eventually found this Adam-styled piece in a Wiltshire auction room.

She opened the plain lined notebook and read the first page. It was dated February 19th. That had been a Sunday four weeks ago when James had been called to Downing Street for an evening meeting with the Prime Minister. Almost a month ago, it was the week before

130

she had gone with him to lunch at Chequers and met Angel in the street afterwards. She had written:

Can one love so violently, in so short a time, after so few meetings? How can one know when something is deeper than lust, beyond the body? Why do I think of destiny and fate? Why is a stranger so much a part of myself?

The next page she had written last week the day before her dinner with Sir Arnold. She read:

I always believed some people could find their twin soul, someone who is so much their counterpart that they are bound indelibly for life. Yet, I always thought life was showing me that this was not for me, that I was alone in the universe, untwinned. Now I have found this ideal, I am traumatized, shaken into pieces, transformed beyond belief. I thought I had experienced heights of passion and sexual fulfilment. But nothing was like this, this volcano of feeling, this soaring of sensation like a religious inspiration, this obsession with another person and their life, this agonizing incompleteness when we are apart.

She turned to a clean page and took up her pen. She put in the date and then, without hesitation or conscious plan, wrote:

> Something entered my body
> And speared my soul;
> Something not ordinary
> Though without a goal,
> Scored a perfect mark.

Does evil come to the unwary or is destiny always good? I have been caught like a fish on a spear, simply and innocently and unwarily. Does the fisherman's shadow fall too late across the lake for warning? Or was the foolish fish a-dreaming of its fate and making dreams reality?

How did I come to this impossible surrender to my opposite. His intense male to my female, dark to light: two worlds in collision. Two beings impossibly attracted. Like ones gods would destroy.

Is there some way of escaping fate? Is it right to run from something that seems to challenge the fundamental laws on which I base my life? Or am I meant to confront this, as one faces a mirror, and find the darkest image of myself, and in doing so redeem it as one saves a drowning cat?

What is buried within me that I fear so much when I see its counterpart outside? What makes me shake and shiver when I meet him? Desire? Desire for what? For death. No. It is fear. Fear of death. Fear of the death of the self I am now. Fear for the birth of the self I will become after the passage from womb to world of the innermost secret.

She laid her head on the desk. Pain flooded her and yet there was a strange joy, like a reminder of promise, a blackbird singing in the snow.

*   *   *

The rain had thinned to a misty drizzle. She stood in a doorway on the corner of Hill Street and Waverton Street, her coat collar turned up around the tightly wound scarf that covered her hair. She had taken refuge here, both from the rain and from the cruising drivers who assumed that any woman hanging around the streets of Mayfair was for hire. It was 2.25 a.m. She had come by cab and gone up to the flat but he was not there, so she had gone out again. She had been waiting thirty minutes and was growing both anxious and angry. He had never kept her waiting before: but she made excuses for him. She had never met him so late and he must be detained at his club by something important. Surely? She alternately accused and excused him. But she would give him five more minutes and then hail a cab.

She thought of the warm comfort of her father's house less than a block away. It was ridiculous to be standing

132

here. If her father drove past after a late night, he would see her. She wondered if he had ever seen the Aston parked in Waverton Street on any of her earlier visits. Of course, he had no reason to drive around this way to get to his front door. Anyway, she hoped he was asleep, now. He had been looking very tired.

When he came she was cold and it seemed to her that only her rising anger had kept her blood circulating. She saw the gold Rolls coming fast up Hill Street from the direction of Berkeley Square and her heart thudded into exuberant life. It looked as if he were coming from the Sirocco, as he had told her he would be.

He did not recognize her with her hair hidden and the coat collar masking the lower part of her face. She stepped out onto the kerb and waved him down. He stopped and she went around to the front of the car and put her hand on the radiator. It was quite cold. So he probably had come from Bruton Street.

He got out quickly and came to her. He said anxiously, as if he were afraid of her anger, 'I'm sorry I'm late. I had some trouble.' He looked around him, 'Where's your car? You shouldn't be standing around on the street.'

She said, 'I came in a cab. Half an hour ago.'

He gave her a guilty look. 'I'm sorry. I thought . . .'

She cut him off curtly. 'Never mind. Let's go in now.' She could tell he did not like her manner.

They went up the street together not touching. In the lift he tried to kiss her but she turned her face away. He put his hand out and touched her cheek. It was as cold as her manner.

He unlocked the flat door and they went in. She led the way into the drawing room, turning on the lights which seemed bright and brutal after so long in the dim street. The air had the stale smell of an unused room. The heavily swagged curtains were open to the street, as always.

She turned to face him. 'Who owns this flat?'

He shrugged. 'A friend.'

'Doesn't your friend ever use it?'

'He's away.'

She smiled stiffly. 'Anywhere nice?'

'South Africa, actually.' He turned away, acting nonchalance.

She absorbed what she was sure was a lie. 'Who else uses it?'

He had drifted away from her and was examining a picture. Now, he turned abruptly towards her. 'No one else has keys.'

'Does anyone else ever borrow them from you?' Her voice was cold and quiet.

He turned away again and she saw him loosening his tie. He said, 'Aren't you going to take your coat off.'

'I'm still rather cold.' She heard her own voice as if it were another person's and heard the anger in it like fractured glass that was ready to break at a single vibration of a tuning fork. She felt even colder than she had done on the street. Then her anger had been lit by a frisson of fear. Fear that he would not come. Now she felt like metal under ice. There seemed to her to be no source of warmth in the room. Her blood barely seemed to move. She felt as if her heart had stopped.

He came towards her and suddenly folded her completely in his arms, holding her close and nuzzling her face with his lips. Her coat was very damp. He started pulling the scarf away and then started struggling to open the tight button at her neck.

She pulled away. He said, 'Catherine. What is it?'

She walked over to one of the long white sofas and sat down. She felt exhausted. He followed her and sat next to her and began very gently to undo her coat. He pulled the scarf from her and kissed her face gently and repeatedly. He whispered, 'My baby's angry.'

She leaned her head on his shoulder and closed her eyes. She said quietly and with the complete defeat of fatigue in her voice, 'Do you use this place for your whores?'

She felt him freeze. He took hold of her by the shoulders and shook her slightly. He was looking hard into her face. He said, urgently, 'What are you talking about, Catherine?'

She was smiling sadly at him. She said, lazily, with a

134

half yawn. 'I mean, is this where your whores bring their customers?'

'What makes you think I have whores, Catherine?' He shook her again.

'Don't you?'

He let go of her and stood up. He walked across the room and opened the drinks cabinet. He took out a glass and went out of the room and into the kitchen. She heard him banging about and heard the tap run and he came back with water in the glass. He sat down opposite her and put the glass down sharply on the low table between them. He leaned forward and looked at her. He said, 'You have to understand something, Catherine. I run a night club. I have hostesses in my night club. If they want to do business when they leave my club that's their affair. But they don't use this place.'

She lay back on the sofa, her head resting on the cushions. Her legs were crossed at the knees and he could see up her skirt. She was wearing black stockings under a short black dress. Her blonde hair fell attractively over the black trenchcoat. He wanted her. She was smiling very faintly but her eyes were sad. She was looking at him from a long way off. He stood up and went around the table and sat next to her. He put his hand on her knee and moved it slowly up under her skirt.

She did not move. She seemed not to notice him. He got up and went to the master switch by the door and turned out all the lamps. Now, the room was lit only by the amber glow from the street. He came back and sat down in the same place and leaned over her. He kissed her gently. It was like kissing a sleeper. He put his hand on her leg again and slid it slowly up the thigh. Her legs were still crossed at the knees and he pressed his fingers between them. He wanted her badly now. He began kissing her exposed throat, licking and mouthing and half biting her until he felt a response, a movement, a sigh. He undid his trousers and pulled out his swollen cock and put her limp cold hand over it. Then he pulled her legs apart, and ran his fingers into the warmth of her protected place. She was wearing nothing under her dress

135

except the suspenders and stockings, but whatever had been in her mind when she left home, she was dry.

He dropped onto his knees on the white carpet and pulled her forward by the pelvis with one swift lift of an arm around her buttocks. He put his mouth onto her and ran his tongue into the delicate petals of her rose. She tasted of salt and surrender. He felt her soften under his tongue and heard her sigh become a moan. He took her then without difficulty, pushing into her with one hard thrust that made her gasp and bringing her to a swift climax, coaxing her with his hand while he jabbed into her. He watched her face the whole time.

To Catherine, looking back into his face, he seemed, in the reflected light from the street, to have a look of desperation and anguish. His eyes, like black olives in his pale face, searched hers, hungry, pleading.

She threw her head back then and felt herself loosening, like a space traveller, casting off from her ship, her only hope of gravity and life and air; letting go as if letting go of life itself, not caring what lay beyond death, going into some blackness peopled with warmth and consuming fire that was becoming pure light, devouring and enlightening and merging.

He came with her and entered the same space. And they looked for that timeless second deep into each other and saw, reflected in each other's glistening eyes, the image of themselves, belonging as two halves of a single sea shell broken by the waves is suddenly by some trick of the sliding sand brought together in its exact whole form and recognizes itself once more for what it is, until the next wave destroys the certain knowledge of its completeness.

*　　*　　*

In the car, as he drove her home, she said, 'I wish you would share yourself with me more. I want to know you.' She was watching his profile as he drove. She saw the anxious movement of his jaw and ripple in his throat as he swallowed. 'What are you afraid of?'

'I'm not afraid. Of anything.'

136

'Liar.' The word cut between them like a drill.

He turned his head and saw her looking at him with a look that tore his fiction from him. 'You know I tell lies, Catherine,' he said, softly, a teasing seductive note coming into his voice. He reached across and put his hand on her leg and moved it slowly up, lifting her skirt.

She took the hand and said, gently, 'Could you try to lie less, do you think? I find it rather insulting to be lied to. No one likes to be taken for a fool.'

He laughed. 'A good liar flatters you by telling you really clever lies. A better one lets you make them up yourself.'

She snapped, 'I prefer the compliment of being trusted with the truth.'

'Ah Catherine, you might not want me any more if you knew everything about me.' He kept his eyes on the road. They drew up in Queen Anne's Gate around the corner from her house. He said, 'Did your father buy you that house?'

She said, 'If I wouldn't want you after knowing the truth, what makes you think I want you knowing you're a liar?'

'I don't tell lies all the time.' He was smiling roguishly at her.

'You don't lie when you make love.'

He smiled mysteriously. 'I might, sometimes.'

She said, angrily, 'I mean, your body tells the truth.'

'About what?'

'Your feelings. Bodies can't lie.'

He leaned towards her and held her shoulder firmly. 'Yes, I have feelings for you, Catherine. You know I do. But.. .'

She waited but he said nothing more.

She leaned over and kissed him, sliding her hand down to where the stiffening penis was already pushing against the cloth of his trousers. She said, 'That doesn't lie.' And looked into his eyes.

He looked back and for a moment there was complete complicity between them. Then he grinned delightedly at her and moved to free himself. 'You must go in. And I must go back to work.'

'It's almost four. When does your place close?' Suspicion again.

'It's closed but I have to check the takings.'

She nodded. 'Of course.'

She moved to get out of the car and he pulled her back. He looked into her eyes and said, 'I can't be what you're used to, Catherine. I'm what I am. You shouldn't have got mixed up with me if you wanted something better. I can't change myself.' A police car came past them from Birdcage Walk and one of the officers turned and stared at them. He said with a bitter note in his voice, 'You'd better go home, Mrs Waring. In case they think I'm trying to kidnap you.'

Taking it as a joke, she said, 'Do they know you that well?'

Viciously, he said, 'They think they do.'

He accelerated the car around the corner. The police had vanished. He stopped sharply outside her house.

Her hand on his shoulder, her voice musical with her appeal, she said, 'Please remember what I've said. I want to know you. We're friends and I love you. Don't treat me like a child who can't be told what the grown ups are doing. Take the risk that I won't like the truth. But realize that, so far, I've not . . . been affected by anything I've learned. I still want to be with you. You may not think I ought to love you, but I care for you enough to want to know you despite knowing some things about you . . .'

He caught her arm and challenged her. 'What do you know?'

She smiled. 'Just little things about your night club. Things any half-witted little cub journalist could find out in five minutes.'

He looked anxiously at her and she reached over and kissed his cheek. 'Don't worry. I'll get used to it. . . . So long as you tell me things. Don't force me to find them out for myself.' She squeezed his hand and swung quickly out of the car, closing the door with a wave.

He watched her with a thoughtful expression until she had gone in. Then he slid the Rolls into gear and drove slowly out of her street.

23

Gerald ran his hands down the girl's back and let them settle over the curve of her small buttocks. His breathing steadied. She had been considerate. He had expressed none of his special needs. He had undressed, lain down and closed his eyes and she had used her mouth to stiffen him. She had slipped his cock into a tight, thin condom, as briskly as a nurse, and then sat astride him and brought him to climax with surgical simplicity while he dreamed of . . . no one in particular. His fingers found the small aureole in the crack of her neat bottom and gently teased.

She sat up and lifted herself off his penis. 'If you want more you pay again,' she said in a matter of fact voice. She had a northern accent. Manchester, he thought.

He said, 'Maybe I do. Don't rush me. I'll pay you well.'

She stood by the bed, quite naked as he had asked her to be. She was astonishingly flat chested and her hips were barely curved. He guessed she'd had plenty of customers with his interests. Her dark hair was cut very short and her jaw was boyishly strong. She was very young. At the club she had been wearing a black sequinned sheath that showed her narrow body's flat contours and covered her neck and arms. Its back had been exceptionally low cut, in a narrow wedge that ended where the crack of her buttocks began. She knew her market.

He said, 'I'd like some more.'

She shrugged and came back onto the bed, kneeling next to him. 'What do you want this time?' Her voice was flat and bored, like that of a waitress in a cheap coffee shop.

He smiled. 'Do you like your work?'

She grinned. 'Do you want to beat me for being a bad girl? Or do you want to put on the dog collar and convert me?'

139

'Turn over,' he said, feigning excitement.

She did so, adroitly, and he slapped her behind a few times until she squealed.

'Spanking's double,' she said.

'Turn on your side,' he said. He wished he was at home asleep. He had no erection. He did not find her attractive. Which one of us is the bigger whore, he thought, and smiled. He curled himself into her body's shape and pushed his limp penis into the space between her long thighs. 'See what you can do with that,' he offered.

She stroked him carefully.

'What's your name?' he asked, quietly.

'Sandra. But they call me Sam.'

'How long have you worked at the Sirocco?'

'A year.' She was squeezing him between her thin thighs and deftly manipulating the tip of his cock with her fingers.

'What goes on there?'

She laughed. 'What do you think? Men come in for a good time and we make a bit of extra by bringing them home.'

'Who runs the club?'

'You must have seen him.'

'Which one was he?'

'The big tall bloke with the nigger hair do.'

'What's his name?'

'Angel. Christopher.'

'What's he like to work for?'

She laughed and her voice rose into a squawk. 'Ere. What do you want, a fuck or a bleedin' conversation?'

'I'd like a bit of both,' he cooed, and to show willing began rubbing his fingers over her clitoris. He felt clumsily inept, like someone trying to make a crucial speech in a foreign language.

He said, 'Have you got a dildo?'

'Of course I have,' she laughed. 'I charge extra for that, though.' He put a hand down through her buttocks again. 'That's extra, too,' she said.

'All right,' he said. 'In a minute, maybe. How much are we running at the moment?'

'About three hundred, with the spanking.'

He said, 'I'll pay you five if you'll tell me what your boss does apart from run the Sirocco.'

'How would I know?'

'You work there.'

'I've never been close to him. I'm not his kind of woman.'

'What is his kind?'

'He likes women to be women. Not like you.' There was no censure in her voice. It was flat and normal as if she was talking about people preferring milk in their tea.

'Does he go for any of the girls?'

'Not him. He thinks the goods are only for paying customers. Most club owners bonk the girls, but he keeps business and pleasure strictly separate. He's a secretive bugger anyway.'

'Does he have a woman? A wife, maybe?'

'I heard he was divorced a few years ago. She tried to take the business from him, but he did something clever. Something financial and all she got was a cash deal.'

'Who told you that?'

'Cilla, she's the manageress, told one of the other girls. She's been with him for four years, Cilla has. She's after him I reckon.'

'Will she get him?'

'What do you care? What's all this anyway?' She stopped working on his penis and looked around at him, twisting her shoulders.

He said, soothingly, 'Don't stop. I'm enjoying it.' He made a playful thrust with his pelvis against her buttocks.

She said, grudgingly, 'Your time's nearly up.'

'I'll pay you for your time,' he murmured, and bit carefully into the back of her neck. 'Just keep doing what you're doing and answering my questions.'

She laughed softly and continued.

He said, 'Does he do drugs, your Mr Angel?'

'He's dead against drugs.'

'Does he maybe do a little trading in this and that, maybe?'

''Ere, you're not a cop, are you?' She was alarmed.

Gerald chuckled, 'I'm sure I'd be getting you for nothing, if I was.'

'You mean, on the house?' She was grinning.

'On the Sirocco or on you?' He put the barest hint of a question into his voice.

'Both.' She sounded disgusted. Then she added, 'Well, the Guv'nor does give us a bonus for that kind of extra.'

'Does it happen very often?'

'Some of the girls do the odd favour for him. If he's got a friend in town, p'rhaps.'

'Or he needs to please a policeman?'

'Yes.'

'What kind of friends does he have?'

She shrugged. 'All kinds.'

He could tell she was getting bored. 'I'll give you another five hundred if you tell me what kind of people he runs around with and what other kind of business he does.'

'You what?' She was incredulous, her mouth open, her head half turned towards him again.

'But I want the dildo thrown in,' he added. And he took her hand and pulled it around until it reached his buttocks. He pulled her fingers gently down into the crevice and made her touch him.

'Now?' She wanted action. She wanted her money, to be rid of him.

'In a minute. Tell me about his friends first.'

She told him then about the big Mafia connection from Miami who had been in town for a few weeks three months ago. 'He only came to the club twice. But one of the girls went round to his hotel now and then. That was all on the house. The second time he came was just to pick out another girl. He had a few of his friends in and they did an exhibition, him and the two girls. Then the friends had a go with the girls.'

'Did your boss go to that?'

'I dunno.'

Gerald said, 'Did he pay the girls anything?'

'They did all right.'

'Are you sure it was on the house? The customers didn't pay Angel?'

'I don't know that, do I? Neither did the girls. But we thought it was favours for a business partner, like.'

'What did the Mafia do for Angel to merit that kind of favour?'

There was a pause, then she said, 'How do I know you're going to give me that money?'

'You'll just have to trust me.' He got off the bed and went to his clothes. He took his wallet and counted out five hundred in fifties. 'That's on account,' he said. 'You get the rest after.' It had been a shrewd move to go and raid the office safe before going to the Sirocco.

'How much?' Her ridiculously young face wore a sly and greedy expression.

'I told you, another five hundred.'

So she told him. He thought she could be making it up, but that was the risk. She told him the American played a relatively small part in it compared to the local people. She said they would kill her if they found out she'd told anyone. She made him promise to keep it to himself. She said, if she had to disappear he would have to help her.

He waited until she had finished. Then he said, 'How do I know you're telling me the truth?'

She spat, 'You can ask my friend.'

He was not sure he liked the sound of that. He said, 'All right. Now you can get the dildo.' He lay face down on the bed while she strapped herself into it. He looked at his watch. It was just after four. He might have to go in late tomorrow.

*

He retrieved his car from the parking garage and started to press his way through the pre-lunch traffic. The day was flickering with a stark spring light that went on and off with the passage of the flying clouds and reflected from glass towers and the windshields of moving cars. Here, in the winding canyons of the City's streets, the sunlight was sliced by deep shadows where the March wind bit with surprisingly icy teeth. He had no thought for the City and her drama of rushing feet and hot-breathed secrets. He liked the pulse of money being circulated. That he could understand on his own terms. The rest was part of that conspiracy of the privileged, the educated, the well connected. That he scorned like a clever child who has no skill at sport, and who sneers in secret at his more robust peers, but envies them.

It was a fear, really. He barely recognized it as such. Feeling only derision for the arcane games of finance, he held himself back and called the players crooks. But he knew the true crooks were few. Most were dominated by greed and the contest for survival. And these no more damned the City than himself, were no more prerogatives of the well heeled than of the poor.

Perhaps one expected better. He thought he did. Those who had been dealt the better hand of background and birth should be content with that bounty and not grub around for more. Not dirty their manicured hands with the gutter's silt. They should leave the greedy, tricky scrabble for money to those whose entire lives had fitted them for nothing better. He slammed a tape into the deck and the car shook with the pulse of a loud rock beat that detonated his train of bitter thoughts. On Holborn Viaduct he pulled the Rolls into a gap and accelerated. That was better. He'd left the City behind him. If he could drive at a hundred miles an hour now he might just lose the devils he had brought with him. But the traffic would not allow it even if the law did, not that he cared anything for the law, other than not being caught breaking it. As the car was caught in crawling traffic on Holborn he tensed again with anger.

What he had been told, no, ordered, to do was an insult. How dare the man who was no better than he was, who was perhaps worse because of what he had done all those years ago, make him this impossible ultimatum? Knives sharpened in his heart. He wanted to kill the man. No. He did not want to kill him, only to destroy him. He wanted to crack that elegant, oh so polished mask. He wanted to rip off the carefully constructed disguise and show the world that man's true nature.

He turned onto New Oxford Street. Then on an impulse he lifted the car phone. He knew what would make him feel better, knew what would take away the bitter taste. Knew what would assuage the indignity of the offer he had just received. Her cool upper class voice reached him through the car phone's crackle. He could tell she was pleased and that restored his sense of control. His power over her was his evidence that class guaranteed nothing, that there were more dynamic forces than those accidents of birth. Forces that could imprison and command and drag down even the rich and powerful. To feel her body completely and helplessly in his control was a kind of revenge for everything that had been done to him.

He would never hurt her. She was too precious and wonderful to him, had been so almost from the beginning, for that to be thinkable. But there were moments when he almost hated her. Sometimes those moments came just before her climax, when she cried out for his domination over her, when she would seem to do or say anything to have him go on, to have him penetrate her innermost being. It was as though in those moments she would let him kill her, as though she begged for annihilation, as if his cock was a bayonet that would finish her.

Then, he would feel his power rising in him, would feel some surge, like violence, passing through his head

145

and into his cock, would want to possess her, imprison her, even kill her by loosing this energy into her like a lightning bolt. It was some driven need to be her, to enter not only her body and her womb but her mind and her heart, to have her open every page of her life and herself to him, to let him be welcome in her.

He had no feel for books, read little, yet to him she seemed a precious book, whose leaves were edged in gold and whose covers were bound in the finest white silk. She was a book whose thin pages he wanted to turn and finger, reading the words at random, knowing that he had a whole eternity to absorb this precious thing that had been given to him. Given as a reward, he had no idea what for. Only, it seemed that he held this thing inside himself like a lighted lamp that steered him through the dark nights when everything in his past seemed ready to overflow and overwhelm him and drag him down into its dark undertow. This book, this lamp, this woman was some secret knowledge, some personal guide to another world and another life. How could he ever let go of this woman who seemed a magical treasure, a key to something beyond his understanding that would somehow save his life.

His cock was hard. She told him she was working, bringing out an edition. She was not planning to have lunch. She would be free later, much later.

He said, 'I want you now. I'm coming to get you. I'll have you back in your office in an hour. If you're not outside I'm coming in. I'll fuck you in front of them.'

She laughed softly, protesting, but she had felt his intention and his certainty.

As he turned into the Piazza he saw her come out into the street her red cape flying in the bright wind and her pale hair like a flag. He stopped close to the barrier and she saw him and came running over the cobbles in her high red heels, laughing. And he knew then what she was to him.

*

25

The Bill was published the next day. James told Catherine when he met her in the kitchen that morning. He was up early and she was running late after working until 11 p.m. getting the June issue to bed, thanks to her stolen hour with Christopher.

'They're expecting some trouble, I believe,' James said drily as he retrieved two boiled eggs from a pan of water and ran them briefly under the cold tap.

She looked up from making her tea. 'Who are?'

'The police. The Home Secretary has some reports of organized agitation. They'll be on full alert. The demonstration is planned to start from the Bank at noon.' He buttered his toast with emphasis.

Catherine watched him, smiling, not without affection. James was too like a schoolboy in so many ways, not only in his emotions. She said, 'So much planning and the Bill only just published. What are they going to do when you start the second Reading?'

'I don't know.' He frowned.

She said, 'What else has the Home Secretary told you, or am I not supposed to hear that?'

He looked up and she saw the anguish in his eyes. 'It's a lot of trouble, Catherine. The intelligence shows left wing types are behind the organization of the protest groups. O'Leary is a key figure. He is a USSR trained operator, you know.'

She put her tray down on the table instead of taking it upstairs as she had intended. She sat down and cupped her face in her hands. She looked at her husband expectantly, but he resumed eating. She said, 'Why do you think the left is so keen to stop this piece of legislation, darling?'

'Surely it's obvious.' He sniffed and hit the second egg an unnecessarily brutal blow. It resisted robustly.

147

James liked his eggs hard.

She smiled, suddenly demure. 'Not to me, dearest.'

He looked across at her and scowled. 'Do I have to . . .'

She cut in sweetly, 'Just the edited version, please.'

'I thought you were a political woman.'

'I am. But only in my spare time, nowadays. Give me the inside expert story, in three sentences.' James's tendency to take explanations to literary length had to be curbed in advance.

He finished the second egg and mopped his mouth with his napkin. He leaned back in his chair and fixed her with his most serious Ministerial expression. 'In a nutshell, Catherine, the reds want to destabilize the Government by hitting at our hard-core plans to revitalize the inner cities. The extreme left, despite its rhetoric, does not want more jobs and better housing for the underprivileged. It wants more unemployment and less housing because it wants to foment violence and revolution.'

'And get a Labour government elected next time?' She poured weak Oolong from her Wedgwood pot, studiously watching the flow of tea into the cup.

'If not sooner. Assuming they have seen all the moderates and elected a new and hard left leader in time.' He stood up and flushed his eggshells down the waste disposal, then bent down and put his dishes into the dishwasher.

James' obsessive neatness was sometimes useful, she reflected. She said, 'So we're in for a rough ride?'

He straightened up and started out of the kitchen. He said, wearily, 'All I know is, I'm going to be bucking violent protests right through. There's more, but I can't tell you, yet, except . . . it could stop the Bill.' He gave her a look of deep mourning and went out.

'And that won't help your career, young James Waring,' she murmured to herself. Come to think, it wouldn't help anybody very much. She wondered what the Home Secretary was planning to do about it. She took her tray and the papers and went upstairs. She was staying home today to write her Person to Person interview for the July issue and she intended to start by eating her breakfast in bed. Yesterday had been a crazy rush. June was a very big issue and there had been that hour taken out at lunchtime. The memory of how he had forced her down on the hall floor without even closing the flat door sent a tingling ripple of sensation out from her groin, suffusing her whole body in a sensual glow. She pushed the thought of him out of her mind and picked up the nearest newspaper.

* * *

The demo began at noon, right on schedule. A crowd of about a thousand, of well mixed race and including mothers pushing babies in pushchairs, began the long dusty walk from Bank to Parliament. Everything went very calmly. The march was orderly and kept to the route agreed between the leaders and the police. It was only when the front end of the march was half way down the Strand that radio reports started coming in of a second demonstration marching over Lambeth Bridge.

As O'Leary had forseen, the police had to divide their resources. Officers controlling the agreed march had to be lifted over to Millbank. Reserve detachments were called in from outside. But things happened fast, before any extra force could reach the area.

As the front end of the second demonstration reached the House of Lords, police cars tried to cut them off, but the protesters, quite different in composition from the first group of marchers (no mothers and babies in this lot) broke into a run and simply went around the blockade. As the front runners reached St Steven's entrance, the tail was heading down Horseferry Road towards the Department of the Environment. Shortly after, O'Leary's third group broke out from the Westminster Underground and underpass and ran towards Parliament Square.

The police on duty at the gate to New Palace Yard were quite unable to stop this very tough-looking group of youths from forcing their way in. Once in they began chanting and hurling missiles at the windows. They were joined by the Lambeth group who had stormed

149

St Steven's entrance and raced down St Steven's Hall.

Police on motorbikes and in cars came screaming up Whitehall and tried to force their way into New Palace Yard, but they were blocked by protesters. Fighting broke out both inside and outside the gates.

Soon all the police that could be spared from other duties nearby were sucked into the battle. Arrests were being made, but serious violence was developing as some protesters used bottles as missiles and then used broken glass as weapons to fend off the police trying to arrest them. Knives were seen and it began to look as if the police had seriously misjudged the demonstration's potential.

Riot shields and other equipment were not on hand as nothing more than routine crowd control manoeuvres had been anticipated. Questions would no doubt be asked later in the House and out of it. The more especially since, it seemed, the Home Secretary had received enough advance information of probable trouble to request extra police to accompany the marchers.

By two-thirty, the battle was so intense that there was little chance that anyone would notice a fourth group of people arriving in a variety of vehicles near the north end of Queen Anne's Gate.

Catherine had just finished the first draft of her 2,000 word interview and was in the kitchen at the back of the house, getting together a light lunch. She heard the sound of shouting coming closer and started into the drawing room. She was halfway to the window when one of the Georgian panes was shattered by a stone. More followed and she retreated, making for the stairs and going up them two at a time. She ran into her study which overlooked the street and looked down. A mob of maybe fifty young men, many of them black, was jostling and yelling outside the front door. More stones were being hurled through the ground floor windows. She picked up the phone and stood back rather than attract attention, then dialled the security hotline number. It took a minute or more to arouse them. Meanwhile she was calling 999 on the second line. Altogether, fifteen minutes went by before the first police car turned the corner into Queen Anne's Gate.

This mob acted quite differently from the other groups. As soon as they saw the police they ran for their vehicles which they had parked and double-parked up and down the street. They vanished before anyone could catch them.

As James remarked afterwards, the operation had clearly been timed exactly and carried out to a very well-ordered plan. All that was found in the street, apart from broken glass, was the stub end of a reefer, a small square of tissue paper containing traces of cocaine and a crumpled piece of paper on which was written the number of a Brixton phone box.

26

'The 24 hour police guard went on within half an hour of the windows being broken. I don't think that's so bad.' James' voice was pinched with indignation.

'I'm not referring to your present security arrangements,' Sir Arnold said tersely. He was treating James with the weary patience he often adopted when losing arguments with his son-in-law.

Catherine sat quietly. They had just finished the main course of their Sunday lunch. Sir Arnold's favourite rare roast lamb seasoned with fresh garlic and rosemary had kept the men quiet for some minutes. Catherine, eating the less demanding dish of cheese soufflé, had been describing the attack on the house.

Now they had resumed the argument begun in the study over drinks. Sir Arnold thought the Minister's house should have been guarded pending the demonstration, anyway. James maintained that all reasonable precautions had been taken and that no one had

had any reason to anticipate a personal attack.

'The main thing,' Catherine said, 'is that we are protected now. So please don't worry, Daddy dear, about what might have happened.' She touched his hand and smiled at him. She was concerned that he was looking so very tired.

This was the first time they had all been together since the previous Tuesday when the demonstration had happened. Sir Arnold was extremely upset when he learned that Catherine had been alone in the house at the time of the attack, and this was the main cause of his anxiety, now.

Clive brought in the dessert of meringues floating on raspberry puree and the men were quiet again. As they finished, Sir Arnold said, 'Have the police come up with any new information about the marchers' organization?'

James dabbed with his napkin at his mouth before answering. 'They suspect widespread drug-taking among the demonstrators. A number have been charged with possession of cannabis and cocaine. Alcohol was involved too, of course.'

Catherine laughed.

James said, primly, 'I fail to see the humour of the situation, darling.'

She said, 'It seems more like the assault on the Knights of St John of Malta by the Ottoman Emperor Suliman, than a protest march.' Both men looked questioningly at her. She had only brought that up to upstage James. He really was becoming more and more boringly patronizing.

She smiled and said lightly, 'Seventh Century soldiers high on drugs making suicide attacks on the fortress of Medina.'

James said sourly, 'I hardly think that's relevant, Catherine.'

'Suit yourself, but I think it could be an appropriate analogy.' She smiled and stood up. To her father, she said, 'I'll be in the drawing room. James can tell you the rest.'

She gave her father a quick peck on the forehead in passing and went out. Once in the drawing room she

152

closed the door and went to the telephone. She dialled Angel's home number and let it ring twenty-five times before hanging up and dialling it again, just to be sure she had not misdialled. This was the fifth attempt she had made to reach him at various times of day and night since Tuesday, including one call to his club, where she had not left a message. She wondered why he had not tried to reach her. He must have read reports of the attack on her house. Surely any normal person would call and check she was all right. Most of her friends had rung the office on Wednesday and a few had called her at home on Tuesday night.

She sat down at the piano her father kept for no reason, and ran her fingers softly over the keys. She felt disturbed and anxious. It was not only Christopher's silence. She was also quite sure now that she was being followed.

She had first noticed a small grey van with a plumber's trade name written on it in faded dark blue in Queen Anne's Gate one day about three weeks before. Next, it had followed her from Mayfair the night she and Gerald had waited outside the Sirocco. It had not entered Queen Anne's Gate, but she had thought it more than a coincidence to have seen it again the next day as she left Covent Garden and drove home from work.

She had not seen it since, but she had noticed a black saloon several times. She was also sure she had been followed while walking around Covent Garden. At first, it was more a hunch than anything definite. Men followed her, often, but they always approached her eventually. Women did not follow her and she was sure she had seen the same woman several times, walking not far behind her and stopping to look in shop windows whenever Catherine turned round.

She had had some experience of being followed in South Africa, where the police were not particularly subtle and could usually be spotted quite soon. Here, she had been less certain. But then she had less reason to expect she would be watched. After three weeks of careful observation of the streets behind her, she was, however, sure there were several people involved and this worried her as it suggested a round the clock watch. An expensive operation. This had become more evident in the past week. She was now fairly certain but she still had no direct evidence, nothing she could point towards if she wanted to tell the police.

The only other problem, she thought, was the motive. Did someone want to kidnap her? It was always a possibility. Her father would certainly be good for a few million as a ransom. Or was there something or someone else? Someone who had a reason for wanting to know her movements. James? Did he suspect her of having a lover?

She dismissed the idea with a short laugh. James barely noticed the colour of her clothing. Why would he care if she took a lover, other than she might endanger his reputation? She doubted he ever gave the matter a thought. Then there was the possibility that Christopher would have her followed. Was he jealous enough to care if she was seeing anyone else? He had once asked her if she had any other lovers. But he seemed so sure of her, so sure of himself in her affections. It seemed unlikely he would have her watched.

She heard the men approaching the drawing room and got up from the piano. Caught by her thoughts, she had stopped playing after the first few arpeggios. She decided it was too early yet to mention her worries to either of them. It would only cause the most tremendous fuss. James dismissing her fantasies and her father wanting a major investigation by Scotland Yard.

She smiled to herself and sat down by the fireplace. The gas flames were flowering like orange lilies around the ceramic logs. She reached across to the thermos left by Clive, and poured two cups of coffee for her menfolk.

*

27

'I still don't understand why you suddenly decided you wanted to go riding, Gerry.'

Catherine was riding a long legged grey, her own horse which she rode once or twice a week, usually at weekends. Gerald was mounted on a gentle black mare that tossed her head repeatedly under his nervous hand.

'Let her go a bit. Loosen up and she'll stop doing that,' Catherine said.

'That's what I should say to you, but in life, rather than on horseback.' Gerald let the reins out a few inches. He ran an admiring glance over Catherine. Her poise and grace were evidence of her control and confidence. She wore a brown tailored jacket and brown velvet riding hat, beige jodhpurs and black boots, a pink silk shirt and a paisley cravat held with a gold and pearl pin. Her blonde hair was held back in a fine net. Her make up was impeccable. She was from Central Casting, as always. The perfect act.

Catherine smiled, looking ahead. They were riding from Lancaster Gate. It was just after 7 a.m. on a beautiful Saturday, almost two weeks after the demonstration. Gerald had invited himself for a ride saying he thought it was time he did something healthy, and Catherine had suggested the early morning since she was flying to Marbella for a party that afternoon.

She said, 'Are you up to a canter?'

He looked doubtful but nodded. 'Okay, but, promise to pick me up if I come off.' He had not been riding for seven years and would not have bothered now except that he wanted a relaxing situation in which to talk to Catherine. He had not seen her since the night they had sat outside the Sirocco. Catherine was unaware that he had anything to tell her and he had delayed. She had said nothing to him about her lover on the phone and it would have been easy to avoid telling her the things that would cause her pain. He had brooded over the weekend and all week and decided she should know what danger she was involved in.

She led off at a gentle trot and then began a slow controlled canter. He followed, bouncing, glad she could not see him. As they slowed to a walk again at the end of the sand track, he began to wonder if the ride would, after all, give him the opportunity to talk to her.

They turned along the Serpentine and Catherine urged her horse into a trot. They went side by side along the tarmac. It was a good rhythmic trot and Gerald's unpractised muscles began to warm and function. The early air was rain-washed clean and the harsh wind of recent weeks had slackened. Daffodils grew in clusters in the grass alongside the sand track. Blossom was beginning. There was pollen in the air. He could see Catherine's enjoyment in her smile of pleasure, and worried that what he had to say would spoil it. He began to doubt again. Would it change anything if she were warned? Or would it just intensify her anxiety?

She kept up the brisk pace all the way along the Serpentine and almost as far as the gates into Park Lane. Then she turned right and they walked towards the start of Rotten Row's famous Mile.

Gerald's eyes took in the patterns of white and purple crocuses spread like crochet on the sunlit grass. The horse's gentle walk rocked his hips. Damn it, he had to tell her. He said, 'I've never told you what happened after I left you, the night we waited outside the Sirocco.'

She turned and stared at him. The horses walked on. She laughed then and said, 'I didn't know anything had happened.' She seemed to return her concentration to the horse, making him arch his neck and walk diagonally sideways.

They reached the sand and turned right, the horses' walk quickening as they anticipated the long canter to come. Gerald's mare trotted to catch up with Catherine's horse. He bounced, feeling undignified. As it slowed, he said, breathlessly, 'I went back to the Sirocco and I went home with one of the tarts.'

'What?' Catherine reined her horse to a stop. He came alongside her and his own horse stopped too. She was laughing. Then her eyes narrowed and her chin lifted. 'Have you brought me out here to tell me something?'

One did not argue with that look, he thought. He smiled, bashfully. 'Don't you want to know about my night with a woman?'

She said, 'Let's circle here and keep the horses moving while you tell me. We can canter all the way up, afterwards.' She walked her horse towards the wide end of the Row at Hyde Park Corner and then continued in a slow wide circle. Following alongside her, Gerald went through the brief details of how he drove the girl back to her flat in Charles Street where she lived in a seventh-floor walk up studio a few doors from Catherine's father. About how she had told him she worked on the streets sometimes during the day although she had some regulars who called her by phone.

Catherine was listening but glanced at her watch and around her.

He could see her distaste. So he stopped stalling and told her the story quickly and simply. Until he came to the things he knew she would not like. He stopped his horse and she looked back at him. Her attention seemed to sharpen and she turned her horse in a slick pirouette. They stood facing each other like knights about to joust.

He said, 'Your friend is involved in crime – handling drugs and maybe stolen bullion. I don't know how deeply tied in he is with organized crime, or whether he does any of his own organizing. He is thought to do a bit of trading now and again and he has some dubious connections.' He mentioned the Mafia type from Miami but left out the sexual details. Catherine was silent.

He said, 'The girl could have been making it all up. She knew I wanted information and was paying for it. There is something that I'm sure is true, though.'

Catherine had started making her horse move sideways and backwards in simple dressage movements. She continued with her glance fixed ahead of her, her expression concentrated. Gerald said, 'Damn it, Tsarina. Stand still a minute, would you. Let me tell you the rest and then to hell with it.'

Catherine wheeled her horse around in a single swift circle. She faced him and he saw the fear in her eyes.

'He's bribing policemen. I suppose everyone in the night club business does it. Well, anyway . . .' He shrugged. 'I guess it takes two to make a bribe.'

She went on looking at him coldly as if he were confessing some awful misdeed of his own. 'And?'

'He has a policewoman he visits, has a relationship with. It's been going on some time. Before you. He gets information from her about police interest in his activities.' He stopped. It was out. He had known that would be far harder to absorb than the stuff about crime. She was all ready to accept the worst about his life and his dealings. But like all women, she would get mad at the mention of another woman.

Catherine breathed in deliberately and let the breath out again. With a rough growl of rage in her voice, she said, 'Do you suppose he does it purely for practical ends, or does he like it?' She spat the last few words. She turned her horse to face The Mile. 'Now that's over, are you ready?'

He nodded. She went ahead at a fast canter and his horse followed. Catherine went faster still and her horse went into a gallop. His own followed. He had no choice. He bounced uncomfortably and hoped to God the mare would not shy or he was gone. The land rose gradually for about half the distance and then levelled. Gerald was tired by then and finding it hard to keep his grip as his horse had slowed to a fast springy canter that needed a more practised seat for comfort. The mare must have been equally uncomfortable because her pace slackened and she dropped back into a jerky trot.

Catherine reached the end of the Mile and waited. When he reached her, pufffing and mopping sweat from his face, he said, 'I thought galloping was forbidden in the Park.'

She brushed dust from her cheeks with the back of her gloved hand and grinned. 'It happens sometimes.' As they turned onto the road and started back towards Lancaster Gate, she said, 'I'd like to give you the money you had to pay the girl.'

'Don't be silly,' he said. 'I enjoyed the experience. I'm just sorry it took me so long to get around to telling you.'

'You knew I'd be upset.' She grimaced. 'And I am.'

'Does what I've told you change anything?'

She glanced at him. 'Should it? Did you tell me all this so that I'd give him up, for my own good and maybe my family?'

He shrugged. 'I just wanted you to know. I wasn't sure if I should tell you, but in the end . . . I thought you had better be warned. The crime business, he's dangerous to know. If anyone knew about you . . .' They were going along side by side over the Serpentine Bridge. His sentences were fractured and torn away as cars buzzed past them. He was apologizing, explaining. He should not have told her. He regretted it. She would go on with it, but be more unhappy.

She turned her head and he saw angry eyes above cheeks still pink from her gallop. She spat out her words, 'I'm glad you told me. He wants me. I'll swear he wants me as much as I want him. But he has to fuck some police-woman who feeds him information. No wonder I haven't seen or heard from him for three weeks. Who knows what other women he services for the favours they do him? Or how many of his night club hostesses and whores he tries out. How am I supposed to feel? How much love and forgiveness do I have to have for that kind of cheap behaviour?'

She did not care about blackmail, about being hurt by someone wanting to get back at him, about the risks. Behind her neat head he saw the Serpentine stretching east like a long pearl and the distant prospect of Westminster, the Abbey and the House, lit rose by the rising sun. She cared about being betrayed. He said gently, 'Has he ever told you he was faithful to you?'

'No. But . . .'

'But, like all women you expect it. Even though you have a husband?'

She was indignant. 'He knows very well I have no physical relationship with James. And I don't have anyone else. I don't have to be nice to anyone once or twice a week to keep my business end up.'

'You women are too possessive.'

'What do you know about women, Gerald?'

His horse danced as a passing car hooted. Catherine's remained impeccable. She held out her crop and signalled they would cross the road. He followed.

When they reached the park again he said, 'I know lots about women, Tsarina. I don't have to fuck them to understand them, you know. As for you, you have always had far too many men in love with you. It will do you good to know some men have other priorities.'

She said, 'I'm going for another canter. Are you coming?'

He sighed. 'Take it easy this time, please. But, tell me one thing before you go. Just why do you think he loves you less because he has someone else?'

'Damn it, Gerald. You talk about women. Men are all the same. A woman is only a woman, a fuck is only a fuck and love is an inconvenience that may cost some money one day. Don't you think there is such a thing as a bond of trust between people? When a relationship is special, when it's this powerful, why dilute it? It's not as though I'm his adored wife and he has to roll in the muck with a whore to . . . to satisfy his baser lusts.'

'It's your pride, Tsarina.'

She went off again. The sign said clearly, 'Riders, No Galloping', but she jabbed her heels into the horse's side and it leaped past the sign. The loose dust kicked up and formed a cloud into which she seemed to vanish like a bad tempered fairy.

Gerald's mare took off after Catherine and he hung on, desperately hauling in rein, wondering where or when she would stop. She was waiting for him near the exit path. She said, 'It's not my pride, Gerry. It's the thought

160

that if he can fuck one woman for the sake of business
or money, how do I know he's not after something more
than loving from me?'

'Do you mean your fabled wealth, Tsarina?'

'I do, indeed.'

'You have a few other assets a man could find exciting.'

'Yes,' she said, bitterly, turning her horse towards the
road, 'and so, no doubt, does the useful policewoman.'

28

Warm sea air drifted over the dance floor, blowing away
the cigarette smoke. The music pulsed with the underbeat
of an African drum, a slight melody lacing in and out of
the percussion like a charmed snake. Lights like small
stars dotted the floor under Catherine's dancing feet and
those of her partner. She felt lost in rhythm.

The music tailed off and her partner took her hand
and drew her towards the bar. He had met her a few
minutes earlier and throughout the dance had not stopped
looking at her. She wore a brief strapless dress with a
tight ruched grey chiffon bodice from which sprang
pointed layers of pale and dark chiffon in several shades
of grey studded here and there with rhinestones. She wore
little jewellery except an irregular platinum collar from
which trailed fine threads of seed pearls of various
lengths. Her hair floated with elfin fineness over her bare
brown shoulders and her eyes seemed the colour of the
noon sea.

He said, 'You look like a creature from the sea.
A beautiful fantasy creature. Are you real?' He spoke
with a deep, heavily accented voice. She could not tell
its origins.

She smiled and looked back at her new companion.

He was a tall, lean, well muscled man of about forty-five whose handsome face was tanned and trellised with long hours of exposure to strong sunlight.

She said, 'Yes. Are you local?'

He laughed. It was a deep, baying laugh. 'I am, in a way, though in another I am not.'

She smiled. They were leaning against the bar. He turned now and signalled to the barman. Catherine was drinking Perrier. It was late and dancing made her thirsty.

'The same,' he said to the barman. 'Two Perrier, one without ice.'

She said, 'You live here but you are from another country. Is that what you mean?'

He bowed towards her. 'That is right, beautiful lady.' He took her hand and kissed it. 'How wonderful to be so beautiful and also clever.'

Catherine smiled at his Latin lover charm. 'Are you Italian, maybe?' The accent was not right, but there was something that made her think of Italy.

He laughed the deep laugh again. 'Ah, dear lady, you are close but wrong. I was brought up in Rome for some years of my life but that is not the whole story. The Italians have had some important cultural influences on my life, and my tastes, but my genes,' he emphasized the word, revealing perfect white teeth as he did so, 'my genes, are from another race.'

'You are mysterious.' Catherine laughed and waited expectantly for a further clue. The drinks came.

'Let us sit down and look at the beautiful romantic sea.' He took her elbow and steered her towards a table overlooking the water. 'Ah, the moonlight is spectacular. How divinely clever of the Principe to hold a party at the full moon, when not only is the Marbella Club so beautiful and the evening so hypnotic, but there is that madness in the heart and mind. That imminent possibility of rapture.' He took her hand and, gazing into her eyes, kissed it with a studied sensuality.

She felt a shiver of desire go through her. She thought he might quite possibly be a remarkable lover. 'You were going to tell me about your lovely genes.'

'Ah, quite so. My lovely genes, as you call them, are from quite a mixed source. My father was a Serbian who became a refugee during World War II and fled to Greece, where alas, he was not so lucky either. The Germans were everywhere. However, it happened that he found a ship going to Alexandria and he went with it. This gave him the chance to meet my mother, who was Algerian, not French but a Berber, travelling with her family from Marseilles. Of course the Germans were in North Africa too.' He smiled his brigand's smile as if he held a knife in his teeth.

'Alas, I am afraid my father was a naughty boy. He stole into the young woman's cabin at night and made love to her. Then when they disembarked at Alexandria, he persuaded her to come with him. Her family, of course, would never have wanted her to marry a non-Muslim, let alone a penniless peasant from Yugoslavia. But the Serbians are irresistible lovers.' He squeezed her hand and held her eyes in a long intrusive stare. 'In the end, my dear lady, after many trials and tribulations, and dangerous war time voyages, they ended up in Morocco, in Casablanca, actually, where I was born.' He leaned his hand on his knee and looked pensively at Catherine. 'You are very quiet, my dear lovely lady.'

She said, 'It's a remarkable coincidence. My father ran off with my mother, too. But my mother was a Russian Countess and my father was an Austrian. I don't know what he was in Austria exactly. He was very young when he left. He was a refugee too, you see. Isn't it a coincidence?'

He laughed. 'Ah, my dear lady, think how wonderful it would be if we were to have a child together. What a mixture. Think of all those lovely genes.'

She tried to withdraw her hand. He drew closer to her. 'I have no children, yet. My first wife, who is now living in Argentina with a farmer, did not give me any. I have no heirs. Have you children? No? Why not? A woman as lovely as you, it's a waste. A terrible waste. You should hand on your beautiful genes, yes?' He laughed again and threw his head back.

163

She smiled.

He said, 'You would not like children?'

Her face saddened and she said, 'Yes. I would. My husband is not very interested, however.' She felt a pang of realization. She wanted Christopher's child. Was this the first time she had known that?

'Ah. So you are married.' He gave her a searching look but seemed not in the least put off by what he saw in her face. He continued, briskly, 'But let me complete my story. My father, who became quite prosperous, died when I was five and my mother, who was very beautiful, married a French diplomat. He became the French Ambassador in Rome after the war and so for many years I lived in Rome very comfortably and very happily. Now, I live here. But also, I have my place in Maroc. In Marrakesh. Perhaps you will visit me? Already now it is too hot there, for Europeans, but in the winter it is very nice. I have a villa with beautiful orange groves . . .'

Catherine smiled. She thought longingly of Marrakesh and orange groves. He said, 'Oh, now let us dance again. I see you are bored by my chatter.' He took her hand and raised her gently from her stool and led her to the dance floor. It was a slow dreamy number and he held her close. She felt his body's wiry strength and the sensuousness of his movements. He pressed her against the hardness in his trousers.

She thought longingly of Christopher, and then closed her mind to his memory. The affair was best forgotten. There had been too much pain. There was too much suspicion and secrecy. Too much unexplained absence. Perhaps that was his way of leaving her. So, for her, it was easier to return to her own life and mingle with her own kind of people, international people like this man whose name she still did not know.

After the dance he led her back to their table and they talked on. He told her that he lived in Puerto Banus on his yacht. He ran what he apologetically described as a small shipping line but which sounded fairly large as it included three cruise liners, fifteen freighters and an oil tanker.

Catherine agreed after a slight hesitation to visit the yacht. 'Tomorrow, perhaps,' she said, firmly, looking at her watch. She was surprised to see it was only just 1 a.m.

'It's early, yet,' he said. 'In Malbella we live twice, by day and by night. And the night has only just begun. I think you should see my yacht now. With the moonlight on the water what could be more romantic and beautiful? You are welcome any time, of course. But tonight would be too perfect.' Once again, he took her hand and gazed into her eyes.

He seemed to read her decision there. 'Good,' he said. 'Then come. The Prince will not mind you leaving his party for a while.' They walked up the short path to his car, a black Bentley into which he handed her as though she was a piece of fragile glass.

The yacht was much bigger than she had anticipated from his description, the size of a small cruise liner. There must have been room for fifty to sleep aboard, but about this he was vague. 'I don't try to have many guests. There are the crew and my personal staff of course, the chef and the valet and so forth, and just myself, mostly. I move her to Monte Carlo sometimes or to Cannes. We can go to Tangier. We could go tonight. Would you like that? The sea is very calm. And the moonlight is so beautiful on the water . . .'

She laughed. 'You're kidnapping me. I can't allow it. I must get back to the Marbella Club tonight.' She lied gracefully, 'I have to leave for an appointment early in the morning.'

'Of course, of course,' he said. 'We must not kidnap the lovely lady. But now at least, let us have a little good champagne.'

He led her into a spacious saloon furnished like a hotel lounge with groups of white sofas and chairs, small tables and lamps. There were huge flower arrangements in several places. White lilies and carnations, white roses and sprays of yellow mimosa that perfumed the whole saloon.

He spoke briefly into a telephone and then joined her on a sofa that was placed so that its occupants looked out over the ship's stern. They sat admiring the ocean which was lit, as promised, by the moon.

A white-coated waiter appeared and placed a silver tray with a silver ice bucket containing a bottle of Dom Perignon before them. A second waiter brought a silver dish of caviar on ice and some slivers of melba toast. The first glasses of wine were poured into the fine crystal and the first helpings of caviar placed on the delicate china plates. Then the waiters vanished like ghosts.

He took up his glass and smiled over it at her. 'Your very good health, Isabella. I shall call you Isabella until you reveal to me your true name.'

She said, 'It's Catherine. Catherine Clyne. What's yours?'

He took her hand again and kissed it. 'Ali Lazic at your service, Principessa Caterina. But I prefer Isabella for you.'

He said, 'Come to the deck and let us look at the moonlight.' He led her out onto the after deck and they leaned on the rail staring out at the sea's pewter sheen. He said, 'It is interesting, is it not, that this place which attracts the famous and the wealthy, royalty and entertainers, beautiful people of all kinds also has its ugly side. The criminals who live here, many of them British, who escape arrest because they came here before the extradition treaty, are busy doing their evil work. Gold from robberies passes one way and drugs pass the other way and the profits are all going into banks in Switzerland and Luxembourg and Vienna and Lichtenstein. And London, yes, even London, I believe.'

She was listening intently. He said, 'Yes, I happen to know that the Spanish police have been taking a keen interest in the drug traffic quite recently. I believe Scotland Yard has requested their assistance. They have already been working closely with the British police because of the IRA connection with the Basque terrorist group ETA. There is some theory that political violence in London is being encouraged by supplies of drugs. Do you know anything about this?'

She made her confession of interest.

He drew her close to him and laughed. 'Come inside and let us have a little more champagne.'

He filled her glass, handed it to her, picked up his own and then took her hand and led her through the salon. 'Come, I want to show you my beautiful yacht. You shall have a personal tour and I will tell you some interesting stories about my life as we go.'

He took her straight to his state room, took her glass from her hand and carried her onto the bed. He seduced her with even more sensuality and voluptuousness than she had predicted and he found her very passionate, and every bit worth his most avid attention.

29

'Yes, I interviewed the King of Spain for Vanities. And I spent the night with a shipping magnate on his yacht in Puerto Banus and I woke up in Tangier next morning and had to fly back to Marbella and then hijack a ride to Madrid with the Prince of Monaco. Yes. Yes. It was lots of fun, lots and lots of fun. So exciting. Yes. I'm looking forward to dinner next week.

'No. James is going to the Outer Hebrides on some vital mission to do with inner cities. Yes. Of course I've got it wrong. How do I know what James is doing? Just something boring down at the House or in his office at the DoE, I suppose. Hush, you're not supposed to talk about that. The Prime Minister has actually said it's definite. But we must wait for the oflficial announcement before we break out the champers. Bye now. See you Thursday week.'

And my heart is breaking.

'Of course we're bringing out the first issue of Lives on time, November. Don't be silly. The first issue of

French Vanities is coming out in September. No. I'm going to New York for a party that weekend. And coming back on the Queen, so bumpy in October. First Class, of course. I gather it's all pretty awful anyway. But just five days of doing nothing, looking at the ocean. And no jet lag.'

And my heart is breaking.

'No. I want the First Lady for the September issue of British and French Vanities. I'll have to fly over and do her whenever she can give us a date. Well, of course I'm doing her for Private People too. I can't afford to miss out on either the TV or the Magazine. Lives is a whole other bag of stuff. Much later. I can't tell you who we're having in the first issue. It's top secret. Yes. I'll see you at the Cartier Party. Well, if not there then I'll be at the House of Lords for the . . . What? Not that! You can't tell me Joan Collins said that. I'll be seeing her at Annabel's next Thursday. Yes. It's Michael Caine's birthday thrash. Bye now.'

And my heart is breaking.

'Janie. Get Stephanie to hold these damn calls. Now do a few things for me right away, would you? Tell Moto I want a fitting on Wednesday. The red suit. About noon, here. And ask Saint Laurent if they have a size eight in the black velvet cocktail. The one we featured last month. I need one very fast. For Saturday. No. Don't tell me the pictures are late for July. I don't want to hear it. Make them unlate. No, I don't want to rethink the cover. Charlotte Lewis is perfect for that swimsuit number. No. He won't do. I want the sexiest man in town for the centre spread in August. You tell me who is the sexiest man in town. Am I supposed to do all the thinking? No, another town will not do. This is London Vanities remember?'

And my heart is breaking.

'Daddy. Don't give me this stuff about cash flow today. Are you my banker or my creditor? Think the difference, dear. I can't talk money on the telephone. I'll have to get Bill Waites to ring you. He's my accounts genius. No, he does not fiddle the books. He counts the money we make and pays the bills. If you want to sort something out do it with him. I'll come in later and we can sort out the broad parameters for Lives. They've already sold half of November. The first issue. Yes. That's it. Now please, Daddy. Be an angel. Get off my back. Bye then.'

Angel. Angel. Angel. My heart is breaking.

'Janie, I thought I said hold the calls. Who let my father through? No calls means no calls. I don't care if it's the Queen. Who? My husband. Definitely not in.'

Why don't you call? My heart is breaking.

'Janie. I'm having lunch with Commander Armstrong tomorrow? All right. I need his bio. Haven't they sent it yet? Get them to bike it round. If not, send one of our own bikes. Now. No, not in a minute. Now now now.'

Now. I need you. And my heart is breaking.

'Gerald. How did you get through? No. I'm not taking calls. Yes. But you are different. Yes. I did have a lovely time in Spain and I took a lover. You know what I feel. Don't probe me on the phone. My heart is breaking. You're the only one I can tell that to. I'm alone for five seconds or I wouldn't tell you either. How are your aching muscles? Are you coming riding again? I thought not. Well, serve you right for not telling me all that awful stuff over a nice hot dinner somewhere.

'No, I haven't forgiven him. I haven't heard from him for three plus weeks. He's probably moved in with her. They're probably bonking in a cell down at St Marylebone nick. I don't admire his taste either. He doesn't deserve my class is right on the nail. You said it. But I'm agreeing with you.

'Of course that's why I took a lover in Spain. Revenge is sweet and sex is necessary. I know. I think it's time I started a Spanish Vanities, then I can move down there permanently. He was wonderful. He asked me to marry him. The morning after. Imagine. He wants an heir and I think he rather likes me, besides. I'm not being cynical. He's coming to see me in London. Love him? Don't say that. You'll make me cry and ruin my face and I'm right here in the middle of everything. I can't cry now. I'm in the middle of July. Bye darling.'

And my heart is breaking.

'Janie. I'm going to the Health Club. Yes, I know it's only four-thirty. But all I'm getting here is interruptions and I'm tired after flying back last night and I'm anxious to get to work on my transcript of the King. Is it all typed up for me to take with me? If so, I'll start this evening. Just get all that stuff on the Commander, will you? Tell them to bike it to Queen Anne's Gate and put it through the letter box. Or give it to the police guard. I'm through for today.'

Maybe for life. And my heart is breaking.

30

Catherine moving through the early rush hour. The Aston creeping up Regent Street. Shops, still open. It's Tuesday. She has left the office early, has her mind on other things than clothes. Spain. Marbella. Ali Lazic. Loving and being loved. Distraction. Easing of the pain, of sexual tension. Wonderful, ambrosial experience of being touched and sucked and licked and kissed and fucked softly, smoothly, silkily. Seamlessly. Getting to the right places at the right time. Like a lover in a dream. No, not a dream. Dreams frustrate. Never get sexual fulfilment in dreams.

Catherine. Conscious of going the wrong way to the Health Club. The car knows where it's going. It's going up Portland Place, then along New Cavendish Street. Slowly. So silly going so slowly in this very fast car. A car for killing oneself in. Drive very fast late at night. Death wish again.

No. Life wish is drawing her here. He is life. Where is his street? Right turn and right again. Ah yes. Here is his house. It's daylight. It was night before. And winter.

Night and snowy. Now it's daylight, soon to be dusk, and spring with window boxes everywhere. Daffodils, tulips, crocus. Late late crocus. April is here. April Fool. That's Catherine . . .

I'm watching your house. Waiting for you. Hoping to see you. Driving down your mews but there's no sign of life. No golden Rolls or Mercedes. What happened? Where did you go? Why don't you tell me? Is there some reason you have to hide? From me. Why hide from me? I love you. I'd die for you. Couldn't you have said goodbye? A last kiss. Farewell and if forever, still forever . . . Final rites.

If you don't tell me, I'll kill you. I'll wait for you one night and kill you. Kill you for leaving me. Kill you for having another woman. Kill you. Kill you.

Catherine, parking, walking over the cobblestones in black suede high heeled shoes and tight black skirt. Black lace stockings and silk and lace underwear sliding like fingers over her skin. Her body remembers his touch, moistens, opens. She's looking at his house. Standing back and staring at his house. Sees no movement. Goes close and stands at the door and knocks?

She hears nothing. Then the dog gives a deep Woof Woof. So he's still living here, hasn't done a bunk. Why are you never at your Club? Why don't you answer the phone? Three weeks since I saw your eyes, took your big cock in my mouth, in my cunt, felt you fucking as if you wanted to die or kill me or both.

Two nights ago, I met another man. I tried to let him steal me away from you. But he didn't succeed. He made wonderful love to me but I could only think of you. I could only come by thinking of your cock oozing its spunk into my womb. As if I was your whore and you sent me to him. For your favour. I can't get away. You're in my head and in my heart and in my cunt. Are these your thoughts following me to hell and back? What am I going to do? I'm going to have to kill you to get you out of my mind. I'm going out of my mind. I'm mad. I've been mad since the first time you touched me. I'm going to get a gun and shoot you. It's the only way. Or shoot myself. Or both. I can't let anyone else have you.

Catherine walks to her car, drives away. She doesn't see the man watching her, following her, driving after her where she goes next. Catherine Clyne. They are watching you watching. Who is watching you, Catherine Clyne?

31

She drank champagne with dinner. By herself. She was exhausted. Her light went out before eleven. She sobbed into her pillow. She got up and went to the bathroom and stood under the shower and sobbed and sobbed some more. She looked in the mirror and said aloud to herself, 'There. Now you are ugly. No one will want you. You can forget everything like that. Just get old and forget love. Just forget life too. Life is hell.'

It was raining a still cold windless rain. There was snow on high ground but tomorrow would be sunny. It had rained for six hours when Catherine put out her light for the second time. She lay awake for a while and listened to the rain splashing on the window ledges and trickling out of the gutterings from the blocked overflow. She heard distant cars sloshing their tyres on the wet roads. She heard Big Ben chiming quarter past eleven and half past eleven and eleven forty-five.

The House was still sitting. James was in a meeting in one of the Committee Rooms. A highly respected fellow, James. A very up and coming man. She thought about James becoming Prime Minister and thought about living in Number Ten and thought she did not want to live that long. She thought of taking a knife and sticking it into her middle. Hara Kiri, the Japanese called it. You take the sword and plunge it into your Hara, the seat of life, the solar plexus and that's it, relief. The blocked energy flows again and you bleed onto the floor and your soul escapes from prison. Big Ben chimed midnight. Catherine fell asleep with her nose blocked and she snored. Not like Catherine to snore. But what can a girl do when she's cried herself to sleep? Not for the first time. Or the last.

In the slick black wet street outside, a sly and skinny cat slid secretly along the walls under the house where Catherine slept and then dived across the street in front of a car that came quietly down the road with its lights off. The car stopped outside Catherine's house, on the opposite side of the street, and the man inside stared at the windows for a long time. Had the policeman been at his station at the door of Catherine's house he would have seen the man's pale moon of a face in the strained white light, expressionless as it looked up at the windows of the first floor, the eyes like black olives. But, the man watched and wondered and longed to pick up his car phone and call, but dared not.

He had been given an offer he couldn't refuse. Not yet, anyway. He had to stay away from her. Until he could sort out that little problem. He looked at the windows for a long time. Then he drove slowly out of the street.

As the Mercedes left the street another car replaced it and the man inside stared up at the windows of the house. It drove away again just as the police guard returned from taking a leak at New Scotland Yard. He'd radioed for a replacement but no one had come. He could have peed right there, he supposed, but he hadn't liked to do that. He might have been spotted. A member of the constabulary urinating outside the Minister's house. Not dignified.

*

173

32

At eleven-thirty next morning, Catherine walked the short distance from Queen Anne's Gate to New Scotland Yard through slow cold rain. She arrived dispirited with damp feet and was led by a young policewoman to Commander David Armstrong's private office.

The view out of the fifth floor window behind Armstrong's head was of grey skies full of turbulent cloud layers, and of the grime-streaked building opposite. Catherine felt cold and unattractive. Her body moved awkwardly, lacking its usual grace. She stepped stiffly towards Armstrong's large pale hand extended from behind the large blond desk and met his scrutinizing grey eyes with her own assessing look.

The Commander was clean shaven to within a micron of his life. Catherine almost bled for him. His greying blond hair that had a tinge of ginger was straight and short and slicked down with dressing. He was tall and broad-shouldered, handsome in a way, and prepossessing. He spoke with an anglicized Scots accent and wore a tattersall waistcoat with a gold watch chain.

Her raincoat was taken and hung on the door. Coffee was proffered, tea preferred. The young, broad hipped policewoman strode out in her unbecoming flat shoes.

Catherine thought briefly of Christopher's policewoman. She was probably blonde and attractive. She felt a spasm of jealous desire in her groin. Who was he touching? Who was he loving? What woman lay on her back and took his cock between her thighs? She turned her mind to her work.

Armstrong put his big ringless hands with the short clean nails onto the bare desk and leaned back into the view beyond the window, elbows wide. It was a posture of authority. His face dimmed in the drizzling grey light, putting her at a disadvantage. She drew the hard upright chair closer to his desk and saw him wince at her trespass on his space.

'What can I tell you, Miss Clyne?' he asked. Predictably, she thought. Patronizingly, she felt. But his manner was, in fact, defensive. The Commander may have thought being interviewed by a glossy magazine too foppish for a cop, even one with an upper middle class background that made him stick out like a dandelion in a cabbage patch. But the press people at the Home Office had persuaded him to give the interview. They knew who Catherine Clyne was. The Home Secretary had not had to make a phone call. Armstrong did not like the press, however. And it made him combative.

Catherine responded to the duelling spirit. He was very male. She liked that and allowed him what she thought was a superior attitude to her female professionalism. Even if it was a magazine for men as well as women and she owned and edited it, it was an ephemeral, luxurious world, far apart from his rough practical realities. She supposed he couldn't help having an attitude. He thought himself one of the real men, no doubt. She wondered if he was.

She said, 'Why not start with why you went into the police force.' As she spoke, she crossed one knee over the other. She saw his eyes flicker to her legs in the navy stockings and high heeled courts. She felt dowdy in a neat navy blue suit she had selected because she thought she should not intimidate a policeman with too much style. It was one of the suits she kept for constituency party meetings, but it fitted close to her body and looked good for all that. Now, she was using her legs to intimidate him. If he could not respect her, he would have to want her. Either way, she would have power over the situation.

Without waiting for his answer, she muttered a test phrase into her tape recorder, played it back and put it on the desk. He gave it a suspicious look and she laughed. 'Please don't worry,' she said. 'You can tell me if something should be off the record. I'll respect that. In fact I'd prefer it if you talked quite freely. You are welcome to see a transcript of the conversation.'

His voice levels were much stronger than her own and she did not bother to test him, but pushed the recorder right across to him. She took her notebook out of her bag and opened it on her lap and held her pen poised. She was sure that would make him feel surrounded, but it could not be helped. She had to have her back-up.

He relaxed fractionally at the mention of a transcript, but not enough. Catherine sighed. This would have been much better over a meal, but the lunch had been cancelled at the last minute. She wondered if she could talk him back into it, assuming he had no appointment. The August Person to Person column might look a little stark if she failed to warm him up. The way she felt this morning she needed something to help things along. Lunch might be the answer.

Armstrong was in charge of the Metropolitan Police's fight against serious crime. As she knew from the bio pushed through her door last night, however, he had recently been placed directly in charge of policing the South London Redevelopment Scheme's protest marches. In the hope of angering him out of his reticence, she stabbed at him, 'Why did the police misjudge the recent demo?'

He shrugged. 'We were caught out. We thought we had been given the correct details. They cheated on us. They had three demos instead of one. It was a clever piece of organization. It won't happen again.'

He was a talking rule book. She tried to seem relaxed to encourage him to let go his defensiveness. 'What will happen in future?'

Armstrong said, 'We have to try and get into the minds of the organizers and predict what they will do.'

'You failed to do that the other week,' she snapped.

He smiled a flinty smile and said drily, 'Do I take it you want a personal apology, Mrs Waring?'

She inclined her head and looked at him from under half dropped eyelids and spoke silkily, 'I'm interested in knowing what you might be planning next to avoid being taken so much by surprise. Can you plant spies among the protest groups, for instance?'

He was deadpan. 'I can't give away details of any strategies, but I can tell you we do have some fairly concrete plans for dealing with serious disturbances. We will, of course, be unlikely to permit further demonstrations by these groups, but unscheduled and unofficial riots may still happen.'

She tried a surprise gambit: 'Who's behind these protests? Who's coordinating them?'

He blinked at her. 'I can't tell you.'

'Why not? Don't you know?' She seemed indignant.

'Oh yes. We know. But we are observing strict confidentiality on the SLRS protests at present. We are looking very closely into the riot coordination and into such elements as the high proportion of drug use among those arrested. I'm sorry I can't say more at present.' She opened her mouth but he forestalled her with a superior smile, 'No, not even off the record.'

She felt irritated again. She said, 'I am unlikely to want to quote you on it. It's useful background, that's all. Can you talk about your crime policing more openly?'

'It depends.' He smiled a bland, superior smile and lifted his chin in challenge. He added, 'What would you like to know?'

She felt patronized again. She smiled back with her own challenge. 'Why don't we start with drugs and bullion? By the way,' she added, 'are you free for lunch, after all?'

He looked at his watch, declined, advised her he could give a further half hour and began to talk about big crime. It was a bit of a child's guide, she thought but listened patiently while, relaxing a bit at last, he described the way the master criminal graduates from his youthful bank raids and robberies to planning the big ones.

He talked of the way the goods from big robberies were dispersed and channelled and converted into cash which was then stashed in Swiss and other foreign bank accounts. How the master criminals had, at one time, retired to the Costa del Sol and lived in luxury, but later graduates were no longer able to, thanks to the extradition treaty made after Spain joined the European

177

Community. How these earlier graduates had then got into drug and other criminal activity from there.

Much of this was familiar ground to Catherine but she listened quietly. He spoke of the network of contacts and dealers who would pass bullion and drugs. She began to question cautiously, learning more and more about the intricate web of faceless individuals who took their percentages and passed the illicit cargoes on through yet more middle men.

She felt a chill creeping through her as she listened and fitted what she heard into what Gerald had reported of Christopher's activities.

Meanwhile, she prompted and listened. The Commander was now talking effortlessly. At last. She had discovered his favourite topic, his obsession, no less, the clever villains behind serious crime. The worthy opponents whom he was pitted against by destiny. As he talked she could almost see the flaming sword in his hand, felt the fire of his crusader's spirit, his anger against the people he called society's enemies.

'What makes a criminal?' she asked.

She saw him open. He looked at her with interest for the first time since he had glanced at her legs. He entered his subject, leaning over the desk on his elbows, his chin on his clasped hands. 'They're cripples of one kind or another, all of them,' he said. 'Like other kinds of cripple, they may be born that way or else their early experience damages them. It's easy to go wrong when you come from a bad home and live in a bad part of town, keep bad company. When you don't have a strong moral code, from home or church, to measure everything against. Sometimes, even when you do . . . people from good homes go wrong too: they steal, they cheat, they murder. Maybe it's arrogance. They think other people worthless, fools. Maybe it's inbred in every wrongdoer, a genetic weakness. Maybe they have a grudge against the world, from an early age, against their family even. They weren't loved enough. They felt society rejected them because their parents did . . . They want revenge . . . They want to take by force what they were not given willingly . . .

Or maybe they just have no moral conscience, no compassion, no understanding of other people. They haven't formed a mature sense of being part of society, being responsible, of caring about anyone else. Some never do . . . but . . .' He tailed off.

Christopher. Was he . . .? She said, 'Can a criminal change? Or is it a life sentence?'

'It depends how much they like what they are. Depends why they've gone wrong. I nearly went wrong myself. I ran away from school, I had to steal to survive . . . It's a long story.' He laughed, embarrassed.

At last a glimpse of the real man. 'Tell me.'

'Off the record?' He raised his eyebrows. She nodded and leaned across the table and turned off the tape.

He seemed to soften, a vulnerable flicker in the cold eyes. He said, 'My mother and I lived in Edinburgh and my father was a barrister, a silk eventually, who spent all week in London defending criminals. Getting them off.' His mouth turned down and his shoulders moved into an angry hunch. 'My mother became ill. Mentally ill. She had to go into a home. She never came out. My father moved permanently to London. He put me in a boarding school. A small strict place near Aberdeen where the rain is horizontal and the people . . . well, it was a cold, mean place. I ran away at the beginning of my second year there, when I was about twelve. I walked back to Edinburgh. It took a few days. It was September and I slept rough. I was free for almost a month. I stole my grub from grocery shops and anywhere else I could find it. I was caught in somebody's house one day, with my fist full of pound notes.

'I was lucky my father was a QC or I'd have gone to reform school, for sure. They put me on probation and I came to London and went to a day school and lived under my father's eye. Being with my father wasn't that much better than the private school but I had more freedom during the day.' He stopped and looked at her. He shrugged.

She said, 'So you have sympathy for your criminals?'

'Understanding. I can get their cooperation more easily

because I understand what makes them run. I can often prevent them from succeeding at a crime because I understand how their minds work. I can negotiate deals for information because I can see into their heads.'

'Would you ever let someone go, turn a blind eye, because you understood what had made them do whatever they had done?'

He laughed and shook his head. 'I wouldn't let my understanding of why someone commits a crime prevent me from catching them. Society has to punish criminals and prevent them committing more crime. I'm committed to locking up wrongdoers so they can't do any more wrong. I want to clean up crime and make the world a safer place for law-abiding people.'

Christopher. A criminal? A law bender? Which? Both perhaps. Or neither, just a man who made a living in that murky world, from fulfilling other people's less acceptable desires. Would Armstrong understand Christopher? she wondered. And what would he do if he arrested Christopher for some crime?

By the time he looked at his watch, it was already well over the time he had given her. She thanked him and suddenly found herself liking him, too.

As he led her to the door, he said, 'I'm sorry I haven't time for lunch. You must come and have lunch with me here one day soon.'

She pounced on that. She needed more personal stuff. Secretly, too, she had begun to think the Commander a potentially very useful source of information in her pursuit of knowledge about Christopher, a subject she could not leave alone now. She had to find out, had to harden up or clear up the flimsy theories and suspicions created from Christopher's own hints and warnings to her and the things she had learned from Gerald. When she met Armstrong again, she would try to get him to tell her something more. To see if Angel rated in the Yard's computer records and for what reason. She wondered how she would manage to convince Armstrong to help her.

*

33

'Put on the ear muffs. Make sure they fit nice and snug. Okay, then? Now stand this way. No, like this. Watch me, exactly. Let the knees sag down a bit. Okay, then. Now line up the pistol with . . . Yes . . . That's the way. You're a natural, girl, natural. You ever shoot before?' George crouched and aimed his gun at the target, looking sideways at Catherine to see how she lined up.

She said, 'Yes, but only a rifle. I learned in Africa when I was a child. You can't go wandering around in the bush watching animals without a gun, so they told me anyway.' She grinned.

George tilted his head and gave her an old fashioned look. He had a rough complexion and his eyebrows were bushy and grey, shot with long black hairs that gave him a devilish look. His grey hair and his scrawny neck gave him the look of a dead chicken. But for all that he was pleasing. His tough, rough way of talking with his East End accent and his military style, he'd been a sergeant in the Royal Marines, was oddly charming and he had a smile that could have stolen its way into the hardest of hearts. He gave her a grin now and said, 'What kind of game are you after here, then?'

'I'm just brushing up my skills,' she said. 'For self defence.' She was, still, she was sure, being followed wherever she went. Not that that was the only reason. She had a crazy lust to hold a gun, to shoot, to hit a target. What target? Did she really want to kill him? Was her need for him and her jealousy driving her that mad? Did she intend to seek him out and kill him? Well, she was here. There had to be a rational or irrational reason behind the impulse that had brought her to make the one quick phone call, and then to come here.

The pistol was the first non-sports weapon she had ever touched. She gripped it in both hands as George had told her and squeezed the trigger gradually until it released the bullet. She had a natural gunman's aim. Some trick of the eyesight that helped her to line up sights.

She had a few practise shots at the moving target and scored well. 'For a beginner you're a bleedin' genius,' George told her. 'I'd have had you in my crack outfit if I'd had you in the Marines. I'd like to see you with a rifle. I bet you'd make a right natty little sniper, you would.'

He took her to the rifle range and selected a gun for her. 'Try this. It's light and fairly easy. It veers a bit to the right as you fire, but, well, let's see you try it. Okay, then.'

Catherine had been in the St Marylebone Pistol and Rifle Club in the City for almost an hour and George had given her a tour of the Club, a list of the rules, a viewing of the range of weapons and a discourse on safety. She had been on the pistol range for half an hour and had done enough for a first lesson.

Now she lifted the rifle onto her shoulder. It was a long time since she'd held a sports gun. The moving target started and she did a trick she'd learned as a child. She invented a line connecting the tip of the gun's barrel with the target and let the target pull the bullet into it as she squeezed the trigger. It was as if she was back at the age of nine, when she had been given her first gun and taught to shoot and taken on her first hunting safari. She was on the edge of an open stretch of savannah standing up in the Land Rover, her gun on her shoulder. The vehicle was moving slowly towards a herd of Thompson gazelles. Catherine had her sights on one of the gazelles and was squeezing the trigger exactly as she had been taught in the target practice.

She was nine years old and she smelled the dust coming up from under the Land Rover as it bumped over the parched earth. It was the bitter end of the dry season with the long rains overdue. The gazelle were thin. They snatched at the sparse grass, trying to fill their bellies.

'Come on, Rina. Shoot', her father directed her, impatiently. She took her time. She had never shot anything. Not a live thing. She didn't want to. Not a gazelle. They were so pretty. She wanted one as a pet, not to see its head on the wall at home.

They had seen the lioness then. That uncertain dream light between dawn and sunrise made her seem a ghost: a golden lion face with its bloodshot tawny eyes among the taller yellow grasses near the acacia trees to their left. She emerged and crept, belly near the ground towards the herd. No one spoke. The Land Rover had halted. Catherine trained her gun on the lioness and followed her with her sights. Her father watched, intrigued by his little daughter's hunting instincts. Catherine began slowly squeezing the trigger. An invisible line like elastic now connected her gun barrel with the lioness's head. She did not want the lioness to kill a gazelle. But she didn't know if she could kill her either. It was a young lioness, and beautiful, too. It was a choice and she was choosing. Now.

Suddenly Brenda said, 'Oh no. There are cubs. Cat, don't,' and Catherine suddenly put up the nose of her gun just at the moment the bullet escaped from its housing and the crack of her shot hit the perfect silence of the morning like a spoon hitting an egg.

The gazelle herd was off in a stampede of black hooves. Dust engulfed the surprised lioness who turned now and snarled towards the Land Rover. The driver quickly engaged gear and got moving, turning away. The cheated lioness gave them a look that seemed loaded with disgust and loped back to her cubs.

Catherine felt bad. She had deprived the cubs of their day's meal. Looking back, she knew there were no easy choices for humans playing God.

Catherine squeezed the trigger and linked it with her magic thread to the moving target and seeing in her memory the lioness, almost lifted the gun and gave up the shot, but then replaced the lioness with another image. Then she gave the trigger a final squeeze and shot the target straight between the eyes.

'By God. Was that a fluke?' George cried. 'You're a bloody marvel, you are. Do it again just to prove it.'

And she did. Twice more. She turned to him and smiled.

He said, 'What's the bleedin' secret?'

She said, 'You have to imagine you're shooting at someone you really want to kill.'

George gave her a long look then. He hoped she was not serious. At any rate, he was glad the poor bugger she had the hates for was not himself.

* * *

She sat in the peach-toned room and stared out of the window into the night garden. Warm lights within and cold moonlight without. Stars blown by the wind into the trees' bare branches. Gerald was in the kitchen telling Simon, his manservant, what to give Catherine to eat.

'It's all settled.' He was back. Simon was following him with a half bottle of Tattinger and two glasses.

'Just a glass,' Catherine had said. It was ten-thirty. She didn't want to start swilling champagne on an empty stomach at this hour. And tired, she was so tired. After the shooting club she had been swimming. She had called Gerald on impulse.

Gerald said cheerfully in the manner of a head waiter, in a thick French accent of indeterminate region, 'Smoked salmon and a little endive and watercress salad coming. Perhaps a little old-fashioned vanilla ice cream with ginger to follow, or will it be chocolate sauce?' He dropped back into his normal voice and added in a stern tone, 'When did you last eat, Tsarina?'

'Oh I think I had something at lunch.' She shrugged, vague.

He said, still stern, 'You look awful, my dear. You're losing weight and you're looking haggard. Yes. I don't think you're looking after yourself. You've got to eat, to sleep, to . . .' She cut in, exasperated, 'Gerald, stop trying to mother me. I'm going insane. I need a shrink not a Jewish mother, for heaven's sake.'

'Now, now.' Gerald poured the champagne into chilled glasses. The intricately cut flutes clouded as the cold pale yellow wine bubbled invitingly in them. He handed her a glass and raised his own. 'To a saner Tsarina.' He lolled back against the assorted peach and apricot and orange cushions on the sofa next to her and looked shrewdly at her. 'It can't be the lack of sex, Tsarina. You went for years on nothing until this brute appeared.'

She sighed and said emphatically, 'It is sex. I'm going mad. I'm insanely physically jealous and I haven't seen the man for four weeks. Not heard from him. He gave me no hint that anything had changed. I'm imagining all sorts of things. I can't stand the idea of him making love to another woman. And he must be. He's gone and left me. I love him. I hate him. I want to kill him. I thought he cared for me. What was he after and why has he gone away? I don't understand it.'

'How long is it since the ship owner? A week?'

She nodded.

'Shall we send for a toy boy?'

'Oh Gerry. Please. Stop it.'

'I just thought it might help to stop you going off your head, Catherina. In fact, if I thought it would make you feel happier I'd offer my own services.'

She leaned over and kissed him. 'I do believe you mean it. And I might not refuse. But I do have to be honest; nothing will turn off this aching longing. I feel as if part of me is missing. I just long to hold on to him and have him love me. Just to see him and talk. I love him so much. But my mind hates him for leaving me. For rejecting me without warning, without explaining. Why?' She stood up and began pacing the oriental rug that lay before the marble fireplace.

Gerald looked at her, taking in the curving slender legs in the black stockings and high heeled shoes, the lovely figure in the short, tight black skirt and the flowing white silk shirt and the wide leather belt; the lovely face with its darkened eyes, the long, fine, elfin blonde hair. He could not understand any man leaving such a woman. Let alone a man driven by the kind of passion Catherine had suggested. Was her passion too much for him? he wondered. Was he unable to cope with the consequences of loving and being loved back this much by a woman like Catherine; a moral, steadfast, loyal woman who believed in vows and God?

He said, 'Drink your champagne, oh fairest of them all.'

She reached for the glass that she had placed untouched on the table and then stood against the fireplace. 'May I light the fire?' she asked. 'I'm cold.'

He nodded and she took the matches from the mantelpiece and knelt to light the gas. The flames flickered yellow and blue, adding life and cheer to the room.

Simon came in with the tray of food and placed it on the table, laying a place on the coffee table with a fine linen tray cloth and napkin and Gerald's good silver.

He went out and Gerald said, 'Could he be running away from you? Was it getting to be more than he could handle? After all, Catherina, you are a married woman. He might not want to get involved. Besides, there are your differences, your education, your class . . .'

The flames cast their moving lights over her as she crouched facing them, warming her hands. She said, quietly, 'He knows how things are with James. I don't think I've misled him into thinking I'm happy. I don't think he thinks he's just a fling. I have told him he matters to me. I . . .' She stood up and taking her glass came and sat next to him. 'I don't want, didn't want him to think this was just a bored married woman's adventure with some lower class stud.'

'But you don't look like getting a divorce, Tsarina. And it started just as sex, didn't it? It started that way for him. It was just a sexual fling. You were a prize he couldn't keep his thieving hands off and his hands turned you on. Look at you, Catherina. Are you sure this is love and not sexual addiction?'

Catherine put down her glass and Gerald leaned over to top it up. She looked at him reproachfully, and said, 'Oh, Gerry. No. I thought so for a while. But it changed. It was he who kept asking me always, while we were making love, "Do you love me, Catherine? Do you love me?" Over and over. And in the end, I said, Yes. I knew I loved him after he made me think about it. He made me love him. Created it in me like a light so that he could receive it. If I've never loved like this before it may be

186

because I've never met that much need for love before. Anyway, after that, the sex was even more wonderful. There was beginning to be something spiritual about it. Paradise feelings, strange lights in the head during love and after.'

Gerald looked reflectively at her. 'Ah, Catherina, do you suppose he couldn't take it? Too much light for the man who lives by night. Too much sun. Too much love. Blinding, burning. Hmm.'

She smiled wearily and turned to her supper. 'I don't understand. But more to the point, what am I going to do? He doesn't return my calls. I must assume he's dumped me. For whatever reason, he doesn't want me any more. But then he's not even at his club, it seems.'

He said, 'You've called him there?'

She nodded.

He said, anxiously, 'What name do you leave?'

'Clyne.'

Gerald reached out and took her hand. 'Oh dear. Don't you think it might be best if this is over after all, Tsarina?'

She swallowed a mouthful of salmon and turned a pained face towards him. She said, indignantly, 'How can that be?'

'Catherine. I'd be the first to say this experience was something you needed, to set you alight and make you realize there is more to relationships than being the impeccably virginal wife of some workaholic politician. But have you seriously considered the risks this particular liaison presents?'

She carried on with her salad and he could see only her profile. Her shoulders were rounded, tense and high.

He went on, 'Have you thought about the conflicts of loving a man who works in that business and being married to a member of HM's Government?'

She said, 'Daddy thought of it pretty fast.'

'You've told him?' Gerald sounded horrified.

'Weeks ago. He had been telling me to have an affair, you know. Anything to keep me happy and married to James until we both enter the glorious portals of Number Ten. Then I won't even be able to have an affair, of course. Can you imagine it? Taking the bodyguards everywhere?' She laughed unhappily.

He went on, 'For another thing, can I ask you if you happen to have been using those delightful little rubber things that so turn me on every time I look at one, the power of association being what it is?'

She shook her head. 'No.'

'It didn't cross your mind?'

She leaned back and dabbed her mouth with the napkin. She said quietly and slowly, never taking her eyes off his face, 'Gerry, I love this man. I want all of him. I want the chemistry that happens when we touch. I want to feel his skin on mine in the most intimate way, not insulated by rubber, however fine. And I want his semen in my womb.'

'But, Catherine. You don't know how many women or what sort of women he messes with. In short, you don't know where he's been or where any of his women have been. And he's running a club full of whores.'

She looked at him with tears in her eyes and with a voice that was choked said, sadly, 'I've taken the risk, Gerry. I don't think I've ever explained to you that I'd happily die while he makes love to me. It's not important that I run a risk. The risk is not real. I don't live without him. He is life to me. I was half dead when he found me and didn't know it. I'm dying again now that he's vanished. I don't much want to live. I don't want to go back to that state of numbness that I existed in before. I would rather just shoot myself.'

He was silent. He lifted the almost empty bottle and trickled the remaining drops into her glass.

She said, her voice stronger now, 'Don't think I've not thought of giving it up, myself. Don't think I haven't weighed everything up in my head when I'm away from him. I've tried to tell myself I don't have to go on with it, that I don't need him. He's just another man and I can find another lover.' She held the hand he had given her earlier and her voice rose with an anguished sound. 'But I can't, Gerry. I can't. There's something more than my feelings involved here. It's as though he won't let me go.

As though he's caught me in some net, like a fish, and whatever I do I can only swim around inside that net. I'm not free to leave him.'

Gerald squeezed her hand. He said firmly, 'Catherina, that's not true. You are a free agent and don't get your knickers in a twist thinking you are not. If you really want to free yourself from him you can. But I don't think you do. You are much too attached to him and the pleasure he gives you. And to the love that has turned a lamp on in you and you into a raving beauty, not that you were so bad before. So, to that I say, go on with it, if he returns. And I feel sure he will. But, for heaven's sake, I think you should be more careful.'

She smiled a struggling little smile. He put his arm around her shoulders and pulled her close until her head was down on his chest. He held her there for some time, stroking her silky hair.

34

Armstrong said, 'I hope you have a better idea now of how we work here, Ms Clyne?'

The Scots burr in his voice was stronger today. She wondered why. She thought of the way he had opened up towards the end of their first interview and said, 'I really need to know a lot more about you, about Armstrong the man.'

He flinched. She realized he wanted to go on hiding behind his professional facade. He looked around. They were sitting at a corner table, near a window. No one else was near. 'What would you like to know?' he asked. He tugged at his tie as if to loosen the knot and his eyes showed something like fear.

The Scotland Yard canteen was hardly the place to

loosen up a senior policeman who had no emotional life that Catherine could discover. She already knew his wife had died of cancer, that his elder daughter lived in Australia and his younger one in Canada and that he lived in a small bachelor flat in the Barbican. But she needed much more expression of personal feeling from him. He was completely buttoned up in his role of senior policeman and she needed to pull out the real human being. The real man was in there, she had seen him peeking out, talking about running away from home, about criminals.

She said, casually, 'Have you got half an hour?'

He looked nervously at his watch and back to her face. 'I suppose so.' The 'so' sounded very Scots. Perhaps he became more Scots when his defensiveness was heightened.

'Then let's go to the park. It's too lovely a day to sit inside. We can talk as we walk. So much healthier, don't you think?' She picked up her bag as though the decision were already made and moved as if to get up.

They drove the short distance to St James's Park in the Commander's chauffeured car. The driver dropped them near the Admiralty and they walked towards the lake. It had been raining but now the sun was flaring onto the unshaded paths, the air brisk and blue, and the light wind sprinkled with petals. Small jagged clouds like torn shirt sleeves drifted high in the washed out April sky.

His parents had divorced after his mother had been put in a home for the mentally ill. After being brought to London, following the runaway business, he had gone to a local school and lived with his father in a flat in the Middle Temple. He had not liked his authoritarian father whom he hardly knew. He had gone into the police force. Retrospectively he thought he had done so to spite the criminal barrister whom, he thought, foiled the law.

He said, 'I suppose that's an odd reason for wanting criminals brought to book, to get back at my father.'

They both smiled at that. He said it quietly, almost blushingly. He was more used to asking questions than being asked them, more used to gaining confessions than making them.

They sat outside the little cafe and drank execrable coffee. Catherine faced the lake where a nanny and two small children were feeding ducks. The sun was soothing on her face.

Armstrong seemed more human now. There was less prickliness between them. Once away from the office he had opened to her sympathetic questions. But he had given these facts with evident pain, seeming to wrench them out and offer them with embarrassment, even shame. He would have preferred to forget his past, she could see. Unhappiness had been sealed under a hard veneer. He worked long hours dominated by a puritan ethic, lived an ascetic life and pushed his feelings away. Women seemed remote to him. He evidently had no one close. She wondered what he did for sex.

The conversation now moved on to Catherine's life and she felt bound to give some in return. She told him about her childhood and her own motherlessness. They were closer after that. Something fell away that had been a barrier to sympathy. Perhaps he had not believed anyone as privileged as Catherine had suffered deprivation.

The talk turned to the problems of the Warings' personal security and the recent riots. Armstrong's authority returned. He said, 'We don't expect to see any reduction in the street violence. There is a very experienced organization behind the South London protest groups. They'll be up to all sorts of tricks.'

'It's political, I suppose?' She shrugged her acceptance of the inevitable.

'Not entirely.' He gave her a guarded look.

'Oh?'

He gave a quick look over his shoulder on each side and cleared his throat. 'It's off the record, of course. But I think you personally might like to know that we think there is more than meets the eye in this protest. I imagine your husband must be in close touch with the Home Secretary and that he would eventually tell you everything I'm likely to report to the Home Office.' He gave her a questioning look.

She shrugged. 'He might not tell me anything, Commander. James has a rather tight view of pillow talk. He doesn't believe Government Ministers should give their spouses an opportunity to gossip about State business.'

He looked down and fiddled with his coffee cup and mumbled, 'Perhaps I shouldn't be telling you . . .'

Catherine cut across him. 'You don't have to tell me anything. But if I want to know I can always ask the Home Secretary myself.' She felt suddenly ashamed of the way her temper had sharpened her tone and smiled regretfully at him.

He smiled back and said urbanely, 'Well then, I suppose it doesn't matter if I tell you myself.' He looked at his watch. 'I'm afraid I'll have to be going in a moment, though. Shall we stroll back towards the car?'

They got up. He said, 'We've been doing quite a lot of surveillance on this South London business.' He glanced at her and grinned, 'With the Home Secretary's full permission.'

'Surveillance?'

He meant phone tapping and tailing, but did not say so. She saw the glint in his grey eyes and realized he was quite capable of doing it without permission too, if necessary.

He went on, 'There is a political motive, of course. That's clear. But there is also a strong criminal involvement.'

'Why?'

'The history of South London is not short on crime, bent second hand car dealers in Clapham, robbers hanging out in Deptford are fairly traditional. Now we have the drug barons of Brixton and a few other nasties along the line between. South London is a sort of breeding ground of crime.'

They passed a bed of primulas and the Commander stopped to examine them. She watched him, curious. He turned and gave a nod. His face seemed rounded and softened. 'Nice little flowers, aren't they? I used to do quite a bit of gardening in my spare time when I was living with my wife in Wimbledon Common. Not that I had much spare time. A policeman's life is unpredictable. The job comes first. Wives don't usually like that. Mine didn't.'

Sadness squared his face again and he suddenly straightened his shoulders, threw his chin up and started to walk on. His voice came out very Scots. 'Well, as I was saying, South London is a bit of a rats' nest. The swathe that runs from Vauxhall to Greenwich has its pockets of villains of one sort or another, its networks of supporters with a vested interest in keeping information from the police.' He stopped to examine a shrub. 'Hm, camellias don't look so well in this bed, I think.'

Catherine turned to look at the fountain she had always thought of as the White Lady of St James. It frothed and sprayed in the gusty wind, and the sunlight pouring through it out of the western sky turned it into a dancer, breathing light and life and joy.

Armstrong lost interest in the camellia. He went on, his voice smoother now, 'The criminal fraternities of Deptford and Brixton don't want to see their neighbourhoods broken up by beautiful new offices and housing and invaded by more law abiding folks. They don't want unemployment reduced by new light industries, they feed on unemployment.'

He turned and began walking towards the road again, but very slowly, his mind on what he was saying. He was talking now without addressing her, without any apparent sense, even, of who he was talking to. 'The lesser criminal classes might welcome the chance to earn a decent penny now and then, but their bosses, the big villains, ha, that's not in their interest at all. They've got their manors and their set ups and their nice little see no evil, speak no evil, hear no evil arrangements in their communities.' He chuckled. 'No. Criminal community solidarity will be knocked into fragments by your husband's idealistic plans to turn South London into an urban paradise.'

They were almost at the gate. Catherine could see the black car with its police driver waiting. Armstrong stopped and turned to her. He said, 'I'm telling you all this so that you will realize the background to what I really want to say, which is that the problem we face is that there is some collusion between the criminal elements and the political ones. We know who is organizing the political end. That's no mystery. As to who his masters are, that's a question for MI5. But meantime the matter is complicated and dangerous.'

She said, 'Look, I think it's very interesting but I can't help wondering why you're telling me this. I know it's off the record and I know it concerns me personally, but aren't you sticking your neck out?'

He led her to a nearby bench and sat down. He said smoothly, 'My dear lady, I'm carried away by your charm. Also,' he became very serious, 'I'm genuinely concerned that you should take care of yourself.' He dropped an avuncular hand onto her shoulder. 'There is no doubt in my mind, or that of my colleagues, that some plan is afoot to really stop your husband in his tracks. Now, I don't know what they will do. I don't know how far they are prepared to go, but you should be on your guard. It could be a kidnap, an assassination, anything of that nature.' He took his hand away and seemed about to stand again.

Her eyes widened suddenly. She gasped, 'Heavens.' Then she blurted, 'I'm being followed.'

He looked around quickly, alert and somehow dangerous. 'What do you mean?'

She blushed slightly. 'I keep seeing the same cars and the same people behind me. I'm sure I'm being followed.'

'How long has this been going on?'

'About a month.'

'Have you reported it to anyone?'

'I haven't told a soul. I didn't think they'd take me seriously.'

'Well, I'm taking you very seriously. I'm really rather late now and I'll have to go but I'd be very pleased if you would have dinner with me, perhaps tomorrow. Are you free?'

She was surprised. 'I should take you out. It's my turn.'

'Well, next time, perhaps.' He was protective of her as they walked to the car, his hand under her elbow. He said, 'I'll see what can be done about your tail. We'll have you watched ourselves for a few days.'

They reached the car. 'Can I drop you anywhere?'

'I'll take a cab. I've made you late enough.'

He climbed in and the driver closed the door smartly. As the car drew away, David Armstrong waved. Catherine realized she still had to ask him to help her find answers to the questions that were always in her mind now. She would do that tomorrow. She thought she had found a friend. She felt less alone and oddly reassured that things would, perhaps, turn out well. For the first time in a few weeks she also felt she was not being followed. But in that, she was wrong.

35

Commander David Armstrong did not drink alcohol. He would not even drink spring water. Tap water would be just fine, he told the waiter, with just a touch of smugness. Catherine thought the only thing that turned him on was talking about his work.

They were in the Gay Hussar in Greek Street, Soho. Catherine thought it a strange choice: a Hungarian restaurant often frequented by politicians and rather risque intellectuals and which was once fashionable but now only with an older crowd. Evidently it was the food he came for. He had eaten some rather awful looking cabbage dish with great relish. Catherine had stayed with a simple grilled fish and was following it with strawberries while Armstrong ate cheese.

She had been wondering all evening how to approach her subject, but now something Armstrong said gave her a lead. He ordered himself coffee and then looked at his watch and asked her if she liked jazz. She nodded and he suggested they went along to Frith Street to Ronnie Scott's. He said hastily, 'I don't go to night clubs, of course. But I have always been a keen jazz fan.'

She said, smiling, 'Why don't you go to night clubs, David?'

With Edinburgh primness evident in his voice, he said, 'I can't afford to be seen in dens of iniquity.'

She laughed. 'Isn't Ronnie Scott's a den of iniquity?'

'Not at all. It's the best place in London to listen to serious jazz. There is very little cost to it. It's not a clip joint. It's just a straight jazz club. A place for enthusiasts.'

'Would you go to Annabel's?'

'Oh, no one ever invites me there.'

She smiled. 'Maybe I will.'

He said, 'I'll look forward to that. However, seriously, in my position, I have to be very careful where I go and what I do. The night life world is very risky. It's full of snares for the unwary. I don't want to be in a position to be friendly with club proprietors. It's too dangerous.'

'Why?' She seemed only mildly interested. The conversation was going in exactly the right direction. A fraction too much interest might spoil it.

'Some police officers have been known to become too friendly with club managements and to have found themselves compromised.' Armstrong gave her a hard look.

She tilted her head on one side and leaned it on her hand like a child listening to a story. Her expression was innocent. 'Compromised?' she said. 'In what way?'

He took a sip of coffee and set down his cup. He went on looking intently into the cup as though the answer lay within it. Then with his head still lowered, he looked up at her from under his brow bones and she noticed the thickness of his tawny eyebrows. He went on, 'A police officer who gets known in the night world may be one who has to work in the control of narcotics or other criminal activities which thrive in these places. He may have to spend time in them in pursuit of enquiries. He may have to get to know the people who run the clubs to keep himself informed. But,' and now Armstrong's voice went gravelly and he spoke savagely, 'he may have weaknesses, women, boys, a liking for liquor, even drugs, or just an expensive lifestyle he has to maintain, perhaps he loves a woman who is not his wife and who is turning expensive. The easiest thing in the world for such an officer is to succumb to temptation.'

He poured himself another cup of coffee. Catherine was silent, waiting, her breath held in her throat as if she dared not speak for fear of breaking something. Or for fear of the sounds that might come out.

Armstrong said, 'If that happens, then the policeman is doomed. He is of no further use to the Force. He may continue for years to play his role as an officer of the law, but he has himself become a perpetrator of crimes. He is one of them. One of the criminal classes. He is corrupt.' There was disgust with a smear of sadness in his voice.

Catherine said hesitantly, 'Have you ever had anyone approach you? Try to corrupt you?'

He nodded. 'It happens.'

'Have you been tempted?'

She was surprised when his eyes slid away a moment. He said, quietly, 'Temptation and the devil are always with us.'

She said, very innocently, 'Would you . . . do you think you might ever give in?'

He looked at her for a moment as though he were deciding something. His eyes ran over her face as if he were really looking at her for the first time. His expression was immensely searching, his gaze penetrating and analytical. Then he put his elbow onto the table and rested his fist under his chin and smiled at her through narrowed eyelids. He said, softly, 'Were you planning to make me an offer?'

She laughed. 'Not tonight. I don't know yet how useful you're going to be to me.'

'Och, I could tell you that right now, missie.' He exaggerated the Scots accent. 'I think I'm going to be very useful to you indeed. I'm going to be the vanguard of your protection.'

'All right,' she said. 'Let's put you to the test. I need to know a few things about one particular night club called the Sirocco.'

He signalled the waiter to bring the bill, then turned his attention to her.

'Do you know it?' she asked, blandly.

'I believe I've heard of it. What do you need to know?' He was reaching into his pocket for his wallet.

She said, 'I'd like to know what you have on record about it . . . and the man who runs it.'

He was still reading the bill, checking the arithmetic assiduously. He stopped and looked up at her. 'Dear lady, do you know what you are asking me to do?'

She shrugged. 'Yes. Give me a little clue as to what sort of people are involved with this place and what sort of . . .'

He caught her wrist with a very strong, long-fingered hand, a strangely sensitive hand whose fingers were downy with reddish blond hairs. He said, 'I can't do that, Catherine. I can't give you information from police files. You must have known I'd say that.'

'Isn't it public domain? Couldn't my member of Parliament get this for me?'

He looked astounded. He let go her hand and took up his pen to sign the bill. He said emphatically, 'No. It is not. It is police information which has to remain confidential. An MP can have access via the Home Secretary, for his eyes only. Otherwise, anything we collect about any individual is not available for public scrutiny. You can't police a country if every Tom, Dick and Harry can go along and nose through the files. The police must collect information that can contribute to the prevention of crime. To make it public would be to remove the element of surprise that is one of the few things on our side in finding suspects, making arrests and getting convictions.'

'Well,' she said, hamming slightly, 'I only asked.'

He said, 'Please don't ever ask me anything like that again.'

'How can I get information, then?'

'Hire a private detective.' He folded his wallet away in the breast pocket of his plain grey suit.

She said, 'David. Would you look in the files and do just one thing for me?'

He gave her a closed look. She went on, 'Would you look and see if there is anything about the Sirocco and a man called Christopher Angel? All I want to know initially is yes or no. After that I would only ask that if there were anything that might make that person dangerous to know, that you would tell me again yes or no.' She knew she was presuming on a very short acquaintance. But then they had done a lot of talking in the last few days. Personal talking. Catherine had enough for her profile now. But things had moved further on. It was not professional interest so much as the dawn of a cautious friendship that had brought them here tonight.

She was not sure if her marriage was something that would bother a man like Armstrong if he found her attractive enough. She thought he had strong moral principles but could not tell if that extended to views on adultery. And she was not sure what he felt towards her. He had not, she thought, shown any interest in her as a woman, yet. She was not sure why he had invited her to dinner.

She was curious, also, about her own feelings. He was attractive. But she was not really able to think of getting to know another man. She only wanted one man. She might succumb to a seduction, perhaps, as with Ali Lazic, but nothing more. She was not in the frame of mind for an affair. She wondered, though. Was he looking at her in that way? Or did he have calculated reasons for befriending her. Did he want to meet James, perhaps? Was he socially ambitious? Did he want political connections to further his career? She could not tell and would wait and see. Meanwhile she was waiting for his reaction to her latest proposal.

Armstrong shook his head. 'I'm not even going to ask you why you want this information. I cannot tell you anything. I can't look in the files at your request. I can't tell you what's in them or not in them.

I'm sorry, Catherine. That's the book.'

'Oh well,' she smiled, 'I guess I'll just have to look for someone more corruptible.'

He smiled back. 'If you find them, you'd better not tell me. Now let's get on. We're missing some good jazz.'

36

Big Ben chimed the quarter hour. The small launch pushed up the river against the outgoing tide and the gusting west wind, its narrow bow bouncing on the swift stream so that the helmsman had to grip the wheel tightly in his gloved hands. The water was black and shiny as a whore's raincoat and as untrustworthy as the whore herself. A huge plank was coming broadside down the stream just under Hungerford Bridge. They narrowly avoided it by a swerve that almost capsized them in the swift current. As they approached Westminster pier, a wide sheet of clear and almost invisible plastic that would have caught around the propeller, jamming it, trapping them in the tide's sweep and dragging them back the way they had come, passed millimetres away to their port side.

As they came out on Westminster Bridge's west side, O'Leary turned out the navigation !ights and steered cautiously against the wind and water towards the high wall that protected the Palace of Westminster from flooding. As they reached the wall, he kept the engine idling just enough to hold them stationary. His companion made a note of the time and took a long decorator's measuring stick from the boat's bottom and measured the distance from the water level to the top of the stone parapet.

It was a difficult operation. The boat bounced and swerved as the tide flooded under its light plastic hull, forcing it downstream against the propeller's thrust. The wind was lessened by the curve in the river and the shelter afforded by the high wall and the buildings beyond it. Eventually the job was done. O'Leary let the boat drift back from the wall and then increased the throttle slowly and gradually until he could move her against the wind and tide. Gradually he steered out into mid-stream until they were going directly into the current.

He turned his head and looked back at the Palace of Westminster. The lights were almost all out and the fingers of Big Ben read 3.42. He chuckled. What he was planning would put more than a few lights out in the big house. He intended to drive a bit more hot air through that place than even those bastards were used to. He turned the launch slowly in a big arc to avoid being capsized by the spirited black stream and headed back towards St Katherine's Dock.

As they slipped quickly under the low arches of Westminster Bridge he turned on the navigation lights. Just in time. A police launch was coming up towards them from Charing Cross. It passed them without interest. O'Leary grinned cheerfully. It was a long time since he'd been involved in this kind of operation and he was enjoying himself. It all had to be detailed fairly quickly, though. They only had about a month to go to the SLRS Bill's first reading.

37

Jana Harding's house was just off the number 16 bus route in Willesden. Catherine was able to park almost outside her door. She was a few minutes early and waited in her car before walking up the three chipped concrete steps to the brown front door with the brass knocker shaped like a lion's head. She waited and rang the bell again. The wind that had been blowing hard on and off for the past three weeks was tearing at her white cashmere coat and tugging the tail of her headscarf and knocking the blossom off the small cherry tree that stood by the gate.

At last the door was opened by a small slim young woman with tightly-curled dark hair drawn back into a high thick pony tail. She invited Catherine to come in, nodding, yes, she was Jana. She had an accent: middle European, Catherine thought.

The girl led Catherine upstairs to a room that was filled with heavy Victorian furniture, the windows draped with dark velvet and clotted lace and the walls hung with old photographs of long gone family or friends.

In that room with its various shades of burgundy and claret and sage, that was like an old lady's boudoir, it seemed time was waiting to begin again after some long pause. The silence was astounding. There was no whisper of the traffic that Catherine had left a few minutes ago. They were in another world, some kind of ante room to life.

The girl took Catherine's coat and asked her to sit at a small round table that was covered with a sage green velvet cloth. There was a rose glass with a single carnation to one side and a candle in a brass candlestick. Jana lit the candle and bent her head in prayer. She took Catherine's hands and held them, her eyes closed, her breath coming long and deep. When she opened her eyes she seemed different. Not the young girl who had opened the door but someone much older and infinitely more experienced. She gave Catherine a long searching look and then closed her eyes again, breathing deeply once more.

After a few moments, she began: 'You are waiting for something to happen. This thing dominates your mind. Your life is not important. It is on one side. But this is . . . you are living only for this thing . . .'

She paused and Catherine saw her frowning, straining, her whole face puckered with effort, or was it pain?

She went on, hesitantly at first, then in a rush,

gathering momentum, 'You are waiting for a meeting. With . . . a man. It's a man. You are waiting to hear from him. You are waiting for him to come back . . . You don't know where he is. You are worried, yes, yes, you are very worried, sometimes suffering very much. Sometimes you wonder why you must suffer so much. You cannot bear to be without him, yes, you need him so much. Every part of you is waiting for this man. It is a very physical relationship, yes, but very spiritual, also. He is needing you too, madam. He is very much needing you . . .'

She paused. Her eyes fluttered open. They were dark ovals, lined with kohl, fringed with long silky lashes. Darker, in this light, than Angel's eyes. Darker and yet the same. Catherine saw reflected in them the candle flame and her own pain. She said softly, 'Why doesn't he come to me? If he needs me what's stopping him?'

The girl looked deeply into Catherine's eyes then closed her own again and was silent, frowning, as if concentrating. She still held Catherine's hands in both hers. Outside it was getting darker. The candle flickered in the window draught. Catherine felt cold.

Jana sighed. She said, 'It is very difficult. He is very hard to find. He has many secrets. There is a barrier. He does not want any one to know things. He has to be secret. He does things in the dark, in the night. He is driving. There is a car, a big car . . . he is going down a path, a cliff path . . . by the sea . . . It's night. I hear the sea and I see the white tops of waves . . . I see, there is a small ship, with sails and with engine. It comes at night sometimes. It is coming to shore somewhere. I think it is England. White cliffs. Kent. The South Coast in a lonely place. It is stopping and they are putting, what is . . . the word . . . something to hold the ship so it does not float away?'

'The anchor,' Catherine whispered.

'Yes, yes, anchor. Now they are coming with some boxes, yes, from the ship. I think the gentleman, the one you want, is there somehow. He is there. He does not go to the ship. He is not carrying boxes. Others are there to do that. They are putting the boxes now onto a van. Now he is coming to the people from the ship and giving them something. It's a case. Yes. They open it. There is money . . . A lot of money.'

The girl stopped again, frowning. Catherine waited, her blood seemed chilled. She shuddered. Was it with horror or was it the draught? The girl had hold of her hands. She started again.

'This man works at night. Yes, it is music and dancing and people in a place which is like a restaurant. Sometimes he has something else he must do. He goes away. He is driving south of London. He goes to the country. Kent . . . I think it is Kent, again. He meets people there. He goes to a place where there is a small plane landing. Always at night. He is going to receive something from this plane. He brings something from it. He gives it to some other people and they go away with it. I think it is money he gives them . . .'

She paused and started her deep breathing again. She went on, her words tumbling out, jerkily, unpredictably. 'This gentleman, I think he needs you very much. He is not happy without you. But he has made a promise to someone. This other person, I think . . . I can't see them . . . I can't tell you. This person does not want this man to see you. But you will see him. It will not be easy for you. But I know he comes to you again. I see you are together . . . you are in another country . . . you are by the sea . . . it is very warm and it is night, but . . . there is someone . . . I . . . oh . . . No . . .' Jana seemed to shrink back and her face crumpled as if she would cry. She was silent. Catherine shivered violently.

'What is it?' she asked hoarsely. 'What have you seen?'

Jana shook herself and seemed to smile. Her eyes were still closed. The room was almost dark. The candle glow shone on the women's faces. To Catherine, Jana seemed disembodied, a face floating in a cloud of light.

Jana said, 'It's nothing. I think I was imagining something. But I think you must be careful. There is a gun. More than one gun. Somebody is going to . . .' She drew in her breath.

Panic in her voice, Catherine said, 'Tell me. Don't hold anything back. I must know what you are seeing.'

Jana sighed. She seemed to relax, as if some pressure had lifted. She went on in her soft, accented voice, 'It's gone now. I am seeing a different gentleman. Who is this gentleman who is working very hard? He works in the day and the night. He, oh this poor man is so sad . . . He is so full of problems. He carries so many responsibilities. He seems very old but no, he is not so old either. He is old and young. He is looking always at papers.

'I think you know this man well. Is this man . . . Ah, yes, this man was once your husband. Before the other, the first gentleman . . . Yes. This man is sad because you are not with him. But he does not have time for you. He can't think about you. You are not doing what he wants you to do . . . He has something very big to do with his life. He is going to need a lot of help. Support from a wife. But you do not want to give it to him. You want the other man. You need what the other man can give you, his love. His love is very strong. It makes you alive when you were dead. But not this one. This one is not your husband in your heart.'

She opened her eyes. She seemed almost surprised. 'Is there anything you want to ask me?'

'Is there another woman with the first man? Is it a woman that's keeping him from me? Does he love another woman?'

Jana looked at Catherine and there was an immense weariness in her eyes. Catherine thought of an Egyptian goddess whose elongated eyes seemed potent with the secrets of ages. Then Jana closed her eyes again. She smiled a serene smile. 'There are many women around him. He was married to someone else for a long time and he was very sad when that ended. His wife left him because of another one. Another woman that was important to him. There is someone in his life now. A woman who helps him. She loves him, I think . . . she wants him. She wants to marry him. She is holding him quite strongly. But he does not want that. He is always thinking of . . . his secret passion. His thoughts are with you always . . . he is close and yet he is far away from you.'

She seemed to stare through Catherine's eyes into the distance. 'There is too much between you. There are too many secrets, too many things in the way. He is not able to come close to you because of those things . . .'

Catherine said, 'Can it change? Is there hope?' She felt pain. Her eyes blurred and she fought back tears.

Jana smiled. Her eyes were open. She seemed immeasurably old and wise. She said in a very strong practical voice, quite different from the dreamy, quiet voice of her trance, 'Madam. You always get what you want. You are a woman who has everything except love. If you really, really want this man, he will come to you. But you must be sure, sure in your own heart that you love him enough. And he must be sure too before he will come.'

She closed her eyes again. 'You will have to accept many things to love this man. He is . . . there is a lot of darkness in him and he knows it. He knows how it will upset you to know many of his secrets. He is afraid to tell you. Afraid of losing you. Only you can know if you are strong enough to deal with it. With what you find in yourself when he awakens your own darkness. But to him you seem very light, madam, very high above him. You are a goddess on a stage of light and he is a poor creature fallen into darkness who cannot climb out. He does not think he should show himself to you. He thinks he should stay out of your life. He thinks he cannot give you what you should have. He thinks he can't be what you want . . .

'But, still, he is holding out his hand to you. He is asking you to do something for him . . . You can pull him up into your light but there is a danger too that you will fall into the darkness with him, that if you are not strong enough, he will pull you down with the weight of his darkness. That darkness is hell. Only you can know whether you are strong enough to take the risk and survive . . . and bring him out . . .' Jana let go of Catherine's hands and leaned back out of the circle of candlelight.

Catherine took a deep breath. She felt drained and shaken. The session was over. She thanked Jana, paid and left. Outside in her car she took out her mirror and looked into her own eyes. She saw fear and something she could not read. She put the tape recorder on which she had recorded the reading into her bag, brushed her hair and applied fresh lipstick. Then she started the engine and turned her car into the traffic.

Jana stood in her dark window and watched the Aston drive out of her street. She rubbed her hands over her eyes and yawned. Readings always tired her, but this one more than most because of its dark energy. The lady's powerful emotions, the sexual desires that had overflowed from her and from the man's thoughts had been so violent they had aroused her, too. Then there were the things she had seen about the man, about the future. About what would happen to the man and to the woman quite soon. She had not been able to tell the lady everything she had seen. Not by any means. That would have been too dangerous. One should not know one's fate.

Everything in the future was not fated. There was the possibility that things might change. There was choice, in many things the human will was free. But, on the other hand, she was sure that the woman who had just left her was struggling helplessly with forces beyond her control. There were some things that could not be changed, or avoided.

Jana turned from the window and went to put on the kettle. She shivered and searched for peace within herself. She was glad, though, that she had kept her rule. She never told clients when she saw a death.

*

38

Catherine drives through the mid-evening traffic: thinking, brooding, dazed, disturbed. Jana's far away voice is saying, 'He needs you . . . Someone . . . another person . . . does not want him to come to you.' Who? who? who? Why can they be stronger than his feelings? Why are they so powerful? Why does he do what they want? Who is this person? Who is she? Mother, ex-wife, girl friend, policewoman lover?

Catherine angry, hurt, sad, not understanding, drives too fast with tears streaming. She shouts, 'Why oh, God, why?' in the car's close confines. Has she done wrong? Adulterous, deceiving woman, living a lie. Lies cannot bring happiness. Only truth brings joy. Tears are falling onto her lap, blocking her nose, streaking her mascara. She is drowning. Blind now, the car guiding itself. Suddenly, she remembers. A priest, met last summer at a charity garden party. Oh, the comforting ears of the priest. Someone to listen to her sorrows, give absolution, take away guilt, to tell her what is right and wrong when she has no more moral vision.

She turns down a side street nosing the car, uncertain, searching, then finding the church. She parks her car, almost forgetting to lock it. Pulls her scarf over her head, slips tinted glasses over her tears. She goes to the priest's house, rings his doorbell, waits. No one comes. She turns away, tears flowing more than ever. The church is closed. The priest is not there. God is implacable. Catherine is cast out into the darkness. Starless, un-navigable night. She stands there, torn by wind as if by vultures. Suddenly, footsteps. A housekeeper comes, frowning, what is it? An Irish voice. 'Father is away. I can't help you. I see.' She notices Catherine's distress. 'Wait, miss. I'll ask the other Father.' She goes, clop of flat leather heels on flag-stoned floor. Her voice is a faint burble in the distance.

Another voice, a man's voice. She returns.

'The other Father is here just tonight but he's standing in for Father. He'll see you now. Go around to the church door. I'll open it for you.'

Catherine at the church door, finds it unlocked, pushes it open, goes in, enters the dark church. Silence, sanctuary, one faint lamp lit, incense scents the air. She has never been inside this church before.

She finds her way to the confessional. She enters. The priest is there, hidden.

She speaks. She says, 'Father, I am not a Catholic. I have been raised a Protestant. I have no church, no priest, no spiritual guide in my wilderness. I must confess and have your guidance. I must know God's will.' Her voice wavers and a sob catches in her throat. 'I am adulterous. I have a husband and I do not love him. I did believe I loved him when I married him. But my love died. He gave me no love. He does not want my love. He is like a stone or a machine to me. Not human. Nor loving. I was alone and dying inside my heart like a death of spirit. I could not love life.'

Tears are streaming down her face and her neck, into her silk shirt and down between her breasts. Rivers of silent tears. 'I met another man and he awakened love in me. It was lust then, but now I love him. My body gave a message to my soul. My soul awakened with my body. I never knew love before. I thought I loved but I did not know this passion. To die first for lack of love and then to want to die for love. To live in pain as if with a wound that does not heal.'

She sobs aloud and the priest waits patiently behind his curtain. She goes on, 'I am punished. My lover's vanished. I am waiting and don't know where he is. I am without him. He must have left me. Yet I know he needs me. In the night when I can't get back to sleep I seem to hear him calling me. It seems as though I am being punished. I want forgiveness. I don't know how to ask for absolution. I am seeking your guidance. I don't know how to be forgiven. I must have done wrong. I didn't intend to break my vows. But the need for love is too strong. I want you to tell me what God wants of me now . . .' She sobs and her shoulders shake. Her face is in her hands. She is not speaking any more only sobbing.

The priest speaks slowly. His voice is quavering and old and soft. 'You are fortunate that you can love. Most people cannot love. You have opened your heart to love and therefore to God . . . Give your love to God as well as to man. Go in peace. You do no wrong by loving.'

He falls silent. She gives her thanks and leaves. She wonders who this priest can be who gave her such wisdom. She hovers in the shadow of the door to the street, waiting to see him. He comes out of the confessional without seeing her and goes away from her towards the connecting door with the house. She watches him. He is bent and old, walking with a stick. He has thin wispy white hair and a beard. He must be eighty, ninety, more.

She sees the housekeeper coming, draws money from her purse and drops it into the collecting box. She walks into the empty street. A bright star in the west shines like hope in the windy sky.

39

The cafeteria at Victoria Station is not the quietest or the pleasantest place. But then no one stays long. And no one pays any attention to anyone else. Everyone recedes into anonymity, in transit, belonging elsewhere. Especially in the morning when the reluctant, red-eyed travellers are still recovering from being wrenched by alarm bells from their sleep or are returning home, pale and bruised, after a night's work.

It is a good place, then, to meet unobserved, unless someone is watching for another reason. In this case no one was. The professional watcher was having a meeting with his friend the policeman.

Armstrong sipped an insipid coffee. The private detective drank his railway tea. The rush hour crowd crushed around them. The air was stale and murky with smoke. If anyone had taken a good look at the pair they would have noticed that the tall clean-shaven man with the cropped reddish hair in the crisp beige raincoat seemed to have his older scruffier companion at some disadvantage.

The detective shook his balding head at the Commander's question. He ran a hand over the crown of his head, smoothing the few strands of faded brown hair that were spread there, as if to somehow diminish the shine of his pink scalp. He said, stubbornly, 'I'm being paid well and I can't give you this one, pal.' His voice was heavily Glaswegian.

'Come on, Archie. You've never held out on me before. What's so special about this job?' Armstrong gave his old friend a look of intense scrutiny. His voice cajoled.

'I canna tell you, mate. Isn't that enough?' The detective writhed in his chair and shifted the position of his feet on the floor.

'Now then, Archie,' Armstrong's voice seemed suddenly more Scottish and its cajoling note was stronger. 'You know very well we've been friends a long time and you can't avoid admitting you owe me one.'

The elderly detective gave the Commander a look of dislike. 'You're not going to hold me to that promise on this one, Davie, laddie. It's no' fair on a man. It's no playin' the game.'

Armstrong looked at the detective. He went on looking. There was hardness and reproach in that look and the old Glaswegian had no liking for either ingredient. The reproach made him feel guilty as hell. The hardness meant Armstrong would hold him to his promise. He'd had a favour too many from the Commander. He had known that he only held his licence by virtue of the policeman's intention to put his advantage to some future use. Now that day had come and Armstrong wanted his side of the bargain delivered.

Though why he was so interested in this one Archie Mackintosh could not guess. Unless . . . unless he had some kind of personal interest in the woman? Well, there was no point in guessing. He was on the spot and he knew it.

'Isn't there anything else I can do for you, laddie?'

The Commander shook his head slowly. He went on giving Archie that look.

'What are you gonna do with this information, mate?'

'I don't know till you tell me, Archie. I don't know.' Armstrong kept looking at Archie. He was just waiting, biding his time, the detective knew. He would have to give in. There was no way he would get out of here without telling who was paying him to keep a round the clock watch on Catherine Clyne.

40

Armstrong looked at his watch. 'I'll have to be going, I'm afraid.' He smiled apologetically at Catherine.

It was midnight. Annabel's was filling up. The dance floor was crowded, tables nearby were filled with groups of Americans and the noise level was considerable.

Catherine called for her bill and after another fifteen minutes they got up to leave. Armstrong seemed faintly embarrassed to see her pay. As they walked out she stopped to talk to people she knew in the bar. Armstrong hovered, again seeming embarrassed, just out of reach of her introductions.

As they made the street, she said, 'Were you afraid of meeting someone nefarious?'

'Och no,' he laughed, 'I just didn't want to embarrass you. After all, you are a married woman.'

She smiled. 'They saw you, dear. Anyway, I don't think

212

anyone one is likely to meet at Annabel's gives two pence for that.' The doorman brought the Aston. Earlier, Catherine had suggested Armstrong sent his driver home. She would take him to the Barbican, she said. He had agreed after some hesitation.

They circled Berkeley Square and headed East along Piccadilly. Catherine enjoyed driving the Aston at night, but the streets were still too crowded for her to put on any speed, just yet. Besides, she had not forgotten, had not been allowed to forget, she had a senior policeman in the car.

She had managed to get him to drink a little champagne though she herself drank no more than two glasses, her usual limit. They drove now, decorously, along the Strand, heading for the City.

Armstrong said, 'By the way, I've checked up on that business of your being followed, and you can relax.'

She turned her head briefly from the road to give him a questioning look. 'Really?' she said.

'I've checked you quite thoroughly. You've no worries.'

She said, ironically, 'You mean I'm only being followed by a group of autograph collectors who mean absolutely no harm?'

He said, firmly, 'I mean, you've no reason to worry about being followed at all.'

They were going down Fleet Street. There was little sign of life among the dead bones of the old newspaper buildings. Catherine was still quite sure she was being tailed. She looked in the mirror, but nothing seemed to be following her at the moment. She rounded St Paul's and headed for Moorgate. She said, lightly, 'Does that mean no one is following me? Or does it simply mean I am not being followed by assassins or kidnappers in the pay of the SLRS Protest Coordination Committee?'

He sighed and cleared his throat. His voice heavy, he said, 'I can only tell you we have checked into it and you've nothing to be alarmed about.'

They reached the Barbican. 'Where do I go?'

He directed her and she said, 'I'm still curious. I think

213

I'm being followed and you say it's nothing alarming. Am I right?'

He said, 'Catherine, I'll vouch for your safety, personally, if necessary.' He was very serious. She gave him a glance and he added casually, 'You'll come in for a nightcap?'

She wondered if it was politeness or a genuine invitation, gave him a look and decided on the latter. She wanted to get to the bottom of this tailing business. He was not being straight with her.

'Thanks,' she said, 'I will.' She parked in the underground parking garage and they took the long meandering route to his flat.

In the lift, she said, 'I don't understand what you're telling me, David. You're not telling me I'm not being followed. You're just telling me not to bother my pretty little head about it. And that's not good enough. If you've found out who is on my tail, I want to know, too. And I want to know why you want to keep it secret from me.'

He took her arm and led her from the lift.

The bare corridors smelt of institutional antiseptic. They walked in silence, until they arrived outside his flat. As he unlocked the door, he said, 'Just be patient, Catherine. I'll tell you whatever you need to know to put your mind at rest.'

He took her dark blue velvet coat, revealing again the honey skin of her bare shoulders in the short, blue silk evening dress. He had felt a little outclassed all evening. He said, tersely, 'This is my humble abode.'

She smiled at the cliche. Armstrong used cliches, often. She supposed it was inevitable even for a sort of high flying Mr Plod to talk like a TV copper.

'Coffee?' he asked, bustling in the little kitchen.

'Do you have tea?' she asked. She smiled sympathetically at what she supposed was his embarrassment at being seen to be domestic, and wandered off into the open plan room.

It was furnished simply and without style. One or two pale, tweed-covered seating units were grouped into an L-shaped sofa arrangement around a teak coffee table.

There were some bookshelves, largely devoid of books, some framed family photographs, a TV and a video recorder, a hi fi, a table lamp. It was a man's flat. The home of a man who was seldom at home.

He brought her tea and she smiled at him. She said, gently, 'I'm still waiting for your answer to my question, David.'

He sat next to her and this surprised her. He had been almost afraid to touch her at Annabel's. He leaned his elbow over the back of the seat and wriggled himself into a comfortable position. 'I don't want to prevaricate, Catherine. I'm just telling you, it's of no account. There was someone following you. I've ascertained who they were and who paid them. I can't tell you any more. If you want to know more you'll have to hire your own agency to go out and get the facts. It's beyond my jurisdiction.'

She sipped her tea without looking at him. He had put milk in it and it tasted awful.

He said, 'I'm sorry. I'll have you watched myself if it makes you feel safer.'

'No thanks, David,' she said sweetly. 'One lot of flat feet behind me is quite enough.'

He changed the subject abruptly, catching her with his question. 'Are you happily married, Catherine?'

She turned and stared into his face. He was looking very intently at her, boring into her with his inquisitorial eyes. It was a way of looking she knew she had sometimes when she was interviewing and wanted to be aware of any flicker that would indicate untruth or sham, or that would reveal some deeply concealed feeling.

She put her teacup down very slowly on the table. She said, casually, not looking at him, 'Why do you ask?'

'Because I think I'm looking at a poor little rich girl. A woman who has everything, except what she wants.'

She gave him a quick look and then leaned forward and lifted her cup and saucer up again. 'You don't want me to bore you with the story of my life, do you, Commander?'

He said, gently, 'I won't be bored.'

She turned, surprised and looked directly into his eyes. They were expressive and kindly. She had not seen that in him before.

She said, laughing, 'Your suspicions are correct, officer. My husband doesn't understand me.'

'What are you doing about it?'

She gave him a mock surprised look and a funny little twisted smile.

He was stern. He said, 'I'm serious.'

She went on playing her role, her expression arch. 'I didn't know the CID went in for matrimonial counselling.'

He leaned towards her and put both his hands on her shoulders and squeezed. He said, 'I just want to know the score before I kiss you.' And he pulled her to him.

She let him kiss her without responding. He looked into her face anxiously. 'Have I done wrong?'

She shook her head, unable to speak. His warmth and gentleness were altogether surprising in the stiff and professional man she had grown used to. She felt overcome by his warmth, and attracted to him.

He kissed her again, very gently and now she responded a little. His kiss grew more passionate and he held her close to him. She realized he was lonely and unhappy too, that he needed the same loving warmth and gentleness he was giving her. She felt something in herself give way and crumple. Her gaiety and competence, her hostessy manner of earlier, and her arch games of a moment ago, broke down and she was suddenly without a front. She was a lost, lonely, unhappy woman who needed love.

Tears escaped from under her closed eyelids and rolled down her cheeks. He felt them and stopped kissing her mouth to kiss away the tears. He held her closer and hugged her and rocked her and stroked her head and she cried quietly on.

He stood up then and lifted her up and carried her into the bedroom and laid her on the bed. He undressed her carefully and made love to her very gently and she went on crying silently almost until the end. Then she cried out in her climax as he came with her, and she felt at peace and the tears stopped. They fell asleep with their arms around each other and did not waken until first light.

41

Catherine drives through the grey dawn light in last night's clothes and make up. Almost six on an April morning. The City of London is still unroused. St Paul's reflects the cloud-patched sky. Pearl lights. Misted. She turns along the river, overtaking the sweetly inflowing tide as she fires her silver bullet to 90 mph along the Victoria Embankment's long curve. The mirror shows no one following. She remembers her tears, his loving. His so soothing loving, that caressed her into sleep. A man like that, so hard and solid, dealing with black and white, good and evil, practical, a realist who shows a tender side, loving a sad woman, gently. A man like that . . . worth knowing, worth taking the time to know. Worth loving. If you can.

Why had she let him make love to her? Out of anguish, loneliness, vulnerability, longing for someone who has gone away, who assaulted her with passion and vanished into the mystery he came from. Out of helplessness and need.

I'm not promiscuous. Am I? Yet . . . she wonders. The constant awareness of the emptiness where his body fits. Feeling, in memory, his cock's thrust. Finding any other, almost any other man, a solace, a substitute, something, anything to fill the empty space and bring relief from desire, briefly.

How does a young bride become widow feel? This way. Catherine's way. Her lover lost for ever. The empty place no one can fill. How can I ever be whole again? Believe myself a whole? Is there more than one man to fill this empty torn space?

The Aston slows before turning into Parliament Square. She sees a long beam of sunlight on Big Ben's eastern face, the clock's fingers at 6.13. She passes the Abbey. The door is closed. No absolution today.

At home, she creeps into the house and up the stairs. She strips clothes and make up then stands under the shower a long time, washing away her memories, trying to put the man behind her, trying to think of starting again with someone new. David. Can she love you? Can Catherine love you and forget the other one? The one who vanished. The one who lives on life's dark side. Forget him and love the hunter, the crusader, the man with the flaming sword, with angels, not that Angel, on his side.

She takes a huge white towel and cuddles herself dry. Comforting warmth and cleanliness. She looks in the mirror at the naked face. A beautiful face, good bones, but tired under the eyes. Shadows. Lines forming. Beauty does not last forever. Beauty with which to bait love. Men do not see love. Only beauty. Her eyes are dull. Her soul is not refreshed by love with David Armstrong. Her body is caressed. Her soul is still yearning.

She draws the heavy chintz curtains and slides into her bed. Cool linen soothes like salve. She sleeps, dreaming. Then wakes screaming, 'No. No. No.' Hurling herself around the bed. Big Ben is chiming nine. Sunlight crackles around the curtains' sides. A floorboard creaks as James goes downstairs. Before her eyes she sees Christopher's dark ones, staring as they were in the dream. She hears his voice crying, 'Catherine.' A gun is held to his head.

42

The clerk came back in about ten minutes and put the print-out on Armstrong's desk.

'Thanks,' he said curtly, and the woman went out. He took the sheaf of pages and looked at the name at the top of the first sheet. Christopher Paul Angel, Proprietor of the Sirocco and The Downtown Club. The pages were a detailed account of some of his movements over a period of three years.

Armstrong read steadily down the pages. They detailed the man's court appearances over minor infringements of the law, his arrivals and departures from his various night clubs, cars he travelled in, people who were with him, places he went and people he met. One charge for living off immoral earnings stood out. The police had lost the case. There had been searches on suspicion of drugs being passed at the clubs but nothing proven. There was very little to make Angel look suspicious. Just an ordinary night club proprietor who got into a spot of bother with the law on a fairly routine basis. Clubs were checked periodically on drugs and prostitution.

Armstrong thought there was little to worry anyone in this set of reports. He had called for them because he remembered Catherine had expressed interest in Angel and the Sirocco. He had forgotten all about it until this morning. But this morning was an exceptional one.

He ran his eyes down the most recent reports. Then stopped. Recently there had been a phone tap on the Sirocco. No explanation given. A list of callers ran to several pages. He began to read the names and numbers.

After she left this morning he had not gone back to sleep. It had been a long time since he had been interested in a woman. And it had been some time since he had had a woman who had aroused his feelings this much. He had spent an hour after she had left, over toast, eggs and tea, thinking. He thought it possible he was embarking on more than a casual affair with Catherine. His feelings had surprised him. He had felt a tenderness and affection as well as excitement and desire. This morning he knew he wanted to develop the relationship, wanted to know her better, to make love to her again, soon.

So he had been thinking about Catherine's marriage. He dismissed that quickly enough. It was clearly not working out sexually, and that, he knew well enough from his own sad experience, made a rift, if you were honest. Marriages that had stopped working sexually held together because of children. Catherine's was childless. Her reason for staying in the marriage might be she had nowhere else to jump. Or she liked lunch at Chequers.

Armstrong did not do anything without analysis. He would not put himself at risk of emotional hurt. He had had enough of that. And Catherine was married, even though unhappily, as she had admitted. He had to think about where he stood, where he would stand, where things would lead. He had to think about her life and his. Her high-flying social world: how would a policeman fit into it? Better than the Rt Hon James Waring, MP? Well, no worse. That was when he had remembered her interest in Christopher Angel.

This stopped his daydream. Angel was not a name he knew, but the request for information about a night club proprietor, coming from a woman like Catherine, was something unusual, and the unusual was invariably a clue to something important. A blip on the graph that said, look here, the pattern is not as normal, something is going on. Why would a woman like Catherine Clyne want information about a low life character whose name was in police files? A journalistic investigation? Hardly. The kind of magazine Catherine ran was not interested in that kind of story. Would she work freelance? Hardly, with her money. Armstrong had not been able to avoid noticing her money.

She had mentioned something about a friend. She wanted the information for a friend. That might be a fairly conventional red herring. Armstrong had not got as far as he had in the Force without playing some successful hunches and his hunch was that Catherine Clyne had asked for that information for her own personal reasons. And that worried him. A lot. There had been something about her expression when he had refused her. Some look he had caught in between reading the bill and signing the credit card receipt. Something he now recalled like a still photograph from an archive, something his policeman's mind was long trained to do.

Catherine would no doubt have used the same

technique. She had been an investigative reporter once, she had told him. She should have known better than to ask him, then, should have expected him to react, to be alerted by the oddity of her request. Or was she so entangled she was unaware it showed? Her expression, that was the biggest clue that something somewhere was not right, that emotions were involved here somewhere. That was the still he now recalled into his mind and examined for the answer to his question. Her eyes had the story. In his mind they looked at him again, deep turquoise eyes fringed with black lashes, made up with green and gold pencil. Eyes laden with mystery, seductive and yet sad.

Perhaps she was being blackmailed. Or her husband was, having fallen in with one of Angel's hookers, perhaps. That was a possibility. If so, would Catherine know about it? Maybe. Or was it drugs? He had no evidence that Christopher Angel was involved with drugs, but it was possible he was supplying the Warings. Or Catherine? She did not seem a drug type but you never knew. Cocaine? High-flying people and their chemical support systems. Armstrong chewed his lip and frowned. He ran his eyes down the list. Then suddenly he stopped.

Late in March, there had been a call to the Sirocco about eleven one evening from a number Armstrong recognized as Catherine's home phone, she had given him the number this morning. The caller had not identified themself. About three weeks ago a series of calls from that number had begun. They were as late as 2 a.m. The caller had identified herself as Miss Clyne and left messages for Christopher Angel to call her at her offfice number next day. Once or twice she had questioned the respondent about Angel's whereabouts and when he was expected back. Each time, she had been told no one knew where he was but that he would be given the message.

Armstrong felt a still chill creep over his skin. He buzzed for his secretary and asked her to reach the officer in charge of phone taps. When the man came on Armstrong said, 'Hooper, why do we have the Sirocco under surveillance?'

Detective Sergeant Hooper said he would find out. It took about fourteen minutes for him to come back. He said, 'Clairmont bullion robbery, Sir.'

'Ah, the Home Secretary is keen for action on that one. Any evidence?'

'One or two bits and pieces, Sir.'

'Anything that will stand up?'

'Could be, Sir.'

'Bring the file along to my office, will you?' He put the phone down, swung his chair and stared out of his window at the geometric shapes of the neighbouring buildings, their windows catching the morning light. He had been in his office since 8.30 a.m., after about four hours in the sack. Adequate but not sufficient. He yawned and turned back to his desk. The report came by interdepartmental messenger. Armstrong opened it and flipped through. There was a certain amount of substance though he doubted it was enough for a prosecution, yet. Still, he should not neglect his duty.

He lifted the phone and dialled an outside line. He reached Catherine at home before she left for the office. He knew she seldom left home before ten and preferred to work later in the evening. She had told him that she had recently changed her rhythms to late night and late morning. Going to the office early was too much of a strain when a lot of her business life consisted of obligatory late night functions, parties, dinners. Anyway, she said, journalism was a notoriously late starting, late finishing trade and magazines emulated the natural schedules of newspapers without having the cause of late editions to keep them up. But then, Catherine said, most creative people had late starting metabolisms.

Now he wondered. Could the changed rhythms have anything to do with a man who worked at night? He said, 'Are you free for lunch?'

'That's a good question. I'll have to call you back.' Her diary was in the office. She would ring Janie and have her check. She came back to him quickly. She was free. She would meet him in St James's Park for a disgusting sandwich. Or, on second thoughts, she would bring the sandwiches.

He said that was not what he had in mind but, since it was a promising-looking day, he would go along with it. So long as she would meet him for dinner soon. He caught himself saying that. He shouldn't have. He knew very well he had to wait and see how she reacted to what he was planning to tell her about Angel before he would know for sure whether he could risk seeing her again.

43

They had arranged to meet on the bridge. Catherine had come from her office. Armstrong walked briskly from New Scotland Yard, through Queen Anne's Gate and into the park. The bright sunlight and the cool air invigorated him. He would have felt very pleased with life if it were not for what he had on his mind.

He saw her as he approached the bridge. She wore a long black cape over a short red dress. Huge sunglasses concealed her eyes. She was leaning on the parapet gazing towards Whitehall, the sun brilliant on her hair, the cape flying out in the wind. He came up and put a hand on hers. She said, without turning, 'I do love those little onion domes, don't you? So like a fairy tale palace. A wizard's palace. I always imagine one could get all one's wishes granted there, if one only knew which building it is and could go there.'

'And what are your wishes?'

She turned and pushed the glasses up onto her head, smiling brilliantly at him. 'Just one. I want to live happily ever after, that's all.'

'Ah,' he said, 'poor little rich girl.' He pressed her hand and looked away from her expressive eyes, wanting her again. He took her arm and turned her towards the Mall. 'Let's walk.'

They found a bench and Catherine delved into a large carrier bag she had been carrying under her cape to bring out the promised sandwiches. She said, 'I haven't brought anything to drink, but these are from a super little place in Covent Garden. You can choose from smoked salmon and cream cheese, shrimp with mayonnaise, or cheese salad. All with the best wholewheat bread, of course. I hope you like being healthy.'

They started munching, looking at the lake. The park was blossoming well in the good weather and would soon be at its best. Catherine felt happy. But she thought she sensed some distance between herself and David. He seemed preoccupied and occasionally did not seem to hear what she said. When they had finished their sandwiches, they started walking towards the cafe to get something to drink.

'Let's go the long way.' He pulled her across the bridge so that they would have to walk around the bottom end of the lake. He needed time.

She said she did not mind the extra walk, though, he noticed, she was wearing very high heeled black suede shoes. She also wore black stockings. At least he assumed they were stockings and not tights. She had been wearing stockings last night, and lace underwear. He tingled at the memory.

They walked without touching each other, talking about nothing, the wind, the flowers, the people walking to meet them. They had gone almost as far as the Foreign and Commonwealth Office before he had the courage to ask the first question. 'Perhaps you can satisfy my curiosity about something,' he said, casually.

She looked at him, her eyes hidden behind the glasses. He looked back, watching now for her reaction, and went on, 'Do you remember I told you off for asking me about a night club and its proprietor?'

'Yes?' A question in her voice. But nothing visible behind the glasses.

'Well, I just wondered, really, why you wanted to know.'

To his surprise, she laughed.

'Why are you laughing?'

'I do think you're funny. I asked you this last week and you gave me a rocket for it and now you want to know why I asked. Have you been brooding about it ever since?' She laughed again. It was a merry, happy little laugh. Innocent.

There was a bench coming up on their right, in the sunshine. He took hold of her hand and went towards it. When they were sitting, he lifted the glasses from her face and said very solemnly, 'I want to look at you and I want you to tell me why you want that information?'

'Oh David. So serious.' She mocked him, gently.

'Answer, please, Catherine.' His voice and face were stern.

She became serious, then. 'I just wondered if you could give me some background into something that intrigues me, that's all.'

'Why does it intrigue you?' His manner was intense and he was boring into her with his grey eyes again.

She laughed again. 'Stop giving me the third degree.'

'How well do you know this man?'

'Not well.' That was the truth.

'How do you know him?'

'I met him.'

'Where?'

'David, really.' Catherine stood up, pulling her cloak around her, reaching for her glasses from his lap.

He took hold of her wrist and pulled her down again. He was quite rough and his voice now was that of a parent demanding the truth from a child. 'I'm asking you for your own good, Catherine. I don't think a woman like you should have anything to do with a man of that kind. I'm naturally curious why you should want information about him. A girl like you shouldn't care less about a man in the club world. They're the scum, in the night club life. You know that. Don't you? No, no. Maybe not Annabel's.' He shook his head. 'But the Sirocco, those sort of places where whores work, where the underworld converges . . .' He tailed off. There was

225

disgust in his voice. He sounded very Scottish.

She thought. He's more angry than Daddy. What does he know about Christopher? She felt the familiar thumping in her solar plexus. The fear of a frightened animal trying to get out.

He said, 'Are you being blackmailed, by any chance?'

She giggled, bowing her head over her lap.

He let go of her hand which he had been holding tightly all this time and leaned sideways against the back of the seat, on his elbow, looking at her. He was not getting any answers. When he spoke next, his voice was stiff with forced patience, with the effort to be calm against the thought that was taking hold of him. 'Catherine, you're a beautiful woman, you're clever, you're rich. I admire you. I feel things for you. I want to touch you and hold you and make love to you . . .'

She cut in, her voice brittle with anger. 'Do you want to marry me, David? Do you want to lock me up in an ivory tower and throw away the key? Do you want to be a father figure to me? Do you want to protect me from the wicked, wicked world? To save me from living life?' She was turned fully towards him, looking at him through the huge glasses. The cape had fallen away from her shoulders and revealed the soft draped fabric of her brilliant red dress. Her hair fell back over her shoulders and he saw the plaited gold studs in her ear lobes.

He was puzzled. He said, gently, 'What makes you say that, Catherine?'

'You talking like a heavy father to me, David.' She pulled the cape closed around her neck.

'Catherine, I'm a policeman. I see too much of the seamy side of life. I don't like to think that someone like you should have, by choice or accident, anything to do with those things. Those kind of people. Those kinds of sordid places.'

She said, 'All right, I'll tell you.' She held the cape up around her neck and looked at him with a lowered head, over the glasses. The head went up, then, and her glasses became opaque, reflecting light. She said, 'I met the man we're talking about one night in January. He helped me when I was stranded in the snow. My car broke down in Regent's Park. I'm intrigued by him, that's all. He might make a character in a novel.' She stopped suddenly.

He looked at her expectantly and she said, 'Are you happy, now?'

'Let's walk.' He stood up and took her arm. He had the answer he had been afraid of. At least, he thought he did.

The sunlight was brilliant and the air gentle and fresh. The scent of blossom was almost unbearably sweet. The fountain was spraying and leaping in its many forms like a dancer, dancing for joy on the surface of the lake. So much life, beckoning, yet he could never join it. It was a wonderful day for being happy, if you could only forget. He looked down at Catherine, walking demurely on his arm, and felt a slow ache of regret.

44

'There's a Ms Slight to see you.' Janie stood by Catherine's desk. She was pulling the kind of face which meant, Why didn't I know about this? Janie felt she controlled Catherine's diary. Now this was the second time today that Catherine had sprung something unexpected. First disappearing for a long lunch without telling her where she was going. Now this Ms Slight, who looked to say the least, as though she had got lost on the way to the Social Services, had turned up with an appointment, so she said, but of which Janie knew nothing.

Catherine looked up from the proof of her interview with the King of Spain which was to be put into July with some good colour pictures. She gave Janie a small closed-mouthed smile. 'Okay,' she said, 'show her in.' She went right on reading until Ms Slight was standing in front of her desk. 'Do sit down,' she said, without looking up. 'I'll be through in just a minute.' She made some marks in the margin of the last page and sat back and looked at her visitor.

Ms Slight was about twenty-eight, a blonde with frizzed shoulder-length locks that looked in need of a hairdresser. Her make up seemed smudged as if put on in slightly the wrong places. She wore bedraggled blue jeans and a navy T-shirt under a dirty beige trenchcoat that was too long, too broad and looked as if it belonged to a six foot man. Ms Slight was about five foot three and tending to the plump. She brushed her locks back with her much beringed hands revealing large silver gypsy earrings that dangled over the raincoat's crumpled collar. 'You know where I'm from, Miss Clyne?' Ms Slight smiled. She spoke in a surprising charm school voice.

Catherine looked puzzled. Slight leaned across and dropped a large brown envelope onto the desk. 'AP Investigations. That's your report on the subject for the past one week. The invoice is in with the report.' She said this all with a faintly embarrassed smile and a very plummy accent.

Catherine said dazedly, 'Oh. I'm so sorry. Would you like some tea?' She had not expected a young woman. She had thought the detective agency was operated by men. She had seen a man when she had given AP the assignment.

'Hm. Jolly nice thought,' Ms Slight said enthusiastically.

Catherine buzzed Janie. 'Bring a pot of tea and two cups, darling.' Her fingers moved nervously over the envelope and picked at the opening which was not sealed down. 'Ms Slight?' she said hesitantly.

'Penelope,' the girl said, smiling her lopsided, embarrassed smile. 'All the clients call me Penny and the agency is AP for Andy and Penny, so please don't bother to be formal.'

Catherine smiled back. 'Were you the agent responsible for this . . . this report on my . . . on . . .'

Slight bounced forward in her seat and recrossed her legs. She grinned and said, 'Oh rather. I've been on it all week. Not much excitement, I'm afraid. Leads a bit of a humdrum life, this chap. Had a bit of a hairy drive down the M2, though. He certainly drives like the devil. Sorry to say I lost him just as we got to the Kent coast, on the bendy roads down on the Marshes. My motor just didn't have what it takes to tear around corners like he was. He must have vanished down a lane somewhere between the Romney Marshes and Hythe. I hunted about a bit but couldn't get the right lane, I'm afraid. Bit of a blow, that. The only break in his pattern all week.'

Catherine felt a chill starting in her stomach and spreading out over her body. She said, 'I'd like to read the report now while you're here, Penny. In case there are some questions. If you don't mind waiting. There are some recent issues of New York Vanities just to your left. You probably haven't seen them.'

'Oh gosh. No. That's a bit of fun. Go right ahead. I'll amuse myself with your brilliance while you read my handiwork, poor old you.' She started leafing through a magazine.

Catherine pulled eight pages of typescript out of the envelope and started reading. This was the detailed report on Angel's movements that she had commissioned from AP Investigations a week ago after Armstrong had suggested a detective agency was the best way to get the information she wanted. She had got AP out of the Yellow Pages. The jack-booted rabbit was back in her solar plexus trying to kick its way out. She felt weak. Her legs seemed to have gone to rubber and she doubted she could stand up if she had to. Her fingers trembled as she took the pages and began to read.

Janie brought the tea tray and dumped it rather gracelessly on the desk.

'Pour, would you, darling,' Catherine murmured, looking down at the papers she held as firmly as she could.

Janie gave her a 'Now I suppose I'm the bloody maid as well' look and poured.

Catherine heard her offering Penny milk or lemon. She read down the first page. Angel had been watched from the first pick up outside the club at 4.12 a.m. on the day after Catherine had commissioned the investigation. He had gone to his house in Devonshire Mews and had not left it again until 11 a.m. next morning. He had then driven to St John's Wood and gone into a block of flats. He had come out after half an hour wearing a change of clothing. He had left the Rolls in which he had driven there and got into a gold Mercedes.

The agent, which in this case was Penny – someone else had done the night shift – had gone in and chatted to the porter. She had established which flat the subject had gone into and who lived there. It was a Mrs Sophie Angel. This was the subject's mother, who lived alone. The subject went there often, the porter said, sometimes overnight. His mother thought the world of him, according to the porter.

Catherine read on. There was more mundane movement of no apparent significance. There was one night when Angel had gone to a flat above a shop in Old Quebec Street for about two hours. Penny's night partner had established that this was occupied by a female police constable who worked at the nearby St Marylebone Police Station.

Catherine felt the rabbit kick violently. She took a sip of tea and moved on. The subject had been seen talking to a girl on Marylebone High Street and he had appeared to write something down after the meeting. He had not gone to the Club at all on one night. This was the night Penny had been on his tail and he had driven very fast in the Rolls down to Kent and she had lost him.

The subject met people, usually men, for dinner every evening. One evening he had gone to a restaurant with the girl he had talked to on Marylebone High Street. Catherine winced as she read this. He had gone to her flat afterwards and stayed an hour.

Catherine looked at Penny who was happily munching biscuits and drinking tea while thumbing through March Vanities. She said, 'Have you followed up to find out who any of the people he had dinner with might have been?'

'Sorry?' Penny said, swallowing tea after a mouthful of biscuit and flicking a crumb off her downy top lip.

'Do you know who his dinner companions are?'

Penny seemed surprised. 'Oh no. If you had authorized more than one agent on at a time, we could have tailed the other parties from the meetings. We can do that in future, if you wish.'

'Don't worry,' Catherine said. She put the papers down and forced a smile. She felt sick, both at what she was doing and what she was learning. She reached into her handbag and brought out a cheque book. She wrote the cheque to AP Investigations on her personal account and handed it across the desk to Penny. 'Thank you very much.' She smiled warmly. 'I'm really most grateful for your efforts. I may want you to do some more work for me shortly. But just for the moment, I'm happy with what I have here.' She dropped the cheque book back into her bag.

Penny wrestled herself back into her trenchcoat which she had dropped over the back of her chair while Catherine was reading. She picked up her incongruous shiny black attache case, and stood up. 'Well, then,' she nodded, smiling exuberantly, 'it was a pleasure to do business with you. Hope to see you again, soon.' She turned and walked bouncily down the long room.

Catherine saw Janie coming towards her. She took the report and slipped it back into its envelope, then dropped it into her bag. She returned to her proof and started reading it through again. It was a relief to switch her mind onto her work.

'Well?' Janie challenged her. She leaned her hands on the desk and looked belligerent. Catherine smiled. It was her old smile. Not the cloudy vague and unhappy one of recent weeks. She was aware of a difference in her. There was something final about the sense of relief that seemed to flood her. The relief of knowing things after the uncertainty of imagining them.

She said, 'All right, Janie. I know I've been a bad girl and not kept to the diary. I promise I won't do it again. But, no. I'm not explaining anything.'

Janie picked up the tray and flounced down the room towards the kitchen. Catherine put down her pen and stared out of the window. The afternoon light slanted onto the market building roof. She watched some pigeons pecking crumbs the staff left for them on the sill of the studio's long windows.

Across the Piazza's sunlit and shadow chequered space, life suddenly seemed to open. The day seemed suddenly full of promise. A new cycle was beginning. She had a strong sense of new beginnings and old endings. She felt energy surging inside her. As if the booted rabbit that had been trapped under her diaphragm was leaping into life and cantering through the new grass. She felt a renewed desire to live her own life, as if it was picking up and taking off after some awful winter of misery and suffering. As she turned back to her proof, she felt she had learned and discarded all she would ever want to know or remember about Christopher Angel.

45

Armstrong was watching the street far below him. His eagle's view of the world pleased him. He liked the sense of remote power he got from being in this room several floors above the city's swish and bustle; the eagle's power to pounce, to choose its prey. It helped him think objectively. He turned back into the room and sat at his desk, his back to the view and the changing sky, whose west light, at this hour, at this season, lit his room with amber columns and blue shadows.

He had spent some time reflecting on today's lunch with Catherine. He had reached a decision which had taken some hours of wrangling with the devil within. Catherine was undoubtedly involved with Christopher Angel and that would mean he had to keep away from her. At least until she had stopped seeing Angel. Perhaps always.

Armstrong now had on his desk the report into Angel's suspected links with the Clairmont bullion gang. He had taken the afternoon to assess the position carefully, to talk to colleagues and see if there were grounds for charges, yet. He had then spent an hour or two doing nothing but think. He tried to keep his interest in Catherine out of his mind. To forget that there was something between her and the man whose file was now on his desk, the man whose future he held in his sights. He was not going to allow a private association to influence his professional decision. Yet, he felt it had done so already.

Had it not been for Catherine's interest in Angel, he might never have called for the report to be brought to him. Might never have reached the decision that might rebound on him. Armstrong sighed. His life had never been easy. But once again, on a hunch, he was going to stick his neck out. It was a habit of his to do that. He pressed the buzzer on his desk. It was time to put the word out on Christopher Angel.

46

'I don't believe it. You had the investigator come to the office?' Gerald's face and voice expressed horror and incredulity.

Catherine laughed. 'So what? No one knew who they were and I had already told them who I was. I told them it was an investigation for a special feature we were running and I had to have extra help.' She laughed again. She felt light and free. The heavy depression of the past weeks seemed to have lifted. They were in Greens, Duke Street. It was a convenient stopping off place for both of them on their way home. She had had to tell Gerald of the latest development in her investigations. She now showed him Penny Slight's report.

He said, 'Catherina, what does all this mean? And why are you light of spirit and laughing as though it be the first of May?'

She said quietly, 'Because I've freed myself from an intolerable burden. I'm normal again. I've gone over the threshold of my tolerance, Gerry.' She went on, her voice light and joky. 'I have suddenly been overcome with boredom and fatigue on the subject of Christopher Angel. I'm finished. It's over. I don't care if the clairvoyant is right and he comes back. The door is closed. I can't take any more sordid revelations.' Her voice rose slightly. 'I want to get back to my life. I want to stop feeling guilty about James. I want to start talking to Daddy again without waiting for him to ask me if I've seen Christopher. In short, I want to forget this whole steamy episode and start again.'

'Start again being a frozen rose, Tsarina?' Gerald spoke softly. He was watching her slyly out of the corner of his eye.

'No!'

'Then what?'

She laughed again. 'Find another lover.' She had not told him about Armstrong or about his warnings on Christopher. A girl had to have some secrets.

'Is that all he was to you, Catherina? Just a lover? Not a love?'

She stopped with the champagne glass millimetres from her lips. She spoke to the glass. 'I think he was my only love. But I didn't say I'd stopped loving him, Gerry. I just said I've had enough.' She turned and raised the glass. There was a real smile in her eyes as she looked at him. 'I'm letting you off the hook too, my darling. No more counselling and tear drying. Now, let's drink to love and luck.' She emptied her glass without pausing and put it firmly on the table.

She said, briskly, 'Now I'm going to see Daddy. I just wanted you to know the situation, Gerry. You've been a most wonderful friend. I shan't forget.' She was smiling at him with sweet gratitude.

As he leaned closer to kiss her, he saw the tears in her eyes.

47

Catherine drove from St James's Square, where she had left the Aston, to her father's house. She parked on Chesterfield Hill and walked quickly around the corner to Charles Street.

Clive let her in with a welcoming cry: 'You haven't been here for so long, Madam, I . . .' He put out his hands and took the neck of her cape.

'Hello, Clive.' She swirled out of her cape in a fast pirouette, leaving him holding it, his mouth still open, as she ran across the parquet to the study.

'Daddy, daddy. Ah you're here. I'm so glad.' He was in his usual chair by the fire which was lit against the evening chill, a glass of whisky at his side. His eyes were closed and Richard Strauss's Don Juan was playing softly in the background.

She was at his side in three strides and kissing him.

He jumped and opened his eyes. 'Good heavens, Rina. What is all this?' He sounded irritable, seemed offput by her warmth. He said grumpily, 'Take care you don't knock over my whisky.'

'You are a creature of habit, Daddy.' She dropped to the floor and rested her head against his leg.

'Well, you are not. That's for sure,' he snapped. The tartness in his tone made her feel guilty. He was referring to her three-week absence.

'I'll come and see you more often now, Daddy. I've been so tied up with work.'

'Hm.' She could tell he was not willing to believe her. He was feeling hurt and neglected. And rightly so. She had seen him only once since he had advised her to give up Christopher.

He took up his glass and sipped. 'Have you seen much of your lover?' There was a grave bass note underlying the strained normality of his tone.

She looked up at him. He was staring into the fire, his eyes unfocused. 'I haven't seen him for over a month, Daddy.'

He looked into her upturned face. 'What does that mean?'

'It's over,' she said, and looked into the fire. 'Finished. Dead and gone.' She spoke with such finality she knew she was telling him the truth. And telling herself, too.

She felt his hand stroking her head and knew he was happy. She felt suddenly very sad. Clive came in with her champagne then and there was the ceremony of the chilled glass and the pouring. It took some minutes.

When he had gone, Sir Arnold said quietly, 'I hope you can find happiness, Rina. Everyone needs love. But it must be with the right person. '

Something in his voice made her turn her head to look up at him. He was unguarded. She saw an immeasurable, private sadness in his face. He was looking very tired and somehow older. She said nothing, but she wondered once again how much he had loved her mother and why he had never remarried.

He saw her glance and went on, his voice stronger, his expression more animated. 'Perhaps things will be better with James soon. I understand he is within seconds of being made Secretary of State. The Prime Minister hinted it quite strongly to me a few days ago when I was at Number Ten for tea.'

She did not reply, but sipped her champagne and he continued stroking her head. They sat in silence until Clive called them in to dinner. During those twenty minutes of quiet, Catherine realized it was years since she had felt this close to her father, not since her childhood days in Kenya when they would sit before the log fire in the weekend evenings at the farm with Brenda. She felt a sudden overwhelming longing for those days and the love and security she had received from Brenda and her father. As the tears came into her eyes, she wondered why it was she could not find that kind of love again and why it was that her father, who was at this moment so close to her, had seemed for so long to be so far away.

What was it that had suddenly brought them close? What had she given up that had stood between them? For a moment it seemed she was being what he wanted her to be. Not what she had chosen. And the reward was to be brought back into the circle of firelight and loved. And she saw what she had been missing. The tears made their way slowly down her cheeks and it seemed to Catherine that she was crying as she would if her father had died and she was alone in the world without anyone to love her.

48

The phone beside her bed gave a faint tinkle and she turned to look at it. Then it broke the night's stillness. She had her hand on it immediately, lifting it. 'Yes?' Her voice was husky with apprehension. But it was probably a wrong number. It was after two and even New York was at dinner. It could not be an office emergency there.

His voice came through the fade and crackle of a car phone. Her breath stopped. As in a dream where one tries to scream and nothing comes out, she seemed unable to speak. Her pulse started again, forcing air out of her lungs. In a voice hoarse, just above a whisper, she said, 'Where have you been?'

His laugh came nearer. The car must have changed direction. He sounded full of himself. He said, 'It's where I'm going that counts. I'm coming to see you now.'

She drew air into her starved lungs in a great gasp. The voice trapped in her frozen throat seemed to stutter then leap into life. She said breathlessly, quickly, afraid, 'He's here. Asleep.' He was silent and she felt him waiting for her to go on. In a low near whisper she said, 'But I don't care. Come anyway.' Her voice gathered strength and she added, 'Don't press the bell. I'll be watching. How long?'

He was crisp. It was like a business appointment. 'I'm just around the corner. Three minutes.' He rang off.

She took her red silk robe and went to the dressing table. A trapped bird thrashed in her chest. She brushed her hair, rubbed blusher onto her cheeks, tipped her lashes with mascara, sprayed herself with Opium and went out of the room with her high heeled slippers in her hand. Outside James's bedroom door she waited and listened. His light was off. She heard a sudden snore. He took sleeping tablets to ensure he wasted no time trying to get to sleep when his mind was racing with overwork. She thought he would not hear anything and slipped silently downstairs.

She went into the drawing room without turning on the light and looked out of the window. The street was empty, glistening. A light rain fell. A misty rain to soften the leaves and petals of the park where she had walked with David. A soft, warm rain that had come like the gentle blessing of sleep after a day so bright a spark from a horse's hoof might have exploded it into incandescence. A day in which she had finally decided not to wait for him any more.

She saw him coming up the street and realized she had not told him about the police guard. She went to the door just as he reached it The policeman stepped forward and put a restraining hand on hls arm.

'It's all right, officer,' she said, 'this is a friend. I'm expecting him.'

She stepped backwards into the dimly lit hall and he followed her, closing the door softly behind him. She went on backwards towards the drawing room, as if she were afraid of him, but he caught up with her and put his arms around her and held her with such strength and ferocity. She felt afraid, resisting with her body's stiffness, with its unwillingness to let go her hurt and accept his healing.

He bent his head and put his lips carefully, gently onto hers, kissing her then with such intensity and yet softness that she became still, drinking from his feelings, letting them course through her like water over a dry stream bed. In that kiss she began to remember. Began to learn again what she had tried so hard to forget. She felt the frozen feelings she had stored away even from herself begin to melt. Her arms were around him, stroking him, pulling him close. A soft moan, almost a groan came from deep in her chest.

He pulled open her thin robe and slid his hands over her nakedness, setting her away from him to look at her and admire her honey skin and her lovely breasts, the slender waist and curving hips. Then he was pressing her against the wall, pressing his fingers into her soft wet place, bringing the same fingers back to his mouth to taste her nectar, kissing her again with a kiss that was like slow fire beginning on the lips and then surging into her groin and back through her heart, through her whole being.

She felt her knees giving way, felt herself opening and dissolving, felt herself taken over by desire. He took her hand. She felt him guide it. She felt the hard, hot cock with the start of moisture at its end and she dropped onto her knees and took it in her mouth, sucking like a starving calf at its mother's udder.

She felt him raising her, pulling her to her feet, allowed him to guide her into the drawing room where he had never been, in the house which he had never entered, to a sofa where he made her sit while he threw down his jacket and dragged off his trousers, tearing away the sweater and the shirt, every garment until he was as naked as she was under the wide open robe.

He came to her in that room lit only by the street lights with the policeman standing inches outside the window, with her husband asleep in bed upstairs; in her own drawing room where cabinet ministers and peers of the realm and bankers and newspaper editors and heads of industry had been and sat and talked and considered problems of State and planned the future.

He came to her and rammed his desperation into her and made her cry out and made the tears pour down her face, tears of relief and joy, tears of unspent grief. And her inner tide rose quickly to meet him, and he spoke to

239

her in his low husky voice, told her what he knew she wanted and needed, told her what he was doing to her, told her that she was his and not for any other, told her he would not let anyone have her, told her she was forbidden to anyone but himself.

And she sobbed softly and whispered her need and her longing and told him how she had died again while he was away and how she dreamed of his cock inside her and its silky hardness and its round headed bulk spurting its divine cloud of milky stars into her dark universe. Giving her life. And the will to live. And the searching touch of him inside her was a key turning in a lock that let light into her whole body. And the light ignited this flaming, bursting sensation of being alive but alive only for one purpose, to die under him. She let him consume her like a dry leaf in a fire.

His will powered her. And she felt his will and his love as indivisible from God's love. And in her moved the immense force of that surrender that comes from giving up self, letting go and letting go of every last whisper of restraint, of every last spark of rebellion, of resistance, of ego, dissolving the boundaries, becoming one with something else. She was leaking her soul into the universe, giving up being one, giving up being separate from God or life or love or the other that was her love. Her mind knew that everything else is delusion, that there is only this, this merging, this giving, this sacrifice of self, through this one perfect eternal moment of presence and present now. Past and future were irrelevant. For Catherine, this moment brought annihilation of one knowledge and an explosion of new knowing. She moved irrevocably into another universe, another existence, another way of being. She would never be the same.

They lay together, exhausted. The stored energy, built to an explosive force during their separation, had poured out in those few minutes that had seemed an eternity to both of them. She had looked in his eyes in their moment of climax and known everything, known that for him too this was no transient physical passion, known there had been an irrevocable step taken, known there was an indelible bond of spirit and flesh that no intellectual exercise would allow them to escape. Known how desperately he needed her, loved her, yes, if love was the word for that unslakeable thirst for union with another's soul, even if he did not yet know it himself. And that he too would never be the same.

49

The phone was ringing endlessly. She reached out her hand and silenced it, turning her head on the pillow and dragging the receiver over to her ear.

'Hello?' Her voice was sleepy, drugged. The clock showed nine fifteen. Where was James? Why had he not answered the phone? She remembered, he had gone to bed early last night. He must have had to be up early, had already left. 'Hello?' she said again.

'Catherine. Can I talk to you, please?'

She recognized the correct voice with the Scots terseness. 'David. I'm sorry. You caught me oversleeping. I had a late night.'

Armstrong coughed. 'Not Annabel's again.' It was more a statement than a question.

'Insomnia, actually. Something woke me up.'

He said, 'Would it be very inconvenient if I were to come around to your house now for a few minutes? There's something I ought to tell you. Without delay. It will only be a few minutes.'

He sounded formal and very reserved. Almost as if he were planning to arrest her. She cleared her throat. 'David, dear. Will you give me twenty minutes to get myself up? I'm still in bed. You wakened me.'

'I'm sorry. I forgot you work the night shift. I'll be there at 9.45. Will that suit you?'

She agreed and he hung up. He was strangely unfriendly, she thought. But, she had barely time to wonder about what Armstrong wanted or why he was being so prim, in the rush to bathe and dress and have some breakfast before he arrived.

He refused her offer of coffee in the kitchen. She took him into the drawing room. The cushions on the sofa nearest the door were flattened and the long tie of her red silk robe lay across them. Memory hit her like the heat of a tropical airfield after a long flight from winter. She felt herself soften and moisten, felt that peculiar, will-dissolving languor leaking through her bones.

She saw his eye rest on the sofa and, as if to hide something, she sat on the seat where Angel had loved her. She crossed one knee over the other, waving David to the chair alongside her. He sat nervously, it seemed to Catherine. Was he ill at ease in the elegant room? Was he embarrassed to see her in the house she shared with her husband, guilty about having been her lover? He hadn't touched her today, she realized, had not even given her a peck on the cheek. She had not missed it, but, one would have expected something, surely, some evidence that there had been something between them. He had been warmer yesterday, in the park. Yet she recalled the sense of distance, the look in his eyes when he held her hand and said his goodbye. 'What is it, David?' She was smiling, cheerful, refreshed and energetic in her happiness.

'I'll not beat about the bush. Your friend . . .'

She inclined her head and looked questioningly at him. Whom did he mean?

'Angel.' He saw her expression change and the anxiety come into her eyes. He went on, hesitantly, trying to be concise, 'He . . . you remember I mentioned . . . Well, I didn't mention. I should have. I wasn't very specific, but I should have been. He is suspected of being involved in handling stolen bullion. There's been a warrant out for his arrest, for questioning, pending further inquiries.' He paused for a moment. Her face registered distress. He felt mixed emotions converging in his brain and stopped to examine them, to cool them, lest they tugged at his tongue. Jealousy. Yes. He felt jealousy as he saw that she cared for Angel, loved that scum. And fear for her. And longing to touch her again. To fuck her. He was sitting there doing his duty as a police officer and he wanted to fuck a married woman who was the mistress of a criminal suspect. He felt anger and self-disgust.

He went on, his voice calm and cold, 'I'm afraid he was arrested leaving your house at 3.39 a.m. this morning. He has been taken into custody. Pending further enquiries, charges will . . .'

'David!' She leapt to her feet. She shouted at him, 'Stop talking like a goddamned copper. I thought we were friends. I don't believe I'm hearing this, this official and under the circumstances offensive bureaucratic jargon. Will you stop it and just tell me what happened and why you've come here to tell me anything. Am I a suspect, too? Do you want to arrest me? Are you trying to tell me that I'm going to have to go to court or something? For heaven's sake.'

She was upset, of course. She paced the hearthrug, punching the air with clenched fists as she talked, coming to rest in front of him breathing fast, her sea blue eyes brilliant and opaque. He wriggled in the George III chair and recrossed his legs. His expression and his voice were pained. 'Sit down, Catherine. Don't be angry with me. I'm trying to help you.'

'Then talk like a human being not like a goddamned computer.' She went back to the sofa where Christopher had loved her and sat down with a violent movement, glaring at Armstrong.

He took a deep breath and moved his long body uncomfortably again in the small chair. 'I came here for two reasons, Catherine. One is, I care about you as a friend. I'm attracted to you. I, well, you know what . . . If things were otherwise, I would . . . Well, there's no use in that now.' He paused, swallowed, recrossed his legs again and looked away towards the window for a moment then drew in another deep breath. He looked at her again and his strong features were oddly askew. He went on, slowly, with a visible effort at patience and calm: 'The other is I know you are involved with this man and although I gave you what warning I could yesterday without infringing any law or regulation, I want to tell you now, quite specifically, and unofficially and as a friend, that I recommend you have nothing more to do with him. He is probably a criminal and you are endangering yourself, your marriage, your husband's career, maybe his life and your own for I don't know what you have going with this man.'

She looked down at her hands twisting the red silk sash over the skirt of her black and white dress. She said, gently, 'Thank you, David. I'm very grateful. I'm sorry I shouted at you. I'm sorry about everything. When I saw you yesterday, I was going to give him up.' She smiled at him. 'Yes, really. I was going to let it all go. I hadn't seen him for a month, you see, and I was torn apart wondering why he hadn't . . . why he had left me. I decided not to hope for anything else. Not to wait any more. Not to go on. Then he came last night, in the middle of the night. And it was too much for me. I would have told him. At any other time of day I might have said, No. Go away. This can't work. I'm hurting. I'm going crazy. I don't know who or what you are, except what you tell me. And what I've found out. And the last isn't pretty.' She was looking down again, twisting the silk sash. Her voice dropped to a groan. 'No. It's not pretty.'

'I'm sorry too, Catherine. But it's still not too late to get out of it.' He said it gently and he meant well. She flashed a look at him and bit back the words that would have hurt him. She stood up, smoothing her dress and walked to the window. Looking out into the rainy street, she said, 'How did you know he was here?'

He rose too and stood watching her. He said, 'The constable on the door recognized him. We had put out an alert for him and a description only yesterday. There were mug shots on the board. The PC recognized him and sent for a patrol car. They waited until he came out. I'm sorry you had to be involved. I would not have allowed him to be arrested here, if I had known.'

She spun round as if to shoot him. Her words were hard

bullets flying at him. 'If you had known? Didn't you know? Were you not involved? Who took the decision to arrest him? Who put out that warrant? Don't tell me you knew nothing at all about this when you had lunch with me yesterday.' Her voice was rising again. She walked towards him. Something was building up in her. He thought she might hit him. She stopped in front of him. She seemed small and fragile and vulnerable and tired. Suddenly very quiet, she said, 'Where is he?'

'He's in police custody in the West End. He's talked to his solicitor. He'll have to go to the Magistrates' Court and then maybe they'll release him on conditional bail.'

'Maybe?'

'Probably.' He looked down at her and felt pity. For her. For himself.

She said, 'I want to see him.'

'Catherine, you shouldn't do that. I won't let you.' He put out his hands and held her shoulders gently.

He felt rather than saw her stiffen. She looked at him with eyes that were as hard and cold as gun barrels and her voice was as brittle as the click of a trigger. She stepped back as if to take aim at him. She said, 'I intend to see him even if I have to ask the Home Secretary to intervene. You may care to help me by arranging it yourself.'

She seemed to be staring right into his brain. He could feel her eyes penetrating his head. He sighed, 'All right, I'll take you there. But you mustn't be long. And I don't want anyone to hear of this, least of all your friend. If he asks, you tell him the Home Secretary got you in. Not me. Okay?' He gave her a hard look, then smiled a sad, closed-mouthed smile. He went to her and dropped a light kiss on her mouth. 'I could have loved you, Catherine,' he said and turned away. Feeling swelled his chest and blocked his throat.

'Thank you,' she said, and blushed. 'I'll just phone the office and get my coat.' She went out quickly. That left him respite to sort out his emotions.

* * *

He went in with her. The sergeant in charge was very respectful and arranged quickly for her to see the prisoner in an interview room. He did not ask what it was about. The Commander said he would not wait for Mrs Waring.

She was in the interview room already when they brought him in. He wore the clothes she had last seen him in but he was unshaven, with a dark shadow around his jaw and he looked pale and sick.

They had not told him who was waiting to see him. The constable ushered him in and left, locking the door behind him. Angel stood by the door with his back to it. His eyes seemed darker than ever in his pale face. They stared at her, unfathomable yet overflowing with feeling. She saw his desire for her and his fear of her. His fear of her knowing him as he really was, not knowing what she already knew. She saw he was appalled that she should be there.

She went to him, her arms extended, wrapping them around him, burying her face in his soft suede jacket. He was rigid and ungiving. He patted her shoulder, detached himself from her arms, and moved from her, moved towards the table. He half sat on the edge of it and rubbed his hand over his jaw. He said in a low voice, 'What are you doing here, Catherine? This is no place for a government minister's wife.' There was an edge of bitterness to the last few words.

'They took you as you left my house. I was told about it. I had to come here.' She went towards him again and put her arms around him, hugging him. 'Christopher. What can I do for you? Can I put up bail? Can I bring you something, some clothes, something to eat or drink?' She pleaded with him, gentle and soft, looking into his face.

He laughed a short dry laugh. His voice rising with an arrogance and bitterness she did not know in him, he said, 'You can't do anything, Catherine. You can't do anything for me. I'm no good and you can't do anything to help me. People like me have to help themselves. The world doesn't owe me. You don't owe me. I take what I can. I'm a doer not one of the done to. I'll get out of this.

They've got nothing on me. They're trying it on.' He pushed her arms away and moved away from the table. 'Go, Catherine,' he said. 'Go back to your life and forget about me. I come from a different world. I've got different values. You can't help me because I'm not your kind and you'll never understand me. You deserve better.' He gestured towards the door and turned his back on her.

She ran to him, pulling him round to face her. Her fear that she would lose him had never been greater. She said, breathlessly, 'I won't let you go because of this, because of anything, Christopher. I care for you so much my life hangs on it.'

He put both hands out and cupped her head. He looked gently into her face. 'I won't let you, Catherine. It's time to say goodbye. Finish. I don't want you involved in my mess. I don't want you to spoil your life.'

She pulled his head down and kissed him desperately. She felt his response, felt him want her, felt him holding her to him as his arms slid down to her waist and her buttocks. He held her then in that kiss as if it were the only thing holding him to life. Then he released her and looked long into her eyes.

'Be sensible, Catherine.' His eyes were black as forest pools. She saw her blond reflection in them.

She said quietly, 'I love you. I love you more than life. Don't send me away. I'm prepared to go through anything to be with you.'

He pushed her away and said, 'You don't understand men like me. I'll always be doing something risky. That's how I get my kicks. Life's too boring otherwise. I can't stop doing it. It's me. I can't change myself.'

She caught one of his hands in both her own and brought it to her lips. She said, 'I'm not going to live without you. I'm not going back to that, to walking around as if my life is a dead child inside me. You've no idea what that grief is. To be unloved. To not love those you should love. To be lost in the world that finds you pretty and sexy and important. To have people wanting you, as if you were a toy or a sweet or a piece of jewellery, to enjoy as if you had no feelings yourself. To feel life is over, that there isn't anything more, that that's it. Well, you saved me from that. Oh yes, I still wish I was dead, sometimes, if I think you are with another woman, or, when you were away . . . for this past month, not knowing where you were or what you were doing, not knowing if I would ever see you again. Then, last night I knew what wanting life was again. Feeling God loves me after all. Feeling I'm not cast out of paradise. Not being punished for some ancient sin. Not . . . left out of happiness that others have.'

She held his shoulders and shook them gently. She smiled but there were tears in her eyes and in her voice. 'Oh, my darling love. Am I an embarrassment? You don't want me to love you? Do you just want me for excitement too? Am I just a rich bitch for you to fuck and have your sense of power and use and cast aside to go back to your whores?'

She stopped, aghast at having gone so far and said so much. Too far, too much. But, his face was open, was touched by something, by some wonder, like an orphaned child who finds that after all there is Christmas. There is love. His face seemed to crumple and he swept her to him and pushed his face into her neck. He held her close, her face in his shoulder, rocking her.

Then he held her away from him and spoke in a strong, practical voice. 'Catherine. I want you to go, now. I want you to forget you ever saw me here. I want you to just get on with your life. I'll come and see you when they let me out. It won't be long. My solicitor is working on it. And I have friends in the police.' He gave her a doubtful look. 'I don't want you involved. But I will see you. I want to see you. Just don't get into this mess. Please. Think of your own reputation.'

She said, miserably, 'I don't want a reputation if it stops me doing what I believe is right. If it stops me living my life, or helping you.'

He had his hand on the door knob. He spoke firmly and coolly. 'Now, I want you to go out. They'll come and get me and take me back to the cells.' He pressed a bell at the side of the door and went back towards the table.

He sat on one of the hard wooden chairs facing the door.

She started towards him, but he shook his head. She heard the key in the lock, rattling, that prison sound. The police constable opened the door. He ushered Catherine through. She turned her head to look at Angel. He put one finger to his mouth, kissed it and blew her the kiss.

50

Michael O'Leary reached another six pack of stout from the big old refrigerator and dumped it on the kitchen table. The four men sitting around the old scrubbed pine table passed the pack from one to the other, each taking a can. For a moment, the small room's smoke-thickened atmosphere was enlivened by the pop and hiss of opening cans. The men wished each other Slainte and swigged from their cans, wiping their mouths with the backs of their hands and grunting their pleasure.

'Keep the beer off the plans, boys,' O'Leary said gruffly. He swung himself awkwardly down into the chair at the head of the table that almost filled the room. His stick fell to the tiled floor with a clatter and the young lad sitting next to him reached out and picked it up. He placed it carefully against the side of the table with a deferential glance at O'Leary.

O'Leary leaned out across the table to point with a finger at the large map of the River Thames. His clean well-manicured hands argued with the rest of his appearance. A monogrammed signet ring decorated the little finger of his right hand, legacy of his birthright as the heir to a comfortable Irish fortune. He'd been disinherited in his father's will after the Cuba business. His younger brother now ruled the estate and organized the local hunt and other shannanigins.

O'Leary invariably wore an old pea jacket over cords and a moth-eaten Shetland sweater, except in summer when he sometimes left off the jacket. At this moment, the jacket hung from the back of his chair and he reached back his arm suddenly, groping into the pocket to bring out a pencil. The pencil increased his reach over the map which saved him standing on his gammy leg.

One of the boys slid the map down the table towards him a bit. They were a good bunch, these boys. None of them were local. They were all drafted in from Ulster for this special event, their expertise far surpassing anything the locals could offer for the job O'Leary had planned to take place in two weeks on the River Thames.

Four pairs of eyes watched as O'Leary's pencil drew a line along the river's course. The line started near Greenwich on the South Side and went upstream to Hammersmith.

'Now then.' O'Leary looked around the group to make sure he had their keenest attention. 'The dummy run will have to be carried out under conditions which may be different from those on the day. We can't duplicate the tide and we cannot forecast the winds, either.'

'Can you calculate it on a mathematical model?' It was the big lad with the round face who had spoken. His sing song Donegal accent gave the words an innocence that belied the lad's cleverness. This boy was one of the IRA's top explosives men. His bombs had the exact impact intended. That was why he had been chosen for this job. O'Leary wanted an explosion that was of maximum precision.

O'Leary grinned at the lad whose name was Donald McGuinness. He said, 'I can't but maybe you can.'

There were low laughs around the table. The lad blushed. 'I can try.' He ran a hand through his rather silky short cropped dark hair.

O'Leary resumed his pencilling of the course the barge would take, back down from Hammersmith, terminating at Westminster. He chuckled. 'We don't have to bother about her after that.' He drew a cross in the river that

250

would put her some fifteen metres out from and abreast of the House of Commons terrace.

'What time are you planning for the blast?' A small wiry man of about fifty with a face like a squirrel, sitting at the opposite end of the table from O'Leary, spoke from behind nicotined fingers and a freshly lit cigarette.

'We'll have to wait for the order papers on that, Patrick. That gives us less room to time the operation exactly, of course.' He looked over at McGuinness. He added, 'We want her to go up just as the Bill gets into its first reading.'

'There might be some people on the terrace.' The young blond man who had a squint to his right eye was looking lopsidedly at O'Leary.

'We're not going to have any casualties on this operation, Seamus,' O'Leary said. Looking at McGuinness, he went on, 'It will be up to you, Donald, to get the exact size of the blast right. Don't forget, there's a hospital on the other embankment. We don't want any outraged protests about windows being blown in there. If the distance from the bridges and the distance from the House of Commons terrace is kept to exactly, we should achieve our result without causing a backlash against a legitimate protest movement.' He smiled. 'This is not an act of war, remember, boys. This is a scientifically assisted political protest.' His cackle turned into a cough. Even his pipe was getting a bit too much for old O'Leary, these days, he thought. The others waited for him to stop coughing.

'I don't see how you can be sure of getting that distance right, Michael.' The boy who had picked up O'Leary's stick leaned forward on his elbows. He had a perpetually worried expression which seemed to accentuate the gravity of everything he said.

O'Leary smiled with what seemed like relish. 'Don't worry about that, Peter, me lad. That's going to be my responsibility. I'm going to be the driver of the boat towing the barge. I'll need one assistant who will cast her adrift at the exact right moment. Any of you can volunteer.' He grinned his challenge around the group.

There was silence and then the worried looking boy, Peter, said, 'I'll come with you, Michael.'

'Good.' O'Leary reached over and patted the boy's shoulder. 'That's the spirit. Now.' He looked round the table at the others. 'Let's get down to the serious business. Donald, you can give me your calculations on the tide any time you're ready. The tables are over there near the toaster.'

He tossed small notepads and ballpoints around to his four companions. He looked at his watch. It was just past 9 p.m. He cleared his throat and grinned at them. 'Let's aim to get to the pub before she closes.'

51

'He's no longer here.'

'Thank you.' Catherine started to put the 'phone down. Then as an afterthought she said, 'Oh, when . . . how long ago since he . . .'

'Just a minute.' There was a pause. 'Ah, yes, two days ago. He was just in the one night. All right?' The officer's voice was chirpy.

'Thanks.' Catherine put the receiver down. She felt a weight gathering between her breasts. So he was free. And he had not called her. It was 9.50 p.m. and she was at her desk in Covent Garden. Everyone else had gone home and she had stayed, writing, making transatlantic calls. Now, she dialled Christopher's house. No answer. She rang the Sirocco. It was early but someone would probably be there.

A woman voice answered Catherine's question. 'We're not expecting him until much later, not 'till about one.'

She left her name and her home number in case he should call in. Then she picked up her briefcase and her coat, turned out the master light and went home.

James was at the House. She scrambled herself some eggs and took a tray to her bed. She ate and then lay, flicking through magazines, restless, unable to concentrate.

At 1 a.m. she rang the Sirocco again. She was told he had been given her message and she left another saying she wanted to hear from him that night, that it was urgent. Soon she fell into a light doze with her reading light on.

*　　*　　*

Something wakes her. Her bedside clock says 3.05 a.m. She feels jolted and suddenly alert, her heart beating too fast, fear in her nostrils. Did the phone ring? Could it have been the doorbell? Did James close a door sharply?

Catherine rises from her bed, naked, her hair rumpled, yesterday's make up still on her face, her mascara smudged by sleep. She dials the Sirocco. No, he has not been in all evening. Call tomorrow. No message? No. No message. She dials his home. No answer. She wonders about his mother's place. She has the number from AP Investigations; but she can't call there so late. Besides, instinct says otherwise. He is somewhere else. Where?

She starts to act now as if on a pre-arranged plan, a schedule, as if she is getting up in the middle of the night to catch a 'plane. She moves briskly and methodically, her head clear, her mind fixed on every act as though she already knows the consequences of all that she will do tonight.

She brushes her hair, repairs her make up. She slips a black trenchcoat on over her nakedness, takes a huge red cashmere shawl and wraps it around her head and shoulders, carries her shoes downstairs, puts them on in the hall, finds her keys and lets herself out.

The policeman sheltering from the soft rain under the porch is startled as she comes out. She nods, greets him. Tells him she can't seem to sleep tonight, she's going for a drive. She starts the Aston. The roar seems to shatter the night's fine texture, to tear the web of moisture holding the air in place. James: she watches his window

253

for a sudden light. Nothing. She drives slowly out of the street and turns towards Victoria Street.

Amber lights from wet asphalt, mingled with the reflected colours of shop signs in blues, reds, greens and white faze her tired eyes. She drives past Hyde Park Corner and up Park Lane, going fast and easy in the empty streets. She swings into Mayfair, crosses Oxford Street, clipping the amber lights, never slowing to find her route, going like a homing bird to Devonshire Mews.

His house is dark, silent, empty and shut. She creeps into the space near his door and stops her engine, dowses her lights. She uses the car phone to call his number, rolls down her window and hears it ring and ring and ring inside the house. She gets out of her car and rings the doorbell, uses the knocker. Somewhere close to the door, the dog barks, then she hears his ferocious deep woof and his paws striking the door. She steps back, looks at the house. Where is he? When will he come? He is not away. He is not far. She is sure. She thinks of the policewoman in Quebec Street and closes her mind. She takes the cashmere shawl and wraps it around her head and shoulders. She sits on his doorstep. Why not sit in the car she thinks. Why not stay dry? She wants to be close to him. His doorstep is the closest she can be. She hears the dog again and talks to it. It quiets and snuffs under the door to scent her. Friend or foe. Friend. Always friend.

She looks at her watch. It's almost 4 a.m. He must come soon. He must come soon. She closes her eyes and thinks of falling asleep in the snow. Thinking of death again. Now thinks of the gun. In her mind she opens the car, unlocks the glove compartment. The gun is there, wrapped in a silk scarf. Loaded. Yes, loaded. Why wait to load when you need to fire?

She leans her head against the post and tucks her knees up. The rain has stopped. The air is moist and cool. She closes her eyes. She feels drowsy. Her shoulders are warm under the shawl, but her legs are cold. She tucks her knees under her chin under the trenchcoat. She falls into a doze, drifts into sleep. She doesn't hear the car come into the mews, doesn't see its light swing, picking out her shape huddled as if dead on the step. She does not waken when he comes running over the cobbles, doesn't hear him gasp or see his fear.

He kneels by her. Fear in his heart. They have killed her. This is their revenge for what he has done to them. How did they know of her? His secret passion. His love. He stares at her with horror and grief. He whispers to himself, to her, but she cannot hear him. 'Oh my baby, my precious baby, my love,' then he shakes her, he's touching her, looking for moisture, looking for blood. Nothing. 'Catherine, Catherine.'

She hears his voice, feels him shaking her. She is so still and so cold and deep asleep, so tired, sleeping at last. She is dreaming, she is on a night flight from New York, sleeping in her seat, cold, still. Don't wake me.

She groans and her eyelids flutter. Is she drugged? Is she poisoned? Is she all right? 'Catherine?' He orders her awake. He stands up and leans over her. He unlocks his door and opens it. He pulls her to her feet. She puts her arms around his neck, sleepy, trusting. She murmurs his name. He lifts her, carries her up the stairs into the house.

He drops her on a sofa that is also a bed, made up and ready for sleep. He pulls her coat open. He looks on her body for wounds. He strokes her neck, her breasts, her belly, her thighs. 'Catherine.'

She groans and opens her eyes. She puts her arms around his neck. She pulls him onto her, kisses his face, his lips, reaches for his cock, strokes the stiffening thing under the taut trousers. He tears open his trousers, he enters her, aroused, afraid, so glad she is alive. He goes on and on and on as if he cannot stop, pulling her to him, his arm squeezing her buttocks together to tighten her sleeping muscles around him. She comes awake, alive, cries out and writhes under him. He brings her to climax and lets go, lets go, lets everything go into the void, into the eternal darkness, his mind suddenly released from the madness, clear and sharp and free for a moment from all desire and need, then falling on her, his eyes sliding up into their lids like a dead man's.

255

He falls into a sleep and she lies, holding him, fully aware, fully awake, knowing everything in her heart as if it were written on the wall across the room and she could read it. Knowing she cannot leave this man.

*   *   *

Catherine was awake first as the light grew in strength through the uncurtained window. The dog was sleeping on the rug beside them. Christopher lay face downward across her, his weight pinning her: but she would not move, would not break this spell and the marvel of being with him, sleeping with him, letting his wandering soul supervene in her mind over his body, feeling him to be like a great light surrounding them both.

She looked around the room. It was just one big room with a kitchen at one end and a bath, she could see the shower curtain through the open door, at the other. There were no pictures on the walls. Another sofa lay against the opposite wall behind a white fur rug and a glass coffee table. A telephone sat on the rug.

There was little else in the room apart from a large TV, video and Hi Fi unit under the window. A long row of built in closets lined the back wall of the room. So this was where he lived. When he was at home.

He snapped quickly into wakefulness, looking at her with misgiving. She could see he felt insecure that she was here, in his solitary place. His secret self was exposed as much as this impersonal room could expose anyone.

She stroked the springy head. 'I love your hair, Angel'

His eyes held disbelief. He shook his head, then a small smile forming, said, 'You like my hair?' He stared at her, bemused, then his eyes hardened and he said, bitterly, 'Black man's hair.' A child's misery from racial jibes flickered between them.

She caught the hair in both hands and pulled his face down onto hers. She kissed his lips and felt his response, felt him harden and in a moment he was inside her again.

*   *   *

He went to make her tea and to find her a towel for her bath. They showered and dressed and said little to each other in this strange departure into domestic life. He was awkward and gruff with her. It was as if he were only sure of himself with her when he had her down under his cock, when he was her lover. Everything else left him inadequate. He was not sure how to behave.

They sat together. She wore a towel and he was dressed in a fresh pair of jeans and a sweat shirt. He had walked the dog and bought newspapers while she showered and soon, he said, he wanted to make some phone calls. It was still only 7 a.m. She wondered about James. Would she meet him on the way in if she left it any later? She thought she should go. But there was too much unresolved between them, too much unease and she felt, on his part, regret. She thought he felt violated by her presence. She had intruded into his secrecy.

She stood up and let the towel fall and he looked away from her naked loveliness. She felt rumpled, had no brush for her hair or cream for her face. She reached for her trenchcoat and slipped it on. He looked at her and it seemed he wanted to say something. She found her shoes and put her bare feet into them, then took her shawl from the bed and wrapped it around her head. She smiled at him.

There was a moment's complete stillness between them. It was as if something hung in the balance, something unsaid which would decide the future consciously or unconsciously, would force them to go along some path, make some choice.

He said, 'You're leaving now?' He did not get up from where he sat, his legs stretched out under the coffee table, his head resting against the sofa cushions. It was as if he had not the will to move.

She took her decision then, took events into her own hands. She took the shawl away from her head and stepped towards him. She sat beside him on the sofa, perching on the edge of the seat, and looked at him, smiling, free at that moment of all anguish and pain and desire.

He looked back at her and she saw in his eyes that warmth of love that she had waited for.

She said, 'No, Angel. I'm not going, yet. There's something we have to talk about.'

52

'I might be going to prison, Catherine,' he said, 'if they make this bullion thing stick.'

'How good a chance do they have?' She asked him gently, but her eyes focused keenly on his face. She did not ask him if they had good cause. Her instinct for drawing him out had been right. She had told him she had to know more, had to have some real insight into his life. She could not go on imagining and fearing the worst. He had responded. But his trust was a wild fox.

He stood up and walked over to the window. 'It depends,' he said, looking out into the bright morning mews. He would not face her.

She said, softly, 'Come back here, Angel. Tell me.'

He half turned his head and said, 'There are some police who want to get me. For anything. Whatever they can. I'm not their number one pop star. They'd like to see me out of business.'

'Why?'

He laughed and turned to face her. She could not read his face, contrasted against the brilliant window, but she heard the violence in his husky voice. He said, 'It's the story of my life. I've had nothing but trouble all along. I've done nothing but fight for my survival.'

Again, she said, 'Why?'

'Because I made some mistakes early on. I started out

badly. I've had to cut a few corners.' He laughed. It was a brief, angry sound.

She went to him and put her arms around him. 'Does everything have to be bad? Do you always have to lose? Can't things change? Can't you turn around and leave the past where it is, walk on into tomorrow?'

He gave her a quick peck on the mouth and his eyes were thoughtful, looking over her shoulder as if at someone else. He said, 'I have to make a living, Catherine. You can't make money, not any real money, by being honest.'

She pulled him from the window back to the sofa and made him sit. He was uncomfortable, wanting to get up and go off into his day. He looked tired. She realized he had had, perhaps, two hours' sleep. She had at least napped at home for a couple of hours and again on his doorstep.

He put his hands on the back of her neck over the silky hair and searched her face, his eyes coming to rest at last on hers. He said, quietly, 'You've got to realize something about me, Catherine. I like being a crook. I enjoy it. I enjoy outwitting authority, the law. It's my game. It's what makes life exciting.'

She looked back into his seemingly open face, not knowing how much to believe. Not knowing what he was really saying. Not knowing what being a crook really meant. Half the nation fiddled its taxes or fiddled its expenses. Was that being crooked? She thought it was. But it only became criminal after a certain scale had been tipped. It was quantity not quality of behaviour. In Christopher's case, she asked, what did being a crook involve?

He said, 'Catherine. A nice girl like you shouldn't be with a man like me. You should be with nice people. You have your nice life, your husband, your magazine. I have my life and I'm a crook. I don't break laws but I bend them. I do things that, well . . . I like to see what I can get away with.'

She looked steadfastly at him and said, 'Women love all kinds of men; murderers, thieves, fraudsters. They don't choose who they love, Angel. They love. And I love you. So don't try to persuade me you're not worth it. Don't try to convince me to go and look for a nice little barrister or a banker or a Baronet to give me happiness. It's not as if being out of the right class or background, or being nice, can bring happiness. Loving someone is what makes one happy. I love you as if I've never loved a man before. And I've been in love. I've been sexually magnetized, hooked on a man. I've even married a man.' She smiled a wry, twisted little smile. 'That was my main mistake,' she said, looking down.

She looked up again, the window light full on her face dazzling her. His eyes were unreadable under their heavy lids. She went on, 'I've never loved like this before. I've never had my head blown off by sex. I've never gone into near mystic trances or felt heaven open like I do when you come and waves of light ripple up my body. I don't know what it means, but it seems worth more than respectability. It seems to be more important than things like bending or not bending the law. Maybe it's important enough to hold onto even when things are a lot worse than bending the law. I don't know. I don't know if I'm strong enough to take the pain of losing you to anything, whether it's prison or another woman, or death. But all I know is I'm not going to lose you to a sense of bourgeois respectability, to some silly idea that there are nice people that live separate lives from the rest and that I belong with them, whoever they are.'

He was smiling, happy, almost like a child being given a treat. His face had colour and his eyes were shining. He took her hand and held it to his lips. She went on, 'I'm not giving you up because of what you are. You are what I love. Therefore I love what you are.'

He kissed her very tenderly and warmly on her lips. Then he stood up and pulled her to her feet. He said, 'I'll see you soon, Catherine.' He gave her a squeeze and then abruptly let her go, turning her shoulders towards the stairs and guiding her gently towards them.

He let her go down on her own. She heard him start to use the telephone as she went down the stairs. Out in the street she was suddenly conscious of her nakedness under the black trenchcoat. She pulled the shawl around her head and made it to the car without encountering anyone. Miraculously she did not have a ticket.

She gunned the Aston through the morning traffic and was on the home straight down Birdcage Walk within twenty minutes of leaving him. It was eight-thirty. Outside the house in Queen Anne's Gate, the police shift had changed, mercifully, and it was a different constable who greeted her this morning from the one who had seen her leave during the night.

She walked into an empty house. She was hungry and went first into the kitchen to get her breakfast on a tray to take upstairs and have while she dressed. James's dirty breakfast dishes were in the sink and not the dishwasher as usual. He must have been in a rush. She found the explanation in a note leaning against the kettle. It said:

Darling,
The PM rang at the crack of dawn and ordered me to Number Ten by 8.30. The Sec of State made a frightful ass of himself the other day in Question Time on the SLRS and I think his head is on the block. Wish me luck and you may be dining with the new Secretary of State for the Environment tonight. I'll ring you at the office to let you know the result.
Love,
James.

Catherine took the note and sat down at the table to read it again. 'Oh God,' she groaned, and dropped her head onto her arms. James a Cabinet Minister, maybe soon to be Prime Minister, while his wife was the lover of a self-proclaimed crook.

*

261

53

The hedges were full of hawthorn, and white stitchworts tangled with early bluebells among the lengthening grasses along the steep banks lining the lane. The ebullient rush of her departure from London along the M40 had gradually slowed as the roads grew increasingly winding and narrow. This lane seemed to be a maze, switching and turning on itself, the hedgerows too high to see over. Only the curving line of oaks and beeches and the telephone wires seemed to prove it went somewhere.

She passed the cottage before she realized she had reached it. There was a moment's space where hedges were lower and clipped, some topiary, a giant peacock, she thought, and a monkey tree and a gate set low between them.

Brenda's directions had been accurate. Catherine drove on looking for a turning place. It was two miles before she found one. She had reached the village, such as it was, a shop, a pub, a church and some scattered cottages, a telephone kiosk and the driveway of the big house marked by high gateposts of golden Cotswold stone surmounted by winged griffons.

The church clock read seven minutes past three. She was twenty three minutes early. The road had been easier than Brenda had said. Besides, Brenda would not have realized how Catherine's need for speed would cut her journey time. She parked in front of the shop and went in. She had come empty handed but now she found a box of chocolates she thought Brenda would like. She bought some ice cream and biscuits and a jar of ginger in syrup. She had not given Brenda much warning and she wanted to save her the embarrassment of having nothing to offer her for tea.

She put the gifts into the car and then wandered around

the open space that was the hamlet's centre. The afternoon was still and silent. The sun drifted among large lugubrious clouds. Catherine had not been in the country for months. The last time had been the previous September when she and James had spent the weekend in Wiltshire with Lord and Lady Chorton. She felt suddenly aware of her city tensions and preoccupations and adrenalin driven pulse. She seemed to vibrate with a jarring, discordant energy. She started breathing deeply, letting herself slip down a gear, letting her mind find a level closer to the country's vegetative patience; to that sense of cycles of seasons and growth that cannot be hurried by mind's intervention.

She walked, without real purpose, towards the church and then through its gate arched by yews and down a yew-lined avenue towards the heavy Gothic door. It was open and she walked through it into the still presence of a timeless certainty. Into a sense of something always being, through the transience of lives passing in and out from font to altar to grave.

She felt suddenly tired and sat at the end of the last pew nearest the door. The stained glass window at the east end depicted a crucified Christ. Catherine gazed at it and as she did so the sun broke through the drifting clouds and lit the world outside, highlighting the window's brilliant blues and golds and reds.

She felt an immense presence of moment, of the now, of being without past or future. She sat unmoving for some ten minutes before becoming aware that time was, once more, demanding she move on. She rose and went to the door. As she did, a country housewife came bustling in, smiling, rosy, breathless, carrying a huge scented bouquet of white and purple lilacs. She was about Catherine's age. Catherine smiled at her as she passed and felt a sudden pang of envy for that life, for the routines and simple duties of an ordinary life. She did not know how or where she herself would find such contentment. Or peace. Or simplicity. Or solutions to her dilemma.

She walked slowly up the path under the yews.

The sun was behind a cloud and the air suddenly chill. A crumbling headstone close to the path caught her attention and she went to it. She read it.

'To Catherine, beloved wife of Samuel James, born January 1729 died April 1748.' Catherine felt sadness for the other Catherine's short life. She looked at the small mound and thought of the poor bones beneath the earth. The grave was overgrown and the headstone leaning. Catherine picked a daisy and put it at the headstone's foot. As she did so, she felt a sharp impulse of joy that seemed to come from outside time. Perhaps, after all, the other Catherine's life had been complete, a story neatly told. A happy life. She went from the churchyard full of intensity for life.

As she climbed back into her car the sun suddenly spilled warmth over her and lit the village. She drove quickly back along the winding lane, feeling less doubt now about her meeting with Brenda. She had rung Brenda last night before dinner and invited herself down for the afternoon. She had not told her why she was coming, had not given a clue of the enormous moral dilemma that had been holding her down for the past two weeks since James's promotion. She was still unsure of whether she could tell Brenda anything about her problems, let alone receive the guidance she craved and which no one else could offer her.

Gerald had been some help, but he had dropped the problem straight back in Catherine's lap. 'You have to fight this one on your own battlefield, Tsarina. You know you have a decision to make and until you know what is right and wrong you are not going to be able to make it. No one else can make a moral decision for you.'

'But I do know what's right and wrong, Gerry. I just don't know what the right decision is. Do I leave James now that he's got his Cabinet job and the green light to stand as Prince Regent in a possible leadership election next year? Is it fair?'

'Fair to whom?'

'To James, of course, silly. Will his chances be damaged by a divorce? It's not so much the actual divorce as the emotional and material upheaval at a time when he needs all his wits about him, with the SLRS and everything else. Then there's Daddy. Daddy will make life difficult, too.'

Gerald said, 'The very fact that I have to ask you who your decision would be unfair to, should make you think, Tsarina. You say you must be fair to James. But have you thought about what's fair to Catherine?'

She had not heard that. Not listened to it. It came back now though and made her think as she navigated the twisting lane. She had said to him, 'And I have to ask myself what I'm wanting a divorce for. Christopher may not want me, except as a mistress. He may prefer me unattainable. Perhaps he likes the idea of a lover who has a political husband. How do I know what he thinks or wants? He doesn't talk about it. He. . . .'

Gerald had stopped that train of thought abruptly: 'Tsarina. You can't have both. You don't have to marry Christopher, but you can't stay married to James and go on with Christopher. It's potentially too dangerous. Imagine the scandal if anyone found out. It would just take one diary story. Do you have enemies? Of course. And James has plenty. Well, imagine the possibilities. Yes, you have, I know. It's a choice, Tsarina. A risk both ways. But you must look into your heart and find the answer. Your heart is, if you like, your unconscious mind, another part of your intelligence. It knows the truth your conscious mind can't know and that truth is what's best for you. Not James. Not your father. You, Catherina. You. This is your life and your happiness. You come first. Even before Christopher.'

She had looked at him in wonderment. She knew what her heart wanted, but the moral burden was still too great. She could not release herself from her sense of obligation, or responsibility. Could not put herself first if it would hurt others.

And so she had come to Brenda. To Brenda who had taught her her moral code. Brenda who had brought her up, who had been both a mother, a governess and her spiritual tutor. Brenda who had dominated her African

265

childhood, who had taught her there were no racial superiors, only equals before God. Brenda who had, even while she was at boarding school in England, always been there, as her father's housekeeper, to give advice. To be her mentor and her guide. Brenda who had woven the ethical fabric of her life, who was the author of her morality. Only Brenda could help her untangle this net that held her. Only Brenda could free her to give herself permission to do what Gerald had said she should do.

The cottage, which Brenda had named Heaven's Door, stood about a hundred metres back from the lane. It was a white-walled, timbered, square-fronted cottage with a central door, a low thatched roof and a small garage converted from an outhouse to its right. Catherine pulled the Aston into the grassy driveway behind Brenda's little estate car. She picked up her packages from the passenger seat and went along a small gravel path that ran under the window to the front door.

Brenda was waiting with the door open. She held out her arms and folded Catherine in them, holding her a long silent moment. As she stepped back, Catherine saw tears in Brenda's eyes. But they were blinked quickly away behind laughter and exclamations of joy and admiration. It was two years since they had last met on one of Brenda's rare visits to London.

The small hallway was low ceilinged and dark-panelled. It had a bare flagstone floor worn to a dull shine, on which lay some of Brenda's African rugs. It led right through the cottage to the back door which opened onto a large garden. Brenda led Catherine through the cottage and out into the garden.

'Will you be cold if we sit out?' she asked, smiling.

Catherine wore a wool jacket over her pleated skirt and cashmere sweater. She was warm enough now. Brenda led her to a bower, sheltered from the light wind and facing the afternoon sun. As Catherine admitted to driving straight through without lunch, it was decided she would have scrambled eggs and toast before the ice cream and tea.

Catherine followed Brenda back into the cottage and

into the small kitchen to talk to her while she bustled about among what seemed, for a traditional thatched cottage, an extraordinary amount of high tech equipment.

Brenda looked thinner than Catherine remembered, though she had always been slender. She was shorter than Catherine and seemed more so as she wore flat sandals and Catherine her usual high heels. Brenda was in her late fifties, but her hair was barely touched with grey. Worn in a long thick, plait, it was still the same sandy yellow that it had been in Africa, and Brenda denied artifice. 'I'll go grey when it's time to go grey,' she said.

Her face had the faintly yellowed, brittle parchment quality of skin that has been exposed for long years to strong sunlight. But her eyes were still the same honey gold they had been when Brenda had been a young and, Catherine remembered, rather beautiful woman, much pursued by the White Hunters and farmers of Nyere district. There had always been plenty of Land Rovers driving up to the farm at Nanyuki towards sundowner time. Perhaps more during her father's absences than at weekends when he was up from Nairobi. Catherine did not know if Brenda had ever succumbed to any of these pursuers during long nights lit by wood fires and stars. Or why she had not married.

They carried the trays into the garden and Brenda went back for blankets to wrap their legs against the slightly chill May air. Catherine felt that sense of security and comfort that comes even to adults when they go back again to their mothers and receive food and love. She ate her eggs hungrily and sipped her tea and enjoyed ice cream and ginger and some of Brenda's fruit cake, a remembered treat. Brenda had always made the cakes. She said their Kikuyu cook did not have a light enough touch.

Catherine acknowledged her relief at being cosseted and wondered why she had stayed away for so long. It was not that she had to tell Brenda her troubles. It was simply that she could be with the woman who had been almost her mother and bask in her love and slip back into that old, restful relationship of daughter to parent.

267

She became a child again with her father sometimes, as she had that night two weeks ago when she had renounced Christopher: but usually he challenged her too often and provoked her combative side rather than allowing her to indulge her sense of being his loved daughter. She had always fought with him, silent as well as verbal tussles. Her rebellion against going to Oxford had been one of the silent kind. The rowdier kind, they had plenty of those, too. He said it was their Continental blood; fiery spirits of un-English culture always expressing themselves and their emotions. Anyway, she had never fought with Brenda. Brenda had been her loving instructor, ever patient and kind.

Catherine held her face up to the sun and basked while Brenda chatted about the garden and her life in the Cotswolds. She had decided simply to enjoy the visit and forget the problem that had brought her here. She did not see how she could bring her story of sexual passion and sordid night life and marital infidelity into Brenda's quiet garden.

Brenda had come here five years before after deciding she had had enough of London. Sir Arnold had been sorry to lose his housekeeper of so many years but had bought her the cottage and given her a pension and here she was, she said, with her lilacs and her roses and her memories and dreams.

Catherine was suddenly aware of the nostalgia or was it wistfulness in Brenda's voice. She opened her eyes and looked at her. Brenda's face wore a look of hurt and regret masked by pride and courage. Catherine impulsively reached out her hand and touched her. She said, 'What is it, Brenda? Why are you sad?'

'Oh, my dear.' Brenda dashed a tear from the outer corner of her eye with the back of an impatient hand. 'Seeing you has made me realize how lonely my life is . . .' A sob caught in her throat. She leaped up and took hold of the tea pot. 'I'll get some hot water. I won't be a minute.' She ran towards the cottage.

Catherine stared out at the gentle hillside beyond the wooded end of Brenda's well loved garden. Clouds' shadows drifted across like thoughts across her mind. A cuckoo called in the distance. She felt Brenda would tell her something. Had to. She, Catherine, had to persuade Brenda to explain her sadness. But would she, then, after all, tell Brenda what she had come here to tell? She had wanted for weeks to have Brenda's strength and moral voice to guide her. Yet she hesitated because she had felt Brenda would apply her rigid moral code without comprehension of how passion had moved Catherine's understanding of love beyond the reach of ordinary morality.

It was only now that Catherine felt her own ability to take a moral decision had been derailed by so much emotion, that she needed to hear the voice of her childhood, needed to drink again of the well from which her own life's meaning sprang. Perhaps, after all, she would tell her.

Brenda seemed composed as she returned with fresh tea. She sat down and poured them each a cup.

Catherine said, 'I didn't know you were lonely, Brenda.'

'Oh, yes,' Brenda laughed. 'Everyone is lonely sometimes, of course. But I have my darling dogs.' She gestured to the two golden retrievers gambolling at the end of the garden and looked at Catherine with a smile that did not hide her hurt.

She said, 'Oh Brenda, I can't bear this. I didn't know. Won't you come and stay with me for a while? Come and live with us if you like.'

Brenda cut her off with a hand on her arm. 'No, my dear,' she said firmly. 'It's not that easy. Just being with people is not the answer, even people one loves. You see, I made a big mistake once and I can't go back and change it. It's too late. At my age, there comes a moment when you have to admit that it may be too late for some things. And I have. I'm lonely because I suppose I always thought God's love was enough. I never acknowledged that human love is a bridgehead to the divine. And somehow, these days, without love of a man, I seem to have got further away from God. Oh, don't think I've given up going to chapel or my morning prayers or anything like that. It's just some phase of life where I feel in darkness. And it's all my own fault.'

Catherine said, hesitantly, 'Did you ever love a man? Did you ever want to marry anyone, want to be with someone very much?'

'Oh yes.' Brenda was looking towards the sun. She went on, without looking at Catherine who saw only her profile, fine and unblemished by age, firm and dark as bronze against the light, 'I have had my moments, my love affairs and, yes, there was one important love in my life.'

'Why did you . . .?'

'Never marry him?' Now Brenda turned and stared directly into Catherine's eyes. 'I would have,' she said and her voice was deep with restrained emotion. 'I would have, but he thought it was best that we did not. He did not feel good enough for me. He thought he would spoil my life.' She took an enormous breath which became a sigh and turned her eyes back to the horizon.

'Oh, Brenda.' Catherine felt deeply for her. She could not avoid the thought that perhaps she had inherited Brenda's pattern of loving someone who felt unworthy and who would reject her because he could not accept himself.

'Oh, don't worry yourself, Cat. I was happy enough for a few years. It's only now, now that I have so much time and so much love to give, and no one to give it to. No. It's not even that, there are enough people and children in need of love. I could go off somewhere and work for the needy.' She paused and stared blindly towards the sunlit hill where the clouds still played their game of shadows. She said, 'But I can't seem to give love any more. It's got all choked up inside me like an unused fountain. I seem to have stopped loving everything. I'm not able to unblock the fountain. So, not I, nor anyone can drink that life-giving water. You see, love needs to be felt all the time at every level of life. One loves God by loving the grass, the birds, animals, strangers who pass you by. But without one constant source of love in your life you lose the knack of loving.'

She turned again to Catherine and her eyes were tear-filled. Her mouth quavered. She said, 'That's why I'm in this darkness, you see. When one cannot love anything, one cannot be loved back by God. The universe is reciprocal. You love and it flows back to you in a pulse. We get back everything we put in. I just can't put anything in any more.' She gave a small laugh. 'I probably ought to die. That's one of the symptoms of death, spiritual death. Not being able to love. One of the signs that you have gone beyond your time. The body should let go its cargo and die for the spirit to find new life beyond time and space.'

'Oh, surely not!' Catherine cried out. 'I was like that once and I wasn't dying. I felt as though I was dying but I wasn't. I was alive. My body was alive. Yes, my soul was wilting for need of love or someone to stir love in me. But not dead. Only wanting. Surely that immortal thing can survive in the desert for ever, if it must?'

Brenda turned a clinical scrutiny on Catherine that she had not used since Catherine had been a young girl and Brenda had wanted to be sure she was telling her the truth. She said, 'When was this, Cat?'

Catherine felt a burst of confusion in her mind. 'Oh. It was . . . you know about Jan, don't you?'

'The South African?'

Catherine nodded. She said, 'Well, that was a very strong love, but it can't have been really strong or I would never have married James. You were still Daddy's housekeeper when we married. I don't know how much you thought I loved James, but, well, things have not gone well. There's nothing left there, now.' She paused and looked carefully at Brenda's face. She saw no trace of censorship or doubt. 'I felt like you say you feel. I felt dead. I felt I had a dead child inside me all the time. As though my life was over, as though there was nothing else, nothing worth being alive for. There was no one I really seemed to want to be with. People amused me for a while and then I would have to leave them, go home and be by myself. I had to talk to everyone at parties

271

and things, and, you know, James's functions, all those terrible important captains of our destiny.' She laughed briefly. 'But it was as if I was a machine, a perfect conversational machine. My life wasn't in it. My heart wasn't in it. My mind wasn't either. I used to go blank in the middle of a conversation with some Cabinet Minister or someone, as if my mind was trying to home in on something more important. It was as if I had a real life that was going on somewhere else and I wanted to join up with it.' She gestured towards the horizon. She had been talking fast as the thoughts came tumbling out. She swallowed and drew a gasp of air and went on, 'I . . . James and I more or less stopped making love. We were not getting on well. We still don't have much to do with each other. He's well, he's working very hard and so am I. I go to functions with him but otherwise we lead separate lives, pass each other on the stairs, sometimes, that sort of thing. But . . .' She stopped, wondering whether to go on. Brenda was still giving her that X-ray look.

Brenda said, 'You don't look as if you are in that state now. What's happened to change things?'

Catherine told her. She told her everything, beginning with her conversation with Sir Arnold about wanting a divorce, to the agonies of love she had experienced with Christopher, and the pain of his recent absence. While she talked, her face was lit with love and her animated beauty evoked such feelings in Brenda that she got up and came over and put her arms around her and held her close and wept silently into her shoulder.

The two women held each other close for a while, neither able to speak. Eventually, Brenda drew back. She said, 'What are you going to do now?' Catherine flinched and all the conflict of her feelings flashed into her face. Brenda saw this. She said, 'Are you going to leave James?'

'Oh Brenda.' Now it was Catherine's turn to weep. She told Brenda of the extremities of her dilemma. Of Christopher's background and his arrest, and of her fears for James's political career.

Brenda said, 'That's not a problem.' She sounded practical and authoritative.

Catherine looked at her, amazed and anxious. Would Brenda advise her to give Christopher up?

Brenda smiled at her with glowing eyes and gave her a great bear hug. 'You don't have a dilemma, Catherine. You can't possibly stay with a man you don't love for some ideal of holy matrimony and his career. Or for your father's ambition. Don't listen to your father on this. He would have wanted you to be Prime Minister if you had gone into politics, which you almost did. He never accepted how disappointed he was with you for backing out but he did succeed in marrying you to a minister. He wasn't thinking of you then so much as himself. He's always resented the attitude of the Anglo-Saxon Establishment both in Kenya and Britain, to his own origins and self-made success. And he is determined to break through the class barrier and have his daughter at least as the Prime Minister's consort.' She chuckled. 'The only thing better would be to have married you to the heir to the Throne.'

She took Catherine's hand. 'Now, I'm sorry to appear to speak ill of your father, Catherine. He's a wonderful man but he has always allowed his head to dictate to his heart, and well, not with the best results in his own life. But that's another story. Anyway, I don't see why he should ruin your life by applying the same calculated approach to your future.'

There was a kind of anger in Brenda now. She let go Catherine's hand and stood up and started loading the tea tray, brisk and clattering. Catherine was too stunned to do anything but watch her. Brenda spoke with the no-nonsense manner of Catherine's childhood nanny. 'All you have to do, Catherine, is make your mind up whether you can have a decent lasting relationship with your Christopher or not. He sounds as if he has exactly the same complexes as the love of my life. He thinks he's not good enough for you. He thinks he can't reach your standards. In my case it wasn't class or education. It was something in the character. Something the man had done

273

in his past that he carried with him like an open wound.

'If he had only allowed me, I could have healed that wound with the power of my love for him. I still could. Nothing is ever too late while we live. Living is the only chance you have to change yourself and redeem your ancient sin. No one changes in paradise. Or in hell. The Purgatorial path of life is our great chance, our divine opportunity. Not many people realize it. Your love may be one of the few who will risk taking on the challenge. You seem prepared to do so yourself and you must allow him the choice of doing so too.'

Catherine was silent. Brenda stopped loading her tray and turned sharply to her. She said, aggressively, 'Are you? Are you prepared to accept him completely, whatever he is? That's the main barrier between you now, you know. He will be able to come closer if you will let yourself accept everything about him. I mean everything, Catherine. No reservations. No anxieties. Love risks all. And love redeems all. You then give him the choice of taking the same risk, and redemption. If he refuses it, he bears the responsibility. Not you.'

She lifted the tray and marched towards the cottage. Catherine took a last look at the sun, now partly obscured by a heavy cloud, picked up the blankets and followed her indoors.

54

The launch moves steadily upriver against the tide. It is 2.25 p.m. on Wednesday, the day of the First Reading for the SLRS Bill. The reading starts at 4 p.m. The launch tows the barge, loaded with crates under tarpaulin. They are empty. Save for one which has the bomb in it. And the timer. Donald McGuinness has done his work. And he's plotted the tides. The wind is from the west, now pushing the launch and the barge back downstream with the tide. They pass the Palace of Westminster. They look at it and laugh. They make way upriver and are still in good time.

At Hammersmith they hove to and wait a while because the outgoing tide with the wind behind it is a shade fast. Their timing must be perfect. If the bomb goes off too soon or not soon enough, they have lost.

At 3.20 p.m. they cast off and drift down on the tide, putt-putting the engine to keep ahead of the barge which coasts on her own. They keep her straight. It's not easy. They don't want to go too fast. They should have had a tow behind as well. But that would have been too tricky for the getaway. They have to time the getaway right. Or get blown out of the water.

They come down under Battersea Bridge, then Chelsea Bridge and steadily on towards Vauxhall. They reach the broad stretch of river that passes the Tate Gallery and Millbank Tower. The river is the colour of wet putty. O'Leary is at the wheel. He catches sight of Big Ben. He looks at his watch. Something is wrong. His watch does not read the same time as Big Ben. His watch is slow. By God, they are behind time. The bomb. They have one minute. Less, fifty seconds, perhaps. O'Leary guns the launch. She rises on her stern. The barge puts up a bow wave, resists the increase of pace. They are going faster than the tide and the wind can carry them. They are fighting to hold her straight. O'Leary has to get closer in to the North Bank. He pulls the launch towards the left arch of Lambeth Bridge. He hears Big Ben striking. He puts on a burst of speed. It's too late. They won't make it. He yells to the boy to cast loose the barge. The boy scrambles to the stern of the launch. It's too late.

*   *   *

'A barge was destroyed in an explosion near Lambeth Bridge this afternoon. The barge was being towed by a smaller motor launch. The launch was capsized by the explosion. One man was killed. Another was rescued from the river by a police launch. He is helping with police enquiries into the cause of the explosion which is thought to have been a bomb.'

Catherine waits to see if there is anything more. The newscaster turns to another topic.

* * *

'James? What was this explosion about?'

'Some kind of mistake, I believe. The Home Secretary is keeping me informed. The police say it's linked with the SLRS protests. Michael O'Leary was fished out of the river in remarkably good shape. They're holding him for questioning. Some poor devil was blown up. God knows how O'Leary survived. But then, old soldiers never die, they say.'

55

The phone rang four times before he reached it. 'Hello?' His voice was faint, cautious, as if he were expecting trouble.

The voice he knew well said, 'You have broken our agreement.'

He said nothing.

The voice went on, 'You know the penalty?'

'Why don't you spell it out.' He spat the words out, contemptuously.

'An agreement was made and I kept my side of the bargain. You have gone behind my back and broken yours. The penalty is death.'

The line went dead. Angel looked into the receiver. He laughed a short bitter laugh. 'Mine . . . or yours?' he whispered. He smiled as he put the receiver back in its cradle. But as he went back to the business of dressing to go out to dinner his face was anxious and his mind preoccupied.

56

Penny Slight did not seem to have changed her clothes since her last visit. She came up the long room with her loping bouncing walk carrying a Marks and Spencer's carrier bag and her shiny black attache case. The big raincoat flapped open and tailed out behind her like a sail in a dying wind.

Catherine gestured to the chair. 'Do sit down, Penny,' she said and smiled. 'What have you got for me today?'

Penny sighed. 'Not a great deal, I'm afraid. But interesting. He is an interesting chap, your subject.' She heaved the attache case onto her lap and clicked it open. She rummaged among the densely packed papers and brought out a cardboard-backed brown envelope that said 'Photographs Do not Bend' in red on the front.

She handed Catherine the envelope with a cheerful smile and then sat back while Catherine slit open the seal with a brass paper knife.

The pictures were not very good, but they were good enough for Catherine to get an idea of what the Sirocco was like. Some of the shots showed hostesses draped around drunken-looking middle-aged or elderly men. Another was of the topless floorshow. One showed Angel at a table with some men and a girl who looked like a hostess.

The report was a single typed sheet tucked in with the glossy prints. Catherine scanned it quickly. Penny had done some good work. Angel had two clubs and two escort agencies as well as a number of minor interests in several bars and restaurants. Eight years earlier, he had been prosecuted for living off immoral earnings, but the police had lost their case. A prostitute had made allegations that he was her pimp and that he had extorted money from her but they had not been substantiated and the defence had shown that the girl had a grudge against Angel.

It was sordid. Catherine felt the sick weight in her stomach. She looked up. Penny was gazing around the busy room. Catherine said, 'How did you gather this information?'

Penny smiled brightly. 'Oh, I didn't. It was Andy, my partner. He went along to the Sirocco with a couple of friends and chatted up some of the girls. He took most of the pictures.' She leaned across and rifled through the prints on Catherine's desk.

'Here they are. They got one of the hostesses to take a shot of them.'

Catherine smiled faintly through her sickness. The picture Penny held out to her showed a table of three jolly looking young men, two of whom had girls on their laps.

'And the information about the escort agencies and the court case?'

Penny grinned. 'Andy had to go home with one of the girls and offer her some extra dash for spilling the old beanies.'

'Dash?'

'Oh, that's West African slang for a bribe. My parents were out in Nigeria when I was a baby. I was born there, actually. Up country. In a two men and a dog colony up near Kano. Bloody primitive, if you ask me. I was born with the help of a couple of the local mamas. No quack for miles. I must have some super antibodies to have survived it.' She laughed. It was a loud, jolly laugh that made heads look up right down the long room.

Catherine said, 'I was born in Africa, too. But in the East. My mother had the best doctor in Nairobi but she died giving birth to me.'

Penny said, 'Gosh. I am sorry. What a blow.'

Catherine nodded. 'It was for my father. I didn't know any better.' She went back to the typed sheet. 'How did you get the stuff on the court case?'

'Public records. Once the tart told Andy about the case it only took a tick to track it down.' She leaned over the desk and pointed at a footnote to the last page. 'You'll see there that the tart apparently claimed your chap is also the keeper of a brothel and the girl Andy took home substantiated it. But as we have no documentary confirmation we left it out of the main body of the report.'

The jackbooted rabbit hit Catherine's gut. She leaned back and smiled. She said, 'Well done. How much do I owe you?'

Penny blushed. 'It was rather an expensive evening, I'm afraid. The champagne is over a hundred a bottle and they had to have a couple. Then there was the dash . . .' She tailed off with a guilty look.

'Don't worry. That was inevitable.' Catherine reached for her cheque book.

When Penny had gone, she sat staring out of the window for a few minutes, her eyes unfocused. Then she got up from her desk and picked up her jacket. She called to Janie, 'I'm going out for a bit.'

The noon streets were crowded with pre-lunch crowds. Catherine walked through brisk sunlight across the Piazza and down King Street. She turned onto Garrick Street and walked down until she came to Nathan's, the theatrical costumiers. She looked around to make sure no one was watching her and then she went inside.

57

She parked the Aston in the NCP car park in Audley Square. In the dim chill of the underground garage she pulled the canvas holdall containing the wig and the raincoat out of the boot. She slipped the coat on over the short black skirt and sweater and belted it tightly. Then she sat in the driver's seat and rolled and pinned her blond hair tightly back the way they had shown her at Nathan's. The wig fitted tightly over the top. So tightly she wondered how long she could stand it. She pinned it carefully to her own hair. In the driving mirror it looked quite effective, completely natural, made her a different woman. She put her dark glasses on, smiled at herself in the mirror and swung her legs in the black lace stockings and the high black patent shoes out of the car.

She walked out into the street and headed down towards the Hilton. She had heard it was a popular place. She wondered if she need really have dressed up quite so much for the part.

*   *   *

No one asked her to leave. But then she was only in the lobby a few minutes before the heavy-set man approached her. She stood by the lift, looking outwards. He was about fifty, not tall, but very dark and broad with a smooth pale face and a small bushy moustache. She could not decide whether he was Arabian. He walked towards her, looking her up and down with obvious assessment. Then he stood beside her, looking at the lift's brass doors. She took off the dark glasses and his eyes met hers. He gestured at the doors as they opened and she went in ahead of him.

They were alone in the lift. He pressed the button for the top floor and stood back, leaning against the lift walls, looking at her. Then he moved quickly to her and pressed her against the back of the lift. He pushed his hand under her skirt between her thighs. She wore no pants over her stockings and suspenders and he quickly found what he wanted.

She gave him a little push which he resisted, pressing her against the wall. He had his cock out, a thick, heavy cock. She felt no desire.

No excitement. She said into his shoulder, 'It's £500.' He stood back and looked at her, pushing his cock hurriedly back into his trousers as the lift slowed. The doors opened and a tall, elderly couple stood outside looking in at them.

Catherine's companion said, 'Going up. You want?' His voice was heavily accented.

'No,' they chorused innocently and shook their grey

heads. They were American, from the South.

The lift resumed its journey to the seventeenth floor. There, the man took Catherine's hand and pulled her after him at a fast trot to the penthouse suite. He unlocked a door on the left which led into a bedroom, and pushed her in ahead of him, closing it with a bang and locking it quickly. He went to the closet and reached a neat brown briefcase which he unlocked with brisk movements. He counted out the cash in fifty pound notes and then locked the case and put it away. He took his jacket off and laid it on a chair and put the money in the uppermost pocket, sticking out.

He said, 'It's yours if you do what I want.' He grinned at her. 'Now take off all your clothes except the stockings and put the coat back on.' He went out into the reception room and a few minutes later came back with a scotch and soda.

He started taking off his own clothes. He had a lot of hair on his body. It grew in tufts from his muscular shoulders and curled thickly over his broad, well-fleshed chest.

She held the condom ready in her hand as he came towards her, but he pushed her to sit on the bed and stood in front of her, his legs apart and his belly pushed towards her. He forced her head down to his hairy groin. She took his penis, obediently, in her mouth and did what she knew would give him pleasure. His body smelt faintly of onions. She had a strong desire to get up and run out of the room and forget the whole thing.

As she tasted the first sea-slick taste of semen leaking from its tip, the man snatched his swollen cock out from her mouth with a sudden movement that startled her. 'Not yet,' he said breathlessly. 'Not yet.'

He held her hair, the wig, in a tight grip behind her neck. She felt sure the pins would not hold, but miraculously they did. He pulled her upright and held her against him so that she could feel his hardness. Then he turned her around and threw her face down on the bed so that her feet still touched the floor.

He pulled up the skirt of her plastic coat and put one hand on her shoulder, holding her down. She realized

281

she had not yet put the condom on him and started to move. But he knew what to do. He took it out of her hand and she heard the silky snapping sounds as he stretched it over the head of his penis. Then he pushed her legs wide and entered her from behind. He was slow and methodical in the way he took his pleasure. She heard his breath in husky spasms and lay inertly, relaxed, accepting. He put his arms under her pelvis and pulled her to him but did nothing that would give her pleasure. She gasped as he drove hard into her, hurting her, but he took no notice of her responses. It was as if he were masturbating. She knew then what it was to be used. To have her body treated as a convenient device for someone else's release. She thought briefly of Angel, turning her mind quickly from him as she felt a spasm of desire. She did not want to feel desire. But she remembered the last time she had lain under him, two days ago in Hill Street, how she had suddenly felt she would do anything he asked at that moment, even allow another man to enter her.

The man came to his climax grunting and then letting the air out of his lungs with a strange long gargle like a death rattle. He sank onto her then got up abruptly. 'Wait,' he commanded. He went into the bathroom. She heard water run. He came out wearing a towel. She was sitting on the edge of the bed. He said, 'You want more business?'

She opened her mouth but no words came out. He went to the phone and dialled a short number which must have been another hotel extension. He spoke in a rapid guttural language which she realized was Spanish. He came back to the bed and pulled her up. 'Take a bath,' he said.

She went into the bathroom and showered herself until she felt as scrubbed and clean as a dish. When she came out, dressed once again in the stockings, her high heeled shoes and the coat, there was another man in the room.

He was much younger, perhaps twenty-five, tall and slim built with longish silky dark hair. He was naked and she saw his cock stiffen and jut towards her as he saw her.

Her first client had been back into his briefcase. He

put a pile of notes on the chair by the door. She could see it was double the original amount.

The young man came towards her while the first man watched. He pulled the coat off her shoulders so that it trapped her arms and pushed her backwards onto the bed. He slipped a condom onto his long erect penis and was in her quickly. He was as fast and urgent as his companion was slow.

Catherine was not involved. She moved as she felt he wanted her to move. Without desire of her own, she used her skills to excite and pleasure him. Then something happened.

The first man joined in and pushed the younger one aside. They jostled for her this way repeatedly, first one entering her, then the other. They turned her over and took her in turns from behind, then, on her back again and the older man snatched the condom off and put his cock into her mouth while the younger one rammed her deeply, panting, coming again and again in multiple waves of contractions that still seemed to leave a residue with which to begin again.

She felt oppressed, choked by the cock in her mouth, sticky with sweat, the coat still pinning her arms, the boy stabbing her painfully with staccato blows of his long narrow penis. Then Catherine suddenly awoke to the contagion of their desire. She began to participate. She raised her hips and contracted her internal muscles, holding and sucking the young man into her. She pulled her arms forward against the coat's restriction and ran her hands over his buttocks and between his legs over his strong thighs and under his balls. She pulled and pressed him into her, guiding and directing him so that he became her lover, moving to her time.

She let herself feel the full desperate need that drove him and let herself become engaged in his lust. His eyes were almost insane as the older man pushed him away and wrestled him to get into her. And she cried out with frustrated desire for the younger man as the older pushed his thick cock into her. Then she began to respond as if in a trance to her new lover.

The younger was holding her breasts and rubbing his cock against her side and running his fingers over her clitoris close to the other's plunging cock. And she felt for the young man's cock with her hand while the other held her legs over his shoulders and came again, dripping with sweat and braying.

She held herself back for the younger one and felt a wild exultation as his long pointed penis found its deep mark, wriggling its way into the secret channel to her womb. Then she let herself start a slow ripple of contraction that built and built around the boy's pulsing cock and she longed to tear the condom away and have the hot semen he had to give her. He gave himself with a tremendous cry, hugging her hips to him and penetrating her secret place. She surged around him and felt herself rise like a star, free and innocent of desire.

The men were still at last. Catherine was able to get up from the bed and dress. She took the money from the chair and went out to the lift. She felt tired, but strangely untouched, no more involved than after a session in the gym. But she was oddly exhilarated, as if she had achieved something important, although she could not say exactly what.

'You're nuts, Tsarina. Nuts. I don't want to believe what I'm hearing.'

'Why are you so upset, Gerry? You actually used a prostitute yourself one night, if I recall.'

He snapped back, 'Yes, but I wasn't the tart and I didn't get paid for it.'

She lolled her head back on the sofa cushion and said languidly, 'You were just as much a whore as the girl.

You were doing it for information. Anyway, what's the difference between the whore and the one who uses a whore?'

'Thanks, Tsarina. Thanks.' Gerald glared at her.

She smiled. 'Well, I'm not criticizing you for that, darling. I'm very grateful, as you know. I just don't want you to think there's so much difference between what I did and what you did.'

'Well, we know why I did it. Why did you do it?' There was acidity in his voice.

'Aha. Good question.' She drank from her long glass of Perrier and focused her eyes beyond the window.

'It wasn't for the money by any chance.' He grinned. It was the first sign he had a joke in him since she'd told him about last night's adventure.

'As a matter of fact, the money has gone to a little-known charity for prostitutes.' Her tone was light and teasing.

He put his glass down on the side table and clapped his hands together above his head. He said, loudly, too exuberantly, 'I applaud that! Now, come clean, why did you do it?'

They were in the drawing room at Queen Anne's Gate. The street outside was in shadow: but long beams of early evening sunlight tripped over the roof opposite and ricocheted from the windows on their side of the street to the ones on the other and back again into the drawing room, filling the room with a limpid, watery light that seemed to ripple over the blue furnishings and their faces. It was as if they sat at the bottom of a lagoon.

Catherine smiled at Gerald. It was a serene smile that seemed to express some kind of remoteness, some kind of celestial detachment from things of the world. Her eyes were clear and her face as open and fresh as a rain washed daisy. She stood up and walked to the drinks table and refilled her glass with Perrier. She walked back and stood on the hearth rug facing him. She said, 'Three reasons. One, I was curious. I've been curious for months ever since you told me about that girl from the Sirocco. I suppose I wanted to know what being a whore feels

285

like.' Her calm voice took on a harder edge, 'Since my lover's in the business.' Her voice rose slightly, her words more emphatic, 'Two, I was angry because I couldn't stand the thought of what he's doing. I really hated the thought of him hiring those women, assessing them for what they've got to offer, maybe, probably, being tempted . . .' She threw out her free hand. 'How do I know what he might do? He might find he had to have one of those women, the way he had to have me. How do I know what goes on in that world? Maybe he tries them out whenever he feels like it.

'Then there's the policewoman. He goes, or went, to her to get information and I suppose that makes him a whore. All this has been going round in my head making me furious. So, I suppose I wanted to get my own back. To say, all right, I can do it, too. I can sell myself. I can make commerce out of sex. I can meet you, be your counterpart. I'll punish you for making money out of whores. I'll turn the woman you value and desire into a whore who lets anyone have her for a few hundred pounds.' She was still standing, leaning against the marble mantle. Behind her the silver framed family photographs posed normality.

Gerald, looking at her in her own drawing room surrounded by these family things, seemed to express outrage in the way he sat and looked at her. Then, he also stood up and paced around the room. He said, 'Those aren't good enough reasons for a well brought up, beautiful, well-married woman with aristocratic blood in her veins to go hanging around the Hilton in a black wig and a plastic mac and getting paid for being laid.'

Catherine laughed. She was unused to Gerald's indignation. 'All right, so there's a third reason. Brenda said that if I really want him, I have to accept him completely, whatever he is, and I felt I could only do that if I put myself in the situation, did the thing I despise him for being involved with. That I could only understand it, that world and the way those people are, forgive it and accept it, if I swam in the sewer myself.'

He was silent, eyes doubtful.

She paced slowly across the carpet towards the window. 'So I've done it. I've been there. I'm not the pristine Mrs Waring from the other side of the tracks any more. I've tasted something else. I've tested myself. I've . . .'

'Don't kid yourself.'

She was surprised by the derision in his voice.

He went on, aggressively, 'You haven't really been there at all. You tried out being a whore without having the mentality of the whore. You didn't sell yourself. You simply took a trip, by having a debauched couple of hours with two total strangers. You should have paid them because it was they who gave you the experience you wanted.'

'Well, Gerald dear,' she said, 'I'm intrigued at your reaction. I suspect you are appalled that any woman you know could have sex for money. I wouldn't have thought you capable of these bourgeois feelings. But I can tell you this, I am no longer horrified by Christopher's world. I feel a lot more comfortable with it. It may be you are right, I should have paid them for giving me the experience I sought. But whatever the reality of last night's games, I feel more able to meet my lover on his terms. I can accept him and what he does. He doesn't have to keep me on a pedestal or in a glass case, like any other man who has to use a whore to express his baser feelings towards women, meanwhile keeping his wife in some Olympian isolation and giving her a duty fuck once a week.'

He opened his mouth. But she lifted her hand. She was glimmering on and off in the darkening room, like lightning on the horizon. 'Don't interrupt, I know you know as well as I do that half the bankers' and editors' and politicians' wives who invite us to dinner parties are in that position. Maybe they're lucky if their husbands screw a female whore and don't go creeping around the highways and byways looking for little boys.' She spat out the last words.

He said quietly, 'So do you approve of him and what he does?'

'Oh, yes, I think so. Someone has to service all that

secret shame and lust. If people want whores, let the market provide them. Why are we so prissy about what people want? Sex without love may not be for you or me, but it seems to be a positive need for some men even if they have loving women in their lives.'

Gerald sat again and crossed his legs. He held his fingers with their tips touching, like the Gothic arches of a church. He said coldly, 'And women? Do all women want loving sex or are there some of them who just want a good bang with a few cute little perversions thrown in?'

She smiled a grim metallic smile full of angry energy. 'Oh, yes, my darling. Oh, yes. There are women who want the other. They want to be fucked for lust and not for love. They have violent feelings they want to act out with strangers, faceless men who they never see again. They fantasize about being ravished and loving every minute of it. The trouble is most women haven't the courage or the facility to indulge their needs.'

Gerald looked unhappy. He said, almost pleadingly, 'But Catherine, love is the alchemy that turns lust into divine energy. It makes mere copulation a spiritual act.'

She dropped to her knees on the carpet in front of him. 'I know, and once those feelings have been experienced there is no substitute. Just ordinary sex, after the real thing, it's like a nun fornicating to try and duplicate the mystical ecstasies. Sex and mystical experience use the same energies. You told me that yourself, one day, remember. And I know it. I know it's real.'

Her expression was as lambent as her words, alive with passionate conviction that what she was saying was true. 'Why do you think I have reached this point? Don't you think it strange that a woman like me, with hidebound views, with a rigid indoctrination about the taboos of sex and marriage and good and evil, should come into the hands of this sort of witch doctor? Should tangle with a sex merchant and find a state of spiritual grace through lust transfigured into love?'

Gerald laughed now. 'I don't think it so strange, Catherina. You were a sexual volcano waiting to erupt.

Your Christopher was the earthquake. That's all. Your passion happens to have been translated into the spiritual because you are a deeply spiritual woman.'

She sat back on her heels and smiled at him. 'Oh surely we are all seeking the spiritual in sex? That is what we glimpse that makes us fall in love. That's what makes addicts of us and keeps us hunting madly for our fix if the special partner leaves or dies.'

'Tsarina, you are becoming a psycho-sexual evangelist. And as dangerous as any other religious nut.' He was half serious.

She exclaimed indignantly, 'Nonsense, I'm the first to admit that pure erotic pleasure, and wild lust, and psychological twists also influence what people want and do to each other. It's part of the excitement and delight of sex. Anyway, you are the one who told me sex is both black and white magic. You don't think people who want to express the plain erotic and psychological side of sex should suppress their desires, do you? Is it black magic to be purely physical?'

'Maybe.' His eyes were sliding about the room.

She sensed his confusion. She said quickly, 'Then what about you? Where do your sexual needs come in all this? Is it normal or right or spiritual to do what you do? Or is it purely erotic? Or a psychological need?'

'No.' It was a short curt sound. A refusal to open himself. She was stopped by its starkness and vehemence.

He said, terse and bitter, 'I'm an aberration. I'm a freak of nature. I'm not in any way in a position to argue with you.' He bent down to give Catherine a kiss and added lightly, 'I think this conversation has gone far enough, Catherine, and I'm going home to play with myself.'

'Oh, Gerry.' She laughed. 'Stay to dinner.'

'What? And face that po-faced husband of yours, knowing what I know about his wife? Not on your life, Tsarina. I'm off.'

She saw how disturbed he was. But she was happy. She felt able to accept Christopher's life now that she had tasted some of its pungent flavours for herself. Her experience had demystified his secret world and made it seem infinitely less glamorous and exciting than it had appeared before. In fact, she thought, it was probably the resort of the banal and the bored.

She smiled. She could recommend to any married woman who knew or suspected her husband used a whore to go out and be one herself for a night. The thought of her husband paying for sex would never make her feel inadequate again. Briefly she wondered about James. Was that what he did?

59

She ran a fingernail lightly down the centre of his back to the tip of his spine. They lay on their sides, looking into each other's eyes, noses almost touching. This closeness, his willingness to stay longer after lovemaking, had grown up since her night at the Hilton. She believed it was her own changed attitude towards his life that made this possible. Accepting him, she had dissolved barriers.

But there was still a pent up secrecy about him. He suggested occluded radiance, like a brilliant light shining from behind a heavy screen, casting an impenetrable shadow before him. The things he did not know she knew of and many more of which she still knew nothing and could only guess, despite Penny Slight's industrious efforts, weighed in him with the intense pressure of water against a dam.

There were moments when she seemed to contact this reservoir of secrets directly. It was like diving into a dark deep lake. She could see nothing only feel the cold threat of the dark water around her. It was like that when they lay together after love and she seemed to merge into him, limp and warm in his arms, aware of the mysteries swimming within him, threatening as sharks.

It was like that now. It was as if the dam must burst. She felt something bubbling to the surface, some need to tell her something, a wish to speak. In the dimly lit room, she saw what seemed shadows of thoughts flickering like moths across his eyes.

She said, 'Tell me.'

'Tell you what?' His eyes opened wide and he assumed a pretence of innocence, a childish look that also contained mischief.

'Whatever.' She kissed his soft lips.

He responded and then kissed her neck and shoulders, her breasts and belly and the flow of touch and response began again between them, that far deeper dialogue than words conveyed. Their now familiar responses and their bodies knowing sense of each other brought them closer each time to some perfect union in which it was becoming impossible to separate the pleasure of one lover from the other. There were times when Catherine was not certain if her climax was her own or his. This was one of those times. After, he covered her face with kisses and then lay on her and she held him tightly and felt she would never allow him to leave her. She had forgotten now that she had thought he wanted to speak. His unease with words was always overcome by his lovemaking. It was as if the thoughts and feelings he failed to articulate built in him and poured through his body in the act of sex.

Perhaps his power to communicate with her even when they were apart – she was now always conscious of his thoughts, of his eyes apparently watching her, anxious and hungry as a neglected dog's – lay in the wordless energy of his need. Emotions he could not trust to speech built up in him like that other dam of secrets and turned a powerful turbine whose energy reached her each time he touched her with hand or thought. His physical presence, especially before their lovemaking, held some imminent threat. As if the tumescence of his cock was merely the expression of some other swelling violence whose only outlet was his sex. When they met outside the flat, he seemed, always, tautly controlled, as though some pack of wild predators hurling themselves against the restraint of chains were waiting to be released from within him at a terse command.

It was there, even now, as he rolled away from her and turned his back, sitting on the side of the bed looking, as if lost in some thought, out of the window, whose curtains they never drew because he wanted to feel the world could witness his forbidden possession of her. Even now, there was a tension and a readiness Catherine likened to that of a soldier whom she had loved briefly in Rhodesia, before Jan, who had razored his nerves in the bush war's anticipation of ambush. Angel, too, was like a man going out to fight, in danger of his life, never relinquishing his guard that was like armour he only took off to make love. Never knowing from which direction death would come.

She watched him, from where she half lay leaning on her elbow and he got up and went into the bathroom and closed the door. She began combing her hair and tending her face. When he emerged, wrapped in a towel and freed by the shower of their mutual scent, she felt his preoccupation had deepened. He was not even with her now. And yet there was still that sense of something unsaid.

She took her turn in the bathroom and when she came out he was dressed. He waited, silent, while she pulled on her stockings and the white silk cocktail suit in which she had been to a perfume manufacturer's reception. Silent while she slid on her shoes and picked up her bag. Silent while they walked the length of the hall to the entrance. Silent while they went downstairs in the lift.

He walked her to her car and helped her in. As she sat before the wheel looking up at him, mouth pouting for a kiss, he said, 'Let me in on the other side. I want to tell you something.'

So he did want to talk. She leaned over and opened the door and he walked around the front of the car and got in beside her.

He closed the door and sat looking ahead, down Waverton Street. He said, 'I'm going away.'

She felt pain kick in her stomach and a rush of blood

to her face as her heart leaped into terrified response. She put her hand out to touch his hard broad thigh in the dark blue pinstriped wool and he held it in his own warm soft one.

She spoke into a silence that lay between them like a field of thin ice over a lake. 'What do you mean?' Her voice held the tremble of fear. She was looking at his profile.

He spoke into the distance, as if to the high wall at the street's blank end. 'I'm leaving London for a bit.'

Quickly, panic rising now, her voice breathless, whispering, about to scream, 'Why? Why?'

He turned then and held onto her and pulled her close across the gap between the seats, nuzzling his face into her hair.

Calmer, louder, her heart grinding to a stop, her breath held, frozen, time going on without her, she said, 'Tell me,' and pushed him away to look into his eyes. 'Tell me.' Angrier, pleading, 'Don't keep me in suspense.'

He was looking out of the window over her shoulder. His voice was distant as if he spoke already from far away. 'It's business. I've got one or two problems that can be solved best if I go away. Things are difficult here, so, I'm going to the States. There are a couple of deals I've got to see to. The business here will go on without me for a while.'

'Don't lie.' She shook him gently. 'Don't lie to me now. Don't leave me with a lie.' She buried her head in his shoulder and he stroked it gently. Her voice was muffled by the cloth of his jacket. 'I can come too, you know. I can just leave things in other hands and come with you. I can go to the New York office and join you more easily wherever you are from there. You can come to me, stay with me. I'll rent an apartment.'

He caught her hair strongly behind her neck and pulled her head back. 'Catherine. I don't want you to. I've got to go alone.' He looked hard and searchingly into her eyes. 'I'll come back. I promise.' He stroked her hair where he had held it.

She groaned and the groan turned into a howl and

then she sobbed and flung herself back into her seat and leaned her head back on the rest and sobbed as if she were alone in the universe.

He sat silently. He took her hand and held it. Then he took her by the shoulders and pulled her back towards him and held her close.

He said, 'I don't want to go, Catherine. I don't want to leave you. I have to. But things will change. I'll come back.'

'When? How long?' The tears were drying on her cheeks. She felt weak and tired and finished. She was curled in his lap. She heard his voice coming from above her.

'There's something I have to think about, maybe something I have to do. Then I can come back.'

She lifted her head. She said, suddenly remembering the charge that was still against him, 'I thought the police had your passport.'

He smiled. 'I've got that back. I've got friends in the police.' He laughed softly.

She drew in her breath. Her eyes searched his face. He said, 'I've got a friend quite high up who fixed that for me. The charges have been dropped. I'm free. A free man.' He laughed again.

She sat up and spread the tears across her cheeks with her fingers. 'I'll miss you.' Her voice, dense with unshed tears, was defeated.

He caught her to him and kissed her gently. 'I'll miss you, too.' His eyes told her he was not lying.

60

She entered the empty house and went upstairs. Her body rang with his presence; the sense of his touch, his semen still deep inside her like a secret treasure. She did not want to wash, to lose him under a soothing flow of hot water. She wanted to sleep in this memory of his scent and touch. She took off her clothes and cleaned her face with creams, then slid between the sheets. In her mind she was lying in his arms, could feel his presence, the softness of his relaxed body and his arms around her. Even her hair smelled of him, evoking him as it lay around her face and spread over the pillow. At last, she turned out the light and lay in his radiance.

She must have heard James close his door. It was after 2 a.m. She lay for some time in the dark, trying to slip back into sleep, but remained stark awake, her eyes closed but seeing him through their lids. Seeing his eyes looking at her in farewell. She thought she might never see him again. After so much understanding. So much distance travelled. So much emotion. She could not let go her pain. Or her love.

She thought longingly of a hot drink, soothing chamomile tea, or vervain to bring her sedation and sleep, a kind of absolution to wash away her pain. She turned on her light and climbed out of bed, slipped on a robe and crept out of her bedroom towards the stairs. As she passed James's door she saw the light under it. She started down the stairs in the semi-darkness and heard his door open behind her.

'Catherine?'

She turned. 'Yes?'

'Oh Cat. I'm so glad you are awake.' There was both strain and relief in his voice.

'What is it, James?' She turned and came back up the stairs, holding her robe up.

He looked tense and exhausted. 'I can't sleep. I've got something I'd really like to talk to you about . . .'

She said, 'Now? Must it be now?'

'Well. You're up. Are you going back to bed now?'

She shook her head. 'I'm going to make some vervain to help me sleep. Would you like some?' She spoke as if to a guest.

He nodded. 'It might help.'

She moved off again. 'Wait, then. I'll bring it. Then you can tell me.'

The kitchen light was too bright for her night state. Jarringly real. She made the tea and carried it upstairs with biscuits James liked. He was in bed and she went over and sat on the edge of the bed, putting the tray down beside her.

She said, 'What do you want to talk to me about?'

He said, 'Things are getting rather unpleasant with the SLRS. I'm getting some organized opposition inside the party, now.' He paused and gave her a significant look, then said acidly, 'Adrian Haslam is leading the affray.' Haslam was James's main rival for the leadership if and when the PM decided to retire.

Catherine poured the golden tea into the delicate cups and the bitter scent of vervain rose around them. She handed him the biscuits and he absently took one, dipping it in his tea and sucking it, like a child.

He went on, 'Also, there's some gossip that isn't helping.'

'Oh?' She looked up from her tea. The rabbit kicked her diaphragm. Her blood leaped into life. The chemistry of fear and hope combined in her brain. She was being followed still. A possibility she had not considered before lit up her mind. Would Haslam have her investigated, to get at James? Oh, God.

James said, 'Some rumour about Arnold being involved in another group of investors, apart from the Consortium, I mean. Word has it he is buying property in Lambeth, that there are plans for a big hotel on the water. It doesn't look good, Cat. If he is, it just doesn't look right. It looks like family influence. The PM is worried rigid about that sort of thing.'

Relief. I couldn't stand the guilt of being his downfall. Disappointment: I want a divorce. She said, 'Does the PM know about this rumour?'

'I don't know.' He looked troubled.

'It's not against the law if Daddy buys the whole of the SLRS area, James.' Her voice hardened.

He coloured and came back crisply, 'You know very well that if he buys just one house, men like O'Leary will say I have a vested interest in getting this bill through, to enrich my family.'

She said with spirit, 'Well, you could tell the Michael O'Learys of this world to go and make their own damn investments instead of trying to oppose a progressive scheme to enrich the general population and their environment. Wherever is your fight, James? Stop cowering in the bushes and get out there with your big stick. By the way,' she added, 'where is Michael O'Leary since the explosion?'

'In police custody.' He smiled briefly. 'Giving the law a few answers to some sticky questions. I understand he's a mine of information.'

'Let's hope it's not a mine field.' She laughed.

James said, 'I'd still be a lot happier if Arnold would keep his sticky fingers off the sweets, Cat.'

'You'd better talk to him about it, then.' She refilled their cups, and lifted the tray from the bed.

He said, alarmed, 'You're going?'

'Well. You've got your tea, the teapot's empty and I don't really want to hear you bitching about Daddy for the rest of the night. I'm going to try and get some more sleep.'

'Stay with me, Cat.' His voice was low and pleading. His eyes carried sadness and hurt like a lost dog.

'Oh, James.' She put the tray down on a chair and took her cup and saucer in her hands, lifting the cup, sipping the warm soothing liquid. She looked kindly at him. 'Why now? Why, after all this time?'

'I need you, Catherine. I need you to . . .' His voice changed, grew stronger as he made some effort of pride to stop crawling to his wife for sex. Or was it love. 'It's all a bit much at the moment, darling.'

'Haslam?'

'It's vindictive. Yes. I'm feeling down. Under attack from everyone. I never seem to see you any more. We never have dinner together unless we're with other people. What's happening to us, Cat?'

She shrugged and then shook her head slowly from side to side. 'Oh James. Poor James. Have you never wondered this before?'

'I've noticed you are always too busy nowadays,

297

Cat. You don't want to talk to me. And you've grown hard.' He reached out a pleading hand and touched hers. 'Won't you . . .?'

She looked at him with compassion. His expression was miserable and lonely and torn. He looked what he was, a man bereft of love, who had only just noticed that his wife was no longer his woman. After how long? He had not tried to touch her, other than a light kiss on the cheek, for . . . maybe, a year. Had he noticed her emotional change? Had he noticed how she had glowed and gone haggard alternately over the past months? Did he wonder if she had a lover? Did James, did any man, notice these things?

Her father had. But then he had a more considered approach to her. And he was less pressured. James was always in the thrill of battle, the constant adrenalin rush of skirmishes with the Opposition, battles within the Ministry and now, when he was, at last, rid of his main opponent inside his own department, it seemed his other rivals were after his blood.

If James had noticed anything he would not have registered it for long. His other preoccupations would have overgrown any sprouting hint that his wife might have a lover. She wondered what he thought she did for love, and sex. And what did he do? Did he fuck his secretary? Or was it someone else? And where was she now, if there was a woman? Or was she a whore, or whores? Did he remember how long it was since he had last touched her body, last been a man to her woman?

She stood up and saw his anxious pleading eyes follow her. She put her cup and saucer down on the silver tray. She turned to him and let her robe fall open, let it slide over her shoulders and slip to the ground. She stood in a pool of crisp white silk and lace, like Aphrodite in the surf. A bride. The eternal virgin. Then she stepped over the fallen robe and came towards him.

It was the last thing she wanted in the world. To make love to anyone, to disturb and dilute the treasure of Angel's last gift. She could not bear to pollute the sanctuary. But she saw her husband in his need and could not refuse him. She went to him with kindness, let him touch her and enter her and quickly satisfy his need without considering any of her own.

Then she held him in her arms and waited for him to sleep. When he was breathing rhythmically, she eased out, carefully, from under him. He slept with a tiny smile of contentment on his tired face. She went to her own room and lay, stiff as a mummy, in her own lonely bed. Tears flowed silently down her cheeks and soaked her hair and her pillows.

At last, she was still and calm again. She put out her light and lay in the darkness, seeing across London, searching for him, crying out in her mind for him. For forgiveness at what she had done to broach the sanctuary of the inviolate treasure in her womb. She had never felt more of a whore.

61

Armstrong paced his office. Outside it had been dark for some hours and Victoria Street's bleary lights conjured Dickensian ghosts on its damp, unpeopled pavements. Armstrong looked down at the transcript as he walked back and forth across the tired green carpet.

The tape he had requested as an adjunct to the transcript was still playing. O'Leary's warm Irish voice, full of the gutsy character of the wily old man, echoed around the bare room. He had been interviewed in the hospital where he was taken initially, to recover from shock and exposure after his ducking in the Thames.

Armstrong had requested both tape and transcript because he wanted to hear the emphasis put on certain words to avoid placing his own interpretations on the ambiguous printed word. He wanted to know not only what O'Leary was saying, but how he was saying it.

There was one section in particular that Armstrong went over several times. The Irish man was describing how the bomb was meant to detonate and with what effect, politically. No one was to have been hurt but a point was to have been made. That was what the protest coordination committee had not been able to agree about, O'Leary said. Some were for the bomb, most were against. But the minority had got together and done it anyway, under their own steam.

Then he had said that key phrase that intrigued Armstrong. He said, 'The backers approved it.' Had he said the backers or was it the tape's quality? Maybe he had said 'the buggers approved it.' That was why Armstrong wanted to listen to the tape over and over again. He wanted to be sure.

The man from Special Branch interviewing O'Leary seemed to have missed that. Perhaps he also thought O'Leary had said 'the buggers'. The Irish accent would have masked the real word and it was easy enough to assume he was simply referring to the coordinating committee. If the word was really 'backers', Armstrong was sure it had been a slip. Not the deliberate red herring of which he was sure, thanks to MI5's dossier on O'Leary, that the Irishman was likely to use to deceive and mislead the investigators.

Five had O'Leary's history on microfilm and a print of that also lay on Armstrong's desk. O'Leary had been picked out and trained by the Russians when he was a nineteen-year-old student at Cambridge in 1948. He'd been to Russia during his undergraduate years and that had not put him off his Marxism. He had become a key figure in Russian undercover exploits in the British trades unions, hence his period as a construction worker (during which he had received his leg injury). That had been followed by a job at Ford in Dagenham. He'd done a bit of damage there before he'd been rumbled.

His Cuban adventures were a diversion, brought on by his friendship with Che Guevara who had introduced him to Castro, before, O'Leary believed, Castro had had him murdered, pushed out of a plane over the Atlantic.

Armstrong was puzzled over the phrase 'the backers approved it.' He believed O'Leary must be referring to the big fish behind the plan to frustrate the Government's programme in South London. These were the people Armstrong really wanted to tangle with. He felt he would have to have a word with O'Leary himself.

Then there was another section of the transcript which had Armstrong turning over mental stones. The interviewer had begun asking O'Leary what he knew about the source of the drugs found on a number of the violent demonstrators on the day Parliament and the Waring house were attacked.

O'Leary said he knew nothing of any drugs or any source. Then the interviewer had claimed he knew that O'Leary had visited a certain basement flat in Brixton on a night in February. He had been seen leaving the flat and shortly after a man known as the Flick, thanks apparently to his speed with the knife, who was a known drug connection, also left the flat.

O'Leary said he knew no one of that description. It must have been a coincidence. Or an error. The man had come out of a different flat. Not the basement where O'Leary had been visiting his friend. The investigator told O'Leary that he knew the man who lived in the flat was also a friend of the Flick. O'Leary had continued to maintain the force of coincidence was operating.

Surveillance of O'Leary by MI5 had been revived since he first appeared on the protest committee in Brixton in November and got his name in the local paper for demanding that housing for the poor and not the rich be created by Government in South London. Not an unreasonable request, Armstrong reflected. But when made by a man of Michael O'Leary's history and reputation, instantly suspect. Armstrong had the detailed report from Five of O'Leary's movements from that date. He now sat at his desk and devoted his attention to that report. It made sometimes surprising reading and set Armstrong's brain seething with ideas. He reached a large lined notepad and began to make a list of questions he

301

wanted answered and the people he wanted answers from. The first three names on the list after Michael O'Leary were Catherine Clyne, Sir Arnold Clyne and Christopher Angel.

62

Armstrong sat on the sofa facing the door so that she would face the light when she talked to him. Anna brought him the cup of unsweetened black coffee he had said he would like when she offered him tea, and he drank it, savouring its bitter strength.

Catherine came in dressed in a tight fitting navy blue suit with a white blouse frothing out over the neckline. She was going to the office in half an hour and she had agreed to give him a brief meeting. It was strictly business, he had told her.

She sat on the sofa opposite and crossed one dark blue stockinged leg over the other. She looked very beautiful, but somehow more remote than he remembered her. There was a coldness in her now that ran deeper than her formal and rather distant manner with him today. It was something else. Some change had happened in her. She seemed less approachable, untouchable, an ice queen.

She smiled and it did nothing to diminish her frozen texture. 'How are you, David?' she said, and for a moment there was a glimmer of warmth. A memory of the flames he had experienced at her hearth.

He said, uncomfortably, 'I'm well, thanks. Are you?'

She nodded. She was looking at him serenely, evidently waiting for him to explain his visit. He felt awkward and uncomfortable. He said, 'Look, Catherine, I'm afraid this is rather difficult. Are we entirely alone?' He glanced over to the open door.

Catherine got up and closed it. She said, 'James is not here. There's only Anna. But, if it makes you feel happy . . .'

'Ah, good.' He coughed and shifted in his seat. 'Then, I can talk freely.'

She sat sideways on the edge of the sofa, leaning her back against the arm. She smiled a polite smile that did not quite conceal her impatience. 'Please go on, David.'

He put his empty cup down on the coffee table. He cleared his throat and said, 'I have to ask you some questions about your friend. About Christopher Angel.' He watched her carefully and saw her surprise.

She turned large alarmed eyes on him. 'How can I help you there?' Her voice was uneven with emotion.

Armstrong launched out. 'I'll not beat about the bush. Your friend is a dealer, a middle man for a number of unsavoury customers. He . . .'

She cut in, coldly, 'Are you sure? Do you have evidence or are you guessing?

Armstrong was surprised by her response. She was aggressive in Angel's defence, protective, even. He said, matching her coldness, 'If I may go on, he appears to be involved in the supply of drugs to the people who have been demonstrating against your husband's pet development scheme. I take it you know nothing of this?' He stopped abruptly and stared keenly at her, absorbing every flicker of her response. She'd had a shock. That was easy enough to see. So she knew nothing of his probable involvement in the SLRS drug scene.

That was about all he needed to know from her. There was one other thing, though. He said, 'It's possible I would need you as a witness if we bring your friend to trial. So I should warn you that anything you say could be admissible in court.'

She stood up. 'Do you mean a prosecution witness?'

He said, almost lazily, 'You wouldn't want to be a witness for the defence would you, my dear?' She came and stood near him, looking down. He saw she was very disturbed. Was it anger?

She said in a voice that was dangerously calm, 'Why

303

would you want me as a witness, David?'

'Because you know the man intimately and you can provide a record of his habits.'

'But I know nothing about his habits.'

'Did you hire a detective to look into his life?'

'Why would I have to tell you that?' She gave him a look that combined indignation with a desire to kill him. She moved over to the mantelpiece and he saw the back of her pale hair and part of her profile reflected in the large mirror behind the family photographs and the flowers. She was the portrait of a lady at home. It seemed a shame to drag her into this. But then she had got herself in, as far as he could see. And he wanted to see how far in she really was. Before he let up the pressure.

He stood up and went over to her and took one of her hands in his. She stepped backwards and tried to withdraw the hand but he held onto it. He said, 'Look, Catherine, I don't want to do anything that will embarrass you or compromise your marriage, let alone drag your husband into this. But I do have to tell you that I want Christopher Angel. And unless I find him, I will have to involve you. I think you know a great deal more about him than you admit.'

She snatched her hand away and walked away from him, towards the windows. She leaned against the window-frame and said coolly, 'I don't think you have anything that can drag me into this, David. You will have to prove to a court that I know Christopher as well as you say I do.'

He could not tell her that he had access to a private eye who had followed her to her assignations with Angel for weeks; although the detective had been hired by a third party, his evidence was still admissible. And he also knew that Catherine had hired her own investigators to watch Angel. He had taken sufficient interest in her links with Angel and in her safety to learn that and more besides. But he could tell her none of this.

Instead he said, 'But you have told me yourself, Catherine.'

She whirled around and flashed at him like a lightning

strike. 'In private,' she snapped. She was coming towards him quickly. She came right up to him and stared into his eyes with an astonishing ferocity. She spoke violently. 'Do you use what has been told you in private confidence as professional evidence? If you do, you are an immoral wretch, no better than the criminals you hunt. What is more,' she turned and went to sit on the arm of the sofa he had left, 'you are trying to blackmail me. And I'm not going to have it. If you persist, I'll tell the Home Secretary.'

He laughed. 'Let's stop playing bluff, Catherine. I'll call it quits. You're a tougher woman than I'd estimated. You can tell me something, if you will, though.'

'Oh?' She was hostile. He had made a mistake in his approach to her, he saw. Intimidation had been the wrong stance. He should have come crawling around with a bunch of roses and tried to take her to lunch in the hope she would tell him what he wanted. But then, he had no thought of that. He had reacted like a policeman with a suspect and not a man who wanted something from a woman.

It was probably too late to change his approach but he moved over to her and put a hand on her shoulder. He said, gently, 'Where is Angel?'

For a moment he saw pain flash into her eyes. Then, she looked up at him with an expression that was as bland and cool as if he had asked her the way to the Zoo. She smiled. 'I really don't know, David.'

He looked down at her with his intense scrutinizing gaze and she stared back at him, coldly. For a moment he was moved by her chilly beauty. He wanted to lean down and kiss her. But he stepped back, as if anticipating the rebuff, and turned to leave. He did not believe her.

*

63

The secretary came out of Sir Arnold's office. She walked across the wide reception area towards Armstrong. In a slightly German accented voice, she said, 'Sir Arnold will be able to see you in a few minutes, Commander.'

Armstrong nodded. He had not given Clyne any warning of his call. He had just turned up at the afternoon's end and hoped surprise would be on his side. He was not sure quite what he expected to find out. But he was quite sure he had had to come here.

The buzzer went on Andrea Werner's large mahogany desk. She picked up the receiver on the internal phone. 'Very well, Sir Arnold,' she said. She lifted her head and looked towards Armstrong. 'I can take you in now, Commander.'

She was quite an attractive woman when she was smiling, Armstrong thought. He stood up with difficulty from the low sofa and followed her into Sir Arnold Clyne's very impressive office. The first thing Armstrong was aware of was the good view of the Bank of England. The next thing he saw was Catherine's portrait on the great desk. There was another enlarged silver framed picture of a beautiful blond girl in early fifties fashion of full skirted polka dot dress and large picture hat. She was standing among some hibiscus flowers with a large colonial style house in the background. He guessed it was Catherine's mother in Kenya.

Sir Arnold was standing behind the desk with his back to the room looking out of the window. He turned and came around the desk, his hand extended in greeting, a smile on his handsome suntanned face. 'Good afternoon, Commander Armstrong,' he said. He was warm despite his formality. It was as if they were old acquaintances, members of the same club.

Armstrong shook Clyne's hand briefly and took

306

the chair he was offered, near a coffee table and a comfortable-looking dark blue velvet sofa. He could see the daughter in the father's colouring and deportment.

Sir Arnold took the sofa and sat back easily, long legs crossed. 'What can I do for you, Commander?' The tone of the question seemed to carry a faint warning that whatever it was it should not take too long.

'I have one or two questions which you may be able to help me with. I trust it will only take a few minutes.'

Clyne's eyes narrowed slightly. He shrugged and gave a charmingly raffish smile. 'I cannot imagine what they must be, Commander. Please relieve me of my curiosity,' he said, lightly.

Armstrong reached into his breast pocket and produced some Yard mugshots. 'Do you know these men?'

'Good heavens. Is that likely? Are they criminals?' Sir Arnold leaned forward and peered at the pictures. He pulled a pair of glasses from the breast pocket of the pale grey suit.

'Let's say they might be.' Armstrong was watching him carefully. He was sure he saw recognition on Clyne's face.

Sir Arnold was staring at the pictures. He ran a hand slowly over his fine pale hair. The hand stopped at the back of his neck. He looked at Armstrong and grinned mischievously. 'What are the prizes for guessing correctly?' He leaped up with a youthful movement and walked gracefully over to the drinks cabinet. A silver bucket containing ice, another silver ice bucket containing a bottle of hock, and a decanter of whisky already stood on a silver tray on the cabinet's dark polished top. Armstrong had seen the secretary carry them in after she had announced him.

Clyne turned. 'Will you join me, Commander? I do believe it's after five-thirty. I think we could risk a little snifter without being considered alcoholics.'

Armstrong smiled. 'I'm not much of a drinker, thank you, Sir Arnold, but something non-alcoholic would be very pleasant.'

The banker came back with a glass of hock for himself and a Perrier for Armstrong. He sat down again and

307

sipped his wine. 'Aha,' he said, 'I think we've hit a good one with this last purchase I made. I went to the vineyard myself last summer and tasted the produce. It comes from the very best of the Rhine's wine-growing area. And the vintage is excellent.' He raised his long stemmed glass. 'Your health, Commander.'

Armstrong smiled faintly. He reached across the table and shuffled the photographs until the one of John Leach was visible. He said, 'I think you may know this man, if not the others.'

'Really?' Sir Arnold put down his glass and put his glasses back on. He looked closely at the photograph. 'Where do you think I would know him from, Commander?' He turned the picture around to catch the light better.

'From right here in your office, Sir.'

Sir Arnold laughed. 'You can't be serious? A criminal suspect, working for me?'

Armstrong said quietly, 'I didn't say he worked here, Sir. I meant you had met him here.'

'Do you mean he came to see me about something?'

'I suppose he did, Sir.'

'What do you mean, you suppose he did?' Sir Arnold's accent was becoming more evident. His voice rose in pitch. His impatience was becoming visible.

'Well, Sir, I gather he came here to meet you one day last February, at about this time, I believe. I wondered if you would remember what took place at the meeting?'

Sir Arnold stood up and walked around the coffee table into the centre of the room. He went to the window and looked out. The Bank was catching a ray of afternoon sunlight on its sombre portico. The Stock Exchange tower flashed back brilliant reflections of the Western light from its dark glass.

He turned and walked back. 'If I tell you why he was here I must know that it will go no further. I must have your word that there will be no repercussions from what I have to tell you, that you will not investigate the matter further.'

Armstrong stood up. He moved a few paces towards

Clyne. 'I can't do that, Sir Arnold. But if it's a private matter and of no public account, if there are no criminal matters involved, you can take my word it will not go further.'

'The thing is,' Sir Arnold said, moving back around the coffee table and sitting down again. 'The thing is, I . . . I could bring criminal charges against this man, but I don't want to do so. I must ask you to believe me when I say something extremely private is involved and that this man came here to try to blackmail me.'

He stopped and looked up at Armstrong. In that moment, his glasses caught a reflection of sunlight off the glass-walled buildings opposite. Armstrong could not see the expression in his eyes. He moved sideways to intercept the light. Sir Arnold said impatiently, 'Please sit, Commander. You make me nervous.' He gestured to the chair, and Armstrong sat down.

The banker said, 'It's a long story, Commander, and I cannot tell you all of it but I hope that when I have finished you will understand my position, why I have not tried to prosecute this man.

Armstrong listened quietly to everything Clyne said. He made no notes, nor did he turn on the small recorder, hidden in his pocket. What Clyne said gave him a certain unique insight into the man and he realized he was privileged to have it. When the banker had finished and was sipping at his hock, Armstrong said, 'Did you tell anyone else? Your daughter?'

'Good heavens, no.' Clyne sat up in his seat. 'I wouldn't want to worry Catherine with something as sordid as this. Besides, it has been settled. I don't think I will hear from them again.'

Armstrong's face wore a doubting look, though he said nothing. He was sure he had only heard part of the story.

Clyne said, 'I hope that satisfies you, Commander? And that I do still have your word that this will go no further?'

Armstrong nodded. 'You do, Sir. I would ask you, though, to get in touch with me directly if you hear from Leach again.' He drew a card from his pocket, wrote his direct number on it and gave it to Sir Arnold.

'Thank you. I do trust there is nothing else I can help you with today, Commander. But please don't hesitate to come back if you think there is something else.' He rose. His movement was intended as a dismissal.

Armstrong rose, too. He said, 'Well, as a matter of fact, Sir, there is something else.' He held the pictures in his hand. 'These other two men. I feel sure you must know who they are. Can I get you to take another look at the pictures?'

Sir Arnold swallowed his evident impatience and carried the pictures to the window. He came back, shaking his head.

Armstrong took the picture of Michael O'Leary. He said, 'This man was with Leach when he came to see you. He did not come in, he stayed outside in the car, but they were together. I know because we had O'Leary under surveillance. He's a political agitator. These two are working together on the protest committee. Are you sure you have never met him?'

Sir Arnold shook his head again. He moved towards the door ahead of Armstrong.

Armstrong said, 'This other man is, I believe, a friend of your daughter's.' He held out the third picture.

Clyne turned and came back and almost snatched the picture from him. 'Who is he?' he snapped.

Armstrong said slowly, 'His name is Christopher Angel. He's a night club owner. I can tell you in very strict confidence that he is suspected of involvement in a cash laundering operation which hinges on a three way trade involving bullion and drugs. Drugs supplied to the SLRS protest groups may be coming into the country through his connections.'

'What?' Clyne looked horrified. 'How does my daughter know that kind of riff raff?' His voice was loud and accented.

'With respect, Sir, I think you should ask her that yourself.' Armstrong spoke kindly. He felt sympathy for Clyne. However, he was not convinced by the Oscar-rating performance that what he had told him was exactly news to the banker. Armstrong was, in fact, quite sure that Sir Arnold Clyne knew Christopher Angel and knew what he was to his daughter.

310

64

'So tell all, Tsarina.' Gerald stretched out on the grass and clasped his hands over his full belly. His face wore a contented smile. His voice conveyed the sleepy indolence of summer Sundays. Gerald had just described these as always evoking the rose gardens of a careless youth, some antics of which, including those of his postgraduate days at Cambridge, he had been recounting to Catherine as they ate their picnic.

Catherine lay on her stomach beside him, propped on her elbows. Close by was the hamper, now plundered of its contents of salads, cheeses, smoked salmon and strawberries. A wine cooler containing an empty Muscadet bottle stood near Gerald's shoulder. The air was green with the smell of cut grass.

Catherine turned and sat up. They were in a quiet corner of a hillside. Below them, Hampstead Heath crawled with moving figures. The view of London stretched southwards into the milky distance. Brilliant sunlight highlighted landmarks rising out of the mass of buildings; St Paul's, Parliament, the four stacks of old Battersea power station. She wondered whether she was looking at the past or the future.

It was rare for her to have Sundays free but James was in a very private meeting at Chequers and Sir Arnold was in Antibes. She herself was working very hard to ensure the September launch of French Vanities went according to plan and that her new magazine, Lives, could be brought out in London in November. The picnic was a break she needed. But, inevitably, she always had to talk to Gerald about the thing that lay in her like a beast with claws.

'Well?' Gerald's voice reached her.

She tugged out a blade of grass and sucked on it. 'I'm going to New York for a bit,' she said. 'I think.'

'Oh? Trouble at the office?'

She leaned back on her hands and tilted her head back to stare at the sky. 'I need the change.'

'Rubbish. You're going after lover boy.' Gerald sat up. His voice was no longer sleepy, but expressed the impatience he always felt when Catherine would not come clean. He got onto his knees and leaned towards her, pushing his face into hers, belligerently. 'You can't fool me, woman,' he said triumphantly. 'Just one look into those big blue eyes and I can tell you everything about yourself . . .'

She laughed and drew back. 'You reek of garlic and alcohol.'

'Then it must be time for tea. Come on.' He jumped up and, catching her hand, tugged her to her feet. 'We've been out here long enough.'

'All right,' she laughed.

They quickly packed the hamper and picked up their debris and started back up the Heath towards Gerald's house.

As they walked, Gerald said, 'Have you heard any more about your friend?'

Catherine looked down at her feet in the low wedge-heeled mules. Her voice was listless. 'I have a report from my investigator.'

'And?'

'Some of it covers the last week or so before Christopher left the country. It's rather disturbing. He was bristling with bodyguards, apparently.' She stopped to look into a dress shop window. 'He had someone living with him, which I didn't know about. No,' she turned quickly to him and her voice flashed anger at his assumption, 'not a woman. An ex-Marine, American.'

'How do you know?'

She made a short tired sound that was neither laugh nor sob. 'It's crazy, really. I spoke to him. It was the day after I saw Christopher last, the day before he was leaving the country. I just rang his house, because I wanted to say goodbye again. A man with an American accent answered the phone. I said I'd call back later and did.

I got him again. His name was Joe, he said, and we got talking. He thought I was American and he said he used to be in the Marines. I don't know why I jumped to the conclusion he was a bodyguard, but I did and asked him. He said, yes he was. I said, in that case, why wasn't he with his charge and he said there were two of them and they had to take it in turns: someone had to mind the shop in case the enemy broke into the house while Christopher was out, and prepared an ambush for him.'

'That was pretty rash of him, talking to you that way. Do you think it was true?'

They continued walking down Heath Street, bucking the crowds walking up towards the Heath. 'I guess it was. But he may have thought it didn't matter to tell a woman. I must have sounded like who I said I was, a friend. Anyway, I had my investigator check it all out. It was true.'

She fell silent. Gerald saw her profile set with tension. They crossed the street and started walking up Church Row towards Gerald's house. The trees were hazed with baby leaves. It was hot enough for the road's tar and dust smells to mingle with the blossoms' scent.

Gerald said, 'Any clue as to why your friend needs protection?'

'Penny, the detective,' she smiled at his surprised look and went on, 'Penny says that her sources say he has upset someone. That sounds obvious, doesn't it? But she can't find out who. The source seemed to think he had failed to deliver on something, had reneged on a deal to deliver . . . I don't know. Drugs, I think.' She stopped walking and sighed. 'It's impossibly sordid, Gerry. I don't know why I can't just forget about him.'

Gerald came back and slid his arm around her. 'I know why,' he said, warmly, and hugged her to him. 'You love the silly bastard.'

'Yes,' she said. Her voice was still and dark. She went on, her face set, her sentences abrupt, 'That's why I've got to resolve things one way or the other. I either have to be with him and know everything, or I have to end it somehow. I have to know what he is doing and who he is with. I can't go on imagining what might happen if he's being stalked by someone who wants to kill him or hurt him. I can't go on wondering if he's really a criminal and whether he's going to be sent to prison. I can't go on wondering whether there is some woman I don't know about who shares his life and his secrets. I can't stand it, Gerry. I'm going mad.'

He pulled her through the gate into his garden and led her up the path towards the front door. Outside the door, he stopped and dug in his pockets for his keys and answered her without looking at her. 'You're glamorizing him with your own inventions.' He put the key in the lock and turned it. The door swung open and the burglar alarm started its beeping signal. He kept on talking as he went to turn it off. 'As for going after him, I must say, I do think you're crazy, Tsarina. Clinically nuts. I've always thought you a bit unhinged. But now you're off your trolly completely. How the hell do you hope to find him? And when you find him what the hell do you think is going to change?'

Catherine stood behind him in the hall's welcome cool. He had dumped the hamper on the parquet. Now he walked into the sunlit drawing room. She followed him, stepping out of her mules. She said, bravely, 'I have a couple of leads from Penny and the name of an investigator in New York. I'll find him.'

Gerald flopped down on a sofa, kicked off his shoes and stretched his legs out over the pale cushions. He yawned and closed his eyes. His voice became a slurred drawl of sleepiness again. He said, 'And what are you going to do when you find him, my dear Catherina?'

She was silent and he looked up, startled, wondering where she had gone. She was standing in the big bay window that overlooked the garden at the back. A mist of green haloed her against the light. 'Tsarina?' His voice was plaintive.

She turned and walked back and stood looking down at him. She was smiling, gently. She said quietly and sweetly as if she were speaking words of love, 'It's change or die, Gerry. I'll either bring him back with me. Or I'll kill him myself.'

Gerald lay back again with his eyes closed. 'Put the kettle on, would you, Tsarina, darling. The help is off today.'

She walked with barefoot silence to the kitchen.

65

Catherine was having dinner with her old college friend Mary-Ann Lee Schneider in the Oyster Bar at the Plaza Hotel. Catherine had been in New York just over a week and was living in a suite at the Plaza, within walking distance of the Vanities Fifth Avenue office.

Although it was early in June, New York was beginning to develop the characteristically muggy heat of its summers. However the evenings were still a pleasant temperature and Catherine had so far enjoyed meeting her old friends and business contacts for drinks and dinners on their apartment terraces and roof gardens.

Mary-Ann had been in Catherine's year at Columbia School of Journalism and had helped to persuade her to stay in New York and take the job at the New York Post after graduation. She herself had gone to the Village Voice but was now with CBS as anchor on a daytime chat show. The two had remained close and met as often as possible whenever Catherine was in New York on Vanities business, which, until the past year, had been every three months for at least three weeks at a time.

Mary-Ann was a good looking girl with the square jaw, wide spaced blue eyes and soft curling shoulder length hair, in her case brown, beloved of America's TV anchor women. She had come, originally, from a small town near Minneapolis but had become a real Manhattan sophisticate with a smart west side apartment and a wardrobe of designer clothes. Her voice still had a strong,

315

clean cornbelt farm girl sound, good as a bugle for calling the men in for breakfast. But melodious.

Just now it rang out across the Oyster Bar with a less than melodious shriek. 'I don't believe it. Catherine Clyne is having an affair. At last!'

Several heads at nearby tables turned and several pairs of eyes stared at Mary-Ann. Catherine ducked her head into her hands and laughed helplessly. Fortunately no one in the room was likely to know that she was the Catherine Clyne referred to. Anyone listening would be bound to assume the name belonged to a third party.

Mary-Ann clasped a hand about her mouth and gazed with stricken wide eyes at Catherine, who shook her head in mock despair. 'Mary-Ann,' she said quietly. 'I promise to tell you everything so long as you give me your word of honour you won't do that again. It really is a secret.' She did not smile.

'I promise,' Mary-Ann whispered huskily. She looked shamefacedly around her. 'Gee, Cat. You just gave me the biggest shock. I still don't believe it. You were the next thing to a professional virgin.' She giggled. 'Married but chaste as a nun.' She paused and gave Catherine an assessing look and went on, 'Come to think of it, though, you have acquired a sort of post-nuclear explosion glow and you do look a touch more lived in.' She leaned across the table, her eyes wide with speculation and whispered, 'So tell me about him. I can't wait.'

Catherine was sorry she had confessed her secret. She begged Mary-Ann never to repeat a word of what she was going to tell her and began, more painfully than she had expected, to tell her story.

She did so because now that she was away from Gerald, she had no one to talk to. And she desperately needed a sympathetic ear and some practical observations to help her see more clearly what she should do. She could not, however, express her desperation to Mary-Ann. She was afraid of what she had made up her mind to do and would have liked to confess everything. But her feelings were so intense that she did not dare begin to let them out in a public place for fear she would cry.

Mary-Ann said, 'You're crazy about this guy. I never thought it would happen to you. Do you remember Buddy Harrison? What he used to call you. "Old Fashioned Vanilla." You were the ice cream queen of campus, he said. I don't know what you did to freeze him out, but he never forgave you. I guess you needed thawing out, Cat. But,' she narrowed her eyes and stared at Catherine, 'I'm not sure you know how to handle it, honey.'

Catherine wanted to get up and run out of the room. She seemed to feel Angel trying to talk to her. It was as if he was trying to say something. Her mind kept blinking on and off. She could not concentrate on Mary-Ann. Life was elsewhere. Not in this room. Life was with Christopher. And death, too. She shuddered, but Mary-Ann did not notice.

Catherine smiled a composed smile that said, Don't come any closer than that. I'm not telling you everything. She had not told Mary-Ann about Angel's criminal links. She said, 'I don't want you to ask me why but I'm afraid he may be in some danger and I want to find him. I've got someone trying to track him down right now.'

Mary-Ann gave her a long hard look. 'I guess there are a few major things you haven't told me, Cat. But what I want to know is, why are you telling me any of this if you don't trust me with it all?'

Catherine wanted to apologize, to say, It's not your fault really. I just can't tell you about this violence inside me. Instead, she said, 'I want you to give me your feeling on it, that's all. Maybe I should turn back to London and forget everything. Just give up and hope to meet someone I can amuse myself with until the pain forgets itself.'

Mary-Ann said, 'You look so goddamned tragic. Like an old movie heroine. But you can get control of the situation, can't you, Cat? A woman like you doesn't have to sit and wait for a guy to call her. Get after the bastard and corral him.'

Catherine shook her head, then leaned it, wearily, on one hand. 'I wish it were that simple.' Then she told Mary-Ann about the arrest and the police enquiries and the bodyguards.

'Wow!' was all Mary-Ann said.

'And there's something else. I've been followed off and on in London for months. I've never found out who it is. The police, a friend in the Force, looked into it but wouldn't give me a straight answer. They said I didn't have to worry. I thought for a while I must have been imagining it. And for a while, recently, it stopped. I wasn't followed after Christopher went away a month ago. But the thing is, Mary-Ann, I'm pretty sure I'm being followed again now.'

Mary-Ann's voice was a remarkably restrained stage whisper. 'Here, in Manhattan?'

Catherine nodded. 'It's been going on all week. It's the same face. I keep seeing this same man all the time. Anyway, I'm getting a bit nervous. I want to buy a gun. Can you suggest . . .'

'There's a telephone call for you, M'am.' The bellhop stood next to Catherine's elbow.

She excused herself and went out to the lobby and took the call on one of the house extensions.

'I have some news for you, Ms Clyne.' It was the detective agency. 'We've located your party. He's in Miami Beach. If you care to stop by the office in the morning I can give you all the details.'

She promised to be there by 9 a.m. Then she called US Air and reserved a seat for an afternoon flight to Miami and went back to the Oyster Bar.

Mary-Ann had ordered coffee. She looked up as Catherine came in and followed her progress to the table with an anxious expression on her lovely face. Catherine sat down and Mary-Ann said immediately, 'What's wrong?'

Catherine said breathlessly, 'They've found him. Now do I go to him or do I run?'

'You go to him, stupid,' Mary-Ann growled. She took Catherine's limp hand and squeezed it. She took her hand away suddenly and said, 'Oh yes. And before I forget, this, you dangerous livin' lady, is where you go get your gun.' She handed Catherine a piece of paper from her notebook, on which she had scribbled an address. She grinned. 'Can you use one?'

Catherine nodded.

'Good girl. Then I won't worry about you shootin' yourself in the foot.' Mary-Ann snapped shut her bag with a deafening click, grinned a satisfied grin and went on in her cornbelt bugle, 'And the way you're living these days, honey, don't leave town without it.'

Catherine gave her a smile that seemed to exude the calm determination of the old Catherine. 'I won't, Mary-Ann,' she said, 'I won't.'

66

The long grey limousine paced the causeway's undulating miles, moving with the grace and temper of a hearse, keeping well under the speed limit on the hot, dead asphalt. Water, pale as dead fishes underbellies gave back the sky's white brilliance. A curdling haze of overheated air shimmered over its surface. The car's interior was a frigid tomb. From within its funeral isolation Catherine looked back. The sun was an incendiary token slipping into a slot between the downtown towers, turning them dark and threatening as the crags of an abyss into which she seemed to be falling. When the token fell into place, night would come swiftly.

She stared out of the windows at the huge ships moored to her right. Cruise boats, casino boats, pleasure vessels, towering like apartment blocks out of the satin bay. To her left, islands, packed with red roofed villas and white mansions; yachts, sea planes tethered at their feet. Clouds as dense and white as Andean peaks were building on the Eastern horizon towards which they drove. Below them she saw the older hotels of Miami Beach, a broken row of yellowed dentures guffawing at the sky. She shivered.

The soft gold kid bag lay innocently on her lap. In it was a copy of the letter that had already gone by courier to her London lawyer with the codicil of instructions for the execution of her will. She slipped her hand into the bag's silky lined interior. She felt the letter's sharp outline. Her fingers roved, touching her passport, a hairbrush, her wallet. She groped for the silk scarf in the bottom corner and her fingers sensed the hard outline lying within its folds, like a secret gift.

She gripped the gun, feeling its cold muzzle through the thin scarf, letting her hand slide until she held the thing firmly as it should be held, outlining the trigger with her index finger. The car swept gracefully on, a cold steel and glass coffin, shining and hard as the gun itself, over the blistered road branded with palms' shadows. Villas, gardens, a golf course, a bridge, passed like the flickering of a backward running film. Catherine's frozen mind held only one image. She saw herself standing, as she had been trained to stand by George at the St Marylebone Pistol and Rifle Club. Feet apart, arms extended, steadying the gun, aligning it, finger squeezing the trigger. Saw him move forward. Saw him fall. Saw the gun's muzzle now raised and pointing towards herself, saw it move out of focus, felt the cold touch, almost a caress of gentleness between her brows. Felt . . .

There was a soft clunk.

'This is the Fontainebleau, m'am.' The driver was holding the door open.

Catherine withdrew her hand from the bag and stepped out of the car. Waves of sensual heat enveloped her, returning her to life. She was surrounded by noise and bustle as hotel guests entered arriving cars or got out of others. Doors slammed, voices were raised, bus boys moved briskly with baggage in and out of the hotel lobby. Bemused, she walked slowly up the red carpeted steps towards the revolving glass doors. Her hand sought the thin straps of her bag, which she had slid in habit over her left shoulder. 'M'am. What time do you want me to pick you up? M'am. M'am. Miss Clyne?'

She turned. The driver's voice reached her through the

mental fog that cocooned her. He was calling her, she realized, now. The trance in which she walked flickered and clicked off. She turned. For a moment she saw everything clearly. Too clearly. With hypnotized clarity. What she saw was like a still photograph that you stare at again and again when you want to discover something otherwise hidden in detail. Some truth. Some secret in the way people stand or move or look at each other. Some expression fixed for ever, lifted out of insignificance, from a fleeting instant, enlarged and made eternal.

In that micro second, moving from slow motion to a sharp focus still photograph, she saw the driver in his grey livery and the long silvery grey limousine that stood between them, its driver door open, the chauffeur leaning on it. She saw cars, a beige Oldsmobile, a black Cadillac, a small blue saloon, parked behind the limousine. She saw the fountains, dashing white spume into the unnaturally blue pools, saw the street with its stream of glittering metal stopped for the lights; the brilliance of water in the canal beyond; the sun, red and low over the houses opposite. She saw a man in the left field of her eye, standing quite still, looking at her. Saw his short trimmed greying brown beard, his light blue blazer, his dark blue shirt and white trousers. Saw him start slightly.

She was, in that focused moment, acutely aware of herself like an actress who has walked onto a stage to utter a single line and walk off again. Standing in her white cotton shirtwaister and high heeled courts, her dark glasses masking her eyes, her long pale hair drifting over her shoulders, the soft gold bag, a little heavy, swinging from her left shoulder.

Then she was looking only at the driver, a young man, Latino with dark brown eyes and a gigolo's face, leaning on the car, looking up the steps at her like a man in a snapshot. Her brain was suddenly hypodermic sharp. She knew in that instant everything she must do and not do. She smiled. It was a smile that combined regret and dismissal. She spoke in her clear English voice with the hint of American vowels, the voice that always seemed so much more English when she was in America. She said, 'I can't give you an exact time now. I'll call when I need you.'

'Okay, M'am.' The driver nodded and slid into his seat.

The car glided away and the frozen world melted and moved again. Catherine went on into the lobby. Here it was cool again. Ahead was a big bar area, set in a huge curved window that overlooked gardens and the sea. She saw people sitting at the tables, saw the banks of white cumulus towering over the horizon. A single, white sail hung like a question mark on the darkening ocean.

For a moment Catherine's intense purpose wavered. She had an impulse to walk over to the bar, pull up a stool, order a drink and sit, gazing at the view, at life. To be like others. To be free of her fate. Then the fog once more seemed to close over her mind, the trance returned. She walked stiffly to the left, following signs to the reception desk.

The reception area was crowded with arriving guests. Catherine drifted among them in her slim white dress and dark glasses, seeming apart and untouched by the milling crowds, vaguely lost. Her hand held the straps of the gold bag on her shoulder. As she stood, gazing helplessly around her, she saw the concierge suddenly free and walked quickly towards him.

'Mr Angel, M'am?' The concierge was an older man, grey haired with yellowed teeth and rimless spectacles. He exhaled a stale nicotine odour as he spoke in his singsong Southern drawl. He turned to his keyboard and tapped in Christopher's name. He smiled at Catherine. He had no hesitation in giving a room number to this distinguished and beautiful lady. She had more class than he was used to seeing these days at the Fontainebleau. 'Suite 17C,' he said, leaning towards her, gusting nicotine. He pointed over her shoulder. 'You go up those stairs, past the ballroom and turn right. Take the elevator to the 17th floor. Is the gentleman expecting you, M'am?'

Catherine smiled. 'No. It's a surprise.'

The concierge smiled and nodded. Not the kind of surprise any guy would refuse, he thought wistfully. He did not think he had had a sight of Christopher Angel, but he sure would not be disappointed to see this lady, whoever he was.

She followed his directions, winding through the thinning crowds and up the wide pink carpeted staircase flanked by marble statues and banks of artificial azaleas. She crossed the cavernous ballroom lobby whose high ceilings dwarfed the Louis XIV tables and mirrors and marble goddesses, standing along its walls. She turned right and came to a bank of three brass-doored elevators.

As she entered the centre lift she turned to look at the mural encased in glass on the lift's brown wall. It showed tropical leaves, huge and dark in rich greens and browns. She did not see the stocky, bearded man who had followed her from the reception lobby.

On the 17th floor, the lift doors opened onto a hushed dim lit hallway whose walls and ceilings were dark sepia brown. Catherine turned left. She heard nothing except the hiss of air conditioning. Huge brown ceiling fans turned slowly. The air smelled fusty and old, like in a tomb or a museum. The whole corridor felt as if it were deep underground, as if light and air would never reach it. She felt oppressed and afraid. The door of Suite 17C was like the door into the chamber of a pyramid, painted the same dark sepia brown as the walls. A spy hole was a bead of brilliant light in its sullen secrecy.

She stood in front of the door and stared at the bead of light. She knew the room beyond would look out onto the sea, was still lit by sunlight, reflecting off the water. She had seen him rarely in daylight. He could be out, but then she had chosen this time as one when he would probably be in, when most people in hotels went to their rooms to prepare themselves for dinner.

She was alert and focused again, now. She removed her glasses and slid them into the gold bag. Her hand now caressed the gun in its silk womb. She pulled it from the bag and unwrapped it, slipping the scarf back inside.

She stood perfectly still, examining the gun in her right hand, letting her fingers clench and unclench on the bulbous handle. She saw how ugly it looked. She turned her hand and saw the ring her father had given her for

Christmas, two weeks before her first encounter with Christopher. For a moment her face flickered with pain. Then the dream walker's blankness returned. She had programmed herself for this moment, rehearsed over and over again what she would say and do. The gun was already loaded. She slid off the safety catch and let her finger hook around the trigger. Then she let her arm drop along her side. Focusing her attention on the spyhole, she lifted her left hand and pressed the bell on the left of the door. She waited.

He was a long time coming. She saw the light from the spyhole eclipsed, felt rather than heard a gasp of surprise, then heard the locks being undone. Then the door swung into the room and he was behind it. Her eyes filled with the brilliance of the evening sea and sky and for a moment she was disoriented.

He must have been sleeping. She saw the blurred look on his face as he turned from quickly closing and locking the door. He started towards her, his hands extended, his face bemused and happy but bearing reproof. She swung around to face him, backing away. Her back was to the fading light. Her face was in shadow.

She saw his expression change abruptly as she raised the gun with her two hands. He froze. His eyes were watchful, calculating, baffled. She could see he was confused. She stood silently watching him. His expression changed from suspicion to fear, then to anger. She saw resolution take over. His shoulders dropped. He seemed to relax. He took a step towards her.

He said softly, 'What are you doing, Catherine? Put that away.'

She backed towards the window. She said, 'Don't move, Christopher. I'll kill you.'

'What's this about? Who sent you?' His voice was abrupt, rough.

She said quietly, 'No one sent me. I want you to tell me the truth about yourself. Everything. I want to hear the real story of your life, how you make your money and the people you are with.'

He gave a small exhalation that was almost like a gasp

of relief. His face relaxed again. He moved a step nearer. She tensed her arms, targeting him sharply and he froze again. He said, uncomfortably, 'What truth, Catherine?'

'Is there more than one?' Her voice was hard. She stared at him, unblinking.

He smiled then, roguish. 'It depends what you want to hear.'

Her finger tightened on the trigger and she saw the alarm leap into his eyes. He had to believe her. He had to realize that she had planned this to go all the way. She felt saliva caught in her throat. Her voice had a curiously metallic emptiness, like an automaton, when she said, 'I mean it. I'll kill us both. There's no other place to go except the truth. I don't care if you never want to see me again, or I you when I've heard it. I just want to know who and what you are. What I've been involved with.' She paused. Then, into their silence, she said, 'I want to know what I love.'

She saw him soften again. Saw his eyes glowing and gentle. Saw the mouth seem to smile a fraction. Saw the shoulders drop. 'What do you want to know, Catherine? What can I tell you to stop you doing this crazy thing?'

'Why you've been living lies. Why you've loved me the way you have and yet hidden yourself behind a screen of untruths. I want to know who and what you are, Christopher Angel. I want to know what you do with your life. I want to know why you left London. Why you never told me where you were going. And I'll kill you before you finish, if you begin another lie.'

He knew then that she meant it. It made him want her. He wanted her, violently. He thought, I'll never touch her again. She'll kill me. And herself. It's a crazy waste.

She waited.

He was, maybe, eight feet from her. 'Catherine.' He held out his arms towards her. 'Catherine.' His voice had a husky crack. He said, desperately, 'I do care for you, Catherine. That's true. You know that's true.' The need for words choked him. Feelings flooded under his fear's ice, feelings of lust, love, passion, desire for this woman.

325

When had he last touched her? Months ago. He couldn't tell her anything. He had to persuade her. If he could. She waited. He stood looking at her. Fear went. Disgust came. Self-disgust. Self-destruction. Self-loathing. Desire to die. Words, at last. 'I'm not worth it, Cat. I'm not worth your time, your love. I'm not worth this mess. Not worth dying over. Don't waste your life on a man like me.'

She wavered then. His so long self-denied emotion sloshed over her like a bursting dam. She almost whispered it: 'My life is a waste, Angel. I don't want to go on.' The light had faded to a faint glimmer. His face was as pale as the daytime moon. His eyes were black holes into another universe. Into another space and time where everything between them would have been possible.

Catherine was outlined against the window. Faint light from the sky made silver of her hair and her white dress. Her face was in shadow. How long could they stand here like this on the edge of the precipice?

He said, 'I can't tell you anything, Catherine. It would hurt you to know any more than you know now. It could endanger you to know anything about what I'm doing. Why I'm here. You're better off walking out of here. Forgetting all about me and my life.'

She was as still as marble, not seeming even to breathe.

'If you want me dead, leave me the gun and go. I'll finish myself for you.' He shook his head and his voice was full of bitterness. 'You shouldn't have ever got involved.' He felt rather than saw her change. He could not see in the dusk light how her face broke its watchful stillness, how colour washed into her cheeks. But he heard it in her voice.

She cried out, 'Well, it's too late for that. I am involved. We are both involved. You can't change the script. And the truth of what we are involved in must be shared. Must be opened now between us.'

'You're better off not knowing, Catherine. Walk away from it. Forget me and my lies.'

'Forget you!' The words hurled at him in the near darkness almost made him duck. 'I'd easier forget my life.'

His eyes were glowing strangely in the reflected light.

Her feelings leaped into words in a way he envied. 'I was with the walking dead when I met you, though I didn't know it. You gave me new life. Your love has given me the power to love from so deep inside myself I know no end to it. That kind of love is the most profound truth. And that truth inspires trust and openness, and sharing. No barriers. No evasions. No lies. I can't live when you withhold your truth, when you hide and dissemble and distort and evade and slither away from me without explanation. The only alternative ending to this kind of love is death. That's to admit an impasse, that our lives can't be shared, that the truth in our souls must be denied, buried under the living lies.'

He said, gruffly. 'Isn't that love enough, Catherine? Why must you know everything? Just take the love and forget the rest.'

'No,' she shouted the word. Then she drew breath and quietened her voice. 'You don't lie when you touch me. The truth between us when we make love, the truth in our silences and in our feelings for each other, is so profound, so beautiful, so real, that there can't be any compromise. You can't know that kind of truth and then tell each other lies or live a deception.'

He smiled faintly. Hopelessness shadowed his eyes, but she could see him only faintly now in the almost vanished light. His voice was a whisper. 'Is that worth killing us both?'

Her voice came hard as ice from her darkened mouth. 'Is a lie worth living?'

He sighed and shifted his weight. The spell that held him somehow gone, he said with a spark of impatience, 'Catherine, where I've come from, you learn to live by lies. Truth is what makes you vulnerable. You survive with lies. You stop them getting you by telling lies. Truth is a rich man's luxury.'

'Does that mean you have to lie to me? Don't you have any trust for someone who loves you? Am I someone from the jungle, too? Someone who will use what I know about you against you?'

'What have I lied to you about?' He was suddenly

327

defensive, touched with bravado. She saw how his instinct to trick and counter-attack came into play. It was no use. She tightened her hand on the gun, aligning the barrel.

'You lie all the time. You avoid the truth. You think that by not saying anything you don't lie. But you do. Omission on the scale you employ it is a gargantuan untruth. I've found out enough to know that for sure.'

'What have you found out?' He spat the words, angrily.

Her voice like steel she said, 'I'll trade you. I'll tell you what I know, if you'll tell me what I don't.'

He turned away from her, walking towards the sofa. He stopped when he heard the trigger click.

'Don't move another inch.'

He turned and faced her in the near dark room. He said defiantly, finally, 'I can't tell you anything, Catherine. You wouldn't want to hear it if you knew what it was. And for your own good I'm not telling you.'

She braced her legs and took aim.

He said, 'Go ahead. But let me give you some advice. Wipe the gun clean. Take it away with you. Dump it in the bay and get out of town.'

'I have other plans and another bullet.'

He moved a pace back until his legs contacted the sofa. Then he sat down. He needed to sit down.

'Do it, Catherine. Do the world a favour. Blow me away. But get yourself out of here.' His voice cracked. He propped his head on his hand.

Her fingers began to lose their grip. She stood, arms outstretched, legs apart and saw only the light catching his eyes. Her knees seemed to soften. He thought she was going into a crouch, but she went down on them, still holding the gun out towards him. Her head came to rest on her outstretched arms and she seemed to subside. She rolled over and the gun fell out of her open hand.

He leaped up and swooped on the gun, raced to the window and peered onto the balcony. He swiftly turned the lock on the glass door and raced to the bedroom and came back quickly closing and locking the communicating door. There was no one there. If anyone had shot her they had gone over onto the next balcony. He dropped to his knees beside her, putting his cheek to her mouth. But she was breathing long deep breaths. He dared not switch on the light, and so he ran his hands over her body, looking for telltale moistness, for blood. He held her away from him looking for a wound, for a stain on the white dress. He found nothing. He kissed her then, on the mouth and heaved her body into his arms. He said, 'Oh Catherine. Baby. My baby. What happened?'

Her eyes were open now, but she did not reply.

'Catherine, I love you.' It was the truth. He felt her arms creep around him. Felt her pulling him down onto her. He kissed her eyes and tasted her tears. He felt her lips kissing, kissing his face, his mouth, her hands pulling his shirt and searching out the bare skin beneath. She was gasping now, sobbing quietly. He kissed her face, now, her cheeks, her tears, her brow, her chin. Then long and hard, he kissed her lips and licked and sucked at her mouth and felt her life flowing into him.

She pushed him away to look into his face and whispered between soft short kisses, 'I couldn't do it. I couldn't do it. There was so much truth in your face. I couldn't kill that truth. That light. Just then, you knew and I knew what we both are. I had to bring us to this point. We had to get here. It was the only way. I've no more words to explain it.'

He had not seen her sudden failure of resolve. He had thought her shot, from behind from the balcony or the bedroom, even through the suite door from the corridor. He thanked whatever God he knew that she was alive. That the gun was no longer between them.

He ran his hands over her bare thighs and she moaned while he undid the buttons that held the thin skirt together, parting it. His fingers delicately found her softness under the fine silk pants and moved gently over the moist petals. She let out a long gasping breath and muttered his name, letting her thighs fall open.

He tugged at his belt and quickly unzipped the heavy cotton trousers, drawing the stiffening penis out. He lifted her pelvis and pushed it into her before she was open so that she cried out in pain and surprise. He fucked her furiously, with all the pent up energy of fear and anger built up during the past half hour while she had held him at gun point, with all the passion and desire she had made him know he felt for her, and for the absent time of these past weeks in which he had had no desire for other women, because of his worries and his fear, time in which he had been thinking of her and longing for her. He seemed to lose all sense of himself then. He knew only his need for her and her wild response. He drove into her again and again and she moaned and writhed under him, tightening and sucking what seemed the swollen point of his soul into that deep and secret place he always sought and the memory of which drew him to her, over and over and over.

He felt her soften and open and her wave begin and felt his semen rising. And as she dissolved under him he seemed to let go every essence in his body, everything in his soul. He poured his whole desperation and passion and love into her. He seemed go on and on emptying himself into her, spasm after glorious spasm until it seemed he would fill her womb, that his whole life would follow the thick white semen to its target, that he himself would be absorbed into her womb.

And she received him, the warm tide of her rising to meet him, merging into him, opening to let him into her secret heart, taking him as though she wanted never to be herself alone again, giving herself up like a corpse into the flames. And the great spark of their fusion rose through her like a current that charged and transformed them both.

It seemed to each of them, separately, that they would never be the same again after that loving, that as they lay exhausted by their passion and by what had gone before, that they had passed through the fire of love and could never equal that madness and desperation of desire and frantic need. They could never separate themselves from that merging that had occurred in their climax. But that they had given themselves to each other now, utterly, without negotiation, as if to God.

They lay together, their arms close around each other and fell into a deep sleep.

*   *   *

330

When he opened his eyes, she was still sleeping under him. The almost full moon had risen and now carved the room into a chiaroscuro landscape. He lay propped on his elbows gazing at her lovely face, wondering how he had ever deserved such beauty or such love. Then he kissed her gently until she awakened and pulled his face down close so that she could plant kisses on his mouth and eyes and cheeks. And he drew away until her eyes were looking back at him and he could see it was unchanged, what she was to him and what he was to her. And he knew it was too late to go back and undo their lives together and too late to run away and begin again without her.

But he did not know what to do about the things he could not tell her and he knew they would come again and again to stand between them because his life was one he could not ask her to live. And there was the other thing to be settled, the thing that had caused him to leave her. He did not know how that would end.

He saw that she had seen the doubt in his eyes and was questioning it. He saw she also was looking for their future and that she could not find it. He planted a kiss on her cheek, rolled over and stood up, pulling her onto her feet in one lithe swing. She lolled against him, smiling like a sleepy child, putting her arms around him and snuggling her head into his chest as if it were a pillow. His hands were on her hair, stroking her head.

Her voice muffled by his chest, she said, 'Come and walk on the shore with me.'

'Aren't you hungry?' He never knew what she would do next. She was so many women. 'It's dark now, too.'

She said, 'I know,' and looked up at him, her face laughing. 'I know. That's why it will be so good. The night is better for us, isn't it?' Her face grew serious again. 'The night is our time.'

He smiled and broke away from her, distant again, wrapped in himself. She watched him walk to the window. With his back to her, looking out, he said, 'All right. Just for a bit. Can you walk in those shoes?'

'I'll take them off when I get there,' she said and shook her hair back.

So they went down in the lift and walked out of the hotel through the beach exit without going through the lobbies. The garden was moon-soaked with black shadows spilling over the coarse grass. There was a scent of frangipani and the sea. They could hear the shuffling of waves on the shore against the crisper splashing of the waterfall that cascaded into the huge swimming pool.

There was no one in the garden. The air was like a tepid bath and their clothes clung to them, sticky with the moisture of their own bodies and the salt. She put her hand into his, demurely, like a child and he led her up the sloping boardwalk and down onto the sand. Here she stopped him and took off her shoes. She put them close to the side of the boardwalk where she could find them on the way back. Then she put her hand into his again and they walked over the gritty sand that was so rough with shells and coral that she cried out and he lifted her up and carried her down to the water's edge where the sand was ground fine and slipped through her toes.

He took his own shoes off and strung them around his neck by their laces and they walked along in silence, their feet patting the wet sand between the waves while the fresh wavelets rose over their ankles.

She said, 'Let's swim.'

He stopped and looked at her, holding both her hands in one of his. He smiled, ready for adventure. The lighted hotels were a few hundred yards behind them. He said, 'Is it legal?'

'Since when did you care?' She laughed. Then she looked at him, her face serious. It was one of the unspoken things between them that was not a joke. Nothing had been said, yet, about what he did. She had revealed something, shown she knew the nature of that hidden subject.

He smiled and said gently, 'I wouldn't want to get you into trouble.'

'That's all right then.' She started unbuttoning her dress. It opened all the way to its hem and she peeled it off and dropped it onto the sand. She wore only her silk and lace trimmed underwear.

He stepped forward, reaching his hands around her back and said, 'Let me do that.'

She slipped the pants off with a swift slither and stood naked, smiling at him. He so rarely saw her without her clothes on, he was taken aback at her loveliness. In the moonlight she was exquisite, her fine hair stirring softly in the light breeze, falling over her shoulders and perfect breasts.

He said, 'Let me look at you. Turn around slowly.' He liked to look at her buttocks. Their full curves stirred his desire.

She did as he asked, shyly, like a bride.

He said, 'You're lovely. Very, very lovely. Don't move.' He came close and stood near her and ran his hands over her smooth behind, then around her and over her breasts and her pelvis, pulling her against him so that she could feel him hardening against her buttocks.

'Undress,' she whispered, her breath caught by her rising desire.

She turned and watched him, and put her hands on his shoulders and ran them slowly and lightly over his chest and down to his already hard penis. She held the tight balls in her hand and stroked them. Then she dropped to her knees and took the full hard cock in her mouth. She brought him to the edge, tasted his first brackish fluid, and then he stopped her.

He pulled her to her feet. 'We'll swim first.' He took her by her shoulders and gently steered her into the water. They walked until they were waist deep. Then she plunged into a breaking wave and vanished, coming up a few yards away, sweeping her wet hair off her face. He dived after her and they swam and frolicked together letting the waves break over their heads, plunging in the warm phosphorescent water.

At last he took her hand and began tugging her shorewards until they both lost their balance and fell into the surf. He lifted her up and she was still waist deep. He put his hand between her thighs and touched her and she threw her head back, breathing deeply as if she were in a trance. He lifted her over his cock, just under the water,

333

and then pulled her down onto it and she was open like a flower. She curled her legs around his back and let the water take her weight. He took her then, gently and easily, under the water's lip.

A wave carried them inshore and knocked them over, but he kept on, lifting her head above the water with one arm around her neck and holding her to him with the other, pressing deeply into her with an undulating rhythm that was like that of the sea, until he had drawn her orgasm out of her and filled her with his own. They lay in the surf, wavelets washing sand into their hair, limp as survivors of a wreck, clinging to each other as if there were no other hope of life.

At last, unlocking themselves, they lurched to their feet and started out of the water, holding hands. Suddenly she stepped on a sharp shell and stumbled, falling to her knees with a surprised cry. He seemed to lose his balance and fall heavily beside her. She scrambled up, laughing, sweeping the sand-choked hair out of her eyes. He lay, face down on the wet sand, small fringes of the waves curling around his head.

'Come on, darling.' She laughed and bent to reach for the hand that had been holding hers as she fell, clasped it and tugged. He lay limp and heavy, his face in the sand. His body seemed as soft and pliant as a waterlogged rag doll. She tugged again, then knelt, smiling to splash water over his head. He lay completely still.

'Don't play dead, my Angel. You'll catch cold.' She pushed playfully at his soft, unwettable hair with its scatter of sand and weed. Then against his pale skin she saw the dark stain she had thought was a piece of weed above his left shoulder blade. It moved, elongating into a narrow line that drew itself slowly down towards his armpit.

She stared at it, fascinated, horrified. She slowly put out her hand and touched it, felt its sticky wetness. She lifted her hand and saw the dark shadow of the stain on her fingertips. She stared at it and with the slow movements of an idiot child, brought it to her mouth, putting out her tongue to taste it. Then she screamed. She lifted

334

her head to the moon and howled in anguish. Then, holding her breath, she suddenly pushed him frantically, turning the heavy body so that his face was out of the sand, desperately brushing, splashing the sand from his features.

'Oh Angel, Angel, Angel. Oh my love. What happened? My love, my love, wake up. Please.'

She crumpled over him, kneeling in the riveted sand, putting her cheek to his mouth to feel for breath, filling her lungs and breathing into his open mouth. There seemed no response, but she thought he was still breathing. She turned suddenly. Someone was running towards them. She flung herself over Christopher's body.

A man's voice said, breathlessly, 'I saw what happened. I tried to catch him. Let me help you.'

She looked up and saw a man of about thirty with crewcut hair and light running shorts and vest. She stared up at him, unable to speak.

He saw her shock and said gently, 'Stand up and let me look at him.'

She stood, shivering, forgetting her nakedness and the stranger knelt over Angel. Then he put his hands under the limp body and gently heaved it out of the water. He turned to Catherine and spoke urgently, 'He's breathing but he's losing blood. Wait here with him. I'll go for help. Put on some clothes. Cover him with anything you have.' The man sprinted towards the nearest lighted building.

Catherine held her sobs within her so that they emerged like shivering long gasps. She did not understand what had happened. What had happened was what she had imagined: but it was not she who had done it. But who? Who? She took Christopher's trousers and struggled to put them over his limp legs. She took his shirt and draped it over his chest and shoulders and saw the dark stain paint its message of death across the thin cloth. She folded her underclothes into a pad and tried to staunch the dark flow. She put on her dress and knelt in the sand and took Angel's cold hand between her own. Then, as no one came and he seemed to grow colder she lay her length along him and tried to breathe warmth from every inch of her own chilled body into his.

By the time they came, running with a stretcher, her white dress was soaked in his blood. They had to pull her from him. The runner who had gone for help took her and wrapped a blanket around her and led her towards the hotel while the paramedical team lifted Angel's unconscious body onto the stretcher.

As they walked towards the lights, Catherine turned suddenly, panicking. 'I must go with him.'

The stranger stared at her. He saw she was rational. He saw her determination as tight strung as a fine silver wire. He said, 'Of course. I'll just help you to the ambulance.'

They walked through the garden and into the hotel and on through the lobby to the forecourt. Catherine was aware but careless of the stares that followed them. She sat with him inside the ambulance, holding his limp hand, saying nothing to anyone. The blanket wrapped squaw fashion around her shoulders warmed her, but her bare feet were cold and smeared with sand and dirt. She gazed into Angel's face and pressed his fingers to her lips. She took the hem of her dress and wiped the sand from his forehead and his cheeks. Before they took him from her again, she put her lips onto his and said, 'I love you.' She was completely calm when she stepped from the ambulance. Her mind was empty of all thought except the prayer that Angel would return to life. In her head she heard the silent words as if they were spoken in a huge cathedral, echoing under the gothic arches. Her mind repeated the same phrase. 'If God wills it, let him live. Even if I never know him again, let him be alive and whole.'

They went inside the hospital and doctors took him away and she found herself waiting alone, in an anonymous, comfortable room that had padded chairs lining its walls, a TV talking silently at one end and stacks of magazines on a low table in the centre. A nurse brought her coffee and she drank it, forgetting how she disliked it. She said to the nurse, 'I want to be with him. When can I go to him?'

336

The nurse was middle-aged and black. She smiled a smile of professional compassion. She spoke in a crisp, high voice with a Carribean lilt. 'He's in theatre now. It'll be a while. They have to operate. If there is a bullet in him, they have to take it out. If not they have to repair any damage best they can. You'd best relax and watch the TV. They'll let you know the outcome.' She bustled about the room, pillow chested and big bellied with the broad, high rump of her race, pulling magazines out of the tipsy pile on the coffee table. She handed three of the better ones to Catherine. She said with a bossy thrust, 'You'd be best taking your mind off it while you're waiting.'

Catherine nodded. After the nurse left the room, she stretched her legs out in front of her, pulled the blanket close to her neck and closed her eyes.

She shut out her anguish and went over the sequence of horror that had brought her here. She tried to remember every detail of what had happened from the moment she stumbled. She had seen no one in the darkness, had not been looking anywhere except down to where she put her feet in the frothing sea. She had heard no shot. Only the surf sound came back to her probing remembrance.

She lived again the slow motion horror of her discovery of the blood trickling from the wound in his shoulder. She replayed her unbelief, her slowness, her blankness on her discovery. She had known the moment she saw the thick moving trickle that could have been a piece of weed, but she had not wanted to believe it. Still drunk on their lovemaking, high with life, how could she believe in his death? She drew in her breath suddenly at the thought that struck her: whoever had shot Angel had been watching them, perhaps since they left the hotel.

She had stumbled and whoever it was had fired at Christopher at that moment. As she went down, Christopher had taken the bullet from the unseen killer's gun. Had the gunman meant to kill them both? Had her stumbling at that point saved her? Had the killer thought them both hit when he ran from the beach? How many bullets had been fired? Had Christopher been hit more

337

than once? She did not think so. But now she wondered who wanted him, or perhaps both of them, dead. And who might try again. She shuddered.

She wondered again about Christopher's life. She let her mind run over the things Armstrong had told her. She must have expected something like this could happen. Christopher had run from London for a reason he would not tell her. Said he could not tell her. Some reason she could not be allowed to know because it would endanger her. And there were the bodyguards, and Penny's source who said he had upset someone. Someone had been trying to kill him for a while. How long? Why? Who? And how soon would they try again if they found out he had survived?

She chewed her lower lip. The taste of the coffee she had drunk, came back to her and she wrinkled her mouth. Something else was coming back to her, too. Something hesitated on the brink of recall, like someone who refused to enter a room. Something. Her mind went back to the minutes before she knocked on the suite door, the gun in her hand. Then she remembered her gun, sitting on the coffee table. The maid would find it in the morning. She had to get back there before then.

She looked down at her feet. She remembered her shoes sitting under the boardwalk. She would have to get clothes and more shoes from her hotel. She would have to go back to the Grand Bay. Or send someone. The limousine company, perhaps. She closed her eyes. Suddenly, she was looking at a clear picture. She saw the driver leaning on the limousine door, looking at her over the top of the car. She saw him waiting for her answer. She was aware of the people standing around her, all frozen into immobility as in a still from a film. She was looking at the picture as if it were there to show her something, as if her mind had dropped it onto a table and someone had said, Look, what do you see in that picture? There's something in that picture that you need to know. Something that is the key to what you are thinking about.

She was still concentrating on the picture when the police came.

67

Dawn was a dull smouldering event, a high dawn where
the sun had to climb the banks of dark clouds over the
Gulf Stream before it could break out the day. She
watched it from across the bed where Angel lay, his eyes
closed, his lips parted, little puffs of breath escaping in
rhythmic short rasps that were far too tortured to be
snores. His lung had been holed clean through by the
single bullet that had scraped within millimetres of his
heart and the aorta. A fraction lower and the aorta would
have been nicked, would have gushed his blood out in
seconds. She shuddered and looked again at the sombre
dawn. The gold light of coming sunrise cut the black
cloudbank out of the grey sky.

She leaned her head against the cot's cold railings and
yawned. Her watch showed it was just after seven. She
had been here all night. Watching him come out of
anaesthesia and fall into a fevered sleep. Her blanket was
still wrapped around her, concealing the bloodstained,
crumpled dress. Her feet were still bare and sandy. She
had slept, off and on, not wanting to relinquish consciousness. Not wanting to trust that he would go on breathing
unless she went on willing it consciously.

They had allowed her into the room despite Angel's
critical condition, but only after she had thrown the most
tremendous scene downstairs. Her lips curved in a weary
smile of achievement. That had been soon after the police
had finished and she had been tense and tortured, not
knowing whether he would live or die, answering their
seemingly meaningless questions while her soul screamed
its silent desperation.

Where had they been? Where were they going?
Why were they on the beach, in the sea? Who might have
wanted to shoot either of them? What had brought them
to Miami Beach? What were their names, addresses, birth

dates, passport numbers . . . and on and on and on. All with the solemn suspicion of men who trust nothing and no one and who regard even victims of crime as guilty until proven of good faith. This was an attempted homicide, but who knew yet what was involved: drugs were a common cause of shootouts in Miami.

They had someone, they had told her before they left. A patrol officer had seen the gunman running from the beach, had pursued, wounded and caught him. The man was currently in a coma. When he came to, if he did, they would be able to question him. Ms Clyne and Mr Angel would be asked to see if they could identify the man, as soon as they were fit to. The police sergeant had looked Catherine up and down without sympathy. She might have been a body dredged up from the sea lying on a morgue slab for all the human interest he showed her.

Angel's breathing changed then. For a moment it was deep and gasping. He moved his head, tossing it first to one side, then the other, moving the exposed arm with its gruesome attachment of plastic tubes. Then he was still, the rasping breath suddenly silent. Alarmed, she leaped to her feet and leaned over him, putting her cheek to his lips. But the breath was coming gently, still. She relaxed and sat back, watching him anxiously.

His face had a greyish tinge and a growth of beard darkened his jaw and lip. He had lost a lot of blood during that forty or fifty minutes it had taken to bring help and get him here to the emergency hospital in downtown Miami. Thank God, there had been no second bullet, no more wounds. Thank God for the runner who had surprised the gunman before he could fire more shots, and then had come to their help.

A ray of warm light from the now risen sun brought a translucent glow to his pallor. She wondered if the light would wake him. She had drawn the thin curtain back at first light, relieved after the long watch of the night in which she had sat listening to his breath struggling for birth from the wounded lung. She longed for the moment when he would open his eyes. How she missed his eyes.

How important they were to her. She had seen him sleep so rarely, only the few times he had slept in her arms after lovemaking, but then always with the assurance that the long lids would open and the dark eyes look at her with their deep wells of unspoken feeling.

Now as the sunlight began warming the room, lighting the muted greens and creams of the walls and furnishings, the bed cover's stark white, pulling shadows out of corners, he inhaled deeply and tried to move. But the wretched tubes held his arm. His eyelids flickered and at last she saw them open, saw the beloved eyes, bewildered and dull with pain, as they moved rapidly back and forth, taking in the room. He tried to lift his head. She saw panic in his face.

She said softly, 'It's all right, my love. You're safe.'

He had not seen her. But he looked straight at her then. She saw him look at her as he might look at a stranger and with fear. Then he relaxed. His head fell back on the pillow. He stared at her from under half closed lids. She could not read his mind.

She stood and leaned over him and kissed his forehead. She dared not kiss his lips for there was a danger of infection to the lung. She sat again and took his free hand and held it against her lips. She felt the smallest movement and then the pressure of his fingers on her own. She saw his lips curve slightly in a smile, then the eyes closed again and he was asleep once more. He was still sleeping a half hour later when the nurse came into the room.

She looked curiously at Catherine. She had not been on the night shift and knew nothing of the hell Catherine had raised to be allowed to stay the night in the room. She bustled around, checking the drip.

With a leap of her heart, Catherine remembered the gun. She had to get back to the Fontainebleau immediately. But before she could get in there without attracting attention she had to get back to her own hotel and pick up some shoes and fresh clothing. She would make picking up toiletries for Angel her excuse for getting the key to his suite.

341

To the nurse, she said, 'Will the doctor be checking in here soon?'

'I expect so.' The nurse was a young plain blonde woman with a hard face and bony shoulders. Her voice, which matched her looks, was brittle and insensitive.

Catherine hesitated. She hated to leave Christopher, but she had to. She said, 'I'll have to leave for a while now. I just want to be sure my friend is going to be all right.'

'You can't expect no miracles,' the nurse said. Then she smiled, a sudden friendly smile that took all the harshness out of her face. 'But don't you worry about him, now. He'll be looked after.' She paused and gave Catherine a long, searching look. 'Maybe you better look after yourself a bit, now,' she said.

Catherine nodded. She gave a last look of doubt and longing at Angel, and went out.

68

She stood alone in the centre of the bedroom. The mid-morning sun blasted the rose-toned room with searing light. The gun was back in her gold kid bag that hung once more from her left shoulder. She was freshly bathed, wearing a clean white drill dress, severely cut and belted with brass buttoned pockets and epaulettes: a perfect St Laurent. But that was purely a disguise for what she had come to do. She had had no care for her appearance as she showered yesterday's sand out of her tangled hair.

She had arrived back at the Grand Bay while most people were still at breakfast. She had scurried up to her room, still barefoot and blanket wrapped, still trailing sand. She was noticed only by the doorman and a surprised looking chambermaid who was examining the outside of her door as she reached it.

Now she was in Suite 17C in the Fontainebleau. She had expected difficulty, but fortunately, when the receptionist had called the hospital to verify her claim that she was a friend of Mr Angel's who had come to pick up toiletries and clothing for him, there had been no obstruction. She had been given the key and allowed up alone.

She walked to the window and looked out. She could see the bright beach with its stuttering lines of surf, its striped awnings reduced to tiny toadstools. Her eyes searched southwards for the place where they had been last night. She thought she could pinpoint the spot, a few hundred metres south of the hotel's limits. Yet nothing, from this distance, recorded their presence there.

She knew, also, that if she walked down the shore now, past where her shoes from last night must surely still be waiting under the boardwalk, past the awnings and the lookout station, walked down to the innocent sea, she would see nothing. The tide would have smoothed away every indentation in the sand, have dispersed each drop of precious blood, have erased the vibrations of trauma, washed out their passion and her grief.

Had he been dead, there would have been no more sign of their moment there. The warm sea had drowned their agony as easily as it had massaged their ecstasy. It was as if a stage hand had removed the props of one scene in readiness for the next. Yes, she thought, we have moved on. Rather than a new scene or Act, it seemed as if a new play might begin. Nothing seemed the same since yesterday. She was unsure if she was even the same person. It was as though she had a new identity, a new name. Or none. Her body felt light and empty, hollow as a paper doll's. Her head was faintly dizzy. She had eaten nothing since lunch yesterday, she remembered. But her sense of unreality was due to much more than that, surely. The world looked different. Even daylight seemed to have changed its quality and intensity. The blankness of the beach in response to her questioning eyes seemed to suggest another universe had replaced the one where such passion and violence had existed in so brief a space of time. Something had changed, too, between herself and Angel, during the past night's close silence. It was as if their thoughts had continued their dialogue and some new contract had been struck.

The air conditioning was blowing strongly with a sibilant persistence. She turned away and walked to the bathroom. Here it was dim and still, like a haven of rest away from the brilliant day. She wanted to lie down on the soft carpet and sleep. The mirror above the wash basin gave her back an image that was, at a glance, fresh and groomed. But her eyes seemed dull and her expression showed pain.

She lifted his shaving kit from the shelf, his toothbrush and toothpaste from a glass, his aftershave. She looked around. Was there anything else? She saw the heavy long-toothed comb, the black man's comb, and put her hand out to touch it with a sudden tenderness. She lifted it and saw a single tight-curled dark hair clinging to it. An explosion of emotion blew tears from her eyes. 'Oh God,' she gasped aloud. Was it like this when someone died? The simple personal possessions were weighted with pathos. She sobbed aloud, crumbling suddenly, the comb still in her hand, dropping her weight onto the closed lavatory seat, burying her head in her lap, sobbing.

She had not cried. She knew she needed to let the shock and grief of what had happened out of her being. Knew she had to let go of the stored tension, the impossible restraint that had kept her awake by his bedside through the dark hours, waiting for dawn, praying for his healing. Knew she had to cry tears of relief that, after all, he was alive, that he would live, that unless there was an infection or a sudden complication, a haemorrhage or a heart attack or . . .

'Oh my God.' The dangers and possibilities for disaster overwhelmed her. She stopped sobbing. Her tear-drowned breath came raspingly in long deep sighs. She should not think of what could go wrong. She stood up and took the single hair from the comb, wrapped it carefully in a tissue and slid it inside her brassiere. She took his toiletries and walked out of the bathroom, pulling his robe from the hook at the back of the door as she went. A voice seemed to repeat in her head. He'll live. He'll live. He'll live. She murmured the words aloud. Repeated them like a mantra as she crossed the dull rose carpet.

She opened the wardrobe and stared at his clothes. Two lightweight, hand-tailored suits she had never seen, a linen sports jacket, some slacks, shirts, ties, belts. She recognized a tie. Otherwise these were the clothes of a man she had not met. She selected a pair of slacks and the linen jacket, a shirt and tie, then opened drawers looking for underclothes, for something casual like a sweatshirt or a cotton polo.

She found the gun wrapped in a T-shirt at the back of a drawer of underwear. She unwrapped it and stared at it, drawing in her breath and biting her lip. Then she rewrapped it and put it back. In the next drawer, with the cotton polo shirts, she found his passport, some travellers cheques and a bunch of keys.

She opened the third and bottom drawer. A slim black briefcase fitted neatly into it. She started to close the drawer, then stopped. Sudden curiosity made her open it again. She lifted the briefcase out. It was locked by a padlock not a combination. Without hesitation she lifted the bunch of keys and found the only one that could fit the case.

The lid swung upwards easily. It was neatly packed with uniformly packaged stacks of used $100 bills. She counted them quickly. A million dollars can look pretty small. It fits a pretty small briefcase quite easily. There was nothing else in the case. Catherine closed and locked it.

She looked for a small bag into which to put his toiletries and clothes. She saw his empty luggage stacked neatly on the rack. A black canvas suit bag and matching soft case. Everything fitted into the case.

She took her handbag into the bathroom, rinsed her face with cold water, combed her hair, put on some lipstick and her dark glasses. She went once more to the wardrobe and opened the double doors, surveying herself in the long mirror inside. As she swung to look at her dress from the back her shoulder caught one of the suits and the jacket slid from the hanger. As she lifted it from the shelf under the rail, she noticed the weight from the right breast and put her hand inside, feeling the silk lining and the pocket cut into it. A small address notebook fitted tightly into the pocket.

Catherine could not stop herself lifting the notebook out. She opened it at random, flicking the pages. Her own name was absent from the C pages, but she could not help noticing the letters AC followed by her father's private number at the bank.

69

'Lift your skirt.'

She looked up, startled. The magazine she had been reading slipped from her lap. He was smiling at her, awake after a long sleep, without her noticing any change in his breathing.

She laughed. There was joy and relief in her laugh. Suddenly, he seemed better, a presence behind his eyes now. She stood up and did as he asked her. The full red skirt lifted easily. The thin silk wafted as she moved towards him. The black lace knickers revealed a tantalizing pattern of honey skin. As she reached him he put his hand onto her warm thigh, sliding it softly up the blonde down and into the moist tangle under the lace.

She looked down at him, her eyes indulgent, their colour suddenly intense. She bent and brushed his lips with her own, then straightened. 'I shouldn't kiss you yet.'

There was still a danger of infection to the lung. Kisses were not recommended. It was the fourth day since the shooting. She had sat by his bedside all day and every evening, only going back to the Grand Bay to sleep and return refreshed and in a different dress every day. She had made a special effort to look lovely. He opened his eyes so little during those first days and she wanted him to remember what he saw, to have what he saw help him come back to life.

He said, 'Then kiss me where it can't hurt.'

She glanced towards the door. Anyone might look through the glass panel to check on him. She put her hand on him, and felt the hardness, but admonished him gently, 'You're not well enough. Save your strength.'

His answer was to insinuate his fingers gently into her.

She said, 'I want to. But I don't want to deplete you. You must save every scrap of energy.'

He said, 'You make me feel strong.' Then sharply, a command. 'Do it, Catherine. Or I'll get up and fuck you in spite of all this spaghetti.' His right arm was still attached by tubes to the drip.

She laughed. There was a husky crackle of desire in her laugh that aroused him more.

He said, pleadingly, almost whispering, 'Go on.'

She glanced once at the door and then knelt on the bed. She bent her head. Her hair trailed deliciously over his belly and he felt the warmth of her mouth, the rapid movements of her tongue, her lips sliding lower and lower and the rough ridged texture of her palate against the swollen sensitive tip that seemed to be the focus of his whole being. She squeezed and sucked and licked him, biting the head of his cock gently from time to time, running her tongue in erratic slivering ripples over the bulbous end and down its hard sides. Her hand stroked and encircled the lower end of the shaft, the tightened testicles. His fingers under her skirt played delicately with her, sliding in and out of her yearning space. How delicious that was, but how she wanted him.

She remembered the last time they had made love, in the sea, four nights ago, before . . . No, not that. She should not think of that because here he was alive in her mouth, seeping semen now, not blood, gusting his own sea smell into her being. She tasted him, the salt sweet taste of him, felt him rising, the ripple under her fingers, slackening in her mouth, and the sudden warm and salt sea taste on her tongue. She sucked and pulled every drop out of him, drinking him, swallowing him, loving him.

And in that moment, he brought her, crying from the depth of her throat, loosening her grip but still holding him in her warm mouth, brought her to a violent convulsive climax that seemed to go on for ever under his knowing hand.

After, she lay alongside him and buried her head in his sound shoulder while his free arm stroked her thighs and buttocks under her skirt.

He slept then and she lay, drawing her head back and watching his face. Although he seemed deep asleep, his eyes were not completely closed. It was like watching a cat sleep. In the open slit under the dark lashes she could see the amber iris with its onyx pupil and she wondered at his watchfulness, his lack of trust even in sleep.

It was as if they were awake and talking to each other. She was aware of currents of energy flowing between them, everywhere along their bodies' length. An intensity of life and light seemed to fill her and play back and forth between them as if they were rare bodies of magnetically charged particles, flowing and pulsing, a kind of human Aurora Borealis.

When he opened his eyes, she said, 'I've such a selfish reason for wanting you well. To have you make love to me, to have you inside me, filling me.' She looked at his profile and he turned his head slightly towards her gaze. She saw the look of content on his face; but his eyes grew wondering under a slight frown.

She raised her head questioningly and he said, 'I don't know why you want me, Catherine.'

She said: 'You've said that before and I still don't have an answer. You're my happiness and I just want you. I want you, all of you, whatever you are. And to be with you. Isn't that enough?' And she thought of the briefcase with the money and the gun in his suite and the things she knew that he did not know she knew, and wondered

348

when he would tell her and melt the mountain that stood between them.

He said, 'You shouldn't be with me, Catherine. Look at the trouble I'm getting you into. Shooting. The police: they'll be round one of these days asking a lot of questions and you'll be involved. What's going to happen if the British papers get to hear about it? Cabinet Minister's wife, distinguished banker's daughter, involved in a shooting, with some shady character in Miami Beach. Your reputation . . .' He tailed off and looked into her face with troubled eyes that seemed to crave something.

She sat up and swung her feet in their high red stiletto heels to the floor, pulled her skirt straight and walked to the mirror above the washbasin. She stood, staring at her image. She looked flushed, glowing, happy. She turned towards him and her smile radiated love and joy. 'Look at me,' she said softly. She walked back to the bed and sat on the edge looking at him. 'When you met me, did I look like this?'

He smiled, mischievously. 'It was dark. I couldn't see you as well, then.' Serious again, he added, 'You were beautiful, Catherine, and you're even more beautiful now.'

'So you see,' she smiled triumphantly. 'I'm more beautiful now, because I love you. And perhaps because I feel your love?' She made the last a question and waited for his reply.

She saw his face cloud. 'I don't think we should go on hiding from that word, my Angel. Whatever you think it means in terms of obligations and conventions you might want to avoid, and I won't complain about that, we are neither of us conventional, I think we should forget whatever we think those conventions are and simply love.'

He was listening, watching her with eyes that seemed to glow and warm her.

'I suppose the danger, if it is a danger, is that love is the most powerful agent ever invented for the transformation of people's lives.' She wanted to say 'and their souls' but stopped herself. She added, 'Transformation for the better. From inertia to energy, from stagnation to activity, from indifferent to happy, from misery to joy.

Can you risk being transformed, Angel?' She reached out her hand to touch his cheek.

He caught the hand and pulled her towards him. He said, indulgently, 'You're a romantic, my baby. A romantic.'

'You're so right. But I'm also realistic. And I know that love begun has to continue and develop or else great misery results. We have no choice, my Angel. We've had no choice since the first time. Because we knew then, both of us, that we had struck gold after years of turning up lead. Love like ours is alchemy: base metal into gold, lust into spiritual power. Can't you feel it. Haven't you allowed yourself to be lifted up by it, admitted that the things we do together with our bodies are the greatest kind of ritual for finding paradise on earth?'

He nodded. The eyes still glowed like candles in a dark cave.

She said, 'That's why . . .' she was going to say, I thought I had to kill us both, but said instead, 'That's why we can't hold anything back . . . or the alchemy will fail. I couldn't bear that, my love. I couldn't bear what we have to stagnate. I want that prize, that paradise. Do you?'

His eyes told her he knew and understood and accepted. He said nothing but his hand squeezed hers and held it and he looked at her as if he would never let her out of his sight.

70

After a week, Angel was considered well enough to be moved out of the emergency hospital to the Cedars of Lebanon at Eighteenth Street. Catherine spent most of every day with him. He had slept a great deal and she had read or merely gazed through the window at the

Miami skyline, grateful for time to think. She sometimes made caretaking calls to Vanities' offices in London and New York before leaving the Grand Bay. Otherwise, she left him only to take the occasional swim and, each night, to sleep.

She had told her offices she was taking a short holiday so she received few calls. She had heard once from her London lawyer, perplexed by the letter and codicil sent from Miami, and once from her father whom she had not called to say she had left New York. Having called Vanities in New York, Arnold Clyne had found her at the Grand Bay before breakfast. Arnold always knew how to catch people before breakfast whatever their time zone. He had expressed surprise at finding her there. Miami did not seem like the kind of place where his daughter would take a vacation. 'Isn't it a bit rough?' he asked.

She laughed at him. 'It has flavour, Daddy. It's a city of great character and variety.'

'But so risque, my dear. So proletarian and outre.'

'Darling Daddy. You're such a snob. I suppose even Palm Beach is too nouveau for you.'

'You're dead right, sweetie pie,' had been the ham rejoinder. 'I wouldn't be seen anywhere on the continent of America outside Georgetown or Fifteenth Street and Pennsylvania Avenue, Washington DC, or the Upper East Side of Manhattan. Cape Cod is permissible in the summer. Florida and California are too vulgar. The Caribbean is the only accessible alternative for people of quality, and only then in winter, of course.'

She laughed. Her heart was light. Life was blossoming. Christopher was being more open and frank than she had ever dreamed. There was a growing strength in their bond, a closeness she had wished for over months. She felt happier now and more confident in their relationship. The months of doubt and fear, of suspicion and anger, seemed to have dispersed like nightmares with the day.

And each day had brought fresh insights into his real nature. They had begun to talk of the past, his past. She said, 'I want to know everything,' and laughed when he gave her a look of warning and retreat.

'I mean everything about your life when you were little. I want to know about you as a child. I want to know how you were with your mother. I want to know what kinds of things upset you, what you liked. I want you to tell me things you haven't thought about for years.' She wanted him to develop the habit of confession, wanted his truths, wanted to strip him of his burdens, wanted him to let go his past and relinquish his anger, knew that if he talked now, he would be freed of the hold the past had on his actions, on his present, his future, his dreams.

She now continued and developed what she had begun that morning in his house in London, which was subtly to take hold of the relationship, to assume control of its destiny. Perhaps he was unaware of it. He did not seem to resist. But, she had no conscious design. It was an instinct that drove her. Her love guided every word, every need.

Now, too, there were those sensual episodes. He would wake from sleep and pull her to him. As he healed and grew stronger he needed her more often. Her presence was a constant stimulant to desire. And desire was strong when there were few distractions. His usual way of being absorbed by his projects so that his desire was simply a source that drove him on, was lost. He felt his rising energies taking the form of need for her, avid desire for her mouth on him, in the absence of enough strength to take her fully, as she should be taken.

Now they could kiss, too. Her lips on his were her own constant expression of love. One day, he asked her to give herself to his tongue, to sit astride his face and let him take her that way, but she would not.

She said, 'There's still too much risk. Your lung. We'll have time later.' And he smiled, pulling her closer on the bed, pulling up her skirt and touching her tantalizingly, drawing her hand under the covers to find him hard and valiant.

They had talked. Oh, yes, they had talked. And there was more to come. She had heard of his childhood, of the way his mother had suffered with her woolly-haired, fatherless child. After her family's first shock and disapproval, which had left its mark on him as his own rejection of his black blood, they had closed ranks around her. Even so, they must always have regretted his mixed blood and shown it each time they looked at him. Besides, many in their Jewish community had shunned them and he carried with him that scar.

He seemed to feel he was unwanted and blamed his mother, seeming, in turn, to despise her although he remained close to her. She had earned her living cleaning houses, working in Woolworths. They had lived in Walthamstow in north east London. He had gone to school there in the days before there were many black immigrants and been laughed at for his hair, his rare, half cast, black man's hair.

He had hated them. He still hated them. Most revealing, he had hated a blond girl, for whom he had suffered a calf love. A girl of some better class, an older girl, who came home from University in the holidays, the local doctor's daughter. She'd turned him down. Brutally. His anger still lived.

Catherine said, 'Have you punished every blonde you've met since? Have you always wanted to get your revenge on that girl?'

He smiled, innocently, 'I like blondes.'

'She spat on you with her class and her looks. You've never forgotten it.'

He pulled a face and shrugged as best he could under the bandages. 'I wasn't getting my revenge on you, if that's what you think.'

'Not even to start with? All that stuff about rape?' She smiled at him.

With sudden strength, he said, 'I still want to rape you. I'll do it when I've got the strength. You wait, my baby.'

She smiled. His intention penetrated her, awakening in her groin, rising, tingling. She wanted his gentle violence. If he called it rape it was only because he believed he did not deserve her, that he could only have her by force.

She said, cool and detached, so that he would not know how his need for vengeance thrilled her, 'How much

353

more are you trying to get your own back for?'

He widened his eyes, giving a cheeky grin. 'I don't want to get my own back on anyone. I just want to defeat my enemies. I want justice. Not revenge.' It was a game again.

She sat in her chair, close to him, in a vivid pink dress whose tight skirt rode halfway up her thighs, whose halter neck bared her still tanned shoulders, and smiled at him and thought, we must get back to honesty. She stood up and leaned over to kiss him. She said, 'I'm going for a swim. Do you mind?'

He shook his head, smiling. 'I'll sleep a bit now.'

Her lips were light on his. He took her hand and held it and looked long into her eyes and she read the hurt in there and wondered how it could be healed and thought only that she needed time. A lifetime.

* * *

She asked him again about revenge. 'Justice,' he said, again. 'I only want justice.'

'What about forgiving and forgetting?'

He gave her a look of disgust. 'Forgiveness is for wimps.'

'Wouldn't you like forgiveness, sometimes?' 'For what?' It was an angry snort.

She was silent, looking at him, shyly, afraid to give him her views. She said, quietly, 'Forgiveness frees you.'

'Oh? How?' He was hostile.

'Forgiving someone leaves you free of the burden of whatever they have done to you.'

'And where does that leave them?'

She smiled. 'With the responsibility for what they've done.' Her face went serious again. 'But if they want forgiveness and ask for it, it frees them, too.'

There was a pause, in which he looked at her, his eyes black fathomless holes in which she could find nothing familiar. When he spoke, his voice was cold and rational. His words came slowly as if he had to find each one. 'I don't care about them. I don't care about their responsibilities. I want to win. And if winning means beating someone else, doing them down, punishing them, getting my revenge, as you call it, whatever, that's what

354

I'll do. So long as I come out on top. That means putting your enemies where they can't hurt you.'

There was a tense silence while they looked at each other. Then she said, 'Have you ever forgiven yourself?'

He laughed without humour. 'What for?'

She said, smiling, 'I wouldn't know, my Angel.'

He started to grin. He said, 'I've nothing to be forgiven for?' He shrugged his good shoulder.

She smiled back and slowly crossed one leg over the other. She saw his eyes drop to her legs, to the exposed flesh of her thigh. She said, 'It takes a chat with a serpent to reveal original sin. I would be the last person to send you scurrying for a fig leaf.'

He laughed loudly and she saw a thoroughly wicked delight in him. She stood up and walked to the window. It was after sunset and growing dark outside. A large tree outside the window hung a sombre shadow across some parked cars. She turned and he saw only the outline of her fair head against the window. She spoke with infinite tenderness, her voice sunk to a husky whisper that he could barely hear. 'Perhaps you'll begin by forgiving me.'

His eyes followed her as she walked towards him. As she knelt on the bed beside him, he saw her expression. It was as determined but gentle as a mother's, full of an immense love.

She took his hand and moved it softly between her kneeling knees, pulling it slowly between the warm thighs until he could feel her brush under his fingers.

Her eyes were still on his and she said, 'Do you know why I want you to forgive me?'

He said nothing. He was lost. He had lost control. She moved his fingers into her softness. He felt her wet.

She whispered, 'Say it, Angel. Say you forgive me. Forgive me for everything you think I've done to you. Forgive me for thinking you weren't good enough for me. Forgive me for thinking what you are is not good enough for me. Forgive me for being my class. Forgive me for being my father's daughter, my husband's wife. Forgive me for the privilege and the money and the beauty I've been lucky enough to have from birth. Forgive me for all those things.'

355

He jerked his hand away, then, and pulled her fiercely by her arms and then slid himself down the bed until he had positioned her kneeling astride his mouth. Then he pulled her onto his tongue.

When he had tasted her desire and brought her shuddering to climax, he pushed her from him, pushed the bed covers away and brought his determined hands onto her head, guiding her down onto the thing so darkly swollen that it seemed the skin would break. She took him obediently in her mouth and heard him say, hoarsely and exultantly, 'I forgive you, Catherine.'

They both knew that he had done so. And that he was in control again.

71

He still slept often during the day. When he did so she read or paced the room. She rarely left it. She wanted to be there when he awakened, to see his eyes flutter open, to see the first bewilderment and unease switch to relief and pleasure as he saw her.

She had begun questioning him, gently, about his present life. But it was a sealed corridor. Though she guessed its nature, and was armed with what she had learned, she was still waiting for his trust. They had not talked seriously of his present life since she had held the gun on him. She wondered if the time would ever come when he would tell her the things he feared would turn her from him. She thought, if only he knew that I know and accept so much.

So she went on talking about his childhood and youth. His memory was a dark mine in which he hid even the simple and inoffensive details of childhood. His mother had been gentle. 'She was soft on me,' he said. 'But I was hard on myself.'

Slowly, in pieces of unrelated jigsaw images, his story emerged. He was angry at so much of what he recalled. Angry and bitter at the rejection he and his mother had experienced.

Beyond that lay a hostile, rough land where although his skin was white and burned pink like that of white children when exposed to the summer sun, his hair and his chubby Afro build had marked him out as different. A merciless land for changeling children of another race. A half breed; belonging nowhere. And his mother's people liked him least.

He said, bitterly, 'I can't hide my black blood.' And she replied, 'Then stop rejecting it. Value it as I do.' He looked at her with eyes that sheltered hope.

In their scattered hours of conversation, she gleaned fragments of his world. They came in brittle shards that drew memory's blood. Short phrases separated by long silences were like odd clues in a treasure hunt. There was no serial logic. She pieced it together later, as she swam in the nearby pool or at night, lying in her lonely bed.

Each day he tossed another bottle with its cryptic message into her sympathy's sea. Occasionally he told her stories, often against himself. One day he began, 'Once there was a little boy called Christopher with hair like a Brillo pad.' He told her how he ran away from school and no one could find him. How he never meant to go back, even to his mother. He was on the run for a few days, sleeping in niches behind dustbins in people's basements or in the public park. He was eight then and the police had found him, taken him home to forgiveness and tears. It had been a pattern often repeated with women in his adult life. They had all been grateful to have him back, Catherine noted, including herself. It was a way of proving he was wanted, against the contrary evidence.

Later, he ran off again. He got further that time because he was thirteen and had grown crafty and had prepared the ground for his escape. He had enough money, stolen a penny at a time from his mother's thrifty purse, to make the tube journey from Walthamstow to Piccadilly, with some to spare. He had wandered among Soho's bright lights and dingy corners. He had dined off the fallen fruit from barrows in Berwick Street Market. He had slept in a doorway one night, in a locked lavatory in a smart hotel the next. On the third night, wandering in Shepherd Market he had met a whore who had let him sleep in her bed because she was not working. He was a big lad for his age. In the morning she had taken his cock out of his trousers and sucked him before sending him off. That had been his first experience. He had not got very far with girls his own age. But a year later a young teacher had kept him late for bad behaviour and had done the same.

Catherine smiled and said, 'You're obsessed with your cock. Is it the only piece of you anyone ever liked?'

He laughed without humour, then looked at her with ironic challenge. 'Do you like anything else about me, Mrs Waring?'

She looked at him straight for a minute, then, her voice flat, said, 'Yours is not the only cock in the world or the biggest. There might be something else about you that's worth having if you could just stop hating yourself.'

He had smiled then.

She said, 'I love what you are. I'm glad you are what you are. I would not have you different.' And she had just gone on looking at him as if he were an actor in a film and she the director waiting for him to utter his next line.

*   *   *

Every day brought her nearer the place she was aiming for. She did not know what would happen when she reached it. She only knew she must arrive there. It was like an interrogation. And it resembled the steady growth of trust between subject and analyst: there was the steady transfer of guilt from patient to doctor and Catherine's burden grew while Christopher's lightened. Neither noticed what was going on.

She came each day, eager to see him, anxious of what

she might learn, longing for and yet afraid of the inevitable revelation. Sometimes they joked or chatted about Catherine's bed and breakfast life at the Grand Bay. Now and then he had a story to tell her about the hospital, of some idiocy or foolish thing that had occurred in her absence.

She guessed he lay awake at night, from habit. He slept much in the afternoons while she watched him. And now, today, he began at last to walk, with crutches, and was allowed to move out of his room in a wheelchair. It was only a week since the transfer from the Emergency Hospital. The drips had been banished before he left there and he was eating and drinking better each day. Catherine brought him vitamins and iron tonic, fruit and cheeses and smoked salmon, and chocolate which he loved but which she rationed.

He was still weak from blood loss. The wound was deep and cruel and his lung severely damaged. His breathing restricted his movements and he sometimes gasped and coughed as they talked. They made love less often but often she stroked him under the blankets while they talked. Sometimes she lay on the bed beside him to feel his closeness. While she lay this way he would caress her legs and sometimes fall asleep with his hand under her skirt. The nurses let them alone and only came in with meals or medication.

The closeness between them had grown. She thought he had a trust for her now that she had longed for since the beginning. Then at last, he began to tell her the things she was afraid to hear.

He had been intelligent and wild, rebellious and a truant. He had left school at fifteen with little education, able to read and write but not much more. He had seen the dead-end road ahead, the life of little means and boredom and he craved excitement and glamour and wealth.

He knew enough of the beauties of London. He hung around the good streets with their expensive shops. He watched the well dressed, bejewelled women who passed in and out of the elegant hotels and restaurants.

He saw the men who escorted them, smooth and chauffeured and he chewed on his anger like a hungry man chews on a twig.

A kind of violence grew in him. The rebelliousness that had pitted him against the misunderstanding authorities of school and home now turned into the determination of the guerilla. He wanted to undermine and destroy the society that had somehow denied him an invitation. But his lust to destroy and plunder was not political or universal. It was not a cause. It was singular and personal. He wanted not to overthrow the system for another, only to take it for himself. He dreamed of running the country, of disciplining and controlling it, of taking his revenge with power.

This evening they were lying together side by side and the evening light was fading. They had not turned on the lights and she saw his face dimly in the dusk. His eyes grew bright as he described his dream of dictatorship, laughing at himself, yet serious. She saw how much he wanted to change the world that had turned him down without even looking to see what he might have been. She saw the burning frustrated intelligence of the man. She saw how much he hated himself for failing to be what the world wanted. And yet blamed others bitterly for what he was.

He seemed to blame his unknown father for fathering him, his mother for her innocence and the passion that had made him, a mistake, into a human being, always to be regretted, a living reproach to a family and a community: an outcast from the start. His grief and pain as he talked became so evident she took his hand, but he seemed oblivious. He talked with a growing strength and violence. He talked more than she had ever known. About the crooked businessmen and bankers, the sly City men and politicians who bent the rules and enriched themselves, the respected and the knighted, the brilliantly fashionable and feted, and the masks they wore to hide their true natures from the so-admiring world.

She saw, through his eyes, the world in which she moved with ease. Saw it as fraudulent. Saw it as decadent.

She saw its unworth, both in the way he described it and in the pathetic need he had to share its power. Through his cynicism she saw the pompous self-importance of so much that she had accepted. Saw the vanity and greed and pride of those who, living well, see nothing of the other side. She saw the pitiless and brittle brilliance of the social scene she had so long lived with and she realized how she had despised so much of it for so long.

As he spoke and she saw his disgust and disappointment, she found herself also turning away from her brilliant life. She felt again the anger she had lived with as her daily companion in South Africa, against the smug, unfeeling preoccupations of the insulated ones.

'Oh no, we're not all like that,' she told him, firmly. 'Don't think you can type us or justify your own prejudices. Being privileged is not always an anaesthetic against conscience.'

He snorted and said, 'Ah, you clever people and your words.' He told her then about his first forays into crime. Blundering, amateurish crime. He told her how he had been with a group who planned an armed robbery, how he had not gone with them on the day they had shot and killed a warehouseman, because that day was his mother's birthday and he had stayed at home to celebrate it with her.

He told her about the gang he had formed and how it had fought others. She found it funny and laughed.

He said, 'Being shot at with a shotgun isn't funny, Catherine. It's one of the facts of life that you get used to. Or lose out to.' He had learned to shoot with both rifles and pistols even though the most sophisticated weapon he had used was a sawn-off shotgun.

She lay in the darkening room and listened. He made little of it. His voice was without colour. She listened and waited. It seemed she no longer knew how to breathe.

He had got out of that, he told her. It happened that he met a man who owned a night club. He had gone to work there and had been saved from street crime and gang war. And worse. It would have got a lot worse. You learned your trade. You were a professional of a kind, and you graduated, if you were any good, from being on the streets and doing the hitting, to planning and plotting and organizing bigger and better crimes.

Club life was an honest living, of a kind, and a refuge from a more dangerous life. It had not taken too long before he had managed to start his own club. He glossed over the intervening years, but she was still sure it had not been a straightforward run. He avoided her questions about prostitutes and drugs, parrying them with jokes or distractions.

She watched his profile in the room that was now lit only from the glow of lights in the courtyard and saw his eyes, staring at the ceiling. His hand in hers was limp and detached and his voice remote. He seemed to be gearing himself up for something. Her last words had been 'And now?'

She saw his lips moving and heard the words, soft and well spaced and with a silky menace. 'I've told you, Catherine, you shouldn't know me. You know people shoot at me. It can happen again. The kind of people I do business with don't like being messed around. It's better you don't know what I'm doing.'

She stared at his profile and felt her heart thumping against her ribs and against his arm. She squeezed the unresponsive hand, 'Perhaps I know.'

He turned and looked intently into her eyes. He held her shoulder suddenly with his free hand. His voice was rough and tinged with alarm, 'You don't know. I'm involved in something, now. It's been going on for months. I can't tell you any more and I don't want to involve you. So I want you to be a good girl and go back to your hotel and pack your bags and go back to London.'

She lay, rigid with shock. He had somehow taken control again. She had for days been leading him, gently and surely as a counsel leads a witness, to the point of revelation. And now he had made it seem as though all along, it was he who had been guiding the conversation. He who had been leading her. To this point. To the point where he would tell her, now that she knew enough, that she must leave him and go home.

'No.' She sat up, leaning on her elbow, looking down at him. 'No.' She was determined and cool.

'Yes.' He shook her shoulder gently. His face was close. His eyes looked directly into hers. 'Be a good baby. It's not going to be safe for you here with me. I'll be getting out of this place soon and whoever it is will be after me again. You've got to go home.'

'No. No. No. I'm not leaving you.' Her voice was low but tough.

He said softly, 'I'm ordering you, Catherine. For your own good.'

'What is this you're involved in?'

'There you are, you see. You want to get more involved than you are already. Just do as I say and go home. I'll be coming back eventually.'

She clung to him, hugging him to her so that he winced as she squeezed the wound. 'Don't ask me to go,' she whispered. 'At least, not yet.'

He softened under her hands. She heard him sigh. He said, 'Why do you want to be with someone like me? I can't ever do you any good.' He lay curled over now, his head on the pillow.

She kissed the side of his head, kissed his hair, kissed his eye and his cheek, reached for his lips. She said in a matter of fact way, 'I love you, Angel. I didn't choose it. We don't know who we're going to love. We . . . I don't know why I love. It's some lost part of myself I've found in you. Don't ask me to leave you. Please. I love you and I want to be with you, whatever that means. That's why I came here, remember, because I couldn't go on without you. I can't go back without you, now.'

He reached out and pulled her down beside him. 'You must go soon though,' he said quietly.

'I'm going to take you with me when I do.'

He pushed her away from him and stared at her in the darkness. Her hair was a silver skein against the night. One bright star hung behind her. It was like a guiding light. Something he had to follow. He stared at her and at the star for a moment. He shook his head and smiled. He said, 'You're crazy.'

The light came on then. It seemed shatteringly bright. Catherine was staring towards the door, over his shoulder. He turned, blinking, and looked towards the open door.

The taller policeman cleared his throat and spoke. 'Mr Angel. We'd like you to answer a few questions.'

72

Christopher eased himself up against the pillows, his face guarded. 'What can I do for you?' he said.

They were the same two detectives who had interviewed Catherine on the night of the shooting. While she was waiting for Christopher to come out of the operating theatre, they had asked her whether she knew why anyone would want to shoot at either Angel or herself. She had refused to answer questions about Christopher. She thought he was on vacation, she said, but they should ask him themselves when he was well enough.

Now they were here. The taller one, the sergeant, had sandy hair, thinning at the crown, and a bristling sandy moustache rather like a World War II pilot. He had been born and raised in Florida in a small town on the Gulf side and he spoke with a sleepy Southern drawl that countered his red hair and alert blue eyes. 'I'm sorry to bother you,' he said to Angel. 'M'am.' He nodded towards Catherine.

She was standing now, near the bed and close to Angel, her hands behind her back. She nodded slightly in return, her face serious.

The sergeant was looking around for a chair. He saw the one guest chair near Catherine and decided to stand. 'I'd like some details from you, Sir,' he said to Angel in his soothing, sing-song voice.

The younger officer held a notepad and pen. He was short and heavy-set with an olive complexion. The radio under his coat broke suddenly to life. He spoke brusquely into it with a slight Latino accent and it crackled back aggressively then went silent again. He handed the notebook and pen to his senior officer.

'Fire away.' Angel smiled politely at the sergeant.

The policeman went through the preliminaries of name, address, age and occupation. Angel answered, though when it came to his address he gave one in the City of London, not the Devonshire Mews house. He described his occupation as company director.

He told them he was in Miami on a combined vacation and business visit. He was, he said, interested in opening a discotheque in South Beach. Catherine moved over to the chair and sat down. She watched Angel as he spoke. His manner was gracious and informative. He gave the impression of wanting to do everything to help the police. He had a gift of social charm that clearly impressed the two policemen.

The senior officer's manner became more deferential. He said pleasantly, 'Have you any idea why anyone should want to kill you, Sir?'

Angel shook his head and replied confidently, 'None at all.'

The sergeant reached in his left breast pocket and pulled out a small passport-sized photograph. He showed it to Angel. 'Have you seen this man before?' His speech was slower and softer.

Angel shook his head again. 'I'm afraid not,' he said.

The officer leaned over the bed and showed the picture to Catherine. 'M'am. Have you ever seen this man before?'

Catherine stared at the picture. She felt herself sinking into the chair. Her mind went back to the moment when the policemen had come to her in the waiting room. She had been picturing the scene at the Fontainebleau when she had stood on the steps and answered the limo driver. There had been someone in that picture that had seemed important, someone she had to recognize.

365

She reached out for the photograph. Why hadn't she realized it before? After the moment in the waiting room, her mind had not returned to the scene on the steps. She had been too preoccupied with Christopher, with what was going on between them, too busy working out the next steps in their dialogue, analysing what he had said to her each day . . .

She looked up at the sergeant. 'Yes,' she said, her voice barely above a whisper, 'I've seen this man before. He was at the Fontainebleau when I arrived that day. And . . .' she cleared her throat and spoke more strongly but with hesitation, 'I'm sure . . . I'm sure it's the same man . . . I've also seen him in New York. I used to see him most places I went. I thought he was following me around. If it is . . . he was at the airport the day I flew to Miami . . .'

'Who is he?' Christopher snapped at the sergeant.

The junior officer took the picture of the bearded man out of Catherine's inert hand.

The sergeant finished writing in the notebook. He smiled at Angel and said cheerfully, 'He's the man we've charged with attempting to murder you, Mr Angel, Sir.' He snapped the notebook shut and handed it to his junior officer. He picked his hat up from the table where he had placed it next to the vase of red roses Catherine had brought that morning. He turned to Catherine. 'I'll need you to attend a little identity parade, M'am. Tomorrow morning at eleven.' He handed her a card. 'That's the address.' He positioned his hat carefully on his balding head and adjusted it with an instinctive precision. He drawled sweetly, 'Sorry to have disturbed you all, Sir. I hope you're making a swift recovery.' He nodded towards Catherine. 'M'am. Goodnight. I'll see you in the morning.'

The two officers went out and the door clicked closed behind them. Catherine and Christopher stared at each other. Then Christopher laughed.

'What's funny?' Catherine was looking at him with distress.

'Just the cops, my baby. Just the cops.' He chuckled quietly and slid down in the bed.

She said softly, 'I think it's appalling that I led that man to you. Whoever he is, he followed me to you. I nearly killed you twice in one day.'

He looked at her solemnly. 'Don't fret, baby. No harm done. I'll be all right.'

'Who wants to kill you, Christopher?' She stared at him but he would not look at her. He was looking ahead as if deep in thought.

After a moment, he shook his head and turned his eyes on her. They were wide and innocent and he was almost smiling. 'I couldn't tell you that,' he said gently.

She went to him, then, and lay alongside him, her face in his neck. He put his good arm around her and held her close. After a moment, he felt her tears on his bare skin and reached out with his other hand and stroked her head and turned so that he could kiss her cheeks and eyelids. He went on kissing her gently and stroking her until the tears stopped.

They fell asleep together. A nurse who looked in on them an hour or so later smiled gently and turned out the light.

73

The identification process was designed to protect the witness. Sergeant Macnamara showed Catherine into the viewing room and she watched through a one way glass while a line of bearded men walked onto a brightly lit stage. On command from a uniformed policeman, they turned left and right profiles, back and front.

Her man was shorter than the rest. His beard was a little trimmer; dark, greying and pointed at the chin. He was wearing the clothes she had last seen him in, the blue jacket and the lighter blue shirt. When she had last seen him he had also been wearing a pair of dark glasses. That and the complete change of clothes had been among the reasons she had not recognised him as her tail from New York when she glimpsed him at the Fontainebleau.

Now, she could see his eyes. He stared ahead with a cold unflinching stare. His expression was completely amoral. This, Catherine thought, was the fact of the hired gun. Her anger grew as she looked at him, the man who had tried to murder Angel. She drove her thoughts into him and the violence should have killed him. Something of her accusation must have reached him. For a moment, his face altered, seemed to ripple like a face seen under water and she felt a flash of compassion for this cold creature and his dismal fate.

She turned to the sergeant and nodded.

'You're sure now, M'am?' came the lilting drawl.

'I'm sure'. It was the third time he had asked her. Fatigued, she turned to leave. He stood back to let her pass.

She had been back to the Grand Bay for breakfast, a shower and a change of clothing before getting a car to bring her to the South Miami Beach police station. She wore her white cotton shirt dress, the one she had worn the day she went to the Fontainebleau.

They reached his office and the sergeant said, 'Sit down please, M'am, there are some details to take care of.'

She sat, watching as he reached forms and a pen and passed them towards her.

'It's just a formality, M'am,' he said in his slow way.

She did what was necessary to the pieces of paper and signed her name. 'What happens now?' she asked.

'We put the guy on trial for attempted homicide.'

'Do you know yet why he did it?'

'You mean who paid him, M'am?' He looked slyly at her. His arms were on the desk and she noticed they were deeply freckled and covered in long tangled red hairs with a few grey ones interspersed.

She said coolly, 'No. I mean why he did it?'

'He ain't talkin', yet. But he will, I guess. Then we'll find out who paid him and what for. After all, we still don't know whether he was goin' to kill the two of you, do we?' He smiled at her, then pushed his chair away from the desk and uncoiled himself from it. It was like seeing a sitting giraffe get to its feet.

He stood, tall and gangling over her as she stood up. He put out his hand and she gave him hers. 'Thank you for your assistance, M'am,' he said, walking her towards the door. 'We'll be keepin' in touch with you on what happens down here. Now we have your identification we should be able to push along pretty good. Since he was caught a few yards from the beach and runnin' away from the scene still carrying the same gun that fired those bullets into the sand and through your friend's chest, we've got a pretty tight case.'

'Good. I'm glad to hear that.' She smiled. 'I'll hear from you then.' She turned to leave him but he seemed to want to talk. He leaned against the doorpost and scratched his balding head.

He said, 'M'am, you can tell me to mind my own business, if you like, but how well do you really know Mr Angel?'

She turned sharply to face him. He knew she had been sitting on the bed with Christopher in the dark last night before he came into the room and turned on the light. What else did he know?

'Fairly well,' she answered cautiously, adding more sharply, 'Why do you ask?'

'Has he told you about any of the people he knows down here?'

'No. Should he?'

'That's up to him and you, M'am . . .'

'Good, then I'll say goodbye for the moment, sergeant.' She turned away again, putting on her glasses.

His lazy voice followed her and she stopped, her back still towards him. He went on slow and musical, 'I think you should know, M'am, that we have to look into the activities of any aliens that happen to come to our attention. We know who you are and what your interests in New York are. We also know one or two things about Mr Angel.'

She turned slowly again and leaned her back against the corridor's cool wall. She gazed at him through her glasses. His face had a perplexed expression as if he were in some doubt about her reactions to what he had to tell her. Or was he just perplexed about what Mrs James Waring was doing with a man who was not her husband?

'I just thought I ought to mention it, M'am, that you might not realize what kind of people you were associating with. A lady like yourself . . .'

'Tell me what it is you're trying to say, sergeant.' Catherine's crisp words cut into his languid speech. Her voice was bored and weary. She wanted to get out of this place, wanted to get out into the sunshine and back to Christopher, wanted to drink some tea, to telephone New York. She wanted anything, anything rather than hear what the sergeant had to tell her. She leaned her head back against the wall and looked down her cheeks at him.

'I don't want you to misunderstand me, M'am. I'm not trying to intrude into your private affairs . . .' He stopped, aware of the double entendre. He recovered and went on, 'I just feel it is my duty to warn you that the gentleman's associations are questionable. Some of the people he knows here are, shall we say, under suspicion for various crimes. It would not be unusual for these kind of people to put out a contract against your friend, assuming they thought they had a reason.' He stopped and seemed to be waiting for her answer.

'Thank you, sergeant,' she said and stood away from the wall. 'I'll look forward to hearing that you have found out who is behind this attempt to kill my friend. And I bear in mind the implications of what you are telling me.' She smiled and turned from him once more and walked quickly down the corridor towards the rectangle of sunlight. Her footsteps clipping the hard floor had the sound of panic. To the sergeant, she seemed to be running from anything else he might tell her about Christopher Angel.

*

370

74

Miami's business district rose out of the water left and the limo's wheels rumbled on the bridge's metal gridwork. The driver took the right lane for I 95, the fast route over the city, taking her to the Cedars. But she decided to go back to the hotel and make some calls to London. She spoke through the intercom and directed him to go along the water to Coconut Grove. The more scenic slow route would allow her the time and space to decide about one particular call before she reached the Grand Bay.

The driver shrugged and swung the big car left, across two lanes. As they turned onto US 1, Catherine's mind replayed the sergeant's words. She asked herself over and over why she had bolted. Why hadn't she asked him to explain more about Christopher's Miami connections. No doubt one of these would be the big Mafia connection that Gerry's tart had mentioned. What crimes were they suspected of? Murder? Drug dealing? Wouldn't it be better to know? She almost spoke aloud. I want him to tell me himself. Angel, Angel. Trust me enough. So her heart responded. But her mind argued, You should find out for yourself. Find out what you can. Let him tell you. But don't let him know you know. She thought of Penny Slight. Getting information in London had seemed a matter of survival when Christopher withheld so much. But now, surely, it would seem a betrayal of Angel's trust to go behind his back. To go to the sergeant would be to put a third party's views before personal loyalty. She thought, What kind of friend would I seem if I crawled back there and start asking questions? Disloyal. And yet, the awful suspense. The need to know, to verify, to safeguard herself. Then, the arresting question, How can I expect Christopher to trust me, if I don't trust him?

The car swept gracefully along Brickell Avenue. New glass towers reflecting each other like mirages, among mirrored clouds and trees were as deceptive as the images Christopher presented. What was the truth? Did his past matter? What mattered was not what she knew or what could be found out. What mattered was that he should tell her the truth about himself. The details of this or that crooked connection were immaterial. His secret life, his recent past, still stood between them like a wall.

But was the past to be mirrored in the future? Or would he change? She knew she could not, did not want to change him. He could only change himself, from within. Love, his and hers was the catalyst. Her mind turned over and over the same theme. His life had to have reached a turning point. The escape from death marked a dangerous corner rounded. Was his near death to be a rebirth? Was he not different already? Did it matter? Didn't she love him as he was? As Angel had said as she held the gun on him, couldn't she just take the love and forget the rest?

The car slowed and turned in to the hotel courtyard. Did she have to know any more? Her lips made a silent Yes. She had been given the preamble to his story. Now she wanted the rest, wanted the truth she had threatened to kill him for. Wanted it from him. But first, she would make that call.

75

He was asleep, with the late afternoon sunlight making a wedge of gold across his head. She moved stealthily into the room and took the chair, slipped off her shoes and tucked her feet under her. She sat watching him. His face had an unfamiliar anxious look and there was a crease between his brows. Little gasping puffs of breath blew out his lips, making him seem both innocent and vulnerable.

She waited without moving for almost a half hour before he heaved into wakefulness. His eyes snapped open and went straight for the chair as he sensed he was not alone. He smiled and nodded gently then closed his eyes again. She sat still, making a conscious effort to breathe. She did not know how she would handle this. Or where the next few minutes would take them.

At last he opened his eyes again.

'Hello,' he said, huskily.

She smiled. 'Hello.'

He looked at his watch. 'You've been a long time.'

She said gently, 'I had calls to make and then I thought I'd swim before coming here.' She made no attempt to go to him and kiss him. He seemed unaware of any change in her.

She calculated her moment and then, her voice very cool, said, 'I hear you're wanted for questioning in London, about a drugs matter.' It was a brutal thing to do, she thought, to someone who was still weak. But she wanted to force him out into the open.

He looked sharply at her and she admired his self-control. He said, tensely, 'Where would you hear a thing like that?'

'I made a phone call to a friend in London?'

'What friend?'

'I can't tell you.'

He sat up against the flattened pillows and stared at her. His face registered alarm and suspicion. He said abruptly, 'Why not?'

She gave him a long, deep stare. She saw his eyes widen. He had seen her detachment. She was sorry. It set back his trust in her. She was assuming his guilt and judging him; it must seem that way to him.

Before she told him anything she wanted him to tell her more voluntarily. After her return to the Grand Bay she had phoned Armstrong on his private office number. She had not mentioned that she was with Christopher, had, in fact, let Armstrong think she was in New York.

373

Christopher was waiting for her answer. She gave none. He said quietly, 'Who told you that, Catherine?'

She said, 'Did you know they wanted you?'

Now it was his turn to stay silent.

She went on looking at him for what seemed several minutes. It was, perhaps, almost a minute. She felt as if she were suffocating. She took a long, gasping breath and let it out slowly. Then she let go the hardness with which she had been holding in her feelings and her breathing became more normal. Her face once more expressed the love and sympathy she felt for him. He saw it and relaxed.

'Angel? Did you?' Her voice was soft again.

He yawned and stretched. He smiled a twinkly little smile and his voice was casual when he replied, 'No. As a matter of fact, I didn't.

'What I still want to know, though,' he said, turning on his side and snuggling against his pillows, 'is who told you that. Information is only as good as its source. I'm sure you'd agree with that, as a journalist.' He closed his eyes and appeared to go to sleep again, but as she watched him, perplexed at his reaction, she saw him looking at her, cat-like from under half closed lids.

She almost whispered, 'I'm satisfied the source is impeccable.'

'Then it must be true,' he said, and his eyes were closed again.

She waited but he stayed as he was. Then she said, 'You could trust me, you know. You could talk to me. You know I have some idea what kind of stuff you get into. You know it doesn't frighten me away. You know . . . I hope you know by now how much I feel for you. I am your friend as well as your lover. I don't expect you . . . I don't care what you are. It doesn't change my feelings or my loyalty, but I would feel better if you trusted me . . . if you would share.'

His eyes were open now and he was leaning on his elbow, looking at her gently. 'I don't know how much you know about me,' he said.

'It's not what I know that bothers me. It's what you don't tell me.'

374

'Let me work that out,' he chuckled.

She smiled. 'It means I want you to tell me about yourself and your life. It's your secrecy, your trying to hide everything that bugs me and hurts me and shuts me out.' Her voice rose slightly, then fell. 'It parts us even when we seem close.'

He leaned back against the pillows. The sun went behind a cloud and the room was suddenly gloomy. 'Catherine, I run a legitimate business but I'm involved in other things I can't tell you about. Nothing very bad. I don't do anything violent or hurt individuals. I'm no worse than the kind of City gents who fix little deals for each other on a nod and wink basis, who bend the rules to suit themselves.

What I do is less socially acceptable than what they do. But it's no worse. '

'Do you mean like handling cocaine?'

'I wouldn't handle drugs unless I couldn't avoid it somehow.'

'Why wouldn't you be able to avoid it?'

He shrugged. 'Favours due. Offers I can't refuse.'

'Why would anyone want to kill you, Angel?'

He laughed. It was a long, lazy laugh and he was laughing at her. He said, 'You could tell me the answer to that one, my baby.'

She shook her head and smiled. She had asked for that one. 'Other than me?' She pressed him.

'You don't always know who wants to get you.'

'Could you have a guess, maybe?'

He smiled. Then the door opened. Sergeant Macnamara came in, alone. He took off his cap and nodded to them each in turn. He seemed to be more gangling and awkward than before.

'Good evening, sergeant. What can we do for you this time?' Christopher said genially. He sat up and smoothed his covers. There was, Catherine thought, a slight mockery in his tone.

The sergeant cleared his throat. 'I just dropped by to tell you that the, er, suspect, in your shooting, Mr Angel, has claimed his contract to kill you originated in London,

England. We will be handing the matter over to the English police to make further enquiries. I thought you might like to know that.'

Angel said sharply, 'Has he said who issued the contract?'

'He has, Sir,' the sergeant drawled, 'but I'm not at liberty to give you that information.'

Catherine said, 'Why not?'

Angel said, firmly, 'Thank you, sergeant. I'm very grateful to you for coming along to tell me that. Please let me know if there is anything I can do to help further your enquiries.'

Catherine said nothing more and Macnamara said his farewells and left. The sun came out from behind a cloud and lit the room with a rich glow. Catherine stood up and went to the window. She stared down into the hospital yard for a while and then turned back into the room.

Angel had fallen asleep again. She felt suddenly terribly tired. She walked across to the bed and kissed his forehead gently, then she picked up her bag and walked quickly out of the room.

76

He was dressed and sitting in the chair. Behind him, morning light lit the world beyond the window as if it were a movie screen while the room remained coolly shadowed in its soft green tones. His face in repose was sad, and still very pale. His eyes were fixed on the newspaper in his lap, but he looked up as she entered and they gave her his welcome.

She stopped and smiled. 'Goodness,' she said. 'That's a nice surprise. Do you want to go outside into the courtyard?'

He stretched his arms above his head and grinned at her. He said, cheerfully, 'I want to go for a drive.'

She kissed him lightly on the mouth, then sat on the bed and looked at him anxiously. 'What's the rush? A short walk should be more than enough for you. The doctor can't have said you're all right for driving around.'

'I want to go to the beach.' He was serious, determined.

She gave him a perplexed look. 'Why?'

'I want to get that bullet out of my mind. I keep dreaming I'm being shot at.' He gave a small apologetic laugh.

She picked up the phone and called the car company. The limo that had dropped her a few minutes ago could come back for them.

Christopher stood up and walked to the window. He leaned his back against the sill and looked at her. She said, 'I'm sorry I left without saying goodbye yesterday. You were sleeping and I was so tired I just had to go.'

He smiled. 'It's all right.'

There was an awkwardness between them. Unfinished business loomed like rocks in a night sea. She said, 'Let's go down and wait in the lobby.'

She took his arm but he gently shook it free. His walk was rubbery, not his usual stride and now and then he seemed to lose balance and put his arm out to the wall to steady himself. They made the lift in silence, but she watched him from the corner of her eye.

He shuddered. The hospital stank of sickness. In his small room he had somehow avoided the sense of being in such a place. Catherine's flowers and fruit gave the air a living scent. Her perfume pervaded the place, even when she had gone. The room was their place, the place they had been together for the longest hours in their entire association. Leaving it made him feel insecure, as if their bond was loosened by their liberation from its walls.

But it was time to take her away from it. To a fresh stage. There was so much more he had to tell her. He would do it in his own way, free from her promptings and from policemen's interruptions.

*   *   *

The noon beach was glittering and peopled. Heads bobbed among the swelling waves and the water was as slick as mercury under the high white sun. Only where the foam-frilled runnels licked the stony sand was there relief from the light's metallic attack.

They walked hand in hand and shoeless until they reached the spot they thought had been the place. He held her closer as they stood and sensed their history, his arm around her waist, and neither spoke. Wet sand and broken shells prickled between their toes. Children's shouts mingled with the sea's rush. There were no echoes of the bullets' crack, no stains or stumbling footprints. Had they expected anything, any recognition of their moment? Had they thought their own past ghosts would beg them for exorcism? Was that why they had come?

He pulled her back the way they had come, towards the Fontainebleau. Neither spoke as they passed along the beach, or walked through the garden and into the hotel. It was a silence of understanding. They paused only to dust their feet and replace the shoes they had carried with them, almost out of superstition that to leave them would be to tempt fate to aim a gun at them again. He drew her firmly into the hotel and made for the reception desk.

They gave him his key, and this surprised her. He had, as soon as he was well enough to think, asked her to give up his suite and instruct the hotel to store his luggage. Without telling her, yesterday he had told them to put everything back.

Now, her eyes large with anxiety, her voice husky with fear, she said, 'You're not well enough to leave the hospital. Why have you done this?'

He smiled and squeezed her waist. 'I'm not leaving the hospital, yet.' He swayed against her. She glanced up at him and thought him paler. She said, 'You must rest.'

He said, limply, 'I will.'

He knew nothing, yet, of her visit the day after the shooting. As they went up in the dim brown lift she said, 'You know I came back for my gun, don't you?'

He let go her waist and took her hand and squeezed it. He said, 'You're a sensible girl.'

She put her arms around his neck and kissed him on the lips. He leaned back against the lift wall and gently pulled her arms away. But he held her wrists and brought her hands up to his mouth to be kissed. She thought he looked dreadfully weak, and although the air in the lift was conditioned cool, there was a slight perspiration on his brow.

They reached the suite and walked out of the corridor's sibilant gloom into the noon light's glare. The room was cold, too cold, with air conditioning, but the air felt stagnant all the same.

He walked her to the sofa and made her sit. 'Wait there,' he said gently. He went into the bedroom and came out again in a moment with the briefcase in which she had found the wads of notes. She watched him, as with his back to her, he unlocked it, looked inside, then closed the lid. He pushed at the sides with his thumbs and the case opened again, revealing a secret compartment in which she could see papers. He slid his hand under them and then turned to face her. She tried to refocus her eyes. He was pointing a pistol at her.

She flinched and stiffened. Was it the same one she had found in his drawer? He must have slipped it into the briefcase now, in the bedroom. Then he laughed and tossed the small gun in the air and caught it by its barrel. 'It's not loaded, my baby, but I thought you'd like to know, I've got one, too.'

He dropped the gun back into the case, then lifted the sheaf of papers out of the secret compartment and came towards the sofa. He sat down beside her and held them out to her. Her heartbeat was suddenly obtrusive. She put her hand out tremblingly to touch his thigh that was, despite almost two weeks in bed, still well-muscled, though not hard as it used to be. She felt arousal as she touched him but he lightly lifted her hand away and dropped it into her lap without looking at her.

'No,' he said, crisply, 'this is business.' He handed her the sheaf of papers. 'Read them. I'm going to lie down on the bed. Come and see me when you've finished.' He stood up and walked unsteadily into the bedroom and closed the door.

* * *

The papers were copies from police files and she had no idea how he had come by them, though she could guess. She sat, the papers spread beside her on the sofa. They were reports of his activities over some two years. Scattered, often imprecise descriptions of where he had been seen and who with, they detailed a trail of suspicion and catalogued incidents, none of which were conclusive or amounted to evidence about anything, but all of which left a smear.

She picked a sheet up at random and read it again. It was a recent report, dating from a few months earlier. It covered a period of several weeks during which she had seen little of him. She stiffened with alarm. How had she missed this?

He had, as she knew, been arrested after leaving her house. This was reported and the address was noted: her name and James' were down as the house's owners. His arrival time at the house had been inserted after the report of his arrest. It was reported that she had told the officer in charge that he was a friend. The time he had spent in the house was recorded.

She scanned quickly back from this point. He had been missing from her life for several weeks before this. He was reported to have been on several car journeys to Kent, but his whereabouts were not noted.

He had, she noticed, about seven weeks before his reported visit to Queen Anne's Gate, been followed in the City. He had parked his car and gone into the Clyne Johnson Bank. He had been there altogether some fifteen minutes. From there he had driven to Covent Garden. A woman, it was herself, she knew, had joined him and they had driven to Mayfair and gone into a block of flats in Hill Street. She knew what happened then.

There were references to troubles at the Sirocco. There was also a mention of a meeting with one of the men

380

later charged with a part in the Clairmont bullion robbery. The man had been seen leaving the Sirocco, that was all. She scanned the seven sheets. He had been stopped outside his house one night and his car searched for drugs. None had been found. He had been accused by a girl of trying to induce her to become a prostitute. This had not amounted to anything in the end but he had been questioned by the police at some length. It was there, the catalogue of his life, some of which she had learned from Penny Slight. More of the same. Nothing of any great importance, but the record was hardly complete. It showed his life on the edge of crime, of police suspicion and inconclusive investigation. It revealed the simple sordid banality of his existence. Perhaps there were secrets it did not reveal, as indeed she was sure there were. If they knew anything of real importance he would not be here with her now, but more likely in prison. The question remained, had he ever done anything really criminal? Did it matter to her any more?

She piled the sheets of paper back in their chronological order and stood up. She went to the window and looked out. The ground looked very far below and the beach and gardens with their chairs and awnings and gaily coloured crowds were toys she could have scattered in an anger of destruction.

She wanted to know, wanted him to open to her. But every time she learned more she felt physically sick. She wanted to take a shower. Or best of all, to run out of the room and throw herself into the all absorbing sea. To be cleansed of her knowledge, of her fear, of her responsibility towards him, of the burden of knowledge he had now placed on her.

She turned sharply and picked up the papers and walked into the bedroom. He was lying on the bed, on his back, sleeping, his mouth parted, his breath heavy and slow and burdened. She put the papers on the bed and went into the bathroom and closed the door. She ran cold water over her hands and let it go on running until she felt soothed and cleansed. Then she went back into the bedroom and crept up to the bed.

The anguish of the questions she wanted to ask him abated. She was impatient to know what he was doing in her father's bank, why the police suspected him of crimes and had him watched and followed. She felt the compression of pulsing blood in her head. As she looked at him, sleeping, a confusion of emotions tugged her crossways.

What was it that made her want so desperately to hold him, more, to have his arms around her? What made her long for him to hold her close and comfort her? Why did she need comfort for his pain? Had he not given her this to carry for him? How could he heal her of his own ills? Perhaps he hoped that if he told her enough she would sicken of him. Yet it was she who had probed and sought and quested for knowledge of what he was. He was offering her the thing she wanted, his whole self, his past, his present. She stopped her thoughts. Was he offering her his future? Did she want his future? Was she strong or good enough to deal with whatever he would bring her?

She found herself praying. She was looking at him and it seemed the whole of her being evaporated into a prayer that was a single silent cry of longing. It was a pure force of will that seemed to burn like incense and change the colour of the light in the room. In that moment, she took his past and incinerated it in her fire, offered it up like a sacrifice as if it were part of herself to be redeemed. She did it with an impulse of pure love, as intense as a nuclear explosion. And it also changed her. Some dark obstruction vanished. As if through an open window, light could pass through her. Now it seemed the future lay ahead like a green field of dew bright grass.

She watched him sleep and her eyes moistened. Slowly the tears brimmed through her lashes and slid along her cheeks, over her smiling mouth and fell into her lap, into her upturned palms. He moved, then, and his eyes opened and she looked into them with the same desire to go on looking for ever with which, as a child, she had stared into Africa's night.

*

382

77

In the limo he said, 'It's not true. Most of it's inaccurate rubbish.'

They had talked in the hotel and now he repeated what he had said at the beginning. He seemed anxious that now he had cleared most of her concerns, now that she knew his life's fabric, that she should not think him as low as the police report presented him.

'Maybe I don't care, either way.' She turned her head and met his gaze without a smile.

He seemed disconcerted. He looked around and out of the window. 'It makes me sick, that sort of report. It makes you want to do something bad, really bad.' He laughed. 'Maybe I should give them something to really get me for.'

'Did they get you yet?' She sounded uninterested.

He looked quickly at her. Her cool and perfect profile with the small straight nose and the sculpted jaw was a silhouette against blue water as they crossed Julia Tuttle Causeway. It gave nothing away. 'You know they want me now. About the protest committee's drugs.' This was what Armstrong had told her. He was suspected of being a conduit, for cocaine from Miami and cannabis from Morocco. Armstrong had said he believed the deal was through Angel's Mafia contacts, that it was a three way countertrade involving some of the Clairmont bullion. The drugs were paid for in bullion then traded for cash which came from an undiscovered source via the protest committee. The cash went to the bullion's vendors.

Catherine had said nothing of this. 'Do they have grounds?' She was looking out over the water. Only her cheek's soft curve seemed to speak to him.

'They think they do.' His voice was low and bitter.

She turned her head now and looked at him and he looked round to meet her penetrating gaze. Her eyes held him like lights under water that bring fish into a net. He could not look away. Her eyes were darkly blue and filled with feeling. He saw more love in her eyes than he had seen anywhere. He said, 'I'm too risky for a woman like you.'

'Is that an admission of guilt?' She spoke very softly, almost whispering and the lamps never dimmed.

'I'm no angel, Catherine.'

'Did you give them cause, this time?'

He looked out of his window. The sun was lowering over the downtown skyline. The day's molten heat was bleeding away over the horizon.

They had stayed in the suite all afternoon. They had talked, slept, ordered food. She had taken a bath and then just lain beside him while he dozed, watching the sky change. They had not made love in that makeshift way. They had not done so for days. Something had stood between them. Did it still? She looked at him as one looks at an acquaintance, politely interested. He wondered if he had revealed too much.

'Maybe.' He went on looking at the sinking sun, sensing for her response, listening with his mind for her reaction. He was afraid, still. Afraid to lose her.

He felt her hand steal into his. She held it and moved it onto her lap and stroked his fingers.

He said, 'There is something, Catherine. Not anything I can talk about. But it's not what they say. It's not what you think. I can't tell you. It involves . . . other people.' He sensed her stillness. She seemed not to breathe. He said, quietly, 'I'm no good, Catherine. How many times do I have to tell you.'

She drew a breath then, and unfreezing, let it go like a sigh. 'It doesn't matter,' she said and turned her eyes on him again.

He stared at her. He could not hide his pleasure. His eyes lit up and he smiled, trying to hide it. He turned away, looking out of the window and squeezed the hand that held his. After a moment, he said, 'Does he know where we're going?' He gestured at the driver.

She nodded. He leaned forward and pulled the blind down between the driver and themselves. Then he pulled the other blinds on the windows to the side and rear.

She sat perfectly still while he did this and when he came near her. Then he kissed her and held her to him so that she could barely breathe. He gently took her hands and let her feel him. He pulled down the zipper on his trousers and brought her hand inside to touch the stiffening cock. Then he knelt on the soft carpet and pulled apart her knees and lifted her skirt and put his mouth into her softness and melted her with his tongue.

When she was wet and open, he pulled her onto the wide floor and brought his cock close to her, touching her with it, looking all the while into her eyes.

'Do you want me, Catherine?' he whispered.

Her inbreath became a sob, and as he pushed his way into her she broke tears of joy that were, to him, a sudden rain after drought. For days she had been remote. Now he had her. Now she gave her feelings and her love. Now he saw that she was his. More than ever, his. She must be his alone.

He gave all his strength, gathered in the long afternoon of sleep. He leaned on his good arm and pulled her close with the other. He felt and thought of nothing except possessing her. He lost all sense of fatigue or pain. 'Look at me. Look at me. Look at me,' he commanded her. And she looked into his eyes and let her soul rise into them as her body's spring gushed obediently towards him, drenching him in living love, and he sank into her, losing himself in her depths, giving up his being to her in trust.

78

As they approached along the Thames, she watched him anxiously. He was awake, having slept much of the way. His natural pallor was enhanced by his dark beard's growth, but behind that was an unhealthy grey that showed in the discoloured whites of his normally bright eyes.

She knew he depended on regular exercise for his usual health and he had missed it for almost three weeks. But she also knew the wounds under his shirt were healed and the shortness of breath that still came from the damaged lung would soon go. He was a healthy aimal; vigorously physical. It was his mind she worried about now.

As the time for their departure had come closer, he had grown dark and morose. She felt him leave her more and more and go to some place she could not find. He said, more than once, 'I may have to go to prison. If they can prove anything, they might give me five years, but I'll get it cut down. It won't be so bad.' He laughed without humour. 'I can get fit. I can sleep.'

She saw he was far from her, now, his eyes opening and shutting as he fought the need to doze. The stewards were clearing away breakfast. She reached across and squeezed his relaxed hand. He responded, blinking himself more awake and lifted her fingers to his lips, holding them there and letting his tongue play on the spaces between them before turning his head to look at her.

Even after a night on a plane Catherine was beautiful. Even the circled shadows under her eyes that seemed to add sadness to her expression were some kind of artistic plus. They made her look more real, more believable. Usually her beauty was almost a barrier in itself, almost too perfect to be human. Unflawed. He leaned across and kissed her lips and looked into her eyes as he did so. Even in that moment, he felt his cock rising. She was the stimulus that never failed.

He said, 'They ought to market you as an aphrodisiac. Instead of rhino horn. Catherine. Essence of Catherine.' He was tempted to have her in the loo. But the seat belt sign was on. They really were landing. He braced himself. It would not be pleasant down there. What he had to go through would not be a welcome party.

She caught the anxiety in his eyes and pressed his hand again. Her mouth formed the words, 'Love you' and he put his finger to his lips and then to hers both in a kiss and a gesture of silence.

The plane made its final turn, to the west. The early sun fired a staccato burst, through the port windows, dazzling them, making a halo of Catherine's hair before vanishing as the plane finished the curve and the pilot lined up the runway.

He brought her hand to his lips and held it there, as they landed, like a talisman. His eyes looked straight ahead.

She had asked for a wheelchair to meet them. He was much stronger than that now but she had not wanted to take chances with his strength, after the flight and the time change.

He said, 'You're spoiling me.' He climbed in with a smile, happy not to have to walk and stand in line. She followed him with their hand baggage on a trolley.

She caught up with him at passport control and they went through together. The sergeant in Miami had sent word of their departure, of course. The police were waiting at the other side and they came for him. They were very polite.

She said, pleadingly, 'No, no, not now. Let him get some rest. Please. Not yet.'

'It's all right, Catherine,' he said and tried to rise out of the wheelchair.

The sergeant put a hand out to stop him. He said, 'You can stay in the chair, Sir.' To Catherine, he said, 'We don't have any choice, M'am. This gentleman is about to be charged. If you would like to come along, it's possible the court will release him on bail.'

She went with him, of course. The luggage followed on after them. The police car took them to Uxbridge Magistrate's Court. He had been given a moment to call his solicitor from the airport and the matter took only a few minutes.

He was charged with importing and trafficking drugs and with handling stolen bullion. Michael O'Leary had made a statement in which he outlined how the protest committee's drugs were paid for. The Rastafarian called The Flick had been arrested and was giving everything he knew away for as much as he could get in return. He had named the Sirocco as a collection point for one drug consignment. There was no indication of how the police knew of the countertrade involving bullion: Catherine wondered what evidence they might have to connect Christopher with that.

The solicitor, a balding, dandruffy fellow in an unpressed dark suit, said, 'It won't stick,' and shook his head and pursed his mouth while looking down at the floor. He patted Angel on the shoulder before and after the hearing.

Christopher was released on conditional bail and his passport held. Catherine gave surety for £200,000. As they left, Angel looked bravely around him but did not meet Catherine's anxious eyes. In the cab she held his hand but they did not talk about the charges. They drove to his house and went to bed together and slept away the rest of the morning wrapped in each other's arms.

79

She put her head on his shoulder and said in a voice slow with sleep, 'I could stay here a few days. No one would know.'

He chuckled.

'We needn't go out. Selfridges will deliver groceries and champagne. We can hole up in secret, here. You don't have to tell them you're back, do you?'

He said, 'They know already, darling.'

'How?' She lifted her head and peered at him. She had mascara under her eyes.

'I told Roseman to tell Sadie to get you £200,000 by this afternoon.' Roseman was the solicitor. Sadie managed his office.

'You didn't have to do that. Anyway, it's my surety. They didn't say your own would be all right. The Court made me responsible for you. If you run I pay.'

'I don't want you standing bail for me, Catherine.'

'Why not?'

'I don't. That's all.' He looked at the ceiling.

'You're not thinking of bolting?' There was alarm in her voice.

'I don't want you involved.'

She relaxed. She curled her legs around his and wrapped her arms more tightly around him. 'If I could buy you for that much, I would. Just for today. Even just until this afternoon.' She sounded like a child wishing for Christmas.

'You don't have to buy me. I'm already yours.' He turned and looked fully into her face. 'And you're mine.'

She smiled, delighted. 'So you keep saying.'

He kissed her. He said, slowly, 'You'd marry me, wouldn't you?'

There was a silence into which a bird sang. She stared at the ceiling. 'Yes,' she said. 'I would.'

He pulled her close and she saw the joy in his eyes.

She said, 'I'll say I'll marry you if you ask me now. I'll get free and I'll marry you.'

He turned away from her and lay on his back. 'You don't want to marry someone who's going to prison, Catherine.'

'It was your idea, Angel. Anyway, I don't think you are going to prison.'

'It's still my idea but I can't make promises. You don't know what they've got on me. I don't know. Roseman doesn't know. Look at today. It's still today. It's only four hours since we were in court.' He stared towards the window where afternoon sunlight leaked around the dark roller blind.

She leaned on her elbows and kissed his lips. 'I love you. I don't want to have to live without you. Ever again. Not ever.' A sob broke out of her and she ducked her head onto his bare chest and let her tears out. She choked on her words but he heard her. She said, 'I can't lose you. Not now. Not after everything we've gone through.' She looked into his eyes, pleading with him to say it would be all right.

He said, 'It's not over yet.' And his eyes went opaque for a second as he remembered what she had to learn.

He tightened his arms around her and buried his mouth in her hair.

She heard his voice coming through her hair, close to her ear. 'Maybe you won't want to know me after what's coming.'

'Don't be silly. What do you mean?' She turned her head until he had to look into her face.

He said, 'The court case about the shooting for one thing.'

She said, 'That's my passport to freedom. My excuse for divorcing James. Loretta said, you know, my solicitor, I talked to her from Miami, she said I have no choice. James's career won't stand the exposure of my being a witness to my lover's shooting.' She laughed, a light sparkly little laugh, short and lively. 'Stark naked on the beach with the victim. Yes, counsel. We were making love in the surf. Can't you see the headlines, "Cabinet Minister's wife in beach frolic before lover is shot in revenge attack. Blood in the surf as assassin guns down future PM's wife's lover." The Prime Minister will blow a fuse. As it is it will be dodgy, but James will be in the background. Not my husband. My ex-husband or nearly, by then.'

He was silent. He knew she had no inkling of what was coming to her. He held her to him and began kissing her neck and then her breasts and shoulders. He might lose her yet, when she discovered what had really been going on.

He put his hand between her thighs and found her wet and slippery as a slice of succulent melon and he slid his cock into her as easily as if it belonged there always. And it did. But, as he began his slow drive to reach her secret source and before he lost all sense of separateness from her, he thought briefly and sorrowfully that it might be the last time he would do this.

*

390

80

'Don't fuss, Daddy.' Catherine flopped down in the chair facing her father's. They sat in the study and the gas log fire flickered in the grate between them, turned down but still warming the room. As Catherine had only returned that morning from the Miami heat, she found the flames welcome.

Sir Arnold had been complaining about Catherine's lack of communication with him during her trip to the US. 'You vanished,' he said angrily. 'You simply vanished for five days after you left New York. You didn't tell me, you didn't tell James where you were. The offices, both in London and New York, were clueless. Then you told New York where you were, but not me. I didn't know whether you were dead or alive.' His accent was exaggerated as always when he was upset.

She sympathized with his distress. She had been so preoccupied, too absorbed in her private situation to care about anyone or anything other than Christopher, even business. With a sudden pulse of feeling she thought, Oh Angel, I love you.

She said, 'I'm sorry, Daddy. It was all so dramatic. I couldn't start talking to people in England.'

'You'd better tell me the whole story,' he said. He reached out for the decanter by his side and poured a large malt into the heavy cut glass tumbler. His hand shook as he did so.

She said, 'It'll take time.'

He looked at his watch. 'It's half an hour to dinner. Have your champagne and tell me. It can't take any longer, surely?' He grinned at her. It was the first sign of levity she had seen in him since she walked in unannounced and found him drinking, not even reading, just staring into the weak blue flames.

She got up from her chair and went over to him.

'Daddy,' she said, 'I love you so much.' She put her arms around his shoulders and kissed him.

He said, grumpily, 'Yes. Yes. Now drink some champagne and tell me your story.'

She smiled and went back to her chair and picked up the still very cold glass. Clive always got it right. She loved her champagne too cold for good taste. The chill took away the acidity, sharpened the prickling of the bubbles so that they seemed to go straight to the brain from the palate, enlarging the world but not distorting it. She drank half her glass quickly. She said, 'I'm so much in love. I never knew I could love this much.'

He looked at her sharply. 'What are you talking about?'

She told him. She told him she wanted to marry Angel. She told him she had to divorce James and then she told him why. She told him about the shooting and about the coming trial of whoever had hired the killer. She told him about the days in Miami and the things that passed between Angel and herself in the hospital room. She told him that she was happy, at last. She told him she was glad to be alive after so long wanting to be dead. She told him she didn't care what Christopher had been in the past. What mattered was the future. The present was only the transition, the bridgehead, the Rainbow Bridge.

He said sourly, 'I hope you know the Rainbow Bridge was the prelude to the damnation of the gods.'

She got up and went to him and fell on her knees and took his hands and cried passionately into his face, 'I don't care if I'm damned. I love him and I can't leave him. Whatever happens I belong to him. I'm his and he is mine. We are each other.'

He looked at her thoughtfully and then reached out and stroked her head. 'You remind me of myself when I was young, younger than you have ever been, I think. Brenda made you a grown up before you could talk. Now I think you are discovering your youth, your emotions. I only wish you could have fallen in love with someone of your own kind.'

'Oh Daddy.' She leaned her head on his knee and spoke into the fire, 'What does it matter what kind one is? Love transcends everything, class, money, age, race.'

'Listen to me, Catherina.'

A new sound in his voice, gentler, deeper, alerted her to a change of mood. She raised her head and looked into his face. She whispered, 'What?'

He spoke from deep in his throat. 'Love is a kind of madness. It possesses the senses, dazzles the mind, fools the intellect and, I have to say this, destroys sanity.'

She opened her mouth to protest. He held up the hand that had been resting on her head. He was looking into the fire and in his other hand he now held the whisky glass, replenished with another large measure of malt. He drank deeply from it. 'Love, in the case of myself and your mother, was a madness that worked out all right. We were very young and very much in love but we also got on. We weren't the same class, but we had aspirations in common. We had her money and I made good with it. We lived a good life and we grew very close. We complemented each other. It was a good marriage.' He sighed and shook his head slowly from side to side. 'However, love, the kind of mad, impassioned love you speak of, Rina, is not the kind of love to base a life on. It is not the kind of emotion that can lead to lasting happiness. It is not, Catherina, something to put your faith into. It is sex-based with nothing else. What, for instance, do you and this man have in common, compared, say, to what you have with James?'

'I have nothing with James, Daddy,' she said. Her voice was low and slow. She shook her head from side to side. 'Nothing.'

'I disagree.'

As though he had not spoken, she went on, 'James and I ran out of things in common as soon as we were married. Anyway,' she looked appealingly up at him, 'you don't think I could go on with James now? Even if I loved him, well, in comparison to my feelings now, what I felt for James is like a candle to a blast furnace. Anyway, I don't love him any more than I would love someone else's child. He's not mine in the sense of there being emotional ties. He's not my life. My life is somewhere else, a shining stream flowing on another course, over there.' She gestured towards the window and the darkening street. 'Do you understand me?'

He was staring at her and she saw he did not, and yet there was a curiosity in his expression, a glimmer of something, as if he had encountered what she was saying somewhere else, and that this encounter gave it reality, credibility.

'Apart from that, I can't go on. And not only because of how I feel for Christopher, who is my life, who is that shining stream I call my life. It's because of what happened. I can't compromise James. If I go into court, and give evidence, the newspapers will be there. They will report everything. It will be impossible. James will be ruined. Whereas, if I make it clear I am the ex-wife or about to be ex-wife, that the marriage was over already while I was with Christopher in Miami, then the scandal will not affect James so badly. He will get sympathy rather than look a fool.

'The Prime Minister will not be able to shake his head and tell him his wife has let him down. Well, he may do that anyway, but no one will be able to point the finger and enjoin him in my scandal. In fact, I think he will do rather well out of the sympathy he will get when it's learned that I've left him, having got myself into this mess.' She leaned back on her hands and looked up at him. The firelight played on her hair and on her face. The room was darkening now as the outside light went. The lamps had not been lit. Catherine saw her father's face cast in shadows and lit by the flames' reflections.

He smiled faintly into the fire and said, 'You would have done well in politics, my dear. You can twist an argument.'

She said ardently, 'It's not an argument. It's the truth. It's what I know and believe. And Daddy,' she leaned forward again, putting both hands on his knees and gazing up into his face, 'it's what I want.'

'Divorce?' He looked into her eyes.

She nodded. 'I want to be free to be with Christopher in whatever shape or form the relationship develops. I want to join my shining stream.'

He put down his glass and leaned forward. He cupped

394

her face in his two hands and said, 'Don't divorce James for this passing fancy, Rina. There are a dozen ways of avoiding this. You don't have to go into court as a witness to this shooting. This man is quite capable of dealing with it by himself. You don't have to tarnish your reputation by public association with this mongrel dog from the gutter, this criminal scum.'

He spoke with a virulent derision that shocked her. It was as if he had not heard her. She sprang back from his hands. 'No. Don't talk of him that way. I love him. You don't know how I feel when I hear you say those things. You don't know his soul.'

'Sit down, Rina.' He spoke with a dry commanding tone. She turned to the bucket and poured herself another glass of champagne, then obediently sat in the wing chair opposite him.

'Love is a snare and a delusion. You must think of your duty. You do not have to tell the whole truth about what happened. You do not have to admit that you were with him in the way that you were. You can say you were passing, that's all. You don't have to say you knew him, that you were lovers. That is not part of the evidence.'

She stared at him and he went on, 'I think you will find the court is not interested in whether you were swimming naked in the sea with your friend. They only want to know if you saw that he was shot and if you know the man who shot him. Now it would be even better if you were not even there when he was shot, but perhaps disappear from the record altogether. I am sure it can be arranged. We can fix that, I think.'

'Daddy. Stop it!' she shouted at him. 'I want to go into court. I want to tell the truth and I want to divorce James. I cannot live this lie of a marriage any longer. Even if there were no Christopher, no shooting, I would not stay with James. His career will survive well enough without me. He can find another, more suitable wife. He doesn't think I'm a proper wife anyway.'

He looked at her for a moment without speaking. The room was lit now only by the fire's leaping flames. At any moment Clive would call them to dinner. He said, 'You should do your duty to James and stay with him. It is part of your duty to him to avoid going into court. Therefore it is forgivable, morally permissible to lie in order to avoid being a prosecution witness.'

She saw he had not understood what she had told him about life and love. She became stiff and distant. The chair's high crimson back and wings framed her cool beauty with dignity. She lifted her glass and drank a long slow sip, but the champagne did not help. It tasted sour and flat, sobering. She was looking at him and her eyes were cold. She said, slowly, 'I don't think unfeeling devotion to duty measures up to the sacrifices of love on the scale of human priorities. I don't think there is a higher call than love. And, as for lies, I do believe they cringe before the moral power of truth.'

She paused and saw that he was listening again, with a kind of raptness and went on, 'I don't, for one moment, want to do some plastic duty that ignores the most powerful force in the world, the duty to respond to the love in your heart and follow it even into death.' She said the last words passionately, then went on more quietly, but with some formidable strength, 'And truth is surely the highest duty. Before God or mankind.'

They were both silent then. He looked at her and saw her eyes lit by the flames and thought of women who had burned for their beliefs, of the Maid of Orleans and others. She wore that same look. That same stubborn, deified look of the mad, messianic, idealistic fools that died for their beliefs. At the same time, her beauty was more pure and fine than he had ever seen it. She was lit now with a far stronger light than the fire of love for a man. In the dark room, something beyond mere human love now illuminated Catherine. She seemed somehow heroic.

He said quietly, unable to keep sarcasm out of his voice, 'And is the object of your love worthy of the sacrifice you make?'

There was a silence, then her voice came clear. 'The worth is measured by the love inspired.'

There was nothing left for him to say after that. He

smiled and nodded and turned to look into the fire and there was silence between them.

She stayed for dinner and they talked of less personal things, business and politics. She left immediately afterwards. At the front door to which, unusually, he came with her, she held him close and said, 'Daddy. Please understand. I feel alive and I love, for the first time in my whole life. I can't disobey those feelings. They are too strong. Too real. Too important. Too close to the divine. I must follow where they lead, wherever that is, God help me. Please don't be angry with me. Please stay my friend. I'm sorry to disappoint you, to be always your rebel child. I love you too, but nothing in my life has prepared me for this. I am devoured. I am a slave to love, but I don't think that is wrong. One can love God, and therefore the world, more by loving one human truly to the very limit of possibility. I must not fail to respond to the truth in my heart.'

Did he recognize Brenda's voice in her words? He held her very close for a long time and then held her away from him and looked a long while at her face and into her eyes. He said softly, 'I have a feeling you won't have to go through your trial, Rina. I don't think the thing will even get to Court. Go to sleep now and rest. You look tired. Everything will seem clearer in the morning. And don't worry. I suppose I don't blame you for your choice. If I had been wiser when I was young, it might have been my choice to do what you are doing, to follow love to the very end, wherever it should lead.'

She left him with a kiss.

81

Clive rang her at 8 a.m.

She was awake and picked the phone up instantly. James was still asleep: she did not want him disturbed.

'Madam. Mrs Waring. Oh, Miss Catherine. Oh I'm so sorry. I hope it's not too early to disturb you. Oh, I can't do this properly. Dear, dear Miss Catherine. Your poor father. Oh, it's too awful . . .'

She leaped with alarm. 'Clive! Whatever is it? What are you saying?' Her sleepless night's horrible presentiments focused on his words. 'Oh God, no.' Her voice went thin with horror.

'Oh, Madam. Sir Arnold . . .' She felt him pulling himself together and the intake of breath before he went on. 'He has been shot. He is dead. I'm so sorry, Madam . . . I'm so sorry.'

'Clive.' Her voice was suddenly calm and controlled. 'Clive. Are you sure? What happened?'

'I don't know, Madam. He was on the study floor when I went in to draw back the curtains just now. He has been . . . shot. In the head. It's . . . Oh Madam, poor Sir Arnold. He was such a wonderful man.'

She said quietly, 'Clive, Clive. Please don't. Clive, I want you to call the police. Don't do anything else. Don't touch anything. I'll be there very soon.'

She put the phone down as soon as she was sure he would do as she asked. Then she drew back her curtains and let the light in. It was going to be a beautiful day. She went to James' door and opened it. He was sound asleep. She left him and went back to her room.

She picked up the phone and tapped in Christopher's number. There was no reply. Then, she rang Armstrong at home. He answered in a measured wide-awake voice.

She said, her voice clear and rational, 'David. Something terrible has happened to my father. I don't know what exactly. His man rang me. He's been shot. I . . . gather he's . . . dead.' The word stuck in her throat. Dead was not real. Dead didn't happen. Dead was what you feared for the people you loved. Dead never came for real. Dead was not true.

He said, 'Have they rung their local station?'

'I've asked them to. But David, I want a friend. I want you there. I'm going myself in a few minutes. As soon as I'm dressed. Please. Can I still ask you that?' She remembered their last meeting. Was sure he did, too. She had talked to him from Miami, but this was a favour of another kind. She said, pleading, 'David, please come.'

He heard her distress and said he would.

She went into her bathroom and showered. She could feel nothing. She could not believe he was dead. She remembered his eyes saying goodnight. She had known then. Something inside her knew, when he said goodnight. Perhaps sooner . . . How? How could she have forseen?

It was no use speculating. No use anything. She felt numb, cold, automatic. She felt no tears coming. No wells of feeling flooding out of her depths. Instead of the warmth of tears and the release of expressed grief, she felt an emptiness growing inside her. And yet a lightness. Something had gone. Some weight. Some sorrow that had been there like a habit, perhaps for months or longer, had lifted. Something inside her was light like happiness. How could this be? How could she feel this way? Her darling father was dead.

Dead. Dead. What did the word mean? The hot water flooded over Catherine's shoulders and her navel, over her buttocks and down her legs. Her body came to life around fatigue's hollow ache and her memory denied his death.

She dried herself, walked into the dressing room and uncaring, chose something to wear, a dress, a simple dark dress. She slipped her unstockinged feet into high black sandals, picked up her dark glasses and a bag, caught sight of herself in the mirror and ran a comb through her sleep-tousled hair as she went downstairs.

She went out into the sunlight that seemed to mock and defy her icy grief. The world was living and celebrating the day. Not trusting herself to drive, she went into Victoria Street and took a cab to Charles Street.

David was already there. His car, his own car, was on the kerb, illegally parked outside the front door. A police car stood further down. Clive let her in, started to lead her towards the staircase, going to the drawing room. 'Will you have some tea, Madam?' He was impeccable. He was morose. He looked at Catherine with beaten, hurt eyes. Eyes full of pain and rejection. Eyes that said he did not understand why he had been left to cope with this.

'No, Clive. Where is my father's . . . where is he?'

He bent towards her and touched her arm. He shook his head. 'Perhaps it would be better if you did not . . .'

'Where is he?' Her voice rose.

She followed him across the parquet to the study. Armstrong was there and a detective sergeant from Vine Street. They looked up as she came in and Armstrong came towards her. He took both her hands and led her to one side.

He was firm, authoritative. 'Catherine. I don't think you should look. Your father is not . . .' He softened his voice from the professional to the personal. 'It's not a pretty sight, my dear.'

'Show me,' she said, firm and cold. She did not want protection from reality.

But it was not pretty. She fell to her knees on the blue carpet by his spoiled lovely head and stroked his hair. The bullet had entered the forehead and come out at the back. The gun was on the floor near the desk. He must have been standing when he fired. There was no doubt, almost no doubt, that he had done it himself.

The sobs began slowly with a whimpering, snivelling disturbance of her breath. Then they grew and vibrated the centre of her being with harsh jagged sounds that were part groan, part sob. She went on until the tears flowed and until she could contain the sound no more than an explosion can contain itself. She howled as she had howled over Angel's wounded body. More. Howled in anger against a God that could allow this death, this end of life. Howled and beat the floor with her fists.

She let the rage against her father's ending fill her heart and head and fill the house with its sound. She cried her anger in the groaning screams of an ancient grief. And the room echoed with the archaic sound, until at last she was still, kneeling beside him, her head bowed over her lap, quiet, and the room held the split silence of trauma as it must have after the single pistol shot.

When she stood at last, silent and composed, emptied of her rage, numb once more, and barely breathing, she found only Armstrong. He came to her and folded her tightly in his arms. And her breath began again in gasps. And she thought, Thank God, he's here with his strength to help me now.

82

Armstrong took Catherine back to Queen Anne's Gate and waited while she went to fetch James. He was having breakfast, glumly reading the newspapers at the kitchen table and sipping the last of his coffee. He looked up, puzzled at Catherine's arrival and her evident distress. She explained nothing, simply beckoning him. He followed her without a word to the drawing room where Armstrong was waiting.

It was Armstrong who explained what had happened. James looked at a disadvantage standing in his short blue dressing-gown and monogrammed slippers, a day's growth of stubble on his rounded chin. Catherine sat on the sofa facing the window and stared towards the street. Her dark glasses emphasized the pallor of her unmade-up face.

Armstrong said, 'Mrs Waring asked me to help her by explaining the circumstances of Sir Arnold's death to you, Sir. I am afraid there will have to be an inquest and no doubt some publicity will attend that, but I don't believe there will be any doubt as to the verdict. He appears to have shot himself.' He gave the details briefly and as simply as he could.

James said, 'I can't believe it. Whatever can have made him do it? Is the bank in trouble?' He looked at Catherine but she sat still, staring towards the street and beyond, almost as if the walls had disintegrated and she could see into some far place.

Armstrong took the letter in its light blue envelope from his breast pocket. He went towards Catherine, holding out his hand ahead of him with the letter in it. He stood between her and the light and she looked up at him as if he had disturbed her at some important task. He said, 'Sir Arnold left this letter for you, Mrs Waring. I'm sorry that I had to have it copied before you could receive it. But you can keep this now. I promise you the copy will only be used to ascertain that there has been no foul play. It will not be made public.'

She did not move and he put it gently into her lap. He said, 'I'll be off now, if you don't mind. I'm sure you would prefer to be alone.'

Catherine smiled faintly and nodded. James went out with Armstrong. 'Thank you, Commander,' he said. 'It was very good of you to come.'

Their voices receded into the hallway and Catherine looked down at the letter in her lap. Her name, simply Catherina, in her father's elaborate European-styled handwriting, was on the front of the fat blue envelope.

She stood up as James came into the room and went to him. He took hold of her and she let him. She could not cry again now. She was remote from feeling. Limp. She was so very, very tired. She disengaged herself and said, 'I think I'll go to bed. Would you call the office for me, please?'

He nodded.

She went upstairs slowly as if her feet were lead. In her room, she pulled down the blinds and drew the chintz curtains and closed out the brilliant day. She stepped out of her shoes, let her dress fall to the carpet, lay down and fell instantly asleep.

It was 12.42 p.m. when she awoke. The memory of what had happened came back to her immediately. The unnegotiable reality pressed in on her again. He was dead. She groaned aloud and the dull pain of her knowledge seeped through her body until every cell was weighted with despair. She crawled slowly out of bed and went to the windows and drew back the curtains and released the blinds. The day was unbearably fine. It shouted with life.

She reached for her robe and went downstairs to the kitchen. It was cool and in shadow now and gave her a sense of shelter. She had had nothing to eat or drink yet today. She drank a glass of mineral water and made herself some weak tea and sat staring out of the window. She could see the sunshine spilling between the trees onto the cropped green grass and the lake reflecting back the cloudless sky.

The numbness still held her. She could not remember how she had felt this morning in her father's study. Could not recreate her agony and her rage. She had brought the letter down with her. It had lain on the bedroom floor while she slept. Now it reproached her. 'Catherina,' the envelope said. It was time to read it. She hesitated. She was afraid of what it would tell her, of what was written in those pages in a dead man's hand, those words engraved in last night's time and space, yet seeming to come from beyond them. Was she strong enough, numb enough, to learn what they would say?

At last she pulled the bulky envelope towards her. She felt the thick paper under her fingers and lifted the open flap. Her father's paper with his crest embossed in the centre at the top. Her father's writing, sloping slightly, but Germanically round and gothic in its form, easy to read. He had put the time and the date. He had started writing at 3 a.m. She began to read:

My darling Catherina,

I am writing to you now because I love you so very much that I have no other way to tell you the awful truth that has dogged my life. I am not good enough to be your father, or your mother's husband. I was perhaps once, but I ruined what chance there was of leading a life free of guilt when I was only seventeen years old.

It is with shame I write now to tell you that I was a member of the Austrian Brown Shirts and that, in his own apartment, immediately after the Anschluss, I killed an old Jew who would not give me his valuables. It was not intentional. I pushed him hard

403

and he struck his head and that, it seemed, was all he needed to give up his life, poor creature.

In the hellish arrogance of my infected youth, I committed a murder which even then so shamed me that I had no choice but to leave Austria and become a refugee myself, in the hope that by leaving the scene of my guilt I would also leave the guilt itself.

I must tell you now that I never lost it. I have suffered the most terrible remorse for what I did. But the curse of my action has followed me wherever I have been. I have not been free for one waking moment of the knowledge of what I did to a helpless and frightened old man who happened to be one of the hated Jews. Hated for no reason other than that they were the object of some awful sickness, some evil infection that came from a leader who was, I think now, a pure manifestation of the ignored evil in our collective minds, an evil that sought deliberately to create this barbaric madness that destroyed our ability to think and to act decently out of our own noble and civilized European past.

But you, my darling, my precious daughter, need only know this. I was found out. While I was establishing myself here in London after the success in Kenya and just after I had finished taking over the bank entirely from old Johnson, I was approached. At first, I thought it would be possible to buy them off completely. But it was no good. They never stopped. They would not allow me to pay them off. They only wanted more and more things done for them. And the word spread, from one group to another until I became the offficial Banker of Crime.

So the truth is, Catherina, I have, for years, allowed my bank to be used to launder criminal money, from drug sales and robberies of all kinds. No one has known this and I confess it to you now in the hope that you at least will forgive me and somehow understand that I had to remain who I seemed.

I could not have it known that I had been a Nazi, that I had committed murder. I could not have your life blemished, your future risked. And my own vanity was also at stake, though heaven knows, I could have moved on to Latin America or South Africa, somewhere where these things pass unnoticed.

I suppose I need not have told you this except that now you will become the owner of Clyne Johnson and, although it is unlikely you will find any discrepancies as you audit, there may come a time when these people will come to you and apply the same pressure. Recently, I was pressured very heavily to give assistance to the groups working against James's South London Redevelopment Scheme. Yes, I'm afraid I was unable to prevent myself from becoming involved in assisting the criminal elements who were conspiring to obstruct the Scheme.

To counterbalance, I tried to my utmost to make the consortium the best. I believe I may have succeeded in that, anyway. The billions promised by the group of big investors should be a substantial foundation for the Redevelopment Scheme. I wish it well and trust my other actions will be forgiven. It was I who funded the purchase of drugs to pay off the rioters. Fortunately no one was seriously hurt to add to my overloaded conscience.

Catherina my dear, I come to the most important part, for you, the part that explains why you are probably now reading this letter over my corpse. Don't fear, my dear, for my soul. I have never believed in God or the Devil or in Heaven or Hell. I have always considered good and evil to be purely human manifestations, aggrandized by alleged links with superhuman powers.

Catherine paused and blew her nose and mopped fresh tears from her eyes. She had always fought her father on his atheism. Now she thought of him confronted by the reality of his misconceptions, or perhaps annihilated according to his true belief. 'Poor Daddy,' she whispered. She read on:

This, next, I tell you with great grief for I know that I failed in something that was of great importance in your life. I believed you should have risen to the highest place in this land. You are born a British subject, although in Africa, and you belong with the best of these people, who are, as I have always believed, despite their snobbery towards a humble foreigner, the best in the world. I still believe James will become Prime Minister, and Catherina, I still intend you should remain his wife.

She drew in her breath and said aloud with force, 'No, oh please no. Don't bind me to that now.'

That is the prime reason for what I am about to do, to prevent you from having to appear as a witness in the case of your lover's shooting. Not only, my dear, because your lover is a lowlife criminal type whom I have known over recent years and assisted in his nefarious finances. But because, alas, I have to tell you I was the one who ordered his death and hired the gunman whose intended fatal bullet missed its mark.

'Oh God! No! No! No!' she cried out. She stood up and walked to the sink and ran the cold water over her hands. She stared at the tranquil park and felt the convulsion of her horror shake her. The flickering of green leaves moved by a slow breeze seemed like a hand soothing her brow. She drank a glass of cold water, then she returned to the table and went on reading.

So I have to ask your forgiveness for failing to kill the man and thus placing you in the terrible position of having to go to court as a prosecution witness against your father, and ruining your husband's career and your own reputation. And I suppose I must ask you to forgive me for trying to end the life of the man you care for so much that you want to be with him regardless of his criminality.

I did it for the best motives, Catherina. When you

406

first told me who your lover was and I knew it was I who was to blame for advising you in the first place to take a lover, I warned him off. I had you both followed and I knew that he kept away from you for a while, but you got back together again and I found out about it. I warned him again but this time you followed him when he left you, and I knew I had to kill him to set you free. When you left for New York I had to have you followed again for I knew you would go to him.

Believe me, you are and have always been my most precious creature. Perhaps I loved you less at first because you were, in an unintending way, the cause of your mother's death.

I did truly love your mother, Catherina, and I was not able to accept her death. She was so young and beautiful. You were not a fair substitute, a red-faced, screaming brat held out to me by an Indian nurse. And my beautiful Marina Catherina haemorrhaged to death.

But you became as beautiful as she was. And as rebellious. I think if she had lived you would have fought with her more than you fought with me.

Why have I never talked to you about these things? Because I always felt they would intrude on our relationship, which has, I think, grown quite delightfully close since you have been married to James. We could have been closer, perhaps, with some more honesty. Now I see how you respond to the man who is no worse but no better certainly than I, I am sorry I did not try to tell you. But perhaps your love for me would not have been strong enough to overcome the repugnance you would undoubtedly have felt at learning your father was a criminal. Telling you was, of course, impossible. And so we, I, lived a lie.

I want my last words to be more reassuring. I believe you will remain James's wife and that you will, before too long, give him and yourself the child you want who will inherit after you what I have built for you.

Farewell, my dearest Rina. I never really cared for

the idea of growing old. And life was becoming too diffficult anyway. I'm sorry about the peerage, though. I would have enjoyed it and the PM had promised I would have it in the next New Year's list.

I wish you and James both the very best and happiest of lives,

Arnold

She dropped her head into her hands and sat without moving for some minutes. Then she stood, stiff and hurting all over, her body not her emotions expressing her pain. She took the letter over to the waste disposal and began rolling it into a tight tube, preparing to destroy what she could show no one, even James. She was distracted by the telephone and went over to it, still holding the letter.

He said, 'I've seen the evening paper. I'm sorry. I'm really sorry.'

She said, 'I tried to reach you this morning. I want to see you. Can I come now?'

He hesitated for a moment, then said, slowly, 'Come to the house. I'll meet you there in half an hour.'

She put the phone back in its cradle and went upstairs to dress. The letter was still in her hand. She would take it with her. He should read it himself. Perhaps that would put an end to him feeling he was not good enough for her.

83

He came down and opened the door for her and led her back up the stairs. The house had an unlived in mustiness. The windows were closed. It seemed he had only just arrived there himself.

She said, 'Where were you? I called you earlier.'

'I've been out all day.' He looked at her warily.

She delved into her bag and brought out the blue envelope. He guessed what it might be and turned away. 'Want something to drink?' He went to the kitchen.

She followed him. 'Tea.'

He filled the kettle. She watched his broad back and the ripple of muscles under his shirt and wanted him and was ashamed. Now? Wanted him now? She turned back towards the living room and then stood in the doorway as he moved to reach the cups. He had not touched her. She said, 'Do you think death might be contagious?'

He looked up sharply at the bitterness in her voice.

She smiled unhappily. 'Can't you touch me? I need to be held. I need to feel your love.'

'Poor baby.' He came towards her and put warm arms around her. She let her face rest on his chest and let the loving warmth of the man flood her. She was rigid. He kissed her forehead and held her tight and rocked her. He said, 'I'm sorry. Poor baby, I'm sorry.'

The kettle whistled in a long piercing scream and he left her to go to it. He put bags into mugs and poured the water over them. He added milk to his own and carried them through.

She had put the letter on the coffee table and she saw him glance at it and then quickly move his eyes away. As he bent over to put the mugs down on the table she saw the round hard shape of his buttocks and felt desire for him. She had been in the house almost fifteen minutes. It was unusual to be with him this long and not have him bring out his cock and fuck her.

When he had held her she had felt nothing erotic between them. Only his kindness. It made her feel inadequate to be with this man and not have him show his lust for her. In the hospital it had been different. He had been weak. Now, it was as if he had no interest in her. She felt a kind of panic. She did not understand herself or him. She wondered again if sex was all there was between them. After so much, was that the only thing she wanted of him? Or was sex the only satisfying communication, beyond words, which were not his medium, though hers, very much hers?

He said, 'Sit down. Have your tea.'

Her voice and face full of tension, she said, 'Read that letter. I want you to know what it says.'

He was sitting on the sofa. He looked up at her with an expression that told her he was afraid.

She said, 'Go on. Please. Read it. I'm the only one who has read it, yet, apart from the police. I want you to be next. I haven't even shown it to James.'

He said, 'You should show it to your husband before me.'

'No!' she shouted. Then dropped her voice. 'It concerns you more than he. It concerns us. I can't show it to him until I've told him everything about you and me.'

He took the folded sheets of thick blue paper out of their envelope as one would dismantle a bomb. He unfolded them and began to read. It took some time as he read slowly, and he was not used to her father's writing.

She stood and drank her tea, pacing a little but watching him closely. She saw the emotion on his face now and then. At other times he seemed impassive. Occasionally he frowned. When he had finished, he folded the sheets and put them back into the envelope. He sipped the cooled tea and stood up. He went towards the window and looked out into the mews.

'You knew, didn't you?' Her voice was a low choked sound, vibrant with accusation.

He had his back to her. The brilliant day, still undiminished, shone its light full onto him and cast his shadow long behind him. He leaned his hands on the sill and put his weight on his straightened arms, ducking his head around towards her. 'I knew all about your father.'

She stepped closer to him so that the light fell cruelly on her tired face. But he was not looking at her. She said, quietly, without emotion, as if she were reciting a catalogue of facts, 'And you knew who it was who hired your assassin. And you couldn't say. You couldn't say. You let me live through those days in Miami without telling me what I was going to have to face. You let me

410

come all the way back to London to this house and go and tell my father about the gunman. And you still didn't say anything. You let me leave this house yesterday and go to him. You let me go, knowing I would leave his house last night without knowing what he would do after I had told him. You let me put the gun in his hand. You let me kill him. You are a coward and a liar and a cheat.'

He kept his back to her, looking out into the bright sky and said, 'I couldn't tell you, Catherine. I am a coward and I couldn't tell you and I'm sorry.'

Her voice grew stronger and emotion crept into it. 'You let me kill him, Christopher.' She screamed at his back. 'You let me kill him.'

He turned towards her and came to her, holding out his arms. His voice was quiet and reasonable, gentle, kind. He was saying, 'You didn't kill him, Catherine. He killed himself. You were not to blame. I was not to blame. He had enough reason, Catherine.'

She backed away from him and he saw the hysteria come into her face. She screamed, 'He is dead because you are my lover. Because he told us both to end it and we didn't. He's dead because I met you. Because I love you. I killed him.' She started for the stairs.

He leaped for her and caught her by the hair, pulling her back and lashing his arms around her like ropes. He held her from behind and she struggled, trying to kick out at him, but he locked his legs around hers and pinned her completely.

She yelled, 'You let me kill him. You goddamned coward. You damn lying bastard, you. If it wasn't for you he would be alive now.'

He let her shout and scream and he said nothing and he did not release his hold. She quietened and he started kissing her hair and her cheeks and she fought to break away. He walked her, struggling, towards the couch and lay down on it, pulling her onto her back on top of him and locked his legs around hers again. She struggled but was barely able to move, and then he felt her soften and he went on holding her until she was still.

411

She said, her voice heavy with fatigue, 'Let me go please, Christopher. I want to sit up.'

He eased his arms carefully away from her and she turned and slapped his face, viciously. Then she burst into sobs and buried her face in her hands.

A bright red mark stained his cheek. He was shocked but repressed the jolt of rage that shot through him. He forgave the insult and cradled her gently and rocked her until the sobs eased and she began to breathe properly again. Then he began to kiss her face, softly, gently, repeatedly, her cheeks, her neck, her eyes, her mouth. At last he felt her arms steal around him and her fingers opening the buttons of his shirt.

She put her hands inside the shirt and stroked his smooth chest and his nipples and then she undid his belt and his zip and brought out the heavy cock and put her mouth on it and sucked him sweetly and felt him start to stiffen. He felt her breasts under the loose dark dress and then he pulled the dress off over her head and found her naked under it. He began kissing her breasts and shoulders and navel and at last dropped onto his knees on the floor and gently parted her legs and moved the silky hair from her vulva and put his soft mouth there and began to lick her with great tenderness.

When she asked him to, he put his cock into her and let her come to life under his touch and brought her back to sanity with his rhythm and his healing juices and she let the tension that had held her rigid since this morning melt away and let him lift her into her paradise and lose herself in the waves of light and life of their love.

When it was over and she lay under him on the sofa, it was she who fell asleep and he moved away from her gently and covered her with a blanket and drew the curtains to shut out some of the glaring light and went to sit on the other side of the room. He watched her for a while and then his head fell onto his chest and he slept, too.

He awakened to hear her moving around the room. She had on her dress again and her shoes and was groping in her bag for her glasses and a comb. He watched her

412

until she looked at him and then he lifted a hand and waved his fingers at her.

She came to him then and dropped onto her knees and rested her head on his knee.

She said, 'I'm sorry.'

He stroked her head.

She looked up at him. 'There's something else, too. I have to know. And please don't lie to me.'

His eyes showed anxiety.

'When you came out to dinner with me, you knew who I was. You knew I was my father's daughter.' She paused and raked his face with her look. 'I have to know whether you started this relationship because you wanted something, something other than what you . . . I have to know if it was a devious reason. I'm not talking about now. I'm talking about then.'

He shook his head. His eyes had that immense fullness again, that darkness of black holes. His eyes were unfathomable. He said, 'No. It wasn't anything devious.'

She said, 'I can't understand why you didn't say anything.'

He said, 'I couldn't. You would have wanted to know why I knew your father. He didn't want you to know and that was one of the reasons he wanted to break us up. In case I told you.'

'I know.' Her eyes scanned his face, searching for evidence that he was lying. She said, 'I have to be sure. I have to be sure you didn't come after me because of who I was.' She stood up and walked across the room. She sat on the arm of the sofa. She was watching him. Waiting for something.

He stood up, too and moved towards her. 'Do you think I was after your money, Catherine?' His face was both sad and angry. His voice held the bitterness of being misunderstood.

She looked up at him not knowing what to think. 'Were you? I've got even more now. It could be even more worth your while.'

He came to her and caught hold of her shoulders and lifted her so that she was standing. He shook her gently

413

and she saw the anger and the hunger of a man who thought he would never have something he wanted. 'Catherine,' he said hoarsely. 'Catherine, you know that's not true.'

She said wearily, 'I don't know what's true any more, Angel.' She looked down to where her sandalled feet stood on the brown carpet.

He took her face in both his hands and lifted it until she was looking at him. He said, 'I make it my business to know who I'm having dinner with, Catherine. I found out who you were before I came. But I didn't do it because I wanted your money. I came against my rule. My rule is I don't mix business with pleasure. When I found out who you were I shouldn't have had anything to do with you. That was my rule. I broke the rule because I wanted you so badly.'

She searched his face again and found nothing to prove him a liar. She said, 'You left me, twice, when he threatened you. Why didn't you tell me? Why did you just go?'

'Would you have believed me?'

'I should have challenged him.'

'He might have killed me anyway, Catherine. To stop me having you. To stop you divorcing James. I knew your father. I knew that I had better leave unless I was prepared to kill him first. But I couldn't do that. I couldn't kill your father and go on with you. I had no choice.'

She dropped her head onto his chest and slid her arms around his waist. She groaned and then he heard her say, 'Forgive me, then. Forgive me. For everything I've said today. Forgive me for so much more I've thought about you. Forgive me for my anger and my fear. Forgive me, please. I didn't understand. I still don't understand so much about you. And I want to. Forgive me. I love you so very much.'

'I forgive you,' he said, and he hugged her to him. His voice was warm with relief and love. 'I forgive you.'

*

414

84

Armstrong took Catherine's hands in both his own. He sat down on the sofa beside her, still holding them and looked at her with sympathy. He found it hard to make the transition from senior officer to sympathetic friend, all in the space of the four minute walk from Scotland Yard to Queen Anne's Gate, at the end of a hard day.

It was ten days since her father's death. Catherine had asked David Armstrong to call on her. There were so many questions left unanswered about her father's life and his links with crime, and there was the gnawing unsatisfied remnant of the suspicion she had about Angel. She had invited Armstrong for a drink but made it clear that there was a reason, that it was not just a social invitation that he might prefer to refuse or delay.

'How can I help you, Catherine?' Armstrong was still holding her hands.

She looked down at them and saw her own unmanicured thumbnail protruding from the protection of his large warm hand. She had been letting herself slide this past week. She looked into Armstrong's face. 'I want you to help me unravel the rest of the puzzle, David.'

He released her hands. Without asking him what he would like, she went to the drinks cabinet to pour herself a Perrier and, for him, a Highland Spring.

'You know my tastes now, Catherine,' he said with a smile, and raised the glass before drinking a token sip.

She sat down opposite him with her back to the evening street. The room was in shadow and the lamps not yet lit so her face became mysterious in the dimness. Her eyes were points of light without expression and he listened to her voice with greater concentration, hearing its strained timbre. She did not waste time on any preamble. 'I'm unable to rest because I can't follow what has really happened with any logic. There are too many pieces missing in the story my father wrote in his letter.

415

I want to know what you can tell me, so that I can understand. I must put this behind me and be healed. I can do that if I can resolve it and put it out of my mind. But I can't do it until I have the whole truth.'

'I don't know a great deal more, you know.'

Her voice rose irritably, 'Well, you must know what he was really doing with the South London protest groups.'

He spoke slowly as if in pain, his face screwed up and his voice tense and very Scottish. 'I can't see what I can tell you that is going to give you peace of mind, my dear. Can't you just let things be, let him rest in your memory, as you knew him? Forget the rest?'

Her voice stabbed at him like a long sword across the space between them, hard and cold. 'I want the truth. The truth rests easier in memoriam than an untold life of lies.' She stood up and leaned on the marble mantel. He saw, by her left shoulder, the silver-framed picture of her father standing beside her as she sat astride her horse against a background of bougainvillaea, a child in Africa with her handsome daddy.

More gently, she said, 'I didn't know him. I saw only one image of him and missed the truth. It's almost as if I made him up, my darling Daddy. What I have learned this past few days has shocked me into a new vision of him: but it's too incomplete. It's as if I don't know him, don't have anything I can remember because what I thought I knew was just a fraction of his reality, a tiny fragment of his truth. Now, the things I don't know are haunting me. His ghost is nagging me night and day, it seems. Perhaps ghosts are the unrevealed secrets people leave behind them in their loved ones' memories and it's the living not the dead who need to rest in peace.'

She moved and paced the rug. 'But I can't rest in peace while I carry these questions. I can't even sleep. For God's sake, David, help me. Put me out of my agony. Tell me whatever you can. I've begun going through his personal papers. I'm piecing together his past. But it's going to take weeks, maybe months to sort and read through everything he's left in the house, never mind the bank.

For the time being, I can't seem to live a normal life without knowing more, more than I can ever discover from an incomplete jigsaw of memorabilia. David, I need your help. Please.'

He cleared his throat. 'I have a file on your father which dates back a fairly short time. I went to see him a few weeks ago because of a trail my staff were following.' He paused and looked at her. 'We were investigating what we knew about the contacts made by the man we arrested after the terrorist explosion on the Thames.'

'Michael O'Leary?'

'Yes. O'Leary is a Russian-trained operator of some considerable sophistication and he has close links with the IRA and their arms procurement strategies, in which I suspect your father may have been involved. O'Leary was working closely on the South London business with a man called Leach . . .'

She nodded and he saw she knew something of Leach. She moved back to the sofa and sat down, leaning her head back on the cushions.

His voice was heavy with regret and his guilt about the secret he had held for several weeks, the telling of which to Catherine might have saved the banker's life. 'O'Leary was being watched as a matter of routine, because of his IRA links, mainly. He was tailed to your father's building one afternoon some months ago. But he was with Leach and it was Leach who went inside. When O'Leary's report came up after his arrest, I noticed this link and although I wasn't sure that he had a connection with your father, it could have been anyone in the building, I had it checked out. I found out that Leach had visited your father.

'I went to see your father, and I had a longish chat with him. He told me that he had briefly been a Brown Shirt in Vienna and why he was being blackmailed and how long it had been going on. He did not tell me what I learned from his letter, that he had killed anyone in Austria or, more important, that he had been laundering criminal funds for a number of years.

'Anyway, since then I have carried out some investigations. As you are your father's executor, I will now have to ask you for cooperation. We need to make some inquiries, put in fraud officers to check audits and so on. Your father's books may be a gold mine of evidence which will help us to nail some very clever fraudsters and thieves. But, of course, I'm not here for that now, that's a formal piece of office business that will come up later.'

She said, 'What was really going on between my father and the Redevelopment Scheme protest groups?'

'I'm not fully sure yet. But we do know now that your father funded the purchase of drugs and that quite possibly the money was passed to your friend, Christopher Angel.' He paused and waited for a reaction but saw nothing.

He went on, 'As I told you, we suspect that Angel organized the smuggling of cannabis from Morocco and cocaine from Miami. We believe he traded stolen bullion for drugs. These went via Michael O'Leary to the protest groups, as payment mainly. Angel would then have passed the funds received from your father, less his commission, to the bullion's vendors. These were not very large sums because relatively small amounts of drugs were involved in the protests. But there may have been other ways in which Angel and your father cooperated to trade bullion and launder the proceeds. These and much more may be uncovered when we examine the bank records. Your father first knew Angel several years ago, I gather. At that time, Angel was being watched as he was suspected of being involved in a financial fraud, for which we have not yet been able to find enough evidence to bring a case against him. This again is where the inspection of bank records may help. It may also help with several unsolved crimes as I believe your father acted as a conduit for black money, undeclared cash income, quite large sums, in fact, from drug trafficking, vice and big robberies.'

Her voice struggled to emerge from her tautened throat and came out husky and uneven. 'Was Christopher blackmailing my father?'

He shook his head. 'I don't know. To be truthful, I think your father simply became known as "The Banker", that's what they called him, I gather, who helped criminals process their funds. Once he had started, after the original blackmail, he had to go on, because there was a bigger and bigger lump of horror for blackmailers to feed on. If he had only come to the police in the beginning, as with all blackmail, it could have been stopped. But he didn't want anyone to know about the business in Vienna. It would not have become public. It could have been handled quietly. But there you are. People have this terrible fear and guilt and expect to be punished for what they have done. There are probably hundreds of ex-Nazis living peaceful and prosperous lives, even in Britain. Many who did far worse and for far longer than your father have got away with it and will die with their secrets.'

She sat still and silent, chewing a corner of her underlip.

'If he had only been able to talk about it to you, as he did to me, then this terrible thing need never have happened. He was trying to kill your friend so that you would be protected from any danger of learning the truth about his own life. As well as to protect you from a very undesirable association, of course.' His voice stiffened at this point. It was as though he allowed his feelings, disgust and disapproval, to come through, for the first time in what was otherwise a policeman's report.

In a hoarse, heavy whisper, she said, 'Couldn't you have told me, David?'

He responded with some sharpness. 'It was not my business to tell you. Besides, I had given my word of honour that what your father told me would go no further. Had he told me there was this morass of illegal activity going back fifteen years or more I would certainly have had to start an investigation and probably charge him. But, as it was, he told me only that Leach had come to blackmail him over his past as a Nazi, and that he had resolved the matter.'

'Did you not follow up to see if he had paid any money to Leach or done anything else?' She sounded surprised.

He gave her a troubled look. 'Cash is hard to trace. Anyway, I didn't want to start turning over loose stones and starting any rumours flying around about your father. Besides, Michael O'Leary has been our best source for the rest of the story. He has told us all about your friend's part in the SLRS protest, how suitcases of money from your father's bank were handed over to couriers in the Sirocco and taken off to pay the bullion suppliers. How your friend organized the transfer of bullion to the drug traffickers as they brought their cargoes in by yacht from Casablanca or the French coast.'

He added with a sniff, 'Romantic stuff, isn't it? Anyway, I believe your friend liked to courier the money and the goods himself at times. I understand he likes the thrill of the game . . .' He paused and then added with a bitter tone, 'I imagine you were part of that thrill for him, too. Screwing "the Banker's" daughter behind his back must have been quite a turn on.'

She got up and went to the drinks cabinet again. She came back carrying the Highland Spring bottle and topped up his glass.

He was aware that he must have gone too far. But she stood in front of him, holding the bottle and said calmly, 'There was some of that in the beginning. But it's not that any more. I really think the relationship has its own reasons for existing now. There is a great deal of feeling between us which has nothing to do with who we are outside it.'

He said, with a mean sharpness that surprised him, 'You know he has a relationship with another woman. He spends the night with her quite often, in fact.'

She had turned away, now she turned back. He did not seem to notice her reaction. He was holding his glass, ready to take a drink and looking into the fireplace. His voice seemed casual, as if he was thinking aloud. 'He's been with her quite a bit since his arrest a week or so back, since you stood bail for him. Almost living in, in fact. She works for him too, as an administrative assistant. She will be quite an important witness against him, if we can get her to talk.' He laughed. 'But I'm sure he will keep her sweet enough to prevent that.'

She took a step back towards him. She gripped the

bottle as if she were afraid she would drop it. For a moment, he thought she was going to hit him with it. Her voice belied her angry posture. Very calmly, she said, 'No. I didn't know. But why are you telling me that, David? And how do I know you have the facts?'

He said, kindly, 'It's my business to have the facts, Catherine, and I'm telling you for your own good.'

She went back to the drinks cabinet and poured herself a vodka. He watched her slender back in the demure blue linen shift. She threw the liquor back in one swift lift of chin and wrist, and then turned and hurled the heavy glass across the room and past him into the fireplace where it exploded into fragments.

He flung his arms up as small pieces of glass hit him and then leaped out of his seat and went to her. 'I'm sorry.' He was holding out his arms.

'Don't touch me,' she said. Her voice was low and tight. The sound was almost like a groan.

He had never seen such fury, yet surprisingly contained. He saw it would be best to leave. He said, 'I'll ring you, Catherine.'

As he went out into the hall, she was still standing in the middle of the room with the light from the windows making a halo of her hair, but with her fists clenched and violence in every line of her fragile silhouette.

85

She drives to his house and parks her car, slewed across his doorway. She gets out and rings the bell. It is still very light and the mews is busy with summer evening people watering tubs and window boxes or fiddling with their cars. The normality of the scene gives her a sense of unreality. Her mind is in another dimension, stark and cruel and dark with pain.

Why, she asked herself as she drove, does it matter? Why is another relationship a betrayal? What difference does it make to my feelings or those he gives to me, to the love between us? Why do I want to kill him again? The gun is in the glove compartment, wrapped in a silk scarf. Not the same gun or the same scarf as in Miami. Another gun, innocent. Another scarf. No more blood. No more death. Please God. I want to kill him. I want to kill her. I should throw away the gun. I should stop the car and drop it in one of those green bins for keeping London tidy. She did not stop. She asked herself again why she feels this murder in her heart.

Trust, her mind screams. He breached your trust. The lie between you has grown bigger. The betrayal is in the living lie, the absence of confession that this relationship exists, that there is another relationship that matters, that has power over his life, over his freedom, no matter what the basis of its power; sex or secrets held.

This is why he has never wanted to be seen out with her, always met her in secret, not to protect her reputation and her husband's career, but his own secret life with another woman who must not know about Catherine because of what she, this other woman, might do, what she might say to the police, to the court, to damn him out of jealous passion.

Jealous passion is what she feels now. For another woman who feels his cock inside her, who writhes and cries out for his semen, who feels him thrust and flow into her, who rises into paradise and holds his eyes in a bonded glance. Does he say the words to her he uses to me? Does he do to her what he does to me? Does he feel the same things? Is it just another woman to him? Am I just another woman, more exciting because of being from that class that he can't enter by his own right, only by stealth or seduction, rape or theft? Is she exciting and a prize because he feels he is stealing the family jewels of pride and wealth and class, from the Banker by his daughter's ass?

She hears the window go up and he is there, looking down at her, surprise and is it anger in his eyes, those

422

black, unfathomable eyes? Surprised and unwary. Ruffled to be caught out.

The neighbours are about. He looks at her. Then he says, 'Wait. I'll come down.'

She waits and he comes. He says, 'I can't ask you in. I have a friend, we're having a meeting.'

'What friend? Your woman?'

He looks baffled, suspicious, afraid, in rapid sequence. 'What's wrong?'

'I must talk to you. Now. No excuses. Please, get rid of them or come with me in my car to my house and we'll talk there.'

'Come up.' He speaks abruptly. He looks angry, wary, alert. He is thinking about what she wants. What has made her angry. What she will do. If she has a gun. He lets her lead the way.

She stands in his living room in her simple blue dress with a scarf over her head and her dark glasses over her eyes. A long rope of pearls swings to her waist. She is elegant, beautiful, frozen in rage.

He stands there helplessly, in disarray. He looks vulnerable, caught, exposed, shamed. There is no visitor. It was a lie. The TV is on. Papers lie around. His clothes are spread and tumbled on the unmade bed. Coffee cups stand on the table. He takes the remote from the table and turns off the TV. He gestures her to sit on the sofa that is not a bed. He sits on the end of the bed and looks at her.

She sits quietly on the sofa's arm. She is always quieter when she is with him. His presence soothes her and opens her heart to him. Anger is hard. She loves him so much. Now, she feels her love for him washing away her violence. She speaks quietly, taking off her scarf and glasses. 'Tell me about your woman.'

He stares at her. He stands up and walks towards her. He comes around the table to touch her.

She flinches. 'Don't touch me.' Her voice is abrupt but not cold. She is afraid that if he touches her she will lose heart for what she has come to say, to do. To tell him it's over, that she has been made a fool, that she has

423

given him all but her blood: her love, her care, her time and thoughts, her father's life. To tell him he can stay with the other one, the woman who is more his own kind. If he is sure he cannot make the leap he needs to make to reach her, to reach Catherine who now stands away from him, looks down, looks down at the creature who has used her and hurt her and damaged her and taken away her father's life. And whom she loves to death.

She says, 'I love you more than my life. But you have lived a lie with me and left my love in the gutter which may be where you come from but is not where my love should be.'

He looks at her, deeply hurt, and she says, 'You are no good to a woman. You cannot be good. You are, as you said, no good. No good for life. You are a betrayer. You have kept secret from me another relationship while I spent my love and bankrupted my emotions to sustain that love in hell. You took my feelings and spent the strength they gave you with another woman. I let you know about my husband. I tried never to make you feel that my husband came first. Besides, he did not come first. You came first. You were my life. I gave you power of life and death over me. I gave you entry to my soul. But you took my soul and threw it on a heap as if you were a savage who collects scalps.' Her lovely face is a living screen on which her anger plays like fire.

He says, painfully, 'Catherine. Don't say any more. I want you to understand something about me. About what's happening to me . . .'

She cuts across him. 'Understand? I do now. I didn't understand, but I do now. You need a woman of your own kind. You need someone to share your guilty secrets and you think I'm too far above you for that.'

He retreats. His eyes go dark with hurt. She cries out, 'Well, you are wrong. I have sunk pretty low. I have gone beneath even your depths. I am the daughter of a murderer, a fascist and a criminal, a coward who hid the truth about his life under a massive, corrupt lie. Who took a knighthood and would have taken a peerage. Worse, he tried to kill you and even I tried to kill you and would have killed myself as well, two sins to rot in hell for to the end of time. Yes, I am your kind of woman. I am low enough for you to love and share your life with. But I will not share you with another woman. I will not be your wife or your lover and share you. I will not love a man who can betray my trust with lies.'

She stands. 'I wanted you to know. I wanted you to hear me. Now I'm going. You and I have nothing more to say to each other.'

He stands and holds out a hand. 'No, Catherine. You must listen to me. You are still very upset about your father's death . . .'

She spurts anger like a jet of flame. 'It doesn't change what you have done, are doing, to cheapen what I gave you.'

'Catherine, I have to keep her happy for a bit. Until this case is over. Until I know whether I'm going to prison or not. I was with her before I met you. It's very tricky, just now. She could finish me. She can save me with the right . . .'

'Lies?' She spits the word at him and runs on, 'She'll tell the right lies for you. Swear on the Holy Book that you were with her and not wherever the police know you were. Is that it? Would you like me to do that for you? Shall I go to court and lie for you, too? Were you planning maybe I would?'

Her voice is scathing, scalding, cruelly hard. 'No wonder you wanted to give me back the bail money. At least you have some scrap of honour. You couldn't let one woman lie for you and let another stand bail. Another man's wife put up your bail and let her reputation go onto police computer file. Too late to get that back, though.' She puts her glasses back on, walks to the stairs. He lets her go. She stops at the turn of the stairs to look at him. He is still sitting on the bed, his arms fall loosely between his knees, his neck is bent.

He says, sadly, 'I told you I was no good. You said it didn't matter. Do you think I could change so quickly? Change at all?' His voice, bitter and hurt, follows her, as she starts down. 'I thought you loved me for what I was.'

425

She stops. She comes back to the top of the stairs. She says, sadly, 'I'm sorry. Have I betrayed you, too?' Compassion floods her. Anger dies away. Pity, yes and love are there.

He is looking down at the floor. She comes back into the room and goes to him and stands near him, looking down at him. She says, 'Will you, if I allow you . . . if I don't interrupt and insult you . . . will you tell me about it? Tell me the truth this time? No more lies? Will you trust me with truth? Will you forgive me for what I have said to you and trust me to be your friend?'

She has hurt him. Months of work undone, taming the wild animal who fears the human hand. She has breached his trust. He is taut and bitter. His past has come back to him. The old wounds are bleeding again.

He says, harshly, 'No. You are right. I'm just a savage who collects scalps. Women are all just that to me. I use them for sex. I used you. You'd better go.'

She draws her breath, 'Is that the truth?'

He looks up with his black angry eyes and she sees his pain. He says, slowly, 'No. It's not. But if that's what you want to believe, you'll make it true. It takes two to make a lie, the liar and the one who believes.'

She drops down on her knees. 'I never asked you if there was anyone. I assumed that you were free. You never said you had a relationship that was . . . that you were being unfaithful to another woman when you were with me. I never asked because I knew that I was married and that you had your life and I had mine. But things have changed. I am going to divorce my husband. I am free, now, almost, and it has become important. So I've found out you do have someone. Someone who is treated as your offficial woman, like a wife. And I still have to know whether she is important. If she is, I will leave now and not come back into your life. If not, if there is anything for me, can we forgive each other and begin again?'

'I don't know.' He is not looking at her. He stands up and walks away, to the window where the light has moved to dusk. The room is growing dark and a bright star hangs in the sun-lorn sky.

'Then it must be too late for us to begin again. Even if I can accept everything and believe you. And believe I matter. Matter more than . . .'

He turns to her, his hands outspread, anguished and unhappy. 'I might go to prison. You won't want me then.'

She says swiftly, with passion, 'I will. Oh, but I will. I'll wait for you.' She goes on more slowly, 'But only if I am the only woman waiting for you. I can't be part of a . . . a harem of pathetic creatures waiting for you at the prison gates. I must have the dignity of being your only woman.'

He comes closer and she takes a step towards him.

He says, haltingly, 'I can't promise to be faithful, but there won't be anyone . . . like you . . . Just let me get through this . . .'

She goes the rest of the way towards him and pushes his arms away from his body and links her arms around his waist and buries her head in his chest. She says, into his chest, 'No one has ever loved me enough. Even my father, until the other day. I can't go on without love. I have to matter enough to someone, enough to be first for them, before their work, or themselves or another woman. Please let it be you.'

He puts his arms around her, then, and she hears him say, very softly, 'Yes.'

86

A July Sunday: the sun was bright in the park and on the harsh metal of the cars jamming Piccadilly. The day was humid and hot, and the crowds wore shorts and T-shirts, and the cyclists bared pink shoulder blades and ate ice cream cones as they sped along behind the dusty buses.

Catherine was in the cool stillness of her father's house. Mayfair on Sunday is a sleepy backwater. She had given notice to the chauffeur and Clive and Susan had gone away for a while. When they return she will offer the house for rent and they can stay until they have something else. Then she will sell.

She was in the study, reading papers from the safe. She had read almost everything, now. The drawers had been cleared, the wardrobes emptied, his clothes given to charity. She had read letters, private bills, odd notes and a notebook filled with memories of Austria, his childhood days before the Anschluss, before Hitler, before what he did to shame his life.

The safe had a secret safe behind it. A safe within a safe. She had taken a time to find the combinations. At last she had found they were in the codicil to the will which the lawyer gave her. Those and other useful things. Catherine thought, I must do something like this in case I die. Leave proper information instead of the clues and hints and mysteries of most people's daily lives. Like a friend's aunt who died and left her a treasure hunt. Pearls in the tea caddy. Diamonds in the lavatory cistern. Fakes in the jewel box. Share certificates under the lingerie.

At the back of the safe within the safe there were some letters tied in ribbon. Red ribbon. She pulled them out. A lot of letters. Written with black ink on heavy cream paper. Tied very tightly together. The ribbon was hard to undo. The knot was old. Catherine cut it with scissors.

The writing seemed familiar. She took the first letter out of its envelope, carefully, not tearing the paper that was brittle now and yellowing at the edges. Her father had lived in that house for twenty years. Had the letters been in the safe that long?

She looked at the date mark on the envelope and saw, with a start, the Kenya stamp, the datemark Nanyuki, the date 1959. She opened the letter, read the writing the broad-knibbed pen had left in yellowed black ink in the sloping hand on the parchment-coloured paper.

428

My dearest love,

I live for the weekends when we have your presence. On other days I exist warmed by memory. For a day or two after you have gone back to town, I'm happy, aglow with your near presence in time, the feel of you in my body. Your semen still warm in my womb. Then I become colder and lonelier as the days without you pass. I am like the earth going away from the sun in winter, the darkest time is the mid-point when you are farthest away in time from my heart's hearth, like the sun at midnight in midwinter. Then I start to hope again, as if sensing the coming spring, putting out shoots and singing birds of my senses to welcome you back.

I am yours entirely. Living for your love,

Catherine was stunned by the letter's beauty and wistful lovingness. She knew even before she read the signature at the bottom whose it was. Brenda's. The revelation blew blood into her face. She blushed and felt the heat of her shock suffusing her whole body. Brenda Roberts. She looked again at the envelope. Addressed to Arnold Clyne at the Muthaiga Club, Nairobi.

She was stunned. Her father was Brenda's great love. Her secret passion whom she never married. Catherine exploded into tears and shed them over the loving letter, pushing it away quickly to save it as if for a museum.

Such words, such love. Written to her father. Written to the man she had seen dead with a hole in his head on this floor in this room on a fine summer morning just over two weeks ago. Written to the Nazi murderer, the criminal accomplice, the man who she still thinks blamed her all her life for killing his beautiful wife in childbirth. Her father. Arnold, Arnold. Were you the object of this great love? The greatest of love. Love like her own love. Love that sends the body to paradise with the soul. Love that makes earth a heaven until it goes, and then a hell.

Oh God. Brenda. Oh poor, poor Brenda. Living alone in the country. While the love of her life lived and died in another world. Catherine remembered Brenda at the funeral. Brenda stoic and supportive. Brenda saying nothing about the hours Catherine spent with her a month or two ago in the springtime garden where they had wept about their loves. Oh Brenda. How is your grief? And I never knew.

You were young and lovely and I thought your lovers were the white hunters in Land Rovers who courted you over drinks at sundown and stayed to dinner in the farm after I had gone to my little bed, and stayed on with you in the lamplight while the stillness of the night outside became the sound of lion roaring or jackals barking.

The hiss of the first rains welcome on the dried leaves of the hot season, steaming out of the still baked dust, while you lay in your warm bed and the Land Rover left in the first light glow of morning. There were other lovers, Brenda. You were too lovely to waste on one man. One man who left you alone all week like the sun at midnight in midwinter. So well put. You poet. You woman. You secret soul. One man whom you never married. Though you loved him all your life. And love him now, I don't wonder. Alone.

Oh, God. Catherine wept and lay her head on her arms on the desk where Arnold sat to write his letter to her. He wrote no letter to Brenda. Dead love. How near to death her own love had come. She had not seen Christopher since that day, four days ago, when she said those hard cruel words to him and then tried to be forgiven.

He had not called. She had not called. There was silence between them. He had another woman to console him. She had nothing. Only death and dead love and the sweet pungent words of dead love's singing down the years to bring tears and echoes of her own feeling.

She must go to Brenda. She lifted the telephone. Brenda said, 'Yes, of course. Bring your night things. Stay and enjoy the country in its season. The roses are lovely and the hay is cut and the smell at night and the sound of the owls. Please come. I have a new kitten. The dogs think it's a tennis ball. No. Come as you are. I don't want

430

anything. Just you. I'll be happy to have you. Stay as long as you like.'

Catherine put away the papers in the safe and took the letters that were in the red ribbon and put them in her bag. She drove to Queen Anne's Gate to pack her night things and leave a note for James who had gone to a summer fete in his constituency to pat babies and smile at ladies and reassure the menfolk about economic growth.

She propped the note on the coffee pot. 'Gone to Brenda. Back sometime Monday. Love, Cat.'

87

Brenda was right: the roses were lovely, gold and red and orange and pink and white, in beds and trailing over archways and around the cottage door. The kitten was a ten-week-old ball of ginger fur that the retrievers played with too energetically: it had to be rescued twice before Catherine had properly arrived and put her bag down in the hall.

There was time for a drink before dinner in the south-facing bower at the back where Catherine and Brenda had sat that afternoon in early May. Brenda produced a bottle of well-chilled Moselle. Her original liking for German wines had become an educated taste in the years spent with the Clynes, and this bottle was as light and fragrant as the summer evening's air.

Catherine had not told Brenda that there was a specific reason for her visit. So the two women chatted gently about their summer plans. Catherine talked about her work and the plans for the Charles Street house. It was not until after the simple, delicious supper of cheese souffle and salad followed by strawberries and home-made ice cream, during which they finished the iced Moselle, that Catherine brought out the letters.

She had been wondering how to introduce them but no natural development of their conversation had taken her towards the topic of Brenda's relationship with her father.

So, when Brenda suggested they went into the still-warm garden for their coffee, she went out into the hall and brought in the small overnight bag in which she had packed a negligee, some clean underwear and her cosmetics. The letters were folded carefully between the silk lingerie, wrapped in a white silk scarf.

Catherine brought the package out of the bag and went out into the deepening dusk. She sat in the bower, head thrown back and eyes lifted to the stars, inhaling the scent of trailing white roses. She left the scarf-bound bundle in her lap.

Brenda laid the tray of her coffee and Catherine's chamomile tea on the old and peeling table. She glanced curiously at the parcel and started pouring.

The scented air was now enriched with the coffee aroma that Catherine loved so much; it was one of her memories of Kenya. Sitting there, in the garden, it was almost as if they were at the farm. Only the stars were different, never as bright as when shining through the thin pure air. There, on Mount Kenya, 7,000 feet above sea level, you were poised at the earth's centre. You could see the southern hemisphere's constellations processing around the heavens in turn after those of the north as the almost invisible seasons turned.

The near full moon, just risen, cast elongated shadows of trees, like dancers' limbs, on the daisied lawn. In its gentle light, Brenda seemed once more as she had been in Africa. Catherine hesitated. The silence was full of questions.

Brenda broke it. 'I suppose you are getting used to Arnold's not being around, my dear.'

A sudden rush of tension overcame the night's softening presence. Catherine said, abruptly, 'I'm not, Brenda. But there has been rather a lot to digest. I'd like to tell you about it.'

Brenda nodded. She seemed to be waiting for something. As if she knew what was to come. She glanced at the package again and said, 'I'd like you to, Cat.'

Catherine began with the letter her father had written her. She told Brenda about the secret criminal life he had led for twenty years, about the links with Christopher, about what Armstrong had said about the bank, about the investigation now pending there. She talked for ten minutes and, all the while, Brenda sat, first sipping her coffee and then looking out across the moonlit garden as if she were a sailor, watching for some far away shore towards which they were moving with a certain stealth and sureness, white sails filled on a calm night sea.

She never once looked at Catherine. But as her monologue came to an end, Brenda turned her head and looked straight into her face. She said, 'I knew about the blackmail, you know.'

'No! Did you? How long have you known, Brenda?' Catherine's voice was shocked.

'Since it began, almost.' She looked towards the hill where a cloud's moon-shadow hung and went on. Her voice was as slow and dreamy as a hypnotic subject recalling a past life. 'A couple of years after we moved into Charles Street, I walked into your father's study one morning, very early, and went to get a tray left from the night before that was on the desk. I heard voices and I couldn't, for a moment, tell where they were coming from. It turned out he had been in there and left the phone off the hook and then gone upstairs to his bedroom to finish the call. I don't know why he did that. It was the strangest lapse. He must have been very upset right at the beginning of the call and gone to get himself a pill, perhaps, you know he took tranquillizers sometimes, before going on with it.

'Anyway, I was going to put the receiver back on its rest and then I heard what was being said, something about being a Nazi and a murderer. I heard Arnold's voice say, "I'll do what you want. Don't ring me at home again. I'll meet you somewhere." He was given a time and place, some pub in the East End of London, the real East End,

433

long before Docklands were yuppified. I didn't touch the phone then. I just left the tray and went out. I didn't want him to know I'd heard him. But I was very worried. I didn't know what to do. I'd been with you both for over twelve years at that stage and I felt, well, a friend as well as an employee.'

Catherine unwrapped the letters. She said, 'I know you were a friend, Brenda. I found these. I thought you might like to have them back. He'd kept them tied up in a red ribbon. They were in the back of the secret safe. I found them this afternoon. I'm afraid I've read them. I think they're wonderful.'

Brenda's hand flew to her mouth and Catherine saw, for a moment, the girl in her again, in the sudden agitation and blush of memory. She said, reproaching herself, 'Oh, Cat, I never wanted you to know. I thought you'd hate me.'

Catherine leaned forward and touched Brenda's arm. She said warmly, 'I couldn't hate you for loving my father, Brenda. You were a mother to me. More. Maybe you were my father too, because Daddy was away so much in Nairobi while I was very young. You raised me, Brenda. Why should I not want you to love my father, or he you?'

Brenda laughed softly and her face in the moonlight showed relief. She said, 'I suppose I thought you might have an oedipal complex and be jealous.'

'I might have been, if he had given me more of his love to begin with.' She smiled. 'If I'd felt I had something to lose. It took him a long time to love me, didn't it? I wasn't what he wanted. I was a daughter, not a son. And he hated me for a while, anyway, because I killed my mother when I was born.'

'That's no way to talk, Catherine.' Brenda was the stern nanny all over again. She went on brusquely, 'You did not kill your mother. She died, that's all. There was some internal condition, some weakness. She should not have become pregnant. It was hereditary. Her own mother had died of the same thing when she was born, though after two other successful births. One didn't know,

434

I suppose, in those days. And in Africa, where medical attention was not as sophisticated, even in the white hospitals.'

She went on, firm and school marmish, 'No, my dear. You are quite wrong. Your father loved you very much. Of course he was unhappy about Marina's death. He really did love her very deeply. He was very deeply stirred by her and it was not her money that drew him to her as so many malicious folk have tried to suggest. It was a very passionate kind of love.'

'And with you?' Catherine leapt in dangerously.

She hesitated, then plunged on, 'Yes. It was with me, too. We loved each other very deeply. From the beginning. I think we were both surprised by the depths of feeling that came so soon after we first made love. It worked so well between us. We were both quite experienced and very compatible.'

Catherine was surprised at Brenda's readiness to expose her love. She said, 'When did it begin? How long after . . .'

Brenda sighed. 'Oh. We met in Nairobi before you were born. I knew your mother, too. It was not a great friendship with her. We were from different worlds. I was living with my family who were missionaries, away a lot in the bush. It was a very different kind of life from the swinging Kenya social set your parents moved in. When your mother died, I was free and rather bored, so I went to your father and asked him whether I could do anything and he said he needed someone to look after you. He didn't want you brought up by an ayah until you were old enough to have a governess. So I said I would take on the job. We became lovers quite soon. Your father was a very lonely and unhappy man, then. I don't believe he knew at first whether he was feeling for me or for your mother through me. I may have been a surrogate. In time I believe he came to know that he loved me for myself. I knew much sooner how much I loved him.'

'But why didn't you marry?'

Brenda's eyes seemed to glisten in the moon's soft light, perhaps from tears. Her voice deepening with emotion, she said, 'It's a sorry tale. I told you some of it when you were here last. I wanted to be married to him quite soon after we had become lovers. I could see this was a very close and serious relationship that ought to have the commitment that marriage brings. Marriage is quite a big step compared to living together. And a much bigger step than being a paid servant who sleeps with her employer.' A note of denigration crept into Brenda's voice for a moment.

She sighed, resignedly, 'But, he wouldn't marry me. He said he was not good enough to be my husband. He never told me why. I thought it was an excuse. But then he never married anyone else. I seemed to be the only woman in his life and I thought he really loved me. I found out what he meant that morning in Charles Street when you were about thirteen and away on some school voyage, to Scandinavia, I think it was. Or Leningrad.'

Brenda tipped the coffee pot and drained the last dregs into her cup. She took the cup and sipped the strong coffee, now cold. 'It's all past now, Cat. All gone into the wind. I can't change anything. He's gone and I . . .' Her face seemed to dissolve and change its form as she fought the tears that would not be held back. She gave in then and let them roll silently down her cheeks.

Catherine went to her and put her arms around her. 'Brenda. Brenda, darling. I know. I know.'

Brenda choked back her tears. 'I could have saved him, Cat. I could have saved all this. If only I had married him. When he asked me, in London. After I found out everything and I told him I knew what he was and I loved him anyway and he asked me then and I couldn't. Something stopped me at the brink. I baulked. Maybe my love had weakened. Maybe I felt angry at having had so much time wasted, time when I could have had his children, time when we could have been together as a couple instead of as master and servant in the world's eyes.

'Or maybe it was some pride, some fear, some failure of my will to share his darkness, some fear of accepting that burden, which one does, you know. Whatever one's spouse is carrying in the way of guilt or pain or a past full of shadows, you share it. You can't live your own free life, your own free singular destiny again. You carry your share of their fate. People meld in marriage. They become each other. I was, in the final analysis, not prepared for that as I had been before I knew the full and awful truth about your father. I never stopped loving him, never stopped being his lover. But I did not feel strong enough to carry all that unredeemed sin.'

Her words tumbled out, carrying their meaning along like rapids carrying a canoe. 'If I'd done that, shared his life, his crime, his pain, I could have given him the strength to resist those people and to wash away the past. I know I could have. And we would have lived honestly with each other, at last. The lie that stood between us was removed by my accidental discovery. It . . . Oh, God. My wasted life. My wasted love . . .' She sobbed more loudly and the tears ran freely from her eyes and down her cheeks and fell onto the hands Catherine reached out to put around her shoulders.

Catherine said, 'Don't blame yourself. Don't. You don't have to be guilty for his death. I am the one to carry that. If I had not loved Christopher, if I had not followed him to America . . . Arnold would not have sent the gunman to kill him.'

Brenda's voice rang out over the still garden, startling the night into a new rhythm. 'No! No! Don't say that. Stay free of that guilt. He chose to act in the way he did. We don't all send killers after the people who do things we disagree with. There are other ways. Arnold was not a normal human being. He was not a truly sane person. He was so deeply emotional under that cool exterior. He was a passionate man. He had a terrible rage in him. He had incredible self control, but he had a murderous feeling of revenge for those who harmed anything of his.

'He loved you, Catherine, and he knew your lover was just like himself. He wanted to protect you. Perhaps he also wanted to hit out at the people who had been using him, forcing him into illegal ways, depriving him of any pride in his achievements at the bank, destroying his peace of mind, to hit out and frustrate one of them in his own life. And in that world, as he well knew, there are few methods that really work. He used the language those people understand, threat and blackmail.

'Don't regret his actions or take his guilt. The responsibility for that lies further back. I could have taken up my share of his life, perhaps redeemed his darkness. But I did not. I flunked the challenge. He must take responsibility in the end for what he was and what he did. But I had an opportunity and I neglected it. I failed in some heroic quest of love, to redeem the lover's sins and in doing so redeem oneself. I must carry that. But you are free.'

Catherine stared out over the garden. Dew gave the grass a misted sheen under the moon's light. The shadows were shorter now. A pair of squirrels cavorted over the lawn and scampered up a nearby beech. Freedom seemed a gift of nature, not of human life with its duties and responsibilities, its channels and structures, its necessities, inheritances.

She said, 'Brenda, does history repeat itself? In families? Do we reenact our fathers' follies, our mothers' madnesses? Do we, am I, repeating some terrible, fatal pattern buried in our families' psychological make up?' She turned fully to face Brenda and said with energy, 'Am I repeating with Christopher the same failure of commitment or acceptance, that you and Arnold experienced? Are Christopher and I just helplessly repeating some inevitable pattern whereby we reject each other at the crucial moment? Am I failing to accept him for the same reason as you failed to take on Arnold's burden, when it was offered in the end?'

Brenda stared at her, her face wondering and stunned. Catherine leaned back and her voice was desperate and hopeless, 'Are we fated to go on aborting happiness for generations? Until some mutant, some pattern breaker, comes along? I don't think I want a child if that's so. I don't want this monstrous cosmic plot to go on playing out its horror movie on the planet any more.'

Brenda said quietly, 'Cat, my dear. Situations or relationships may be predestined. But we have free will

438

to choose at almost every point. It's just that the tendency to make the same choices may run in families.' She smiled. 'I'm not your family, of course.' Catherine lifted a hand to stop her and she corrected herself, 'There's no genetic link. But family traits may be handed down through learning. You may have learned to react to situations as I do. Learned from me.' She reached out and took Catherine's hand. She went on, 'But you can still choose. Once you are aware of those patterns, you can override them. You are still free, Catherine. Still free to do with Christopher what I failed to do with Arnold, so long as he will cooperate. If he does not, then your responsibility ends. You will have done your bit towards exercising your God-given choice between good and evil.' She lifted Catherine's hand and kissed it. Then she dropped the hand and smiled. 'We should go in. The dew is falling and you will be cold. You aren't used to country air.'

They gathered themselves up and Brenda took the tray and they walked over the dew-moist grass through the night's petalled smell into the still sun-warmed house.

Later, Catherine lay between the fresh white sheets in the small bed in the room with the sloping eaves in the soft lamplight and remembered her nights in Kenya with Brenda still moving about the house. The way the bare polished wood floors would creak and crack with every footstep. Of how the whispered voices in the passageway would tell her whether Brenda's guest was staying the night. And of how, at weekends, she would hear Brenda tip-toe past her door to the big room at the end that was her father's. Of how she had never, for a moment, guessed that they were lovers. Or, until now, remembered those footsteps in the secret night.

*

88

The room fuzzed around her. Faces, voices, seemed to come and go. She put a hand to her head. 'Excuse me. I think I should sit.'

She was with a tall elegant man who owned one of London's grand hotels and who was a potential advertiser for her new magazine. She was in the middle of describing it to him when she seemed almost to faint. He looked anxiously at her and steered her carefully to a small uncomfortable sofa covered in blue silk placed under a large palm. He was solicitous. He thought it was the champagne.

'Are you all right?' he asked. His face was an elegant mask of concern.

'Thank you, Steven. I can't imagine what's come over me. I've had hardly half a glass of champagne.'

'Are you sure? They fill the glasses when you're not looking, you know,' he twinkled at her.

She smiled sickly. She longed to put her feet up. She said, 'I must admit I feel awful. Can you get them to get me a taxi, do you think?'

Gerald came sweeping up. 'Goodness, Catherina, you look green. Did you eat a bad shrimp canape?'

She made an attempt at laughing but felt truly sick. 'I might have: but I've only been here half an hour and no one's offered me one yet.'

Gerald nudged Steven. 'We'd just better get her out of here before the diary people notice. They'll have her drunk without a qualm in tomorrow's papers.' He was joking.

But Steven said, 'There may be more truth in that than you think. I'll drive her home.'

Gerald gushed, 'Oh, do let me. I haven't had a chance to talk to her for weeks. Catherina, choose between the ardent swains who want to drive you home.'

'Oh darling. Please, I don't care. A taxi will be fine.' She wanted to throw up.

Gerald said, 'I'll take her, Steven.'

The tall man shrugged. 'I'm easy. She's yours for tonight, dear boy. I'll pursue her when she's in better shape.'

Gerald steered Catherine out of the Cafe Royale and into the rain-scattered lights of Regent Street. The party, for the fortieth anniversary of one of London's most established dress designers, was going wonderfully. But she was delighted to be leaving. Her legs felt like lead and she could only think of lying down in bed at home.

Gerald's car was parked nearby on the kerb, miraculously unclamped, thanks to a large preemptive tip to the doorman. He led her to it and folded her into the passenger seat, attaching her belt before running around in the rain to get behind the wheel.

Catherine yawned. 'Whatever's wrong with me, Gerry?' she said. Her eyes were closed.

Gerald glanced at her. He said lightly, 'Oh Catherina, you've been through a great deal.' He paused as he swung the car swiftly around Piccadilly Circus and into the Haymarket. 'But I confidently predict you'll make it through the night.' He patted her knee and accelerated through the orange lights and turned for Trafalgar Square.

She said groggily, 'Oh don't go so fast, darling.' She was silent while he surged past South Africa House and beat the lights into Whitehall. She went on, 'I am doing a lot. But I'm getting somewhere, I suppose. I've set up a charity, a trust to dump all Arnold's ill-gotten gains into. I haven't decided yet who the specific beneficiaries will be.'

He glanced at her. 'What, no tiaras for the Tsarina?'

She laughed, a tired, gasping laugh. She searched for the window release. Gerald anticipated her and pushed the button to let the moist night air into the car.

She said, 'Mmm. That's better. Why didn't we think of that before?'

Gerald slowed and drove with uncharacteristic steadiness towards Parliament Square. Despite the jokes he was anxious about Catherine. The demands of administrating her father's estate piled on top of her ambitious work

441

load, Lives and French Vanities due for launch in the autumn, had left her little free time. He had seen her only twice since her return from Miami, once at Sir Arnold's memorial service and once for a late dinner about two weeks ago. At the latter, she had told him how things had gone with Angel in Miami and since. She talked as if she were remote from her experiences, but Gerald was also aware that she was unwilling to open herself. He thought she had had too much pain recently and had her emotions on hold while she recovered. Now, he thought she might be suffering from a combination of fatigue and delayed shock.

They arrived at Queen Anne's Gate. Gerald saw her to the door but refused to go in.

'Go to bed,' he ordered her firmly. 'Are you sure you can make it up the stairs?'

She nodded.

'See a doctor,' he called from the car and gave her a wave. She waved back and went in.

89

Catherine did not like doctors. She lay in bed the morning after Gerald had brought her home from the party, wondering, not for the first time, why this was. Some bad memory of white-coated authority present at her difficult birth, perhaps? There had to be some reason, apart from having pretty good health, why she almost never consulted them. She usually waited for symptoms of illness to go away or else treated them herself by fasting and rest. Apart from three lots of concussion due to horse accidents, she had not been in a hospital, other than as a visitor, since her birth.

She felt awful, though, this morning. She had felt

groggy off and on for a few weeks since Arnold died. Yesterday and today it was worse. She assumed it was stress brought on by her father's death and the shocking revelations which had accompanied it. Perhaps the distance between herself and Christopher which had developed since her last visit to his house was a hidden part of her sickness. She had, since then, begun to feel that he would never be honest enough with her to forge a really close bond. Perhaps their love was not, after all, destined, their bonding not inevitable. There were limitations. In him.

Was she beginning to part from him? Was she in the act of letting him go, releasing him to return to whatever life it was he could not reveal to her, telling him by her silence and her acknowledgement of his own that she was setting him free of her love? Free to go to whatever other woman he could open himself to without fear she would want to change his crooked ways.

Catherine got out of bed and felt the heaviness of her limbs as she stood. This was not natural, surely, she thought as she walked unsteadily to her bathroom. She must be very tired. Delayed shock had caught up with her. Perhaps she should take a holiday. But that was difficult. The preparations for the launch of French Vanities would involve her in several working trips to Paris in the next few weeks. And she was going to Vienna for a couple of days next week on a private project. That would mean she was away from her office for quite long enough without taking any trips for her own indulgence.

Also, the new magazine's dummies would be coming up soon. If they were going to stick to the November launch date for Lives she had to keep after everyone and maintain her adrenalin, and not peel off somewhere and come back too relaxed to needle them. Besides, it would soon be August and that meant crowded resorts and teeming roads, jammed airports and delayed flights. And she certainly did not think she could face the alternative, a few days at a health farm, although that was the perfect way to rest.

443

Above all she needed to keep her mind occupied with work. Thoughts about her father, about Christopher, and the great sadness and tears that would well up like a storm whenever she was alone and idle, were a problem. They would plague her if she went away for a rest. No. She could not be alone with her thoughts and feelings just yet. She would stay in London and work.

She groaned and lay down again on the bed. Work seemed impossible just at this moment. Her mind felt blurred by her body's heaviness. How ever would she get dressed and go to the office? 'Come along, Catherina,' she addressed herself aloud. 'Get up and get moving. You'll feel better after breakfast.'

She took a fresh white cotton and lace robe from her wardrobe, brushed her hair and went downstairs. A smell of coffee and grilled bacon filled the kitchen. It turned her stomach. She went over to the juicer and peeled a grapefruit, turning it into sweet pink juice.

James sat at the round white table with a ray of sunshine falling on his unshaven face, highlighting the bags under his red-rimmed eyes. He was reading the papers. He managed about five hours' sleep a night and surely needed more. She sat opposite him and he looked up and smiled but said nothing. As usual, he went on reading. Of which she was glad. She did not feel like talking.

They had not seen much of each other lately. She had put off plans for divorce and said nothing to him about her father's letter or her love affair. James had tried to spend more time with her during the appalling few days following Sir Arnold's death but then he had had to return to work with extra effort to make up for lost time as the SLRS Bill was in its committee stage and amendments were looming thick and fast.

But now he was looking slightly more relaxed. Opposition to the Bill was now almost entirely from within Parliament. Since Michael O'Leary's arrest and Sir Arnold's death the protest groups had gone silent.

The Bill was now safely on course for its Second Reading and the House was going into recess the following Friday. He would be going up to his constituency in

444

Norfolk to catch up with local problems and then taking a holiday sometime in August.

Catherine sipped her grapefruit. The sweet juice soothed her palate and took away some of the nausea. She had seen Christopher only once since her visit to Brenda. They had gone to Hill Street and made beautiful, gentle love for an hour and said very little to each other. It was as if the relationship was marking time. Perhaps while Catherine processed her grief and reordered her shaken life, that was better for her.

She was so preoccupied with her own tasks and private suffering that she sometimes forgot that he, too, had his problems. He was awaiting further developments of the case against him. Marking time, too, while the police dug for evidence that he had indeed been trafficking in drugs. The strain showed in fatigue and the need to sleep. He could not seem to see the future and seemed to be living already in some prison of his own making, waiting for the next court summons. Not really living. Not himself. She realized that the prospect of a trial and possible imprisonment were affecting his sexuality, which might explain his lack of attention to her. If only they could just lie together and talk and sleep as they had in Miami.

James put a slice of bread into the toaster and the warm scent of toast overwhelmed the other smells in the kitchen. Catherine felt her stomach rising to meet her mouth. She got up from the table and ran to the bathroom and was sharply sick.

As she emerged, James was standing by the kitchen door. 'Are you ill, darling?' he asked.

'I must have eaten something nasty,' she said, smiling.

He nodded and went back into the kitchen. She followed him and took a bottle of mineral water and a glass and went back upstairs.

She sat on her bed, sipping the still cool water and began leafing through her address book. She thought she had the name of a doctor, a homeopath in Harley Street. She looked under D and found several names, recommended by friends. She stopped suddenly. There was the name of June Noble. June was the gynaecologist Catherine consulted routinely every year. Catherine suddenly remembered she was supposed to have seen June two weeks ago.

She went to her diary and turned back the pages. Of course. There was the appointment. She had forgotten because of her father's death, the funeral and everything. But surely she had seen June sometime before going to America? The memory flooded back and sent colour to her cheeks. Of course, June had taken out her IUD and told her to give it a rest. Catherine had forgotten.

She began counting. It was five weeks since she had first gone to Miami. She picked up the phone and rang June Noble's office. She made an appointment to see her that afternoon.

90

The door opened. He took a step towards her and she towards him. They both stopped and looked at each other. Each seemed to be searching the other for some sign. They were like two strange beasts in a wild place, circling each other, sniffing, suspicious and alert for an attack.

'Can I come in?' She took another step, smiling with her eyes but not her mouth.

He gestured as if to say, How remiss of me not to invite you, bowing slightly and sweeping his free arm away as he pulled the door wide.

She walked stiffly into the hall. It had been her idea to come to Hill Street. Neutral ground. Things had gone well here last time, although they had been cautious with each other. She felt the intimacy of the little house had become too intense after the scenes she had instigated. They needed the anonymity of the strange apartment in order to approach again, as they had done in Miami in the hospital room.

Catherine was very conscious, tonight, of the proximity of the empty house in Charles Street. Conscious of the guilt she should have experienced before when she and Angel stole their hours here, a few hundred yards from where her father sat in his study or slept in his canopied bed. Why now? she thought. Why is it important now? Especially tonight.

He stood close to her but it was she who put out her arms and touched him first. She who stroked the lapels of his soft dark suit and then ran her finger over his full lips. Then he pulled her to him and she felt his hard cock through his trousers. He had wanted her but had not let her see it.

He turned her and pushed her by her shoulders along the hallway towards the bedroom, took her in and half-closed the door. He held her and kissed her softly, holding her so kindly, warmly and with love. She let him undress her, lay her on the bed, let him enter her, his expression awed as if he came into a temple. Let him move her to her heaven's door and lead her through it as if from death to life. Let him empty himself into her as though he gave his life away to join with hers in some beyond. She held him close and would not let him move and he slept for a few minutes with his full weight on her and she felt again her love that was like an open wound through which joy flowed, and a strange power like that of the sun, radiating from her centre.

When he opened his eyes and kissed her face again and again with his soft warm lips she said, 'I have a secret to tell you.'

He smiled and kissed her eyes.

She said, 'I'm pregnant. I'm going to have your child.'

She saw his surprise turn to dismay. Felt him recede as though something passed between her and the sun, felt herself shiver with fear at his response. 'Oh, aren't you pleased?' she cried out. 'Oh please be happy. I am. I am so happy. I am so very, very happy.'

447

He sat up and moved away from her. He sat on the edge of the bed with his back towards her and started to dress.

'Angel?' Her voice was a cry of pain.

He turned. 'You mustn't have it, Catherine.'

'What?' She sat up, moved over to him, held his shoulders, kissed his cheek, his lips. 'What are you saying, my love?'

'You're married to another man.'

'I'll divorce him, of course,' she said, amazed, appalled. 'I want your child. I love you.'

He stood up and pulled on his trousers, tucked his shirt in swiftly as if he had to rush. He said brusquely, 'I'm not fit to father any child with you. You don't want my bastard, Catherine. I'm not the man to give a child to you.'

'Don't say that,' she was on her feet, angry, distressed, her eyes wide and dark-circled and her hair in a wild cascade around her face and shoulders.

She tried to go to him. But he moved away. He sat down on the bed, crushing his folded jacket to him like a broken toy. She saw the misery and dejection in his posture, the stubborn anger in his face.

'Get rid of it, Catherine. You don't want my kid. You don't want a part-black, part-Jewish bastard for people to point at and turn away from. No matter what you do for it, buy it the best education money can buy, your friends won't want your kid to mix with their kids. They won't want a mixed blood bastard in their grand houses with their expensive children.' He stood and began to pace the room, his jacket slung over his shoulder, his tie dangling around the open neck of his blue shirt. 'Even you won't be able to go where you go now, those fancy parties with royalty and Establishment types, all those lords and ladies and dukes and duchesses. They won't want you if you've got my little rainbow bastard waiting for you at home.'

She was half dressed now, her back to him. She whirled around and he saw the tears on her cheeks and stopped abruptly. She cried out, her voice full of pain, 'Don't.

448

Don't make this monstrous mountain out of your own experience. Don't pass on your hurt into our child. Things won't be the same for our baby, born with money, given every chance to be like other privileged children.' She flung out her arms. 'Oh, I know he won't be accepted everywhere completely, but things are different now from what they were when you grew up with your mother's parents hating her for having you and your community pointing the finger of shame at her and them and at you.'

He went to her and held her shoulders and tried to hold her to him. He said kindly, 'I know how you feel. I know you want this child. But it won't be happy. You're bringing someone into the world to suffer, to feel unwanted. You're making trouble and misery for yourself and the child.' He shook her gently. 'You've got to believe me. I know. I've been through all that. Anyway, you don't want me as your baby's father. A crook who might be going to prison.'

She pulled away from him and slithered into her red chiffon shirt dress, placed her dark glasses over her tear-smeared eyes, masking herself. She stood and looked at him and he looked back, unable to judge her with her eyes hidden. There was a pause, as if each were waiting for the other to say something.

Then Catherine said quietly, 'If I could make your life right by dying, right now, I would. It would be very easy to have a reason to die that made up for having no reason to live. But I'm not going to make your life right by killing our baby. I want to make this life and make this life right and make your life right by doing it. And no one will stop me. Not even you.'

He shook his head. 'Get rid of it, Catherine. You'll be happier.' He walked out of the room.

She followed and they said nothing more to each other. She walked alone down the street to her car, climbed in and drove away without another glance at him.

He watched her go and a confusion filled his head.

*

449

91

A bat dived low across their path. Clouds hid the stars and the waning moon's late rising. The warm night flickered with fireflies and the rainfresh air was thick with moths and night stock scent. The silence was the held breath of night creatures waiting their moment of life or death in the close dark. Brenda and Catherine stood still in the diminished circle of the lowered lantern. A faint paraffin smell enwrapped them. They had walked the garden's perimeter, swishing their rubber-shod feet through the wet grass, and now stood near a group of high shrubs at the farthest end from the house.

Brenda said, 'You'll leave James, at once, will you?'

'I'll live at Charles Street until I can sort something else out.'

'What's wrong with Charles Street as a permanent address?'

'Memories.'

Brenda put her hand out and touched Catherine's sleeve. She let it rest there and her fingers caressed the arm beneath. They moved together, by some secret accord, turning back towards the house. This was an after-dinner walk. Catherine had driven down that evening and would stay the night.

Brenda said, 'You'll need lots of room and staff accommodation for your nanny and housekeeper. You might save yourself the trouble of house-hunting.'

Catherine shrugged and looked down at her borrowed boots. 'I'd prefer something with a garden, Regent's Park or Holland Park, maybe.' She turned to Brenda. 'You'll come and, stay won't you? For a long time, I mean?'

Brenda smiled. She nodded. 'I'd like to. But there are the animals to consider. And I mustn't leave my garden for too long. Perhaps in the autumn when it starts dying down.' She put her hand out again, as if she needed to keep touching Catherine to be sure she was real. 'When is the baby due?'

'March. It seems a very long way away.'

'You've wanted it for longer.'

'How do you know?'

'One always wants the child of the man one loves so physically, as you love Christopher.'

Catherine turned quickly. 'Did you want . . .'

'Yes.' Brenda cut off the question. 'Yes, I wanted Arnold's baby. But it was impossible outside marriage. In those days one didn't. Now, it's so easy. But you are fortunate that you can provide for your child. You have great wealth. You can afford everything. So many young women who have children without a husband's support don't realize what they are letting themselves in for, the tie, the limitation on working, the great responsibility with no one to share it. I don't believe one should do it really, even now the social stigma has gone.'

'But you've advised me to do it.'

Brenda laughed softly. 'Would any other advice be worth giving you, Cat? You had already made your mind up when you arrived here. You've told me what June Noble said, to keep it, and I think in your case that is the only advice. You love the man too much to be able to forgive yourself for destroying his child.'

'But I'll be alone. He and I are not going on. I don't think it's possible after what he asked me to do. He won't want anything to do with the child. Besides there are too many problems in his life, prison and a woman and God knows what. He's not . . . oh, Brenda. I don't want to think about it.'

'I think things may turn out better than that. Give him time. He may change his mind. Naturally you can't ask James to adopt the baby as June proposed. That would hardly be a happy situation. No, I think you should move out immediately. Be ready to go before you tell him. It may get unpleasant and you don't want to disturb your pregnancy with any more violent emotions.'

Catherine sighed. 'It would have been so much kinder to have just divorced, or begun the process months ago.

451

I needn't have even mentioned Christopher. Now he has to know all this about the baby and everything. It will hurt him. No man's pride can take hearing he's been cuckolded.'

'But he won't argue with you now. You won't have to fight for your divorce. He'll be glad to get rid of you, and he won't have to support you or the child.'

Catherine turned suddenly. 'I don't know what to do about the money now, Father's ill-gotten gains, you know? I was planning to put all the bank's profits into a charitable trust. Now I'm not so sure. I ought to put some into trust for the baby to inherit.' She shook her head. 'I suppose some of the profits were honestly gained.'

'The original investment from Kenya and whatever the bank was worth before the blackmail began and a good proportion of the capital growth afterwards.' Brenda touched Catherine again. 'You mustn't be too purist, too hard on yourself, Cat. Arnold's gains were far from ill-gotten. I doubt he made that much by laundering the illegal funds. Don't flagellate yourself over this. You are entitled to an inheritance. Don't forget the fortune has been built on the original investment from your mother's family.'

Catherine nodded. 'Yes, but I'm doing all right at the magazine, Brenda. I can live on my salary and the business is growing.'

Brenda stopped and barred Catherine's way with her body. The lantern's yellow light shone up on her face showing the intensity of her feelings reflected in her features. 'Don't give it away, Catherine. Wealth is power. Arnold felt this keenly. He knew he was only accepted because of his money. You are different. But the child will need every advantage to overcome mixed blood.'

'Goodness, Brenda. You sound like Christopher.'

'He knows the realities of being brought up poor with mixed blood, though in a less enlightened age than this one. He knows that even now, with his own money, he still can't pass for one of the belongers of this world. Mixed race is a stamp of being outside that no one can hide, in any community in the world. Don't believe this

452

society has accepted it. Just listen to the private conversations in your aristocratic houses and at country weekends. You still have to be white, Anglo Saxon, male and Church of England and to have been to a major public school or Oxford to be a member of their club.'

'Well, I'm making out all right.'

'You were brought up with money and went to a good school. You are beautiful and talented and successful. Your mother, though foreign, was an aristocrat. You are in and out of the Prime Minister's drawing room, and therefore have power. You may not have a perfect pedigree, but you pass. You could probably marry a thirteenth Earl, so long as he had already been divorced from the girl chosen by his mother, and already bred his male heir from the right filly.'

Catherine's laugh cut the moist air into echoing fragments. 'Brenda, you're such a cynic. And such a frightful old subversive. I do believe the only reason you want me to have this baby is to spit in everybody's eye.'

'Where do you think you got your radical muscles from, child?' Brenda put her arm around Catherine's shoulder. They walked slowly in this way with Brenda holding the lantern higher to light their way. She stopped and looked straight into Catherine's tired face. 'You're wrong about my motives, Cat. I want you to have this baby because you want it. Because you love the father and you loved him when you conceived. A child conceived in passion, real passion, that is, spiritual as well as physical, is a special child, whatever its racial mix. I am looking forward to this baby, my dear. Really looking forward to it.'

She leaned forward and kissed Catherine's cheek. 'Come. It's time you went to bed. You must rest now. You've been under an extraordinary strain and you must make up for it.'

Catherine smiled. 'I'm going to Vienna the day after tomorrow.'

'Whatever for?'

'I'm doing some research into Father's past life. I want to write a sort of novel about him. Gerald wants me to do the biography, edited he says, to exclude the criminal

453

bit. But, of course, that's impossible. One cannot tell the story of my father's life without telling the whole beastly truth. So I thought, well, maybe I'll write it as fiction. Anyway, I'm off to Vienna for a couple of days. I really want to see and learn for myself something of Father's past.'

They reached the cottage and went inside. The house was warm and smelled of polish and roses. Catherine felt very tired and went immediately to bed. Brenda brought her milk and oat biscuits and chamomile tea and made her laugh for being so very motherly. But it was good to be cared for again after the long months of trauma. And in a way it was a relief, though tainted with sadness, to feel that Christopher was no longer the centre of her life.

92

'You must tell me where she is.' He had been very patient. Now he was becoming less so.

Janie said, 'Ms Clyne specifically asked me not to tell anyone where she is.' Her voice was plaintive. The man was giving her a very hard time. But as she had no idea who he was she was unsure how to deal with him.

He sighed. 'I'm a friend of Ms Clyne's. I know she wouldn't mind you telling me.'

'I'm sorry, Sir. I have no evidence of that. You could be anyone from a newspaper or just anything. And if I gave you her address, she would never forgive me. I might get fired.'

Her tone was patronizing and he felt insulted. He said coldly and slowly, 'What if I tell you that she will never forgive you if I don't get to her in time?'

Janie was silent. The man did not exactly sound like one of Catherine's close friends. His voice was not, well, was not what Janie expected of Catherine's circle.

Exasperated, he spoke into her silence. 'Who else has authority to tell me? Does anyone know where she is?'

She was haughty. 'Of course. Her husband always knows.'

He was angry now and alarmed. 'Has she gone abroad?'

'I . . .' She saw no reason why she should deny that. 'Yes, she has, actually.'

'Is it business?'

Janie was exasperated. 'Look, I'm really sorry but I can't tell you. Unless you'd like to tell me what it's about and then I'll call her and let you know if she's prepared for me to tell you where to reach her.'

He said, suddenly charming, 'Look. I'm a close friend. I haven't spoken to her for a few days. I need to tell her something very urgently. Can you get her to ring me. In the next hour?' He gave a number where he could be reached.

Janie agreed to ask Catherine's permission to give her number to Christopher Angel and rang off.

He waited. It seemed intolerable to fail now, to fail to reach her. Now he knew he had to tell her he had changed his mind. If she was abroad, did that mean she had had the abortion and was away for a rest, that he was too late already? A ripple of pain crossed his face. What if she had gone abroad to have the abortion? But why would she do that when there were so many facilities here? Perhaps she wanted complete discretion, was afraid someone here would find out. She was, after all, still married to a Cabinet Minister. That must be it. He was tormented.

He busied himself with calls and paperwork. Between calls, he paced the room and glanced often at his watch. An hour passed and he had heard nothing from Janie. He called again. 'What's happening?' he asked, his voice irritable.

She said, 'I'm sorry, Sir, I can't reach her. She's out.'

He said coldly, 'Give me a number where I can reach her husband, would you?'

James Waring answered his private number at the

Department of the Environment. Christopher said, 'My name is Angel. I need to contact your wife urgently.'

James Waring sounded disinterested. 'Would you mind telling me what it's all about?'

'If I don't get to her, a child may die. I can't tell you more than that.'

James seemed to yawn. He said casually, 'Oh well, I suppose I'd better tell you then. She's at the Sacher Hotel in Vienna. I wish you the best of luck. I haven't heard from her in forty-eight hours myself.'

Christopher thanked him and rang off. He put a call in to the hotel but was told Catherine was out. It was 10.40 a.m., already 11.40 a.m. in Vienna. A condition of his bail was that he should not leave the country without written permission, and the court had his passport. But he had another. He got himself on the next flight out. It left at 12.20 p.m. and took two hours. He would just make it if he ran.

93

Vienna was hot. The afternoon streets threw up the sun's heat. The air was humid and oppressive with traffic fumes. A scent of dust mingled with the sweeter ones of coffee, chocolate, torte and cigarettes from the cafes and on the narrower, traffic free side roads.

She had it now, the groundwork of her father's life, in so far as lives are lived before the age of seventeen. She had the documents of his birth and parentage. She had visited his sister's daughter in the suburbs, her cousin, a prosperous butcher's wife surrounded by her comforts, her photographs of the children, her parents and Arnold's, and her garden. Even a snapshot of Arnold was discovered, secreted away. Arnold in his Brown Shirt uniform, proud and strong and handsome, though a little crude and peasanty compared with his urbane recent self.

There was more to come, a Brown Shirt friend to visit again this evening. One who was there the day Arnold killed the old Jew and doomed his future. How had she managed that? To find him in the records. No, no records. It was an accident that she had managed to dig out the old Brown Shirt who remembered Arnold, who remembered that afternoon just after the Anschluss. Who had talked. Who did not forget a single detail of that terrible moment when her father, a teenage bully, killed an old and helpless man. By mistake.

Catherine needed some tea. She wanted to find a cafe where she could sit in the still afternoon and watch the slow matrons of Vienna and the solid men and think of her father as he might have been before that event, and a time of joy he might have known in this place before Hitler came, and try to forget the present and its aberrant antecedents in that afternoon in the old Jew's apartment when the deed was done. And try to make a forgiveness for unknowing acts, forgiving from the present for the past made out of youth's ineptitude. Forgiving the dead for their living sin.

Across the Ringstrasse in the maze of pedestrian streets ahead, she saw cafes. Tables on the pavement, umbrellas, shade. She turned to cross the broad street, her mind asleep in the heat, thinking only of tea and perhaps something sweet to eat and time to pause. She looked one way and then another. She stepped out and hesitated and then someone hurrying past on the pavement struck her with their shoulder as they went and she felt herself slipping, falling, overbalancing into the road.

It was like a dream sequence. She remembered the traffic. She looked as she fell. Looked the wrong way. Then heard the sound of brakes. The moment of slow motion observation when she turned her head and saw the taxi. Saw the taxi swerving and sliding sideways, its wheels locked by its brakes. And the still slow afternoon was winding down, like a film being slowed and the air was thick with dust and people stopped and stared and their open mouths that did not scream were there for ever in her mind.

And she knew then that things happen this way. That you don't choose them. You don't forsee them. That they come to you. Without respect for your plans. That you see, too late, but cannot move, as in a dream. Cannot avoid your fate . . .

94

The Sacher Hotel did not know where Ms Clyne was. She had left her room key this morning quite early – about 9.45 am. She had not left any messages. Perhaps she would be back before dinner. The gentleman would like a room?

He took a room and went up there with his luggage. It was a charming room furnished with the style and nostalgia of the Belle Epoque with heavy red velvet draperies, a large curtained bed and even a red velvet-covered chaise longue. Old portraits hung on the silk-papered walls. Angel knew nothing of the period, or of Vienna. He wanted to find Catherine, and he could not risk waiting. In case. In case . . . she was killing their child.

How could he trace her? The best thing would be to check clinics and hospitals. Gynaecological ones, prefer-ably. He spoke no German and felt absurd trying to talk to the telephonist about what he wanted. He went down-stairs again.

The girl who helped him was a blonde with a short square body and a small square face softened by short curling hair. She did not seem curious as to why the gentleman wanted a telephonic tour of the gynaecological departments of the major hospitals and clinics. They went for the big expensive ones first. It took a good thirty minutes to call all of them, with no result. Angel had been in Vienna for one and a half hours and he had no idea where to find Catherine, apart from wait for her at the hotel.

He went back to his room and unpacked his overnight bag, taking his toothbrush and shaving kit and putting them in the bathroom. He hung up a spare suit and two shirts and dropped some clean underwear and socks into the drawers of the huge old mahogany wardrobe. He then lay on the bed and stared at the elaborately plastered ceiling.

His decision to follow Catherine had been purely impulsive. His intuition, always his strongest sense, had been very insistent that he should do so. Now that he had changed his mind, now that he wanted her to keep the child, it was vital he tell her, before she did something.

By four o'clock he was getting restless. He could not read. He had tried to doze but without results. He swung his legs off the bed, stood up and went into the bathroom. He ran his comb through his hair and began to think of going out. He needed a stroll.

As he was leaving the room the phone rang. He raced for it and spoke breathlessly. 'Yes.'

The clear, bell-like voice of Vera, the square blonde who had helped him, came down the line. 'Mr Angel?' She pronounced it Enjel.

He said impatiently, 'Yes, yes, what is it?'

'I have a location for Miss Clyne. She was admitted to the emergency hospital half an hour ago. They have just rung back. Would you like a taxi?'

'Yes. Immediately. I'll be down right away.' He picked up his jacket from the bed and raced down the hallway to the lift. He prayed to whatever God there was that he would be in time.

* * *

The hospital was in its own grounds surrounded by trees. He thought briefly of the Cedars of Lebanon in Miami where he had lain for a week and a half after the shooting. Catherine told him she had conceived in Miami. Was it

459

in his hotel suite or on the beach before he was shot, or later, in the limo or the hospital? Whatever it was, he wanted the child now, wanted her to have his baby.

At the reception they had trouble locating her. She was not in gynaecology, the receptionist said. She might be moved there later if she was pregnant. But she had been admitted as an accident emergency. She was in intensive care and awaiting surgery. He was baffled and tried to argue. They must have another Miss Clyne. Would they check the spelling. No, this was the only one. What could they do for him? Was he a relative?

He said, Yes, he was a relative. He was Miss Clyne's husband. He wanted to see her and her doctor immediately. He wanted to know what had happened. He had to be told. There was a baby. His wife was pregnant. It was very urgent he see her.

A receptionist led him to the emergency wing. She was about twenty-five, a tall brunette with shoulder length curls that bounced as she walked on her high heels, clack, clack, clack down the long vinyl-floored corridors. He followed her and watched her hips swing stiffly to and fro as she marched. He felt no stirring of interest in her. He was too preoccupied to notice any woman.

They went up in a lift and along some more corridors. Clack, clack. Bounce, bounce. March, march, march. He was completely absorbed in his worry. Catherine, Catherine. My baby. Our baby. Please God, if you are there, let it not be too late. They came to a waiting area and she told him with crisp authority to sit down and wait.

He sat, absorbing the hospital smell, the inevitable hospital colours of dull greens and golds, the cream walls. He leafed nervously through a pile of German language magazines, looking at pictures. He felt appallingly disturbed. He looked up. A white-coated doctor stood in the doorway of the small glass-walled room. 'You are a relative of Miss Clyne?'

He stood up. 'Yes. What's happened?'

The man was slight and wore rimless glasses under a very high wide forehead. He spoke English with an

American accent. He said, 'Your wife has been hurt in a traffic accident. There is some blood loss, from internal bleeding. We have to operate immediately. But unfortunately we must wait to get blood from another bank. There was a big trafffic accident outside the city this afternoon. We had many casualties from one family who used up our last stock of the rare group AB-negative an hour ago.'

'What do you mean you don't have it? Will she be all right? What about her baby? She's pregnant, you know. Did you know that?'

'No, I did not know it. Your wife is not conscious. Please try to be calm, Mr Clyne. Your wife is in good hands. We will do everything we can to save her and, of course, the foetus. It is unfortunate about the delay. We are taking temporary measures, she is on a plasma drip, and in half an hour, maybe . . .'

'Half an hour! No, that's not soon enough. I recently found that I am AB-negative. You can check with my doctor in Miami or London. Or test me now. Don't waste any time, please. Do it now.' Angel took off his jacket and began undoing his cuff links. 'Where do I go? Please take me there immediately.' He spoke brusquely.

The doctor hesitated. 'It's not so simple, I think. Donor blood must be tested for several diseases. I cannot accept . . .' Angel took his arm. He spoke more quietly, insistent, 'My blood was tested recently after I received a transfusion myself. It's clean. My London doctor has the records. You must ring him at once. You must not waste time. If my wife dies or loses her baby I will hold you personally responsible.' He looked at the doctor as if he would kill him with one blow.

The doctor looked as if he would resist, then seemed to crumble under Angel's gaze. He shrugged and said, 'Come, please.' They walked down the long shiny-floored corridor to a small office where a staff nurse was busy with a clerical assistant. The doctor spoke in German to the nurse and she then told Angel, in English, to follow her. They went up again in the lift and along more

461

corridors until they reached the department for blood testing and donating.

The room was cool and lit by strip lights, insulated from the outside by blank white walls. He wanted to throw something, to scream, to kill somebody. What were they doing? Could it take this long to phone London? He walked towards the door. The nurse was coming towards him. 'Will you come this way?' she said, smiling.

They made him sign a form, then took a litre of his blood and left him lying, faint and weak, on a hard, narrow bed.

He asked them, 'When can I see my wife? I want to see her,' and was told, 'When she comes from the theatre. But now, please rest.'

He must have slept then. He awakened to find the same nurse smiling at him. She said, 'Your wife is now recovering from surgery. She has been given your blood. You can look at her but it is best if you do not go in, yet.'

He sat up and the world spun. She helped him stand and held his arm as they walked again along the strangely shining corridors under the too-bright strip lights.

He said, 'The baby. Is the baby all right?'

The nurse said, 'As far as we know, yes. But your wife has to make her own recovery before we can be sure of that.'

He nodded, and the agony returned. Catherine. He might lose her. He might lose them both. When they reached the unit he was able to look at her through glass. Her arm was on a drip. She was sleeping. He saw her face was bruised and hoped it was not scarred. Her pale hair folded under her head on the white pillow was the hair of an innocent child. She looked vulnerable and damaged, like a wounded bird, but at peace, almost as though she had died. He felt a tremendous sadness and wished he could weep.

They told him to come back tomorrow. But he demanded to remain. They found him somewhere to lie down and he slept again. When he was able, he watched her through the glass panel. He did not know what to do otherwise. He was adrift in his grief.

95

There is a haze of light. White light of sunlight on white walls. The window is a landscape of sycamores whose branches, heavy with leaf, hang proudly like crinolines around their thick trunks.

Her eyes, opened suddenly after some long sleep, or was it death, stay with them, held by their timelessness. She cannot remember how she came here. She is lying down, looking at the trees and it is afternoon or so it seems. Perhaps not. Time seems stationary. The light does not change as she looks and light and time are partners in life, moving on together. But why does it not change? Panic rising. Fear, disorientation. Who am I? Where am I? What day is it, if there are still days and nights to live through? A movement on the other side of where she lies, disturbs her. She turns her head and looks. A man is sitting there. Time begins again . . .

He leans forward. He bends over her. He kisses her. He kisses her face, her bruises and her swollen eyes. He kisses her lips and takes her hands and kisses them, too. And the finger where the ring is, the wedding ring, that is so swollen the ring will not come off, he kisses that, too.

'Catherine, Catherine,' he breathes and sounds like sobs choke out between the words. But he is not crying. He blinks back moisture in his eyes. He wishes he could weep. With joy. She will be all right. They have said that she will be all right. And the baby. She must just recover now and the baby will be all right. The placenta is still in position. Nothing is disturbed. They have repaired her body. They have given her his blood. He loves her. And he is happy she is whole again. Her beauty will return.

And then? He looks at her with questioning anxious eyes, his face so close to hers and kisses her again. She takes her hand, the free hand that is not held by the drip and smooths his springy hair. Hair that is like fine moss to her hands, that to him was always like a brillo pad. Her fingers touch his eyelids, outline his eyes that she often says remind her of olives, move around his cheeks and along his nose and jaw and stroke his lips.

He longs for her. He feels his cock stiffening. He sits back in the chair and looks at her. Looks at the bruised face and the pale tangled hair. Sees the wedge of sunlight moving like an inverse sundial over the pillow until it almost cuts across her head. Sees time moving on.

He is afraid of what must come.

96

Outside, the summer heat, yellow light. Inside, the air conditioning and the bustle and throng of the late afternoon airport. Sounds of bustle and commerce near glass-topped counters where perfumes, jewellery and cameras are sold. Gucci leathers and Hermes scarves. Announcements coming over the air in German, English, French.

They sat together near a window at a table looking out over the airfield. Planes were taxiing, others being provisioned and fuelled. She drank lemon tea from a tall glass. He drank rich Viennese coffee laced with fig essence and layered with cream, and ate torte. Sacher Torte.

'I shouldn't. I want to lose weight and I haven't worked out properly for five days.' He had bought some kit and gone running in the hospital grounds, but he missed his weights.

She reached out her hand. 'I'm sorry. That's all my fault. It was wonderful of you to stay.'

He smiled and looked out of the window. The heat rising from the tarmac was a glistening, flickering haze. He said, 'I'm glad you're all right, anyway. And the baby. I'm glad about the baby. I'm sorry I . . .'

Her hand crept over his. The left hand with the still slightly swollen finger, bruised where the wedding band had been. She had told them to cut the ring off and they had done so, leaving a little scratch on her skin where the soft metal had parted too quickly and the tool had cut her.

Their eyes met. He saw it coming before she put the thought into words and flinched as she said it.

'Do you want to give the child your name?'

He shook his head. He laughed a short laugh. 'No child deserves that.' He looked away.

Her hand tightened on his. She leaned towards him. 'That's not true. It's not a matter of deserving. Your child should have your name.'

'I don't want it to.' He tried to withdraw his hand.

She pulled his hand down onto her belly. He felt the slight roundness, the tautness under her dress.

'Give it your own name, Catherine.'

'My father's or my husband's?'

'I deserved that, too.' He leaned over and kissed her and took away his hand. 'But the answer is still no.' He was firm, smiling.

She said, 'Marry me, Christopher.' Her eyes held the hurt of his rejection. She seemed vulnerable, a deprived child.

He said, 'Look, Catherine, I still don't know what's happening to me. I may have to go to prison for a time. I don't know how long for. Maybe I won't have to, but I can't marry you until that's past. I can't be the child's proper father. I'm just the baby's . . . the baby's . . .' He could not go on.

'Stud?' Her voice was ironic. Her eyes had retreated in a face that was full of pain. Her face, now regaining its usual beauty, was the face of grief.

'Catherine.'

She said, 'I don't understand. You give your blood but you won't give your name.'

'It's much more than a name, isn't it? To marry you.'

She shrugged and laughed. The tension broke in her but she was still irretrievably sad, gone away somewhere, remote from him. She stared out at the still hot sunlight. She said, sadly, her voice as far and dreaming as her unfocused eyes, 'If it seems so awful, I certainly wouldn't want you to be around.' Then she turned to face him and said in a harder voice, 'I suppose you have other obligations. Can't you buy her off? Or do you have to keep fucking her?'

He stared at her. A blush crept over his face and he looked down at his unfinished torte.

She said, 'For all I know you've promised to marry her if she sees you through. But then you don't tell me much, do you? I have to guess at how important this woman is to you.'

He said, 'I have enough love for . . .'

She spat, 'You don't. You don't have enough love for anyone. I wouldn't be suffering like this if you had enough love for me.' She hung her head then and said in a voice choked with unshed tears, 'I'm sorry. I wouldn't be here now if it were not for your love.' There was a silence and she added, 'Maybe that would have been best.'

The announcement of their flight cut into the shaken stillness between them. She stood up and he came to her and put his arms around her. She let her head fall onto his chest.

*

97

August came and Catherine stayed in London. Tourists overfilled the spaces left by the residents who took themselves away to the country or the Med. Mayfair, though, was peaceful. Catherine moved to Charles Street a few days after coming back from Vienna. Her Vienna doctor had advised rest. But she persuaded her father's housekeeper Susan to return and help her move in. Clive returned, too, and Brenda came to stay, to make sure Catherine had company that kept her at home in the evenings and sent her to bed early after her working day.

James was away when she moved. She told him, the night of her return from Vienna, about the baby, told him she had almost died a few days before, told him about the symbolic cutting off of her wedding ring, told him about Christopher and the blood that saved her. Told him she would move immediately.

He heard her silently and nodded his acquiescence. He went to Norfolk the next morning and she had not seen him or heard from him since. She had Anna's help in packing her personal belongings at Queen Anne's Gate. Anything else would have to follow. There was plenty of time for disagreements with James when her health was better.

After that, while Susan and Brenda made a home for her in her father's house, she went to Paris and went over the final details of the September launch of French Vanities. She was postponing her new British magazine's launch until after the baby's birth. And she had a plan, vague in outline but growing in insistence with each day. She wanted to go to Kenya.

One day towards the end of August after a few days in the country with Brenda, she saw Gerald quite by accident in Harry's Bar where she had gone alone for a quiet drink before dinner. He came in hot and thirsty and saw her immediately. She was sitting on a stool at the end of the bar in a red sleeveless shirt dress of thick Thai silk. She radiated loneliness. He went to her. 'Catherina, should you be drinking? And alone, too?' He took the empty stool next to her.

'In moderation. Just one glass. I feel sick most of the time, anyway. And I'm sure the baby likes champagne.' She gave an ironic little smile.

Gerald had seen Catherine once, briefly, since her return from Vienna and learned of her decisions, ones on which he had not been asked to advise. He felt slightly miffed but was relieved, too, that Catherine now seemed less prey to emotional conflict. Her father's death and her pregnancy had opened a new path. She seemed to have become more fatalistic, less tormented by doubt and the need to choose between good and evil. He was aware, too, that Brenda's approval had steadied her conscience. She seemed more certain of her own purposes and strengths, as in control of her life as she was of her business. He pecked her cheek and turned to the barman. 'I'll have a glass, too. On second thoughts, make it a half bottle.' He turned to Catherine. 'I can top you up, Tsarina. The baby can get drunk tonight.'

She laughed and shook her head. 'No, no. Just one glass is my rule. Then a light supper and early to bed. It's a bit boring, but for the duration, it's a case of moderation in all things.'

'Including moderation, I hope.' He gave her an admonishing stare over the top of his new bifocal glasses. Catherine was one of the least moderate people he knew.

She laughed.

Casually, appraising her, he said, 'How is everything?'

She smiled with a closed mouth and looked down at her glass. 'Everything is changing quite fast.' She smoothed her hand over her belly. She looked up at him and he saw her trying to be brave. She gave a crooked little smile. Her voice was light and the ironic tone dominant. She said, 'I don't see much of Christopher. He's too busy and he has the sword of Damacles hanging over his head. The charges still stand although the police have no clear evidence, it seems, that he personally was involved in supplying the demonstrators with drugs.'

'And was he?'

She gave him a look. 'James has not made any negative noises about the divorce. I've started redecorating Charles Street since I saw you last. The change of address cards should be going out any day, but you know where I am. I don't think I shall give a party. It doesn't seem quite right with my father not yet settled in paradise, or wherever he is.' She took a sip of her champagne and looked at the wall opposite.

'Catherina,' Gerald said, 'you have been having too much of everything as I see it. Moderation is a slogan you much need.'

She looked down into her almost empty glass.

'Have you thought any more about the book, your father's life?'

Her head came up and she looked directly at him. It was an open, honest look full of sadness and reality. 'Gerry, I can't. You know that. I haven't changed my mind.' She sighed and drank the last of her wine, then turned back to him. 'But I haven't told you what I found out in Vienna. I talked to another former Brown Shirt.' She gave a look of distaste and reached for a nut. 'My father killed that poor man quite by accident. He didn't even try to push him. My father tried to catch hold of the old fellow's arm. He was bullying him a bit, but nothing serious, not hitting him or anything. The poor old man stepped away from my father and just slipped on the polished floor in the kitchen. He hit his head on the open oven door and that was it. He had some weakness in his head, some blood vessel that was too thin and he just had a brain haemorrhage and went.' She looked into her glass.

Gerald was silent, thinking of the elderly Jew confronted by the bullying boy, of his fear and of the boy's horror when the man died.

Catherine said, 'You see, it was almost as much of an accident as the person who bumped into me and knocked me into the path of that taxi. Except that person wasn't bullying me because of what I was. That was the only difference. I'm not making excuses for that or what happened afterwards. But I think it helps one to forgive . . . to forgive a very young boy who was just caught up in some mass emotion, something historic that perhaps took over his will, confused him about what was right and wrong . . .' She tailed off.

'So you don't condemn him any more?' Gerald's voice was a murmur.

She threw up her head. 'Black and white rules don't exist for me now, Gerry. Nothing is either wholly good or wholly evil when you understand its cause. A pure will to evil, or even to good, does not exist in human terms. Both impulses are driven by so many other things, so many experiences and emotions and events outside the person's control.'

He said, 'But there is right and wrong, and most people know the difference, especially you, my little walking Protestant ethic.' He chuckled and swigged the dregs of his wine, reaching at the same moment for the bottle and pouring a second glass.

Catherine's expression remained serious. 'You have to be very mature, very balanced, very morally certain to know what is really right and wrong. To have a true inner morality, you have to believe in something beyond life. If you don't, you act out of confusion, selfishness, or fear. One's moral code may be some rigid thing imposed by a religion or family or school, not based on a personal ethic. So it doesn't make one any better, one's nature is just as culpable, one is still capable of evil, by accident if not by ignorance. I'm no better for all my rigid morality. No better than Daddy. Or Christopher. I just haven't had the same experience, the same tests. And those I have had . . . well, I think I've not done too well.' She was thinking of how she had almost killed Angel and herself.

'Oh, Tsarina. Don't try to baffle me with your philosophy. I know you're just tying yourself up in more knots again. You have the sort of mind that will argue itself out of anything. You were doing it when you became a whore in order to, as you said, totally accept Angel. So

470

that you could save his soul, no doubt.' He chuckled and patted her shoulder and she stared at him with wide brooding eyes. 'You see, Tsarina, with your background and upbringing and nature, you will find a moral argument to justify anything. If you could only not find one, there might be hope for you. If you could do something and accept doing it, without justifying it by some complicated intellectual argument, without trying to make it moral, I would think you had finally arrived.'

'Arrived where?' She was genuinely puzzled.

'At the rest of the human race.' He laughed and refilled her glass. By reflex, she drank from it. 'Relax, Caterina. Some things are totally without meaning or moral justification. They are just life, just events, just IT. No divine cause has triggered them or pulled the strings. No terrible force of destiny has compelled you to be there when they happen. IT is just daisies growing, whether under living feet or on graves. IT is life without cause and effect. IT is being. Being now. And being happy. Being without meaning. Being yourself. Without guilt. Without constant thinking about things.'

'Have you achieved that, Gerry?' Catherine was staring in wonderment at him.

'No.' He poured the last of the bottle into his own glass. His smile held regret. 'I wish I could. I was brought up, like you, with too many inhibitions. But I do believe there is a state of grace, a state of innocence, comparable with the Garden of Eden before the fall, where we can be free of all our guilt and moral rationalization. Where we can do the right things without even thinking about them, and wrong things without calling them evil and damning ourselves.'

She was shocked now. 'But not killing or stealing, or deliberately harming anyone?'

'That was after the fall, remember. I'm talking about innocence. Before original sin was invented.'

'But how do we achieve that?'

He smiled. 'Forgiveness. Of ourselves primarily. Giving ourselves permission to be free of guilt for the past. Forgetting and starting afresh. Then living just as

471

it comes. Naturally. Without forcing anything. Without wanting or expecting anything. Accepting rain and sunshine alike without reacting. Simply being.'

'Oh, Gerry.' She stood up and put her arms around him and kissed him warmly. What Gerald had said was not much different from what she had told Angel in Miami about forgiveness and releasing his past. Why couldn't she follow her own advice? She hugged him. 'You are wonderful. You take all the weight off my shoulders and make me feel young again. Do you really mean I don't have to suffer?' She laughed.

She was teasing him again. Not taking him seriously. He could see she still wanted her guilt. Wanted to carry the world.

She said, 'Come and have a boring healthy dinner with me at Charles Street, and I'll tell you about all my plans to unload the bank to management and the magazine to the staff and go off to Africa and write my novel.'

'What novel?' He was instantly alert.

'The one based on my father's life. Are you interested?'

'You bet I am, Tsarina. Wheel me off to Charles Street and tell me the rest.'

98

It was the first time he had been in a house that was hers and only hers. The fact that it had been her father's was, well, both intimidating and exciting. It made her seem very powerful, very unattainable. He liked that. That was how it had been at the beginning when his compelling desire for her had been spiced by the knowledge of who she was. It had not been easy to handle the consequences of that first desperate desire. His jealous obsessive passion for her. Hers for him. And then love: he had not bargained for that. Rape was what he had had in mind. To fuck the banker's daughter, to put her down under his cock and screw her whether she wanted it or not. And get his own back on the man and the whole class they came from, the moneyed, privileged class who put themselves above the world and above the law.

Well. He'd had his revenge, all right. Now he was visiting the daughter in her dead father's house and she loved him and was carrying his child and wanted him for her husband. It was all too much in too short a time. He needed time. He needed to adapt. He needed to understand what had happened to him. And what was going to happen at any time, when the police decided they had enough evidence for a prosecution. He could make no plans for the future, he was a prisoner of his past.

He was shown in by the butler who led him upstairs to the big drawing room. She was sitting on a white sofa by the window. It was not quite dark outside and the dark blue silk curtains were held back by heavy gold cords and he could see lights in the building across the street. The room was brilliantly blue and white and gilt mirrored, hung with pictures. White marble busts and small statues were strategically placed. The carpet was white. Most of the upholstery was white. There were some small gilt chairs with light blue silk seats. Blue and white rugs. Catherine had told him that she had had the house redecorated to try to remove the old memories. He wondered how it had looked before, done in the banker's taste.

A blue and gold Chinese-style lamp on the table next to her threw a loop of light over her head and caught the sleek pale hair and put shadows under her troubled eyes. She matched the room as if deliberately. She wore a short flared white silk dress, gold sandals and a long double strand of pearls.

She stood up and came towards him and was in his arms before the butler had gone. He felt his pulse jump and his cock tingle with the first sensations of stiffening. He held her close and felt she belonged to him and then that she never could. Then he held her away, took her

473

hand and led her to another sofa, away from the window, and sat her down on it. He left her there and went for the master switch by the door and doused the lamps.

'Why did you do that?'

'I'm thinking of your reputation.'

She laughed. 'Isn't it a bit late for that? I might as well be seen with the father of my child as with anyone.'

He coloured and looked down. There was tension between them. He had seen her maybe six times in the month since Vienna. She felt neglected and unloved. He was tired. He had too many pressures. He could not give her what she wanted, what she needed. Love, comfort, companionship. He was never going to be good enough for her. To be with her and meet her friends. It would never work. Even if he were not sent to prison. He said, 'I'm not the right man for you, Catherine.'

'Let me be the judge of that.' She said it gently. She took his face between her hands and kissed his mouth.

He pulled her to him and kissed her with as much desire as he could ever remember feeling for her. He wanted her as much as he had wanted her that first time. He put his hand on her bare tanned thigh and lifted the skirt slowly. She wore white silk and lace French knickers under the dress and he found his way quickly inside them and touched her swollen place.

She leaned back with a groan and let him feel her moistness and caress her. She said, 'When you touch me like that I feel you own me completely. It's as if I would do anything for you. I feel totally in your power.'

He said fiercely, 'You are mine. I own you. Completely.'

He had his cock out very quickly. She said, 'Not here.'

'Will they come in?'

'They might. Come to the bedroom.'

He slid his swollen cock out of sight and followed her up another flight of stairs into a big well-proportioned room that looked out over Charles Street. She had decorated it in shades of pale green and turquoise touched here and there with shocking pink. The bed was huge and canopied. The banker's bed.

He lifted the loose delicate dress over her head, slipped the knickers down to her ankles then lifted her up and laid her on the bed. She wore no bra. He took her breasts, already bigger because of the child, and kissed them. He stood back and stripped and she lay looking at him, her eyes alive with love. He came to her and lay along her and as their skins touched it was as if they had left a desert and they looked long into each other's eyes. When he slid into her she said softly, 'Be gentle. We mustn't disturb the babe.'

He smiled and was gentle. But he seemed to want something more than he had ever wanted with her. And he had always wanted this. He wanted to reach into her womb. To be there, too. To be wrapped inside her red warmth and belong to her absolutely as if he were her child and would never have to be born from that secure loving place. He moved deep inside her and looked into her eyes and said, 'What do you feel? What do you want? What's it like with my cock inside you?'

She answered, 'It's all I ever want. Nothing else. Just that. I'm happy now. You complete me. You are part of me. You belong with me and in me. I am not whole without you. There is no substitute. I want you with me, in my life, always.'

And he saw the tears shining in her loving eyes and moved again inside her, wanting to be part of her, already somehow jealous of the child, wanting to own her and possess her and make her his bride. And all the while, he looked into her eyes and knew that she would always want him. And he let his life flow into her and saw her drinking him with her soul. And he wanted to be good enough for that fine thing. And knew that he was not. And all the conflicts in his heart rose up into his head and destroyed his wish. He sank down with all his weight on her and felt that he was rotten and unworthy and wished that he was dead.

*   *   *

He did not want to stay for dinner. But she begged him to and he relented. He was uncomfortable with the butler who served them. He was ill at ease with everything. She saw his unhappiness and wondered why he felt so inadequate when he could be anything that any other man who made money could be. Was it guilt? Was the source of his prosperity the cause of his shame? Did he despise himself for his livelihood and yet not know it?

They sat at one end of the long polished table in the soft light of two triple candelabra. She told him of her plans. She told him the bank profits were to be divided into two trusts, one for charity, one for the child. And she told him she planned to go to Africa soon after the magazine launch in Paris next week. 'Will the court give you permission to come with me? I would so love you to see the place where I lived when I was a child.'

He smiled gently. But she saw the withdrawal in his eyes. They were black holes again. Unfathomable. He did not want her to organize him. He would not play her game. She was the prey still. Had to be. He could only go on in his inadequacy if she let go her power and let him make the rules.

She said, 'I'm going to stay up near where we had our farm at Nanyuki in a place called the Mount Kenya Safari Club. It's very beautiful with roses and green lawns and wonderful exotic birds. The wild bush and the forest are just beyond the grounds and the mountain has a snow peak that touches the sky.'

He was smiling at her enthusiasm, his eyes glowing again with that dark light that said, show me what I know I'm not allowed. She said, 'It's more than 17,000 feet high on the equator. I went up there once to the snow line on a horse. It took three days and we camped at night and it was freezing cold and I was weirdly dizzy and had some funny dreams.'

She laughed, and he smiled again, but he did not share her delight. He was always uncomfortable when she was eloquent. It was as though speech was an alien thing to him.

If only he would let go. Not care. Stop being so stubborn. Stop trying to stay as he was as if he had made a promise to the world never to change; to remain, unrelentingly, the bitter, angry, pent up man who wanted his revenge. To change would be to admit that what the world had done to the half caste child was not irrevocable, could be forgotten, even forgiven. Yet it was the way he was that she loved so much. She loved the wounded child in him. Loved the hurt rejected thing. But wanted to heal it and set it free of pain.

Looking at him with anxious, loving, understanding eyes, she thought, free yourself. Give up your stubborn will to stay cast out of paradise. Give in. Forgive yourself. She loved him as he sat there in the candlelight, resentfully, it seemed, because she was in control in her house and at her dinner table and this made him afraid.

Of course, he would not come to Africa. He said, 'I can't. It's better that I'm here in case there are developments in the case. Anyway, I can't leave the business for long. I don't usually take holidays.'

She did not argue. She nodded and put her hand on his and said, 'If you change your mind, I'll be there.'

She gave up then, and when he had gone, kissing her and still arousing her desire with his own, putting her hand on his hard cock as if it were the only thing he was sure of, the only power he had to rule her, she went to her bed and wept. She fell asleep with her hands on her warm taut belly knowing at least, that she had something of him for life. So long as she lived through its birth.

99

She rode the lift to the fifth floor and walked into the reception area. Marie, the receptionist, knew her well now and greeted her warmly. Catherine was friendly but perfunctory. 'Good morning, Marie. Please tell Andrea I'm here.' Catherine walked on through the heavy double doors that lead to her father's private suite. Andrea

Werner rose immediately from her desk at the other side of the Chairman's reception room. 'Oh Miss Clyne, your visitor has telephoned to say he will be ten minutes late.'

Catherine nodded. She looked at her watch. It was 8.40 a.m. She smiled briefly with closed lips. That gave her a half hour, clear. She walked on through into her father's office and went immediately to the safe behind the bookshelves. She opened it and took out a file marked X. She went to the huge desk and sat behind it. She dropped her slim black crocodile briefcase on the floor beside her and turned to look through the window. The morning sun drew a geometric collage of shadows and reflections over the open space below the window. The Bank of England's roof and portico were side lit by the low sun while the streets remained shadowed. She had become familiar with the view.

Andrea came and Catherine turned to face her. Andrea had been on holiday for three weeks in Germany with her mother. Catherine had discovered that the holiday was part of Andrea's contract and paid for by the bank. She had endorsed its continuation and had added a gift of her own, a costly set of matching luggage.

During Andrea's absence Catherine had spent more time than usual in her father's office, often after 5 p.m. when the staff had gone home, or at weekends. She had spent those hours quietly searching the files and had eventually found what she wanted. She was quite sure that when the Serious Fraud Squad started their detailed investigation of the bank's business over the past fifteen years, they would find nothing on one particular group of transactions.

Andrea placed a tray of opened mail before her. 'Thank you, Andrea.' She smiled. Andrea must know a great deal about her father's business, nefarious and otherwise. She had been a loyal friend and employee and Catherine was determined to reward her once she had taken her father's estate through probate. There was a bequest in the will for Andrea. But Catherine felt it should be more generous.

Andrea was well aware of Catherine's intentions. She was surprised and grateful. She knew her job would continue with whoever Catherine and the directors appointed as the bank's new managing director. She also knew her pension arrangements were secure. She had not honestly expected the windfall of a legacy. She returned Catherine's smile and felt a genuine liking for her former employer's daughter and an extension of the loyalty she had felt for Sir Arnold, whom, after all, she had, in her rather distant way, loved. Catherine was now the nearest thing she had to Arnold and in some odd way she felt love for her, too.

Catherine said, 'When my visitor arrives would you give me a moment's warning before you show him in?'

Andrea nodded and went out. Catherine opened file X and began rereading its contents. She had to decide now what she would do with it. Whether to destroy it or . . .? An idea crossed her mind. She had not intended he should know anything. But now she wondered. Perhaps he should. She read for about ten minutes before Andrea announced her visitor. Then she slid the file into her briefcase and stood up.

She walked across the Chinese carpet towards Armstrong, her hand held out. The light was behind her and for a moment he did not realize it was she. The chignon that held back her hair was partly to blame. But there was also a manner, remote and businesslike that he had not seen before. The cool but feminine journalist who had questioned him in his office, the unhappy woman who had slept in his arms, the bereaved daughter who had clung to him beside her father's body, the furious betrayed lover who had hurled and smashed a glass into the fireplace beside him, seemed all roles she had played.

The woman who took his hand now was a formal professional, a businesswoman whose movements and strict black suit suggested a perfectionism that bordered on aggression. But she never forgot her charm. Now she smiled and the animal energy he remembered shone out of her and warmed him.

She led him to the sofa and chairs around the coffee table. 'I'm very grateful that you chose to come yourself,

479

David. Also, I must thank you for holding off the start of the investigation for so long.'

He cleared his throat. He felt embarrassed and inadequate as he had the day he had sat in the same room in the same chair and heard her father's confession of his past mistakes. It was embarrassing to have to do what he had come to do. But she had had warning. He said, uncomfortably, 'I didn't feel you would do anything to obstruct the Fraud Squad's work if I delayed handing the enquiries over to them and gave you time to collect yourself after your bereavement.'

She nodded. 'I believe the news of the investigation has all been kept very quiet so far, David, but once your colleagues begin here, I'm afraid the bank staff will gossip to their friends and the word will be out. I don't see how we can protect the bank from scandal, or my father's reputation, for that matter. It will all come out.'

'Not if I can help it, Catherine. There will be a "no comment" policy as far as the press are concerned. There is no reason why anyone should think the police are in here because of anything your father did. For all anyone knows we could be trying to trace ostensibly legitimate funds which were in here without your father's knowledge.'

She smiled. She was sitting on the other chair, her lovely black stockinged legs crossed at the knee. He thought she looked very attractive in this severe outfit.

Andrea came in with the silver tray holding the coffee filter and the silver teapot and the Wedgwood cups and saucers. A plate of Sir Arnold's favourite liebkuchen stared up at Catherine like an accusation from the dead. Something touching and human. A personal thing that gave the same momentary stab of memory. She had felt this in the house when coming upon a piece of paper with his handwriting, a toothbrush or a soiled handkerchief. They made her cry, these fragments of pathetic private things from a vanished life.

She had a moment's need to weep now, but swallowed it. She did not know why the biscuits also made her feel guilty. It was odd. She offered the plate to Armstrong, who took one.

He said, 'I hope you won't be too much disturbed by the officers' comings and goings. I'm afraid I won't be in charge of the investigation. The SFS are a quite separate operation from my own. I'm handing most of my own files over to Commander Peter Swift. I'll be able to complete my own department's work on the South London business when they've finished here. But meantime, it's off on other business.' He leaned forward and reached for another biscuit. 'May I?' he said belatedly.

She nodded, smiling. She looked preoccupied. 'I'm not going to be here for a while. I'm going to Kenya. I'm leaving the bank to the professional staff and the other directors.'

He looked surprised. 'How long will you be away?'

'A few weeks. I can't tell. I have a magazine launch next week in Paris. After that, well, I'm as free as I ever can be. My staff can handle things. I pay them well enough. They'll no doubt do very well without me.'

'Is it for a rest?'

'I want to start writing a novel.'

'Oh. What's it to be about?'

'I can't tell you that, I'm afraid.' She smiled.

He took a sip of Sir Arnold's good rich coffee, reluctant to leave without finishing it. He had nothing much more to say. She evidently had no great desire to prolong things. He drained his cup and said, 'I mustn't detain you any longer.'

She stood with him and walked him to the door. She said, 'David,' and he turned, surprised at the sudden intimacy in her voice. 'Thank you. For everything.' She held out both her hands. She wore only a simple signet ring on her right hand and he saw the wedding ring was missing from the bare left one.

He held the left hand up and said, 'Where is it?'

'I'm getting a divorce from James. I'm living in my father's house now, in Charles Street.'

His eyes fell questioningly on hers and lingered. Was

481

she trying to tell him something else? He had to know the answer. 'Are you still seeing . . . your friend?'

She said, 'Now and then.' And the memory of last night's lovemaking shivered through her.

He shot her a penetrating look and she blurted it out: 'I'm pregnant, David.' She smiled sadly and nodded at his questioning face. 'Yes. It's his.'

'Are you marrying him?'

She laughed, all her sadness disappearing in a flash of light. 'The conventional question,' she said and patted his shoulder. 'No. I'm not.'

'But you said . . .'

'I know. I know. But he won't marry me. He says he may be going to prison. Do you suppose he's right?'

She saw Armstrong go into retreat, his hand on the doorknob. He wanted out. Then something seemed to click. He turned back towards her and steered her to the chair. He sat down opposite her and put his elbows on his parted knees. 'I don't want any of this to go further, Catherine. But, for your own good I'll tell you, your friend is likely to go for trial next month. I've no idea how the judge will view the prosecution case. It's by no means watertight. There are a number of enquiries that have yielded nothing and there is only one further major source of evidence to be investigated. If that one delivers the goods we will be pressing ahead for a quick trial, and I would advise you to be prepared for the worst.'

She nodded. He stood up. 'Call me if you need anything. I'll do my best. You'll respect my confidence, won't you?'

'Of course.'

He got up and walked briskly to the door. She followed him and he put his hand on the knob. There was nothing more to be said for the moment, but he could not stop himself from kissing her on the lips before he opened the door.

She went back to the desk and took the file out of her briefcase. She read through it for another half hour before she was satisfied. She now knew exactly what she had to do.

100

Catherine reached her office in Covent Garden by 11 a.m. The day was only just beginning at Vanities, but by the end of it the November issue would be away.

Janie came over as soon as she saw Catherine sit down behind her desk. 'Someone called Lazic rang. Ali Lazic. He wants to have lunch with you.'

Catherine raised an eyebrow. 'Today?' She slipped off her jacket and hung it behind the chair. 'Is the air conditioning on the blink? It feels very muggy in here.'

Janie shrugged. 'I'll check. Here's his number. Oh, and Dr Noble rang. Something about a test?'

Catherine's heart jumped, but she gave nothing away. No one at Vanities knew she was pregnant. She looked up at Janie. 'Okay. Get them for me, will you? Lazic first.'

She turned and reached behind her to the small refrigerator concealed in the black-stained wood-panelled units that contained filing cabinets and drawers. She pulled out a litre bottle of mineral water, a quarter bottle of champagne, a chilled flute and a water glass.

Janie, punching in the number of the Savoy where Lazic had given her his suite number, watched anxiously.

Catherine straightened and poured herself mineral water and drank some. Then she popped the champagne bottle.

Lazic was on the line. 'Catherina, bella. Ciao. Va bene?'

'I'm fine. What brings you to London?'

'To see you, my beautiful flower of spring and also transact a little business.'

She laughed. 'Well, I'm delighted to welcome you. How can I help?' Janie, dialling June Noble on the other line watched her. She thought Catherine almost rude on the phone, knew she loathed telephonic chatter. It was eyeball to eyeball for real talk. Calls were cut to minimal length. This morning she seemed unusually terse. And there was the champagne. She had never seen her drink this early. But then Cat was unpredictable.

'Just a minute, Ali. Am I free for lunch today, Janie? Yes, Ali . . . One o'clock in the River Room? Oh dear, one minute. It takes a week to get a table there. Have you booked? You have? Wonderful. I see you have influence in the right places. Yes, I'll look forward to it, too. Bye bye.' She replaced the receiver and looked at Janie. 'Next?'

June Noble was waiting. 'Everything seems all right from the test we did, Catherine. But, there is one slight question about the position of the placenta. I'd like to examine you thoroughly before you go off. Would you come in this week?'

Catherine's heart seemed to stop and then pound into life again at twice the speed. 'Is something wrong, June?'

'No, no. Nothing wrong exactly. I just want to know whether there are likely to be any unusual features to this pregnancy. Since the accident you've come on fine . . . but . . . well, it's just a precaution.'

'You're sure?'

'Quite sure. Don't worry. I don't like my patients worrying. And you have enough worries, Catherine. Enough on your plate.'

'Sure, June. I'll try not to worry. It's like trying not to breathe, in my case. You know I have permanent ants.'

The gynaecologist laughed. 'I can't deliver you of those, I fear, unless you'd like a mild tranquillizer for a while, but I don't recommend that while you're pregnant.'

Catherine laughed. 'I wouldn't touch them. How about champagne?'

'In moderation.'

'That's what I thought you'd say.' Catherine raised her glass and sipped. She told Janie to make a date with June's secretary and cleared her extension.

She punched in his number on one of the free lines. When he answered, she said, 'I've a present for you. Can I deliver it now?'

He hesitated, then when she said it would only take a few minutes, told her to meet him at the house.

'I'm off for an hour, Janie,' she called. 'Back before lunch.' She picked up her jacket and briefcase and swung briskly down the long room and out to the lift. He was going to be very surprised, and, she hoped, pleased.

*   *   *

She parked carelessly across his front door and rang. He came after a short delay. He was wearing jeans and an open-necked shirt and a fatigued expression. He looked her up and down without a smile and led her upstairs.

'Tea?'

'No. I haven't time. But I'd like you to look at this.' She reached file X from her case and handed it to him.

He gave her a glance that was heavy with foreboding.

She sat on the sofa and leaned back to watch him. He read slowly, leafing through the computer sheets and the plain typed ones that went back earlier. There was a lot of material in the file and it had taken her many hours during evenings and weekends over the past three weeks to glean them from the bank's files.

She said briskly, without emotion, 'I think it's all there. The Serious Fraud Squad will want every bit of it, of course. I'm afraid you'll have to give it back to me. They come in tomorrow to start their dig.'

He looked up at her. His face expressed horror and fear. 'What? The Fraud Squad are going into your bank?'

She nodded. She watched him carefully. He seemed to stop breathing. She was sure his natural pallor had increased.

His eyes were black and fathomless. He said, quietly, 'How did you know about this, Catherine?'

'I have a friend in the police. He tipped me off. Since I knew about your connection with Daddy, I thought I'd better take a look in the files. It's taken me the past three weeks to find that lot. I hope I've taken everything on your companies off the computer and destroyed anything remaining to point out any connection between my father and yourself. I didn't know where to look to start with. I didn't know how one thing leads to another. But I hit on the system after a bit. You see, there was a whole

485

secret cache of files in my father's personal safe in his office. That had all the basic stuff. Then I just had to go through the computer records to see if there was anything else on file and clean it up. And then I checked out the paper files. You don't have anything to worry about now. Unless there's anything else you'd like me to hunt down, something I don't know about, under some other company name?'

He was staring at her with a mixture of puzzlement and dawning relief on his face. 'But you want to put it back. You . . .'

She laughed and shook her head. 'I could blackmail you, I suppose.' She shot him an ironic look. 'I could say I'll give it to you after you've married me and given your child your name.'

He came over to her and took her face in his hands and kissed her on the lips, slowly and sweetly, his eyes never leaving hers. 'I'd do that, anyway. You know I would.'

She took hold of his hands and put them to her belly. 'Would? The word is will.'

He dropped onto the sofa beside her. 'You know I can't until after the trial. Until I know . . .'

'Oh, you could, and I'd have you, anyway. Prison or not. But I'm not asking you again. I've made my offer and that's that. The next move is yours. But I certainly don't want you as blackmail payola. Anyway, my bet is there'll be no trial without this little lot. I hope you've destroyed all your own documents. Do they have anything else that will stick?'

Her toughness and lack of sentimentality shocked him. Was this the woman he had known for eight months? His secret passion, his soft, sensitive dove, his death-wish lover? There was no trace of feeling in her today. She was like some kind of adviser. Cold, hard, practical and shrewd. He was impotent in her presence. She was, after all, 'the Banker's daughter'. He was silent, staring at her profile. She was risking everything for him. Risking her reputation, her freedom, because they would charge her if they found out what she had done. She was breaking the law, obstructing police officers in their enquiries, concealing evidence. They would probably only give her a suspended sentence, but still . . .

'Does anyone else know you've got this stuff?'

'Nope.' She looked at him. Andrea knew some but not all. She hoped she was making sure that would never be a problem.

He reached for her shoulders. 'Are you sure? Have you any idea what they could do to you if they knew about this?'

She laughed softly. 'I don't know how long they would lock me up for.'

He pulled her to him and kissed her very tenderly, then reached her hand to his cock. She felt it hardening under her hand under his jeans' harsh tension.

She took her hand away. 'No. This was just a business call. I have a lunch.' She flicked her wrist up and glanced at her watch. She had time, but she was not going to let him. She wanted to leave it this way. She stood up. 'Do what you like with the file but be sure to leave no traces anywhere. I'm trusting you with my secret. And if you try to blackmail me with it in the future, I'll tell all and go down in flames.'

He smiled. He could see she would. Then a thought struck him. He said suspiciously, 'You don't have a duplicate?'

She laughed. It was an enormous, happy peal of laughter. It had not occurred to her. She said, 'Perhaps I should leave you guessing about that.' She blew him a kiss and he followed her to the top of the stairs, but she went quickly down them and out of sight before she could surrender to his need for her that was pulling her like gravity from his bottomless eyes.

*   *   *

Ali Lazic was already at the table, one in a prime position close to the river view and commanding the large light room. Catherine breezed towards him feeling somehow wildly lighthearted. Exhilarated was probably the best word.

487

As she sat down Catherine realized this was the table where she had sat with her father for lunch on that day in January after her snow-bound first encounter with Christopher in Regent's Park. She wondered if there was anything symbolic in that. Was this perhaps the day she freed herself from Christopher and began with another man? The thought made her shiver as if something hung between her and the sun.

She looked at Ali. He was wearing a superbly cut, blue-grey Italian suit with a pale blue shirt and microspotted silk tie. He was very tanned and very handsome. Like a Corsican pirate. She sighed and felt a little shuddering thrill as she remembered his seduction of her. Then she thought of Christopher. Erotic pleasure was not a substitute for love with a man you cared for passionately. Could she care for Ali? Was there any point now that she was pregnant? She gave him a long look which he returned. Without breaking their gaze, he took her hand and raised it to his lips.

They were interrupted by a waiter. She ordered Perrier and stared once more into Ali's intense blue eyes. He was drinking a very diluted Campari soda out of a half-pint tankard on what seemed to be an avalanche of ice. They dragged themselves reluctantly to the menu.

Their conversation began with light banter and went on to accounts of the past few months. Catherine told Ali about her father's death, her divorce and house move, and French Vanities, but left out everything else.

By the time they reached dessert it was clear that Ali intended Catherine to come to his suite. She knew she had to avoid that. She said, 'Ali. I haven't told you something. I'm pregnant. I'm divorcing James because it's another man's child.'

Ali assumed mock distress. His accent became slightly stage: 'Catherina, you have a talent for understatement. And your timing is superb. You could have told me this before I plied you with expensive aphrodisiacs. Have you no shame? When is the wedding? You mustn't wait too long or the child will be . . . well, I suppose no one cares any more. But it would be better, would it not, if . . .'

She put her hand over his and squeezed. 'I'm not marrying anyone, Ali.'

'Oh? May I ask why?'

'There are reasons. I'm not going into them. My . . . he doesn't want to marry me, Ali. I don't care any more, really.' She smiled. 'I'm happy to have his child. It's not as though I need the money. I'll be just fine and I'll love the child. It's a great joy.' She looked past him at the sludgy brown river sparkling in the mellow afternoon. Her eyes lost focus.

She felt him kiss her hand again. His voice came gently to her from far away. 'Why don't you marry me, Catherina?'

She smiled and then looked at him. Her eyes and her mind focused at once. She saw he was serious. She shook herself. 'Ali, no. I mean, thank you. What a very nice offer.'

Ali was acting misunderstood. 'It is not a nice offer. I am serious, Catherina. I was serious when I asked you before. Now I am serious also. I would like you for my wife. We can make beautiful love again once you have had the baby. Meanwhile, you can live in Mayfair and I can live on my yacht. Maybe I will moor it on the Thames.' He took her hand and squeezed it, smiling at his inventions. 'Afterwards we get together more often. But, all the time, the baby has a name. A good name. Lazic is a very good name. Maybe then, after, you have my baby. Is that not a good idea?'

She laughed. 'Oh, Ali. I hardly know you. You don't love me. Nor I you. It might happen in time. But how could I marry without love? I've just admitted one mistake, well, call it two. Can we keep it on the table and try to see something of each other, perhaps?'

He continued holding her hand. He raised it to his lips and nibbled her fingers. He said, 'Arranged marriages are often the best. And since we know how wonderfully suited we are as lovers, I think we have a start on most. Besides, most men would be after your money. And I, dear Catherine, am much much richer than you.'

Soon after this she left him and went back to her office.

The lunch had left her in a happy mood. It was warming and flattering and reassuring to know she had someone who thought she was a worthwhile bride even if it was not the man she loved.

101

'How was Paris?' Brenda kissed Catherine and put down her overnight bag and led her into the kitchen.

'Paris was a complete success. I hope we do as well on the bookstalls as we did for the launch. The publicity was terrific. Jean-Michel did a very good job. I feel happy leaving everything in his hands for a few weeks.'

'Only for a few weeks?' Brenda turned the already steaming kettle on. She poured some water into the flowered china teapot to warm it.

'Well, I can't turn my back on French Vanities any more than anything else, just because I'm pregnant.'

'But that's not the reason you're taking the time in Africa, is it?'

Catherine smiled. 'Yes and no. I need a break. I need time to rest and put my feet up. I'll have to at first, I haven't been at high altitude for years. I'll have to acclimatize.' Catherine walked around the kitchen. She was joyful, excited as a child about her trip.

'What about "No?"'

'What?'

'You said, Yes and no, about pregnancy being the reason for the trip.'

Catherine turned away and looked through the window. 'Oh well, yes, there is a book I want to start writing. I thought it would be a good time to begin that.'

'And?'

'And I want to go home and find myself again.'

Catherine turned to Brenda and there were tears in her eyes.

Brenda went to her and held her close. She said gently, 'What's happening to your lover?'

Catherine caught her breath in a suppressed sob, 'Oh don't, Brenda. Don't ask me about that. He won't change his mind. I've done all I can. He can't make the leap to be with me in that way. He can't change. I just have to give up. I'll still know him. He is the baby's father. I'll still love him till I die.' She pulled away and leaned on her hands against the table. 'I don't know how long that will be, of course.'

'Catherine. Don't talk that way.' Brenda was the nanny again, strict and disapproving. She picked up the laden tea tray and went out towards the garden.

The sun was warm and the air still heavy with the humid weight of late summer. Roses still bloomed in Brenda's garden and the daisies still studded the long grass. But a faint hint of autumn now seemed to leak into the evenings and September's scents brought piquant nostalgia for the heady days of June.

Catherine followed Brenda out into the sunlight. She said, 'I only meant, I don't know if I'll survive the birth. After all, when women of three generations of your mother's family have died in childbirth you wonder about yourself.' She sat on her usual seat in the bower and watched Brenda pouring tea.

'But medicine is much advanced. There is no reason for you to die just because you are giving birth and just because your family's women did. You may not share their weakness, anyway. What does your doctor say?' She handed Catherine her cup and saucer.

Catherine took the tea and immediately lifted the cup to her nose and inhaled its scent. Brenda favoured Lapsang. It went well with the afternoon smells, the smoky beginnings of autumn lurking in its perfume. 'Oh, June says everything will be fine. No complications. I'm not sure I believe her completely. She wants me in London under her watchful eye for the last three months of term.'

491

Brenda smiled. 'I don't blame her. You are a bit of a wild thing, Cat. You might decide to fly by balloon across the Atlantic or something in the eighth month and give birth at 20,000 feet in a basket.'

Catherine smiled. 'Well, anyway, I want to take no chances and so I have something in my bag for you to sign. We'll need a witness. Will the vicar or someone do it?'

'What is it?'

'Just a document of assignation. I want you to be the child's official guardian in the event of my death. All the other preparations have been made. There's a trust fund and all that. Nurses, tutors, school fees and everything will be paid from that. If I die there will be a second trust of my property and business income, outside of any legacies, that is. I won't bore you with the details but I've spent weeks with the lawyers tying it all up.'

Brenda stared at her. 'What about the child's father? Doesn't he get a say in anything?'

'If I die in childbirth he will have to fight very hard to get the baby away from you.'

Brenda looked puzzled and troubled. 'Catherine, I don't understand. I thought you loved this man. I thought you wanted to share the child with him . . .'

'I do,' Catherine cried out as if she were in pain. 'But he doesn't want to. Don't you remember, he wanted me to abort.'

Brenda was horrified. 'But the Vienna business, the blood and all that . . . Doesn't that entitle him to something? I thought he proved how much he loved you and wanted the child then. He shouldn't have to marry you, Catherine, to have any rights of parentage. You're hijacking his child.'

Catherine leaned towards her. Her eyes narrowed and a look of hardness came onto her face. 'It's not that he won't marry me, Brenda. It's who else he might be tied up with. And prison and all that. Just suppose Christopher is in prison and I'm dead. I don't want the child to be brought up by some woman who is not his mother, and who is not someone I can choose and approve in my place.

I don't know what kind of women Christopher will hang out with and I don't want our child brought up to that kind of life.'

'Catherine, my dear.' Brenda's shock left her almost dumb. Then, recovering, she said, 'I thought you had accepted Christopher and his life. I thought that was why you expected him to believe you loved him enough to share his life.'

Catherine put her head down. She stared at the grass under the old table. She said slowly, 'I think I do accept it. But only as part of Christopher. I can't accept it as part of anyone else. I don't want my child and Christopher's child, our baby, to go into that sort of world. Christopher's original reason for wanting me to abort the child was that he didn't think he was good enough to father it, didn't think he wanted another little half breed running around getting rejected by WASP aristos and bullied at school.'

She looked up and Brenda saw the anger in her face. 'Well, damn it, the only way to give that kid what Christopher wants it to have is to keep it away from whatever ex-whore or night club artist he shacks up with and to give it the best, the very best education and opportunity.'

'Oh, my dear.' Brenda shook her head in sorrow.

Catherine's voice was raised, 'I'm being practical, Brenda. It's not a double standard. It's just plain common sense to want our child to have the best. I love Christopher and I want his child to live without suffering the things he has suffered. And he does, too, I know it.' She sat back and added, 'Besides, if there is such a thing as redemption, the child will symbolize Christopher's and my redemption by the life it lives and the world it lives in.'

There was a silence into which a flight of swallows swept, curving down and then up along the currents of insect-laden air. They settled on the telephone wire running across the garden towards a distant farmhouse. Migration time had come again.

Brenda said softly, 'Have you told him any of this?'

Catherine stretched her legs out and linked her hands

493

behind her head. 'No, and I'm not going to.' She grinned at Brenda. 'After all, I may survive and this would really upset things between us. This will have to be a posthumous surprise. Otherwise a secret. Oh, don't worry, I'm leaving Christopher a lot of money, too. And you. Oh shut up, Brenda. I've given half father's fortune away to charity. If it was just me, I'd give the lot away. I hate the whole damn thing. I hate the way money corrupts people. I hate what they do to get their hands on it, even little amounts of it. I'd almost rather be free of the stuff and live with my begging bowl.'

'Now that's a double standard if ever I heard one.' Brenda folded her head over her lap, laughing.

Catherine joined her. She may have given a lot away, but on paper, with her magazine empire growing and the capital value of the bank, she was worth a lot of millions. It was academic to talk about other people chasing money. Or about begging bowls.

Brenda said, 'Is Christopher afraid of your money, Catherine? Does it make him feel inadequate?'

'Oh, yes. And my brains and my class and my style. But, damn it, I can't spend my life waiting for him to stop shaking every time I open my mouth or reach for my wallet. He has to do some accepting now. He asked me to marry him the day we got back from Miami. Now he's running scared. He can have me as his woman with or without marriage. But he has to accept me for what I am and not have to keep bolting off to relax with some woman who has lower standards.'

Brenda thought that since Arnold's death she had seen more and more of him in Catherine. It was as though Cat had had to wait for him to die before she could allow the world to see she had his qualities of shrewdness, toughness, calculation and strength. And brutality. Of course, it was her rebellion against her father that had prevented this. She had not wanted him, or anyone, to see any resemblance between them. She had fought him to prove she was her own creation.

Brenda said, as if making a promise to a child, 'We'll see. We'll see what happens if he doesn't have to

494

go to prison. Perhaps he will be different after the trial.'

Catherine gave her a look which was hard and assessing, but still held the dream of hope. 'Perhaps,' she said, and there was a sudden gentleness and a prayer in that one word that belied everything else she had said.

102

Catherine looked up from the table where she sat writing. Orange lilies and blue delphiniums projected their heads above her windowsill. Honeysuckle tendrils curled around the window from the cottage's low, tiled roof.

To her left, across the tended green with its sprinklers, the swimming pool with its white surround nested in pink and purple bougainvillaea. Umbrellas stood tipsy against the morning sky, casting little puddles of shade between the sunbathers. The short rains had begun a few days earlier and it had already been raining that morning. Heavy clouds had obscured the sunrise, but these had now passed and the sky seemed clear all the way to paradise, leaving the vegetation and the air shining with fractured reflections from a zillion droplets of moisture.

Before her and to the right, the golf course sloped gently down towards the distant trees. Beyond that the forest rose slowly from a dense line along the river, spreading out and thinning on its way up the mountain. High above the tree line the narrowing slopes that looked too easy from the comfort of this cultured garden leaned up into the sky. The mountain's curious white peak, snow-bound in all seasons, small and jagged as a broken finger nail, seemed to point a way to God.

Kyriniaga, the local Kikuyu called it, magic mountain and the home of God. Once, a group of climbers walking above the snow line had met a wild man, wearing only a loin cloth and carrying a bible and burned black as a cinder by the sun. He claimed to have spoken to God.

And indeed, anyone who went up there without oxygen might well do so. It was a matter for argument whether the perceptions of altitude were the wild hallucinations of an oxygen-deprived brain or the true visions of minds cleared of pollution and cares. Whichever, mountains are convenient places for human beings to retreat to and gain perspective.

Was she achieving perspective? Catherine rose from her chair and walked onto the small terrace. She slipped off the loose cotton kaftan that covered her bikini and lay down on the sun chair. She stared at the mountain. It was already October. She had been here now for three weeks during which she had worked several hours a day on her novel, writing longhand with a ballpoint pen, mostly sitting at the small writing table with its view of the mountain.

Important documents and mail from the office in London and anything that needed relaying from Paris or New York was being couriered to her twice weekly for information only. The staff were dealing with it all but she needed to be kept informed. Very little had required her intervention, which was fortunate as the telephone lines from Nanyuki to Nairobi were never good.

Catherine smoothed her hand over her abdomen. At four months, she was beginning to show now, enough to make her comfortable in her bikini only in private. Fortunately the Safari Club had not been very full these past weeks. But the season was beginning now and there were signs of greater activity around the pool and tennis courts and in the dining rooms.

Every morning just before 7 a.m. the sun rose over the hill to the left and every evening at about 7 p.m. it set behind the tennis courts at the back of her cottage. Her life had the same graceful, predictable rhythm. She was awake at sunrise, doing meditation and yoga for half an hour. Then she would send for her breakfast and take her shower. She would eat on her terrace, unless it was raining. She would write all morning, then have a swim.

She would have a lateish buffet lunch at the terrace dining room from which she would watch the day's new safari crowd arriving.

The afternoons would be spent walking in the grounds or resting in the shade, sometimes horseriding, though June had warned her to take it easy and Catherine was aware of the dangers of riding on the wild mountain where buffalo, buck or elephant could startle her horse and cause an accident.

She would change for dinner and go to the dining room about 8 p.m. each evening, eat a leisurely three courses alone and then retire to bed. There was a sweet monotony to her life that gave her time to return to some balance of mind and body and at the same time heal her feelings and reorder her thoughts.

The story based on her father and Brenda's experience of love was taking shape. But this morning, Catherine realized, it had reached some impasse. She lifted her face to the sun and let her half-closed eyes absorb the brilliantly coloured garden. It was as though the story was becoming her own and Christopher's. As though her own life was beginning to unfold in the longhand pages, like a confession. She wondered again if this was because her life was over, her story complete.

She felt undeniably empty. There was a sense of having come through a storm with all one's possessions lost. If she closed her eyes completely and forgot the beautiful garden, the exotic birds and flowers and the mountain's ever-present finger pointing to God, she seemed to be walking across a wasteland where nothing lived. She had made all her preparations. Everything was in order. If she died when the child was born, Brenda had agreed to assume its guardianship and the financial situation was ordered, too. The right people were even now in charge of the bank and the magazines. Everything was behind her. She could walk away from her life now, this moment, and leave no trace of herself. It would all carry on perfectly without her. The world would turn on its axis no lighter and no heavier for the vanishing of Catherine Clyne.

Something tickled one of her eyelids and she rubbed at it with her hand. She opened her eyes and caught the object in her fingers and held it up for examination. A small white fluffy feather, down probably from one of the flock of Egyptian Ibex that lived in the grounds, had floated onto her face. She smiled. It was an appropriate symbol for her wasted life. When she died, it would be as if she had been no more than a feather blowing on the breeze.

If she lived? Her opened eyes fell on the mountain. If she lived, she had no idea what she should do with the rest of her life. Write her story? Then, perhaps others. But surely there was more? The child. Yes, the child, her son or daughter, would be a glowing blooming thing with fresh impulse to live. She would watch over it from a distance, trying not to impose her own bewildered will on its destiny.

She felt as if she could only be a spectator. Life's stream seemed to have left her. She seemed to have been washed up on its bank. She could watch, for a time, the eddied flow rush on towards the falls and not be part of its thrash and turbulence. She had no need to go on building her empire or managing her business. Her father's remaining inheritance and her own accumulated wealth would allow her to remain untouched by life's struggle. She pictured the years of growing slowly old on life's sidelines. It was an appalling prospect, but she seemed to have no strength for anything else.

On the low, white painted table beside her lay the letter which Mathew had brought her with her breakfast. It must have arrived yesterday. It was a private letter, mailed not couriered, and the elongated slanting letters on the square blue envelope were not familiar, were not Brenda's. She could not think of anyone else who would write a personal letter to her here.

She had not opened it. It seemed to demand now that she did. She reached out her hand and took it. The post mark was London EC3. Taking a deep breath she slit the thin tissue with her index fingernail. There was just one sheet, two paragraphs. She looked at the signature. It was from David Armstrong. It said:

Dear Catherine,

I understand from my colleague, Commander Peter Swift of the Serious Fraud Squad, that the investigations at Clyne Johnson Bank are almost finished. A number of arrests will be made as a result. However, you will probably be relieved to know that no trace of evidence has been found connecting Christopher Angel or his companies to any transactions at the bank.

I believe, therefore, that my own department will not be able to bring the planned prosecution against Angel as there is insufficient evidence of his involvement in the supply of drugs to the SLRS protest groups. I am writing to tell you this to relieve the anxiety you must be feeling under your personal circumstances. I hope you will not tell anyone that I have done so and that you will destroy this letter after reading it.

Hoping you are well,

Yours sincerely
David Armstrong

Catherine sat up. A white peacock stood near her, fanning its tail. It was half turning like a bride showing offher dress for a camera. She stood and went into the cottage. She did not want to think about the implications of David's news. She had put Christopher and his trial as far out of her mind as possible in order to rest. Now, images of him loomed, bringing emotions of regret and grief at what was ended.

One day before leaving London she had seen him in the street with a woman. She had felt a moment's jealousy and fear of losing him. But observing them together she had felt these feelings leave her. Christopher was another person with this woman. She felt the gulf between their lives widen, felt the impossibility of what she was expecting. It seemed then that he would always be trapped by his background, unable to accept that he could be anything he wished if only he would let go of his past.

She saw so clearly in that moment in the busy, shadow-patterned street, that Christopher was a prisoner of his own obsession with the wrongs done him in the past. His will to avenge those past wrongs was holding him back from the future, containing him in a present that was itself a morbid re-enactment of his past. His stubborn anger kept his history alive and its shackles around him. Even the powerful feeling between them had failed to break its lock. Only Christopher could throw the switch in his mind that would set himself free. Only Christopher could choose between the past and the future. Catherine had felt herself receding from his life. She had stopped praying for any specific outcome to his troubles and mentally freed him to go to his own destiny.

She had left London two days later without calling to say goodbye. She walked away to her own freedom with the same lack of fanfare as she hoped would accompany her death. As she recalled that day three weeks ago, tears sprang to her eyes. She dashed them away and went into the bedroom.

Her bedside clock showed 1.15 p.m. It was time for her swim. She wound a kanga over her hips, slipped sandals onto her feet and dropped a large straw hat onto her head. She picked up her swimming hat and goggles and a towel and walked over the dry grass to the pool.

People were drifting towards their rooms to get ready for lunch and the pool terrace was almost empty. Catherine slipped into the pool. The water was cool and stimulating. She swam back and forth, exhilarated by the bright contrasts of cold blue water and hot sun. As she swam, the meaning returned to her body. Exercise always had this effect. It brought a sense of joy in living that otherwise deserted her weary mind.

She climbed out and lay for a while in the hot sun. She reflected that one should not, at this altitude, where the air was thin and the sun's rays dangerous, sunbathe in the middle of the day and certainly not without protective creams. But Catherine lay, enjoying the feeling of the heat and light warming her chilled muscles.

She gazed at the mountain. It brought back to her the echo of that emptiness that was with her always now. Small clouds were beginning to gather around the jagged snow peak. There would be rain by sundown. If she could stay here for ever in this place and watch nature work, she might once more recover a delight in living, get back the happiness she believed she had once found in simple natural things.

She felt a listless sadness. A small cloud must have covered the sun and she felt the heat's absence and a shiver of chill. She opened her eyes. Someone was standing over her, looking down at her. She saw the crisp shoulders of a safari jacket in a vividly deep shade of blue. The silhouette against the dazzling sky was of an African head and shoulders. Was it someone from reception? What did they want her for now? Was it a phone call? Was something wrong?

She sat up and as she did so he moved his head and she saw the light fall on his face. She leaped to her feet and stared in disbelief. Her heart was thumping, her knees trembling. He was laughing at her. They stood with the lounge chair between them.

Then she leaped onto it and flung her still wet arms around his neck. He lifted her up and onto the ground. He put his hand up and held her partly-wet hair and pulled her head back so that she was looking into his eyes. She saw tears start out of their corners. When he kissed her, it was with the same fire and awakening as she had known the first time. She clung to him as if to life.

In *The Banker's Daughter*, Nesta Wyn Ellis draws on her experience of the political world and of glamorous international lifestyles. She has stood for Westminster and the European Parliament. She has lived in Africa and in America, travelled to exotic places as a journalist, interviewed world leaders and played with the jetset. In 1991, she published a much-acclaimed biography of John Major. Her other works include *Dear Elector*, *The Truth About MPs*. Her latest non-fiction work is *Britain's Top 100 Eligible Bachelors* and a new novel, *Affairs of State*, is due in 1995.